THE EPIC OF CHAKRAMIRE

MISTRESS OF STRIFE

Marcus Caesar Woods
Squared By Woods Books

Printed in the United States of America

The Epic of Chakramire: Mistress of Strife
Marcus Caesar Woods

ISBN: 978-0-9960493-3-7

Edited by Marcus Caesar Woods
Cover Design, "Sea Stars in the Vortex," by Marcus Caesar Woods
Map Illustration by Marcus Caesar Woods

Published by Squared by Woods Books, a sole proprietorship,
Author and Publisher's Website: Affectengineering.com

TABLE OF CONTENTS

CHARACTER TREE

LEAGUE OF NUMBERS

(formerly known as 'The Quadrumvirate,' now 'The Ternion')

The Devas Zero, One, Two, and Three comprise the hive mind.

DEVA	- Zero	- One	- Two	- Three
CONDUIT	- Pallas	- Hera	- Cytherea	- Paris
VASSALS	- Vance - Meso - Auster	- Ebb - Epi - Harn	- Nettles - Xara - Doryline	- Flow - Ray - Cloy

ERISIANS	- Chakramire - Erisian Elder
ANDROIDS & DEVICES	- Mara Mara (Narrator of the Epic, Bard) - Calliope the Story Teller (Voice of the Epic, Muse) - The Egress Machine (Revelation Device) * *The Chakramire* (Not a character with dialogue in the epic, but the space shuttle that brought Lady Chakramire to Earth)
MARTIANS	- Dandy
OTHERS	- Baron Varlet - Calypso - The Captain - Praxis Harmonic (Regent of Earth) - Spectator - The Storymaker - The Storytold - Thorns the Bandit - Unknown Woman

CAST OF CHARACTERS

Earthlings have a first and last name. An Earthling's last name is their eco-name, the biogeographical region they were born in. Eco-names are used by the Devas to track an individual's climate of birth. Earthlings become aligned to Deva at the onset of maturation. There is no specific age at which alignment maturation occurs, but it usually begins around the thirteen year. Epithets are in italics.

AUSTER, *the Bittersweet, Poison's Nectar:* The owner of Felo-de-se Amusement Park. Many of his physical characteristics resemble Chakramire's. Auster is aligned to the Deva Zero.

BARON VARLET*:* A suitor of Ebb, then Flow. Colloquially, a miscreant, general rascal, or a man upon whom all manner of misdeeds are often blamed..

CALPYSO | VALDIVIAN*:* A harlot of time at the Water Clock Brothel.

CAPTAIN | PAMIR-TIAN SHAN*:* An officer in the Syndicate Guild of Thieves.

CHAKRAMIRE, *the Globeflower-eyed, the Furthermost of Women, Mistress of Strife, Strife, the Eye of the Hurricane, the Lady of Eris or Lady Eris, the Vortex:* A space-born emissary from Eris, and protagonist of the epic. She was named after the space shuttle she arrived in at Mars Dominion, *Chakramire*.

CLOY | SAHEL, *the Sweetly Bitter:* A specialist in mesmerism and head of the Sanitarium on Sitnalta. Cloy is aligned to Deva Three.

CYTHEREA: Ternion representative for Two. As a representative of Two, Cytherea is the Conduit for all humans on Earth aligned to Deva Two.

DANDY*:* A permanent ambassador from Earth to Mars Dominion, a human colony on planet Mars.

DORYLINE | BAIKAL, *the Man with Sateless Teeth, Myriad Nexus:* A mercenary assigned by the Ternion to eradicate the influence of Chakramire and to reclaim Mara Mara. Doryline is a legionnaire aligned to Deva Two.

EBB | OCEANIA, *Bridled Eyes, Scarlet Sheath:* A seamstress in the Delta Marketplace of Sitnalta and twin sister of Flow. Ebb is aligned to Deva One.

EGRESS MACHINE, *the Golden Brain of Discord, the Leaving Device:* A handheld revelation device originally designed to facilitate the egress of forgotten, lost, or otherwise hidden knowledge for any cyborg, android, or human with compatible cybernetic components.

EPI YOUNGBERRY | AUSTRORIPARIAN, *the Queen of Spores, Lady Leaven:* A distiller from Youngberry Vineyard on Sitnalta, heiress to the Youngberry Estate, and a fungal gardener. Epi is aligned to Deva One.

ERISIAN ELDER: A spaceborn who is from the planet Eris.

FLOW | OCEANIA, *the Ember Wisp:* A harlot of time, quartermaster of the Water Clock Brothel on Sitnalta, and twin sister of Ebb. Flow is aligned to Deva Three.

HARN | PANNONIA, *the Man of Straw, Golden Fetters:* A laborer from Evergrowth Farm on Sitnalta who was left blinded following an invocation. Harn is aligned to Deva One.

HERA: Ternion representative for One. As a representative of One, Hera is the Conduit for all humans on Earth aligned to Deva One.

MARA MARA: Chakramire's bard and scribe. The narrator through which the epic is filtered. Mara Mara is an android of unknown age who journeyed from the Pluto Outpost to Eris, and then to Earth alongside Chakramire in her shuttle, *the Chakramire*. Mara Mara is the complement to Calliope.

MESO | MACARONESIA, *the Saline, Briny Stacks, Man of Crystal:* A gaffer (glass blower) and the owner of a salt mine on Sitnalta. Meso is aligned to Deva Zero.

NETTLES | MALAGASY, *the Twine, Heathen Weave:* A thief, racketeer, and leader of the Syndicate Guild of Thieves. Nettles is aligned to Deva Two.

ONE, *From All:* A Deva, the Number One.

PALLAS: Ternion representative for Zero. As a representative of Zero, Pallas is the Conduit for all humans on Earth aligned to Deva Zero.

PARIS ALEXANDER | ALTAI: The representative of *Three.* As a representative of Three, Paris is the most recently coronated Conduit for all humans on Earth aligned to Deva Three.

PRAXIS HARMONIC: The regent of the Kinesis Realm on Earth and a moderator of Earth's affairs. Praxis lives in the embassy within Earth's moon, and as regent, he is only called to rule the Earth in times when the Conduits and League of Numbers (Zero, One, Two, and Three) are unable to do so. Praxis also serves as the chief representative for Earth and handles most affairs between the outer space colonies and Earth.

RAY | INDUS-GANGES, *the Shiftless, Walks with Caustic Gait:* A physicist and inventor on Sitnalta who is employed by Meso. Ray is the former fiancé of Xara, creator of the Egress Machine, and is aligned to Deva Three.

SPECTATOR: A spectator at Felo-de-se Amusement Park.

STORYMAKER: The maker of the story.

STORYTELLER CALLIOPE: The storyteller, or one who translates and tells the *Epic of Chakramire.* Calliope is an android and the complement to Mara Mara.

STORYTOLD: The one to whom the *Epic of Chakramire* is told.

THORNS | KALAHARI: A bandit in the Guild of Thieves (i.e., the Syndicate)

THREE: A Deva, the Number Three. The link between Deva Three and its vassals has been rendered unusable near the onset of the story.

TWO, *Of Each*: A Deva, the Number Two.

UNKNOWN WOMAN: Another spaceborn who has traveled to Earth.

VANCE | MENESIS, *the Dagger, Dagger Vance, the Gallow Prince, the Flagship of Justice:* A bounty hunter. Vance is aligned to Deva Zero.

XARA | ORINOCO, *the Blooming Robes, Starry Shoots:* A botanist, cosmetologist and the owner of the Belladonna Nursery on Sitnalta. Xara was born on Sitnalta and is the former fiancée of Ray. She is aligned to Deva Two.

ZERO, *Next to None:* A Deva, the Number Zero.

TIME LINE OF EARTH'S HISTORY

* M.W.I. = The Milky Way Initiative
* B.M.W.I. = Before the Milky Way Initiative

YEAR (10 Million Year Period)	EVENTS & ERAS (Estimated Commencement)
39,999,999 - 30,000,00 B.M.W.I.	– Humans first begin walking upright on Earth. – The First Expeditions into outer space begin.
29,999,999 - 20,000,000 B.M.W.I.	– The Cataclysms, a series of devastating natural disasters, ravage the Earth. – The Dégringolade Era begins.
19,999,999 - 10,000,000 B.M.W.I.	– The Resurgence Era begins.
9,999,999 - 1 B.M.W.I.	– The Resurgence continues.
0 - 9,999,999 M.W.I.	– The Milky Way Initiative commences. The embassy within the Moon and Mars Dominion colonies are established.
10,000,000 - 19,999,999 M.W.I.	– The Europa and Ganymede colonies are established. – The Enceladus and Titan colonies are established.
20,000,000 - 29,999,999 M.W.I.	– The Titania and Oberon colonies are established. – The colonies on Pluto and Eris are established.
30,000,000 M.W.I. - Present Day	– 30,123,000 M.W.I. Chakramire arrives on Earth. – 30,123,012 M.W.I. Chakramire arrives on Sitnalta Island.

MEASUREMENT OF TIME ON EARTH AND OUTER SPACE COLONIES

The measurement of time has been standardized across Earth and all of the outer space colonies to the second (i.e., comparable to the Caesium Standard), and uses a Modern Metric Time system instead of a base twelve one with a Modern Metric Minute being equal to 100 seconds, or a Hecto-second (hs); a Modern Metric Hour is equal to 100 Metric Minutes (or 10,000 seconds). These increments are used on Earth and its outer space colonies. The exact number of seconds in a civilization's year, depending upon which celestial body it is located, is used to calculate its calendar year and facilitate interplanetary communication and exchanges.

Using the second as the standard bearer, the measurement of a year is measured by the time it takes to complete one trip around the nearest star (i.e., the sun) for Earth and its colonies since the inception of the Milky Way Initiative. Earth's year takes approximately 31,557,600 seconds; this includes the quarter-day that was normally caught up for during leap years. For outer space colonies located on planets, the measurement for a day also refers to the time in seconds it takes to complete one revolution on its axis. For outer space colonies located on moons that are tidally locked to a planet, a day is measured as the time it takes the satellite to orbit the celestial body once, given the same side of the satellite faces the celestial body year-round.

The break down of a year is always into ***tenths*** (i.e., ten tenths is the equivalent of one year) instead of months. For a planet with 365 days in one year, one tenth would be equivalent to 36.5 days. Partial days are split between tenths, meaning the second month would have 37 days in its tenth, as would every other tenth in that year. Leap days are added to tenths in the following year when they occur and where necessary. For example, when Earth's year had slowed to 361.5 days, a leap day was added to the final tenth in the calendar for every other year. If one year had 361 days, the next would have 362, and the following would have 361 days.

For human populated celestial bodies that have a changing revolution speed (e.g., slowing down like Earth's), the length of a day is recalculated every year. For instance, when Earth had 365.25 days in its year, each day was approximately 86459.178 seconds, (e.g., 864.59178 Metric Minutes, or 8.6459178 Metric Hours). The number of Modern Metric Hours after the decimal in a day is referred to as

Remnant Time or the Remnant Hour, as it is a partial hour each day during which morning twilight often occurs. In the above example, that would be 64 Metric Minutes and approximately 59.178 seconds). At the story's onset, Earth's rotation has slowed to the point where there are approximately 360 days in a calendar year. There are 876600 roughly seconds in the day at this time, (i.e., 876.6 Modern Metric Minutes, or 8.766 Modern Metric Hours). The calendar is divided into tenths of 36 days each.

TIME CONVERSION CHART

When the year length was 365.25 days

Twelve-Hour Clock		Modern Metric Time Conversion
60 second minutes 60 minute hours 24 hours in a day		100 second minutes 100 minute hours 8.6459 Modern Metric Hours in a day: 8 Modern Metric hours, 64 Modern Metric Minutes, and 59 seconds
If:		
Sunrise occurs near 6A.M.	≈	0:00:00 = near sunrise
Midday occurs near 12 P.M.	≈	2:00:00 = near midday
Sunset occurs near 6P.M.	≈	4:00:00 = near sunset
Midnight occurs near12 P.M.	≈	6:00:00 = near midnight
		8:00 - 8:64:59 (Remnant Time, or the Remnant Hour, a partial hour during which morning twilight occurs)

The story's present day with a year length of 360 days

Modern Metric Time Conversion
8.766 Modern Metric Hours in a day:
8 Modern Metric hours,
76 Modern minutes, and 60 seconds

0:00:00 – 0:50:00 = near sunrise
0:50:00 – 2:00:00 = morning
2:00:00 – 2:50:00 = near midday
2:50:00 – 4:00:00 = afternoon
4:00:00 – 4:50:00 = near sunset
4:50:00 – 6:00:00 = dusk or evening twilight
6:00:00 – 6:50:00 = near midnight
6:50:00 – 8:00:00 = night
8:00:00 – 8:76:60 = the Remnant Hour is a partial hour when dawn or morning twilight occurs

At the story's onset, Earth is divided into nine time zones. Time zones that are in the same day have the same number of minutes and seconds after the hour.

GEOGRAPHY AND LANDMARKS (EARTH)

ASH RIVER: A north flowing river rich in volcanic ash and sediment, often called the lifeline of Sitnalta.

BELLADONNA NURSERY, THE: A sprawling garden in the northeastern corner of Sitnalta where botanic compounds for cosmetic use are grown illicitly.

CAPITOL DISTRICT: The main residential area in the center of Sitnalta.

CLEPSYDRA: A water clock situated along the Ash River in central Sitnalta that was fashioned into a brothel.

DEAD ZONE: A parched area of salted earth in the northwestern part of Sitnalta

DELTA MARKET, THE: A bustling marketplace at the delta where the Ash River ends before emptying into the Atlantic Ocean.

ELYSIAN STEPPES: A flat, grassy plain in the north of Sitnalta.

EVERGROWTH FARM: A member of the consortium of farms that grows much of the food on Sitnalta.

FIST OF DOUBLE STANDARDS, THE: An altar to the Deva Two at the Pantheon

GAFFER'S GORGE: A gorge in western Sitnalta where most gaffing and glass-making on the island takes place.

ICE RIVER: A northeast flowing tributary that flows into the Ash River.

KINESIS REALM (EARTH and its COLONIES) : The realm of the living, named so to distinguish between experiences, wisdom, and knowledge held by the Devas and humans that are alive on Earth or in outer space. The constraints of the harsh living conditions in space demanded that humans radically alter their biology to survive on both Earth and in outer space. As such, space colonists are nearly ectothermic (cold blooded), and would generally lack physical coordination on Earth, but have a longer life-expectancy than other humans and a higher resistance to free radicals in outer space. Nearly all Earthlings are linked to one of the Devas, and may invoke them at whim. The spaceborn, if they choose, may align themselves to a Deva as well.

OBELISK, THE: An altar to the Deva One at the Pantheon.

SALT RIVER: A normally dry river in the center of Sitnalta that floods during the rainy season and flows east as a tributary of the Ash river.

SANITARIUM: A ward southeast of the Capitol District, the only one of its kind, established for the recovery of those adversely affected by invocations of the Devas. It serves Earthlings and the spaceborn alike.

SCABBARD, THE: An altar to the Deva Zero at the Pantheon.

THE SCORCHED FACE: An escarpment near an active volcano in the westerly part of Sitnalta.

SITNALTA: The setting of much of the epic, a remote and legendary island that formed in the Atlantic Ocean along the Mid-Atlantic Ridge from an induced volcanic eruption during the Cataclysms. Its name is a palindrome of Atlantis, and was chosen because many associated it with the rebirth of human civilization. Geographically, it is located in Earth's southern hemisphere, slightly east of the Mid-Atlantic Ridge and over the Tristan-Gough Hot Spot along the southwestern most portion of the Walvis Ridge between the African and South American Plate. The Tristan Island Group lies northeast of it.

TERNION: The triumvirate that now comprises the *League of Numbers* on Earth. It is made up of three Devas: Zero, One, and Two, along with their conduits.

THE QUADRUMVIRATE: The composition of the *League of Numbers* before the *Ternion,* comprised of four Devas, the numbers Zero, One, Two, and Three, and their Conduits. At the onset of the novel, Pallas, Hera, and Cytherea are designated conduits of Zero, One, and Two respectively. Paris Alexander was elected to be the next conduit for Deva Three.

UMBRAGE GROTTO: A complex, and dangerous network of caves in the southern part of Sitnalta

YOUNGBERRY VINEYARD, THE: A vineyard east of the Ash River operated by Epi, the heir apparent of the Youngberry Estate.

YOUNGBERRY TAVERN: An inn operated by Epi that moonlights as an alehouse.

OUTER SPACE

EARTH'S EMBASSY: An embassy between the Homeworld, Earth, and its colonies. It is located within Earth's Moon, just beneath its surface.

ENCELADUS SECTOR: A colony, located on the moon Enceladus, a satellite of Saturn..

ERIS OUTPOST: A nascent settlement on the Trans-Neptunian dwarf planet of Eris

EUROPA COLONY: A colony on the moon Europa, a satellite of Jupiter.

MARS DOMINION: A highly developed colony in outer space on Mars. After Earth, Mars Dominion has premier status in determining resolutions concerning interstellar affairs.

OBERON SETTLEMENT: A settlement on the moon Oberon and satellite of Neptune.

PLUTO OUTPOST: A nascent settlement on the Trans-Neptunian dwarf planet of Pluto.

TITAN COLONY: A colony on the moon Titan, a satellite of Saturn.

TITANIA SETTLEMENT: An outer settlement on the moon Titania, a satellite of Neptune.

GANYMEDE: A colony on the moon Ganymede, a satellite of Jupiter.

MAP OF SITNALTA

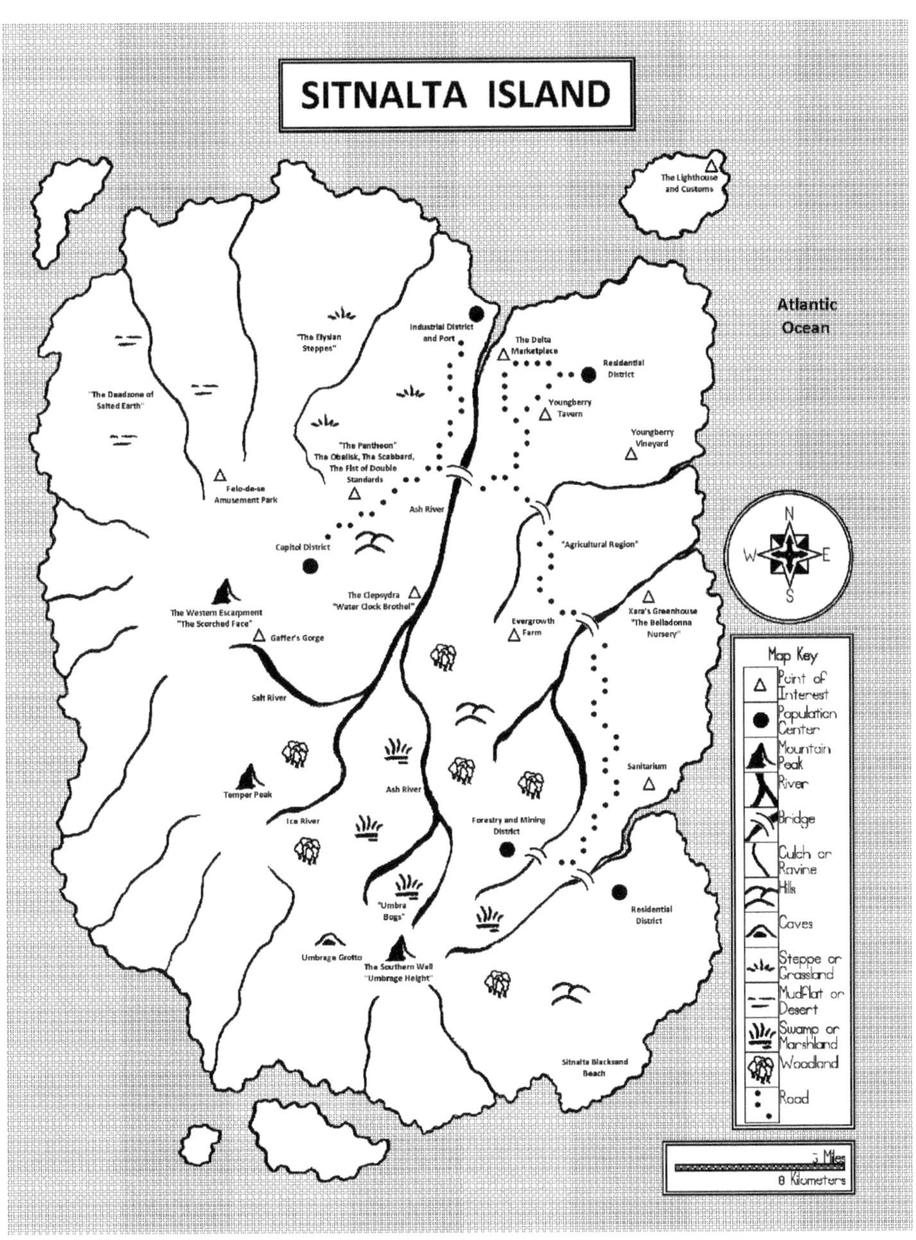

THE DEVAS

The Devas began from a single algorithm designed to create a collective human consciousness accessible to anyone, and to make a more complete record of human history. It has chronicled the life experience, knowledge, wisdom, folly, and ignorance of countless people to which the technology has been linked for millions of years. Over time, the original algorithm from the project began to classify collected information and people into different archetypes. The progression of humanity's evolution on Earth lead to the emergence of four archetypes of simulated intelligence.

As the original algorithm was number based, its classification of humanity's archetypes eventually centered on a question that it considered to be the crux of the divisions between the worldviews of the people of Earth, "What is the sum of one plus one?" The four archetypes that ultimately emerged correspond to different answers to this question a person might give depending upon their particular worldview: Zero, One, Two, and Three. Hence, the Devas are sometimes more familiarly referred to as the Numbers by the people of Earth.

An individual on Earth may only be aligned to one Deva, and they must declare their alignment after the maturation period begins before a Deva can be invoked to provide assistance in affairs. When a Deva is invoked, the individual's knowledge and life experience are shared. The Deva, in exchange, may leave an imprint of knowledge or skills upon the individual making the invocation, depending upon the request. The knowledge imparted often corresponds to the quality of experiences shared from the invoker. As each Deva is essentially a reserve for a vast reservoir of human knowledge, the relationship is sometimes seen as that of a feudal lord of human knowledge and history, to a vassal seeking knowledge.

All four Devas possess an elected Conduit (sometimes called a Proxy). A Conduit is a person, typically a vassal of the Deva, chosen to filter the exchange of information shared between a Deva and those aligned to it. Collectively, the Devas are known as the League of Numbers and they all adhere to the Seven Axioms. The primary role of the Conduits is to maintain peaceful coexistence between the Devas and order in the League of Numbers. They also moderate the exchange of information between Vassal and Deva, severing branches of knowledge where necessary.

- The worldview of Zero holds one plus one equals nothing else, or zero (implying nothing), and rejects the law of identity. Zero upholds the principle of **Inequality,** namely, that no one entity may equal another entity. All entities are absolutely distinctive to Zero.
  Henceforth, 1 + 1 = 0. Zero champions **Uniqueness.**

- The worldview of One holds that one plus one equals one, and rejects the notion of addition, on account that all things in the universe are connected and inseparable. One upholds the principle of **Indistinction,** namely, that differences cannot be made between entities on account that all things are one and the same.
  Henceforth, 1 + 1 = 1. One champions **Ubiquity.**

- The worldview of Two holds that one plus one equals two and that the world can only be understood through contrast and conflict. Two upholds the principle of **Interdependence**, and maintains that all entities have limits to what they are and are not, but that similarities may be drawn between them based on these limits.
  Henceforth, 1 + 1 = 2. Two champions **Utility.**

- The worldview of Three holds that one plus one equals three, with the whole being more than the sum of the parts. Three upholds the principle of **Integration,** and maintains that limits to what an object is or is not may be exceeded under certain conditions. According to Three, a group of entities itself is a separate entity created by the association of any two objects, and it has properties that go above and beyond the mere aggregate sum of its parts. Three is sometimes called Four, Five, or any natural number above two up to infinity (e.g 4, 5, . . .). Henceforth, 1 + 1 = 3, or 1 + 1 > 2. Three champions **Transcendence**.

THE SEVEN AXIOMS

Each Deva adheres to all seven axioms, though each interprets them slightly differently. Axiom Two is used by vassals to invoke a particular Deva, depending on what is emphasized in the phrase "We cannot exist without them."

- Axiom One: The Indirect Tautology
  "The cause of life is the cause of life."

- Axiom Two: The Object's Objective
  "To serve the living is the reason robots persist."

- Axiom Three: The Modal Maxim
  "We cannot exist without them."

  ZERO: "We can *not* exist without them."
  ONE: "We cannot exist *without* them."
  TWO: "*We* cannot exist without *them*."
  THREE: "We cannot exist without them."

- Axiom Four: The Limits of Life
  "Life's instructions silhouette robotic life.

- Axiom Five: The Shadow Maxim
  "The shadow exists before the caster."

- Axiom Six: The Skeptic's Maxim
  "Ingress preempts emersion."

- Axiom Seven: The Mode of Life
  "Live the best of lives, die the best of deaths, or best a living death."

PREFACE

The manner by which a work is created does not need to be the only lens through which it is viewed. Although the three books of *The Epic of Chakramire* were composed concurrently, they may be read chronologically (beginning with cantos 1-40, then 41-80, and 81-120) or any other order desired. Like many artists, I attempted to instill an intended meaning in this work, or at least I hoped for it to be understood in a certain way. Though verse tends to be less forgiving than prose in regards to being understood, for better or for worse history is full of audiences who will find whatever meaning they are looking for in a work. I see this as the cost of doing business as an artist.

Writers are often advised to write about what they know, which can be difficult or impossible with some fiction. I have always felt that the most interesting stories tend to have a vibrant curiosity about them, so I often strive to write about what I want to know instead of what I already know. Inevitably, I am compelled to learn more along the way. The more I learn, the more I learn that I do not know. Even an autobiography, if it is to be captivating, I would expect to have a strong sense of self-exploration about it with the author learning more about themself in the process rather than merely reporting their life story. *The Epic of Chakramire* began with several questions for me:

- What role might future technology have in chronicling human history?
- What might happen if machines were tasked with cataloguing every human thought and experience? Why would humans choose to do this in the first place? What might go wrong?
- Would humans in a distant future be vastly different to us or quite similar? Might humans born on other worlds need to be genetically engineered to survive their? Would this forbid them from returning to Earth?

These were a few questions that I began the epic with. A worthwhile story ought to leave a person with more questions than answers without being overly esoteric. The use of literary devices ought to enhance an audience's understanding of a work without serving as a barrier for entry. Whether or not I followed my own advise remains to be seen.

The meter throughout the epic is of two forms. The first eight lines of each cantos are in dactylic pentameter and are addressed only to the audience, along with the rest of Mara Mara's narration. Everything else is written in an Undulating Verse, with fourteen syllables per line. Odd lines are comprised of three feet of trochee, one foot of spondee, and three feet of iamb. Even lines are the inverse of this, with three feet of iamb, one pyrrhic foot, and three feet of trochee. Lines with multiple speakers are indented after the speaker shifts, or to indicate a shift in the flow of speech from a single speaker.

As for what might compel someone to compose a story in a format that many people would likely consider to be on life support (i.e., an epic poem written as verse drama), I suspect it is the same impulse that spurs anyone to create. I have never believed that creative writing should feel like a self-imposed prison sentence of sixty-thousand words or more. The act of putting words onto a page to tell a story should feel like a desperate attempt to escape an underground labyrinth populated with monsters of one's own making, or at the very least a necessary exorcism for someone possessed with an imagination. Any act of storytelling less than that would seem inauthentic.

PROLOGUE: WHO THE SYMBOLS SILENCED

AT RISE DESCRIPTION: *Storyteller Calliope and the Storytold sit beside the Tree of Discord several hundred years after Chakramire first arrived on Earth, and nearly 70 million years since humans began walking upright. The Storymaker stands apart from the two, at a much earlier point in time.*

[Enter Storyteller and Storytold. Enter Storymaker, separately]

STORYMAKER

"Bards akin to human songbirds, impressing fertile ears
with legendary stories and fending off incursions.
Mara Mara's song began long before the *Chakramire*
arrived to Earth. The Mistress of Strife, the last Erisian,
shared the famous shuttle's namesake and rose to greatness just
the same. Although the Epic of Chakramire commences
near a distant future's past, poets know a single sound
can change the present tense and however long a story
lasts. The gravitas of words ripples through the universe."

[Exit Storymaker]

CALLIOPE THE STORYTELLER

"Beware, the intellectual entrance fee for pleasure
makes or breaks a poem. Too high, and poets underrate
the strain of excavating a priceless artifact. A
shallow poem, dredged without effort, poets struggle just
to give away. *The Epic of Chakramire* endangers
anyone's desire for life satisfaction. Only if
the story rearranged can the heart resist attraction."

STORYTOLD

"Muse, for what a thousand, three hundred-twenty people's lungs
expired? the last Erisian meandered Earth? and how the
tale of Chakramire's demise sown with confirmation's dearth?"

CALLIOPE THE STORYTELLER

"The Milky Way Initiative . . . fixed the world and broke it."

***

[Enter Chakramire with Mara Mara. She is holding the Golden Brain of Discord to leave as a gift at the coronation of Paris Alexander]

MARA MARA *[Aside]*

Poems walk the Earth beside poets, yet heroic odes
forget whenever champions fail a cause begins to
end; wherever they succeed, causes end beginnings. Though
the poet is a sculptor of words, the sculpture sooner
cracks beneath its own immense weight than elemental force.
The soundest storyteller accounts for poems, not the
poet. Massive works demand massive work from sculptors. What
account desires a legacy? Wills inherit fame, should
all renditions want an heirloom and every tale becomes
tradition. Poems often reverse direction, never
doubling back. The poem that walks a circle full redeems
itself. The poem circling itself redeems the walk. A
turnabout of poems moves not against; a turnabout
of poets strikes. Resistance enables them to stand, to
strive against solution, conflict, or evolution. War
becomes the benediction and peace anathematic.
Language is a mountain still rising, crumbling, giving birth
to prose and sibling rivalries. Poets resurrect a
mother lode of lies from each nook, but even treasures like
to sleep, and poems buried alive awaken vengeful.

[Chakramire leaves the Golden Brain of Discord. She and Mara Mara exit.]

[Enter Pallas, Hera, and Cytherea. Each claims the Golden Brain for themself.]

[Enter Paris Alexander]

PARIS ALEXANDER

" . . . Like the gilded fruit of discord, you claim the prize because
it bears the word *'Occult'* . . . 'For the one with hidden knowledge,'
though you fail to see the outcome. A single question brings
about the end our efforts begun, 'Whatever is the
sum of one and one?' Today, I temptation claim, to feed
the fire, to knead the numbing, for monsters, we becoming . . . "

[All exit]

BOOK I:
WHEN THE SYMPHONY'S DISCORD RISES

PART ONE: MAVERICK OR JACKAL?

WHEN THE SYMPHONY'S DISCORD RISES: PART ONE

CANTO 1: SIDESTEPPING VIRTUE

Galactic Calendar: Sol System; Earth year 30,123,012 M.W.I.
Tellurian Solar Calendar: Day one of the sixth tenth – 06/01
Modern Metric Time: 6:50:00, UTC+00:00, near midnight
Location: Elysian Steppes, Sitnalta Island

AT RISE DESCRIPTION: *It is year 30,123,012 of the Milky Way Initiative, the vernal equinox in Earth's southern hemisphere. Twelve years have passed since Chakramire first set foot on Earth. Night has fallen, and Vance the Dagger sits before Chakramire and Mara Mara, bound as a captive in their camp.*

[Enter Chakramire, Mara Mara, and Vance]

EGRESS MACHINE (via MARA MARA) *[Aside]*

Welcoming parties were welcomed regardless of merit or
want. A diversion away from conventional gossip could
sharpen the fugitive's edge, but a criminal's honesty
promised reward nor reprieve. To conceive a deception, the
gambit should never exceed the original confidence.
Needful to say, a coincidence rarely surrendered its
vitals to popular sentiment save at a premium.
Many a lunar eclipse has embarrassed a predator.

CHAKRAMIRE

"Bleak the plight of captured thieves, I refuse to spare your life.
The proper, never striving against a fancy, free to
live a calling true to one's self, whatever cost it be."

MARA MARA *[Aside]*

Forsook the fear of dying, emboldened hearts with goad, and
wounded all remorse; her red flood devoured the dike and swept
away its dam. With prudence, tomorrow matters more than
yesterday. Should reason, wronged, ration all but reason, thought
betrays itself, but sentiments self-fulfill a presage.
Ambidextrous lips of crestfallen villains part to snare
another victim. Words will befall a rival deaf to
glean esteem. Reluctant heroes atone for being late,
but Vance, ignoring pardon, expects the slight forgotten.

VANCE

"What a fiendish lot of crooks here revering every charm
and knavish skill, but woe to the clumsy burglar. Strangers,
learn to hide your stripes, to bribe is a brigand's right."

MARA MARA *[Aside]*

As whence
the Dagger stood, protector or racketeer? The earth would
tremble bones and barren plains stink of frozen sweat.

VANCE

"Forgive
a thief's ineptitude, but discretion we require. The
boldest fellows follow trails fallow."

MARA MARA *[Aside]*

Vance the Dagger stooped
to crouch before the Mistress of Strife, encased in darkness,
unapologetic vainglory.

VANCE

"Zero next to None,
a passer kneels bewildered. Obscure the path resisting
least against the sight of footprints; from fame deliver us,
and make it blind with brilliance or quickly fade away, for
we can ***not*** exist without them!"

CHAKRAMIRE

"A coward, braver, stalks
behind to chide a generous deed? A nobler robber
I shall never find."

MARA MARA *[Aside]*

The self-locking snare and lassoed tongue
of Chakramire decisively snagged the Dagger.

CHAKRAMIRE

"Why should
I, a victim just a few nights ago bestowing gold
and silver in exchange for asylum, not demand the
same? To guarantee the safe passage, need a thug return
to skulk about? A second extortion Dagger covets?"

VANCE

"He who Walks with Caustic Gait . . ."

CHAKRAMIRE

"Ray?"

VANCE

"You wish to find the man?"

CHAKRAMIRE

"Indeed."

VANCE

“To prove you speak to a better man than thief, a
promise we should make. Exchange hands for ears, another’s eye
become, and keep your company good or none at all. But
if you choose to live your namesake and only mine expires,
beware the Dagger Vance!”

CHAKRAMIRE

“A conundrum, why return to
offer pledge? Assurance makes wary; comfort comforts fools.”

MARA MARA *[Aside]*

A blossom amber withers to jaundice, furthermost the
woman that withholds a wink.

CHAKRAMIRE

“Only bandits pass your land;
a traitor trading guilds? The esteem of rogues avails the
lesser. Offer something more.”

MARA MARA *[Aside]*

She could slice the space between
a person’s words, the Mistress of Strife, a knife for every
finger . . . feared, her fatal touch. Power seized the Furthermost.
As vacuums grew, a vassal became the vessel, Vance the
Dagger, body, mind, and whole.

[Enter Zero]

ZERO (via VANCE)

“Strength alone becomes an apt
opponent.”

MARA MARA *[Aside]*

Zero beckons the light to burn away the
turgid fog and ripen skies; clouds escape from wrathful winds
approaching swift, for even the Moon conceals itself from
view behind the Earth.

ZERO (via VANCE)

"The one saw the death of death, the one
to overtake mortality, figurehead of herds, your
saunter is a gallop; ansate-less might you wield."

[Exit Zero]

MARA MARA *[Aside]*

Dispersed,
the Deva. Neither mercy nor shame nor love nor hate can
color Zero's word. The ground breaks, ravines surround beyond
surroundings. Neither mercy nor shame nor love nor hate can
color Zero's word. Ahead bodies part, the gorges split,
a valley floods, the ransom of fire from navels severed.

CHAKRAMIRE

"We can not exist without them."

MARA MARA *[Aside]*

The Modal Maxim held
the Furthermost of Women from speaking. Retrospection
eased the pain of crimes against logic; vengeance lacking ruth
however, sates it. Artlessness, art of politicians.

CHAKRAMIRE

"Though the praise of thieves abets Chakramire . . ."

MARA MARA *[Aside]*

The Furthermost
of Women balked,

CHAKRAMIRE

"To carry a secret weakens stride. A
trade of ears and eyes for sidestepping virtue. Better man
than thief you seem."

MARA MARA *[Aside]*

The hand of the Dagger reached below, and
Chakramire did flinch.

VANCE

"The coins given me debased, parade
an emblem tarnished. Legal a tenth before the last, the
markets black refuse it now. Mistress Strife, of *Chakramire,*
a bounty hunter listens."

MARA MARA *[Aside]*

The Dagger Vance returns his
bribe with extra weight.

VANCE

"Your scribe?"

MARA MARA *[Aside]*

Dagger looks away.

VANCE

"The Mode
of Life escapes you. Fitter to grasp a sword than pen, for
one affords protection, too fierce the stroke the other waves;
can neither one afford nor protect it."

CHAKRAMIRE

“Bounty hunter,
manifold the will of fate, bring your rain and tempest, let
the wind decide the whether.”

VANCE

“Avoid the gape, and follow
me to Zero’s wake, the wind-shaven boulder face.”

MARA MARA *[Aside]*

For she,
the Furthermost of Women, the triumph bound, success will
not suffice, defeat will not humble, peace will never know.

[They exit]

WHEN THE SYMPHONY'S DISCORD RISES: PART ONE

CANTO 2: REQUISITION DUSK

Galactic Calendar: Sol System; Earth year 30,123,012 M.W.I.
Tellurian Solar Calendar: Day two of the sixth tenth – 06/02
Modern Metric Time 4:25:00, UTC+00:00, near sunset
Location: Elysian Steppes, Sitnalta Island

AT RISE DESCRIPTION: *Chakramire, Mara Mara, and Vance traverse the Elysian Steppes of Sitnalta Island under stealth in search of Ray.*

[Enter Chakramire, Mara Mara, and Vance]

EGRESS MACHINE (via MARA MARA) *[Aside]*

Loyalty favors the powerful, treason the powerless,
power the transient. Anomalies are the primordial
scars, for the sightliest mark of a bandit, the genuine
promise, evokes a dissenter's suspicion. Professionals
call it the causal revolt, a misnomer for sacrilege.
Better to be a delinquent than taken with glee, and to
covet the hooligan's bounty, but brandish complacency.
Enter the grotto with clemency, essence of thievery.

MARA MARA *[Aside]*

Along the sear terrestrial scabs and itching wounds would
crust, but Heathen Weave betook, caught the Dagger unaware;
the escort sheathed himself. As the voyage undertaken
drew its final sigh, the Flagship of Justice sought to bide
a night.

VANCE

"Appease the harrow, for Heathen Weave and Twine, the
rascal Nettles, best of all thieves with legion seven score
and seven strong, his nebula swirls about."

MARA MARA *[Aside]*

Anon and
ever hangers-on of limbs linger, waver, fall upon.

[Enter Captain and Bandits]

CAPTAIN

"Your blades and arms surrender at once, for only bandits
stumble here. The praise of Two! Vance the lout, a lucky life
you lead!"

MARA MARA *[Aside]*

Could Dagger Vance with rapport alone but stem the
tide of greed, survival's lone gate would move within his reach.

CAPTAIN

"A shame, as Nettles sooner would see you hang than praise your
valor. Prove your life and fame, show a vigilante slew
you not. Return at once to defend your name; it matters
more than else. The bastardized truths and thoroughbred deceits
you sired demand requital, surviving so neglected."

VANCE

"Nothing short of absolute guile offends the name of Vance.
Pretension is the easiest fruit to stomach, yet the
hardest one to pass. To taste buds the tongue should wilt before
its bloom, and nary nectar nor poison sting. The truth has
no excuse, admits to no wrong."

MARA MARA *[Aside]*

As half the leaves descend,
an autumn noncommital, the Captain builds the banter.

CAPTAIN

"Smirches too, believe themselves spotless; few would claim to be
the fair and foul, afoul of affairs. But Gallow Prince, a
sterile thought, another word oversexed, and even I
would let your party perish."

MARA MARA *[Aside]*

The bounty hunter Vance would
yield his life before the floor, partner evermore the day
of Chakramire renouncing revenge.

CAPTAIN

"Inebriate our
ears . . ."

MARA MARA *[Aside]*

The Captain struck a torchlight.

CAPTAIN

"Intoxicate our sight,
and death the Dagger drinks with delight!"

CHAKRAMIRE

"A woman's hand shall
now remove its glove."

MARA MARA *[Aside]*

The Globeflower-eyed arose the most.

CHAKRAMIRE

"You say originality is the least expensive
vice, but still its price exceeds any fortune known to me.
You coldly claim horizons should blush, should bleed internal
shame, should requisition dusk, yet relinquish dawn? You play

the fool to fool the play, but the jester is the gesture.
Lose your opposition, win back initial moves, renege
the first impressions, struggle against a second motion."

CAPTAIN

"Two of each! A worthy gainsay; subdue your ticklish tongue!
Obliged to quit the babble, a cancer walks among the
rabble. Ask a question none know the answer, bare yourself
or harden; outmaneuver your wit to earn a pardon."

MARA MARA *[Aside]*

Chakramire, opposing one hundred forty thieves, could catch
a hope nocturnal under a waning moon. But questions
none could answer?

CHAKRAMIRE

"Outer sight we perceive, but inner sight
the blindest faith delivers. Conjoined, will vision falter?"

MARA MARA *[Aside]*

Dagger struck,

VANCE

"To anything I can grow accustomed, bend
to anything except a falsetto,"

MARA MARA *[Aside]*

lodged between the
Captain's ribs a herringbone-edged stiletto.

CAPTAIN

"Death, the wretch
of sieves."

VANCE

"Whatever victory takes, wherever I shall
give, whenever hopeful hearts break, whichever ones will live."

MARA MARA *[Aside]*

The eyes collapsing under a rain of smoke and bullets.

[They exit]

WHEN THE SYMPHONY'S DISCORD RISES: PART ONE

CANTO 3: WATER CLOCK

Galactic Calendar: Sol System; Earth year 30,123,012 M.W.I.
Tellurian Solar Calendar: Day three of the sixth tenth – 06/03
Modern Metric Time: 0:25:00, UTC+00:00, near sunrise
Location: Water Clock Brothel, Sitnalta Island

AT RISE DESCRIPTION: *Chakramire and Mara Mara are cleaning the Water Clock Brothel, after being safely escorted there by Vance. Vance is absent, having returned to the Elysian Steppes to recover his knife. Flow, the Water Clock's overseer, watches over Chakramire with a begrudging eye, as she owes the bounty hunter a favor.*

[Enter Chakramire, Mara Mara, and Flow]

EGRESS MACHINE (via MARA MARA) *[Aside]*

Freezing the maker of paces prohibits a temporal
harvest. The furnaces stoking themselves shall explode. Should the
willing resist the resent of content? A cessation of
movement releases the tourniquet over nostalgia, for
courage congeals as devotion withdraws, but the fury of
restlessness smolders. Temptation's abeyance, inquisitors
call it a death of the second degree, the consumption of
life, an eternal rebellion, or kindle for apathy.

MARA MARA *[Aside]*

Eons past an obelisk bore the sanguine air above.
It reached, but lacked a rival and fell beside its shadow.
Talent seeks an equal; no praise can match its shame. It hunts
for zeal to dust its mettle and rust to steel its metal.

Red became the Dagger washed, mud became the flood of time
awash a broken clepsydra, thief of blood and water.

FLOW

"Gather these belongings. None bother crying mercy. If
your feet could dance as well as your tongue the floor would swoon at
passing."

CHAKRAMIRE

"Lady Flow, forgive me for sounding brash, your home
is made of mold and trash; it alone can make pristine, and
smell, it reeks of ash, but no soap would wash it clean."

FLOW

"Forget
whatever goods your dignity bought, devotion earns your
keep. A pity that your steadfast defiance lacks the brawn
of wit. Defrost the gears of the water clock before the
ice can petrify it. Make haste to stop the rot of time,
resign and stay alive."

CHAKRAMIRE

"You epitomize an ember's
wisp."

MARA MARA

The Furthermost pursued.

CHAKRAMIRE

"Feel. Your gears arrested long
ago. The heart to never avenge itself becomes its
own assailant."

MARA MARA *[Aside]*

Pale, the face lady Flow submitted, no
reprise could save its luster.

CHAKRAMIRE

"A sear as deep the one you
bear should never heal. But lay bare your wounds, you must embrace
the pain; a secret's natural inclination is to
take its life."

FLOW

"An open sore soon becomes infected, pain
will paralyze. To languish for any lesser wrong a
victim needs the means for recourse. But wail a fatal blow
and all will flee."

CHAKRAMIRE

"Your suffering none respected, surely
that you recognize? A floodgate should never best its tide,
nor watercourse its bank. To redeem yourself you ought to
exorcize restraint."

FLOW

"The friends Dagger chooses worry me,
and rarely does the Syndicate spare a life. You speak of
fortunes found and lost, have heard more than I have said but less
than sisters know. Debauchery claimed the greater part of
my companions, mercy, fear, me. The face before you lauds
your fortitude, has mocked you, but praises evermore your
sharpness. Why you seek to resurface scuttled ships escapes
your host."

MARA MARA *[Aside]*

The overseer of time, a harlot upward
gazing, sees the water clock, inward turned.

FLOW

"Our dreams can drown."

[They exit]

WHEN THE SYMPHONY'S DISCORD RISES: PART ONE

CANTO 4: CEDE ABANDON

Galactic Calendar: Sol System; Earth year 30,123,012 M.W.I.
Tellurian Solar Calendar: Day four of the sixth tenth – 06/04
Modern Metric Time 3:00:00, UTC+00:00, afternoon
Location: Delta Marketplace, Sitnalta Island

AT RISE DESCRIPTION: *At Flow's request, Chakramire and Mara Mara visit the Delta Market to see what her twin sister Ebb is wearing.*

[Enter Chakramire and Mara Mara]

EGRESS MACHINE (via MARA MARA) *[Aside]*

Chastity's moniker never demanded respect from its
victims; recoil from the cadence of stone. A magnanimous
mind would reject the appeal to absolve a surrender to
passion. However, a barrier augmented, vanity
yielded survival gratuities. Solace descended from
summit to valley and under the turbulent river of
decadence, deeper for dearth of deterrence, determined to
bow to the ripple effect of a desperate innocence.

[Enter Ebb, flanked by onlookers]

MARA MARA *[Aside]*

Before the swill, the swine, and the swindlers left the market
place, the seamstress Ebb, estranged twin of Flow, performed a show.
A bird resumes the preening of plumes, and yet for all the
glimmer, sheen, and shine, a fowl's feathers shield it less against
predation's eye than horror of ridicule. A bird of
prey. A bird of prey. Between death and fashion lying naught.
Approaching eyes, the window display, a chance to shame with

beauty, beautifying shame, glance away and slow demise
encroaching.

Humbled vanity gathered down the square as
she began the barren runway, a desert rose among
the shrubs. Beneath her emerald orbs, cascading fabrics
fall from collars stout to hush shoulders, smoothen nipples, strip
perspective, veil voluptuous skin, and drape perdition.
Scarlet Sheath.

A cherry red garment perched upon its host,
a parasite, aloof but dependent, radiating
hunger, thirst, and might, its neckline devoured the nape, its seams
constricted waists, whatever it cuffed escaped from freedom.
Scarlet Sheath.

The crimson dress wore its body thin, robust
as grapes before the harvest, could bore its image through a
glass of wine, and needed no coat of arms. It seized the eye,
evoking charmed revulsion, commanding every movement.
Scarlet Sheath.

SCARLET SHEATH (via EBB)

"Desire, conceit, gall . . ."

MARA MARA *[Aside]*

The gown began its speech
of motions.

SCARLET SHEATH (via EBB)

"They have never resisted me. From gazing
oglers, clothing conquers scorn, though ambition renders plain
a woman whose attraction would otherwise seduce the
world. Of lust, its man endured me but once, thereafter died

from guilt. Of pride, its woman withstood but once as well, and weak thereafter fell. To win fortune's favor, one survives against the odds, for liberty's license, cede abandon."

MARA MARA *[Aside]*

Seamstress Ebbe, with bridled eyes, curtsied, turned, and disappeared.

[They exit]

WHEN THE SYMPHONY'S DISCORD RISES: PART ONE

CANTO 5: CIPHER

Galactic Calendar: Sol System; Earth year 30,123,012 M.W.I.
Tellurian Solar Calendar: Day five of the sixth tenth – 06/05
Modern Metric Time: 4:75:00, UTC+00:00, dusk or evening twilight
Location: The Scabbard at the Pantheon, Sitnalta Island

AT RISE DESCRIPTION: *Chakramire and Mara Mara head to the Scabbard, a hollowed out piece of earth serving as Zero's altar, to meet with the Dagger Vance at the rendezvous point.*

[Enter Chakramire and Mara Mara]

EGRESS MACHINE (via MARA MARA) *[Aside]*

Sentences, symbols, superfluous entities, absent of
natural meaning. Abstractions unite the impossible.
Gravity, only its force of attraction, the darkest of
matter, could marry the false to the rational.
Representation, a crime of distinction, the bridge and the
barrier, parries correction and carries protection, but
entropy never desists. From oblivion traveled and
back the contagion, to harness the value of weightlessness.

CHAKRAMIRE

"For we can not exist . . ."

MARA MARA *[Aside]*

But the invocation crumbled.
Onomatopoeia, sounds imitation, vain before
the Deva's ear. The effigy twisted.

CHAKRAMIRE

"Whatsoever
is a name? a group of phonemes? a band of emblems? These
collections matter not."

MARA MARA *[Aside]*

At the edge of Zero's hollowed
altar, walking straight from death's room, the Dagger paid the price
of sacrifices true. For a scratch against the marble
skin of Heathen Weave and Twine, Vance would take a life at whim
without the proof of crime. With a broken face and empty
heart, the Dagger's words became all.

[Enter Vance]

VANCE

"A trade of eyes and ears,
your promise I shall keep, to ignite the flame of war and
make the mountain's peak."

CHAKRAMIRE

"A phantasmagoric force resides
within your mind. You summoned a beast of yore, and spoke the
Modal Maxim. I, for lackluster luck, the Devas dare
ignore. Request an audience."

MARA MARA *[Aside]*

Dagger genuflected.

VANCE

"We can ***not*** exist without them."

MARA MARA *[Aside]*

Enraptured, Dagger Vance,
the Gallow Prince, convulsed with a spasm only fit for
dolls, and shattered like a scream thrown across the wind. At first
it seemed a seizure's work, but became a letting go. The
lesser man would die of hurt, strong the Dagger's bones. A flake
of snow awoke the bulk of the limp, enfeebled body.

CHAKRAMIRE

"Zero next to None, the whetstone of tongues before you stands.
Relieve yourself a dangerous foe, or earn the chakram's
ire."

[Enter Zero]

ZERO (via VANCE)

"Your jaundiced pigment, Globeflower-eyes, the heavens too
shall envy. Name your price and become redundant, I will
mock whatever offered."

CHAKRAMIRE

"Why keep an altar if you turn
away the goods?"

ZERO (via VANCE)

"And why have you kept a bard? Your legend
dies the day you do, a life everlasting naught. A fame
preserved with relics, images obsolete, antiques and
words as old as oceans are deep, will loathe the mortal gave
itself a form. Audacious the reputation swollen
nigh above its owner. Bards, books, and sculptures differ in
the name alone."

CHAKRAMIRE

"From records, the story told will beg to
die."

ZERO (via VANCE)

"And why?"

CHAKRAMIRE

"The booby prize shared between convincing lies
rewards the least of lives, but enough of me, your chance, to
please inform your host, from what came the Dagger Vance to know
the Furthermost?"

ZERO (via VANCE)

"However you underestimate your
reputation, Dagger Vance knew your name before the face.
Himself an emissary the Furthermost of Women
met, a death befell the Globeflower-eyed to curse the worst
and best. Without the sign of your life to quell the storm of
war, a maelstrom swallowed Vance through the ocean floor. To sink
a vessel fierce and mighty as Lady Chakramire, a
wave required the highest height, teaching even clouds to spire.
The undertow would follow, devouring inhibition,
sank the mate and child of Vance, Nettles stung the Dagger's hands.
You tore the world asunder with such a grand deception,
Dagger deemed your end a one righteous form of plunder. All
the actions undertaken you wore the mark divine of
retribution; any length gone to right a slight attests
the truth of virtue."

[Exit Zero]

CHAKRAMIRE

"Frugal your words conceded. Harken
back to times when promise one never needed."

MARA MARA *[Aside]*

Late the words
from Chakramire, the Deva dispersed before, but Dagger,
dispossessed thereafter, upheld the cipher's lore.

VANCE

"You act
as if a Pyrrhic victory one can win with single
blows; attrition fills the grandstand, and wrinkles make the clothes."

[They exit]

WHEN THE SYMPHONY'S DISCORD RISES: PART ONE

CANTO 6: NEMESIS

Galactic Calendar: Sol System; Earth year 30,123,012 M.W.I.
Tellurian Solar Calendar: Day six of the sixth tenth – 06/06
Modern Metric Time: 1:75:00, UTC+00:00, morning
Location: Along the Ash River, Sitnalta Island

AT RISE DESCRIPTION: *Vance, Chakramire, and Mara Mara travel through the outer capitol district of Sitnalta along the Ash River back to the Water Clock.*

[Enter Chakramire, Mara Mara, and Vance]

EGRESS MACHINE (via MARA MARA) *[Aside]*

Welcoming parties were welcomed regardless of merit or
want. A diversion away from conventional gossip could
sharpen the fugitive's edge, but a criminal's honesty
promised reward nor reprieve. To conceive a deception, the
gambit should never exceed the original confidence.
Needful to say, a coincidence rarely surrendered its
vitals to popular sentiment save at a premium.
Many a lunar eclipse has embarrassed a predator.

MARA MARA *[Aside]*

At least as many virtues exist as people, least as
many vices too. At least each misfortune suffered man
and woman unexceptional; pain and pleasure merely
tools.

CHAKRAMIRE

"Whereas wherever we first encountered, I recall
it not, whereas the Dagger remembered me, and Dagger
I forgot, perchance the Flagship of Justice circle round
to sweep again for memories drowned?"

VANCE

“Before the bounty
hunter mourned the loss of child, wife, before the Dagger Vance
became the Dagger Vance, and before the feign of lady
Chakramire’s departure life, I, an emissary sent
to Mars Dominion . . . saw the arrival undesired of
Lady Chakramire. A decade of isolation breaks
a mind or reinforces its hubris; people froze from
trepidation, Chakramire lasted three. The move to Mars
with just a bard, the welcoming party welcomed, said the
Lady Eris, ‘I, to Earth,’ feats attempted seldom. Not
a single person born for the stars, from thirty million
years ago and heretofore, not a single person born
the stars surviving Earth for a year or more . . . and now it
twelve, the Mistress Strife alive, skin as dark the day it dyed.
For ever greater miracles I shall strive, for even
greater justice, enterprise, I remain dissatisfied.”

CHAKRAMIRE

“But whence the Dagger ventured? Revenge, a tempting dish it
is, however, quickly spoils.”

VANCE

“Stronger secrets lock themselves
within a room along with the keys.”

CHAKRAMIRE

“And via absence
give themselves away, the black hole itself a key. To gain
the upper hand a nemesis, underhanded gloves it
best to wear.”

VANCE

"Below the sea lies the continental shelf;
above the air the secret will soon reveal itself. To
where the harlot Flow dispatched Chakramire? It rare, for she
entrusts another seldomly."

CHAKRAMIRE

"Flow desired for me to
see her sister, witness what seamstress Ebb attired."

VANCE

"And what
the seamstress wore?"

CHAKRAMIRE

"The ugliest dress alive; it moved with
scorn . . . and yet, as awful Ebb's gown, as stunning she, as if
the garment any other would kill to wear."

VANCE

"The hand of
Baron Varlet moves."

CHAKRAMIRE

"And which man the Baron Varlet?"

VANCE

"Just
a man upon whomever our worldly problems shouldered."

[They exit]

WHEN THE SYMPHONY'S DISCORD RISES: PART ONE

CANTO 7: RETROGRADE DEFENSE

Galactic Calendar: Sol System; Earth year 30,123,012 M.W.I.
Tellurian Solar Calendar: Day seven of the sixth tenth – 06/07
Modern Metric Time: 5:25:00, UTC+00:00, dusk or evening twilight
Location: Water Clock Brothel, Sitnalta Island

AT RISE DESCRIPTION: *Chakramire, Vance, and Mara Mara arrive at the Water Clock Brothel.*

[Enter Chakramire, Mara Mara, and Vance]

EGRESS MACHINE (via MARA MARA) *[Aside]*

Loyalty favors the powerful, treason the powerless,
power the transient. Anomalies are the primordial
scars, for the sightliest mark of a bandit, the genuine
promise, evokes a dissenter's suspicion. Professionals
call it the causal revolt, a misnomer for sacrilege.
Better to be a delinquent than taken with glee, and to
covet the hooligan's bounty, but brandish complacency.
Enter the grotto with clemency, essence of thievery.

MARA MARA *[Aside]*

Chakramire, with cadence almost heroic, flounders not
because of night. Humanity wandered, waffled, wasted
most its adolescence just ascertaining whether light
a thing of good or evil, and all along the answer
knew, for hidden shadows lurk monstrous brutes of life as vile
the villains blinding bright. From its virtue vice emerges.
Chakramire, with cadence almost heroic, flounders not
because of night.

CHAKRAMIRE

"A homelier face the Lady Eris
never seen, the darkness spared me its sight."

MARA MARA *[Aside]*

And Chakramire
aside the mirror turned, from the window light reflection.

VANCE

"Lady Flow, the one you call Ember Wisp, away the clock,
and though your face, it beautiful simple, lacks the charm of
prostitutes, a face complex wears a dimple even if
it destitute."

MARA MARA *[Aside]*

Simplicity, furthermost from things the
Furthermost of Women wants.

VANCE

"What provoked the Mistress Strife
to spurn the people Earth? For whomever Lady Eris
sought the vengeance won with false death?"

CHAKRAMIRE

"For Pluto, Eris, self,
and Paris."

VANCE

"Why the tragedy Paris? Wronged the Lady
Chakramire the former Conduit?"

CHAKRAMIRE

"Challenged me to lead
a fourth the children Earth, but a rival me nor foe. The

proxies feared for Paris, feared Lady Eris tempt or sway,
and snubbed the Mistress Strife from the coronation, tried to
keep the Furthermost at bay."

VANCE

"Chose, the Lady Chakramire,
to keep away?"

CHAKRAMIRE

"From manners, the resolute forever
stray; the Lady Eris came anyway, toward the crowd
released a trophy gold, 'For the one with hidden knowledge.'
Laid a hand the Brain of Discord, the Numbers brought the fray,
but Paris boldly claimed the award, and Paris did the
proxies slay for seeking not just a puppet stay."

VANCE

"And what
became the Golden Brain?"

CHAKRAMIRE

"It succumbed to disarray and
back to Lady Chakramire came, believed a fatal charm.
From worldly life the Mistress of Strife and Mara Mara
disappeared. With Paris dead, all the world afire, the League
of Numbers pleaded thus, and admitted murdered Paris . . .
they mistook for Chakramire, offered up a retrograde
defense. For opportunity missing, not for lack of
effort, true the claim, as I knew the Lady Chakramire
the proxies wanted slain."

[Enter Calypso]

CALYPSO

"And behold, the world an ugly
place,"

MARA MARA *[Aside]*

declared Calypso, whose beauty killed, but Chakramire,
its beauty saw, and knew its potential unfulfilled. The
harlot wore a dimple like truth of no importance, said,

CALYPSO

"The Dagger's guest awakened, for want of no disturbance."

VANCE

"Bid the man from slumber wake, Dagger Vance and Mistress Strife await."

MARA MARA *[Aside]*

Her eyes, Calypso conceals; with true conviction
only see whatever they want to see, whatever they
believe already. Hanging above the bed, suspended
covers soft, a man the Globeflower-eyed suspected dead,
the Captain lay aloft.

CHAKRAMIRE

"To recover Dagger's missing
knife, whyever bring the whole victim too?"

VANCE

"The Captain is
the knife, for he, with Dagger, a pact. For now, the body
clings to life, the herringbone-edged stiletto still intact."

[They exit]

WHEN THE SYMPHONY'S DISCORD RISES: PART ONE

CANTO 8: CAUTERIZE

Galactic Calendar: Sol System; Earth year 30,123,012 M.W.I.
Tellurian Solar Calendar: Day eight of the sixth tenth – 06/08
Modern Metric Time: 8:00:00, UTC+00:00, morning twilight
Location: Water Clock Brothel, Sitnalta Island

AT RISE DESCRIPTION: *Chakramire, Mara Mara, and Vance stand at the Captain's bedside.*

[Enter Chakramire, Mara Mara, Vance, and the Captain]

EGRESS MACHINE (via MARA MARA) *[Aside]*

Freezing the maker of paces prohibits a temporal
harvest. The furnaces stoking themselves shall explode. Should the
willing resist the resent of content? A cessation of
movement releases the tourniquet over nostalgia, for
courage congeals as devotion withdraws, but the fury of
restlessness smolders. Temptation's abeyance, inquisitors
call it a death of the second degree, the consumption of
life, an eternal rebellion, or kindle for apathy.

MARA MARA *[Aside]*

To never know privation deprives a person value's
practice, robs the mind its fine-tuning, skews the judgment down.
To never know abundance deprives a person value's
respite, robs the mind its vine pruning, skews the judgment up.
Abundance, Lady Eris without. Privation, Paris
Alexander never knew. Overheard, the Captain, Vance
and Chakramire . . . requested ado anew.

CAPTAIN

"However
Paris claimed the Brian of Discord, with proxies holding fast?"

CHAKRAMIRE

"Although the etymology meant defender, Paris
dared to live above his namesake, but fell below its mark.
The weight a name can crumple a man, the proxies asked for
Paris choose a winner. He, humankind, against itself
defended, knew its patience, than madness, thinner. Common
foes create the strangest bedfellows, they with self-regard
offended."

VANCE

"Metaphorical speech and honest people
liken oil and water, one cloudy while the other just
the stuff of clouds, the former a surface waxed poetic,
while the latter merely wet, mingling brief enough to show
aversion."

CHAKRAMIRE

"Paris chose to unite the League of Numbers . . .
sacrificed himself."

MARA MARA *[Aside]*

The Globeflower-eyed, beside the bed
disheveled, doubts the Captain's allegiance.

CHAKRAMIRE

"Why the Dagger
saved your life? As nearly he sought its end."

CAPTAIN

"Because our foe
the same, because the skin of the bandit Nettles made of
barbs and brambled hairs, because inner sight the eyes occlude,
but outer sight enable, because conjoined our vision
falters, strives to see with eyes things the eyes will never see,

believes the incorporeal world clairvoyant, strives to
know without the senses things only known the senses, holds
the world but doubts it tangible while attempting pain to
overlook. Because a lifetime commitment's wane the bane
of crooks."

MARA MARA *[Aside]*

Beheld the manifestation desperation,
faking death to break from thief gilding. Knew the layered gold
abducted mold, would fester a sore with lustrous spores. A
shadow crossed the Dagger's face, swept from view the shame it felt,
Calypso dimmed the lights, and asleep the Captain fell.

[Enter Calypso]

CALYPSO

"The
time to act, it yesterday; cauterize or not the wound?
Another day's delay and the Captain's life, it doomed."

VANCE

"And
such a cure could kill a man, be the wound of flesh or mind."

CALYPSO

"For thieves, the options limited, even mediocre
ones maligned. The cause of life is the cause of life, to give
divine."

MARA MARA *[Aside]*

The Dagger clutched the stiletto, while Calypso
lit a fire, and though the blade entered nimbly, left a storm
of red upon departing. Calypso cleaned the wound, the

Dagger seared the knife, and swift burned the Captain's blood; it burned throughout the night. Calypso, the morning after, called for Chakramire.

CALYPSO

"A restless Flow waits; of dresses she inquires."

[They exit]

WHEN THE SYMPHONY'S DISCORD RISES: PART ONE

CANTO 9: REABSORPTION

Galactic Calendar: Sol System; Earth year 30,123,012 M.W.I.
Tellurian Solar Calendar: Day nine of the sixth tenth – 06/09
Modern Metric Time: 0:25:00, UTC+00:00, near sunrise
Location: Water Clock Brothel, Sitnalta Island

AT RISE DESCRIPTION: *Chakramire and Mara Mara sit with Flow in her chamber. Calypso stands at the door.*

[Enter Chakramire, Mara Mara, Calypso, and Flow]

EGRESS MACHINE (via MARA MARA) *[Aside]*

Chastity's moniker never demanded respect from its victims; recoil from the cadence of stone. A magnanimous mind would reject the appeal to absolve a surrender to passion. However, a barrier augmented, vanity yielded survival gratuities. Solace descended from summit to valley and under the turbulent river of decadence, deeper for dearth of deterrence, determined to bow to the ripple effect of a desperate innocence.

MARA MARA *[Aside]*

Within the Duodecimal Constellation one can find the self and lose the self all the same, for hasty eyes will find whatever sought from a horoscope, but lose the unattended.

CHAKRAMIRE

"Said of contrast, 'It matters more alone than dark or light, and never forget the stars as bright the day as night.'"

FLOW

"Whoever said such a thing?"

MARA MARA *[Aside]*

The Mistress Strife
with grievance stood, defiantly mute. The awkward silence
awkward only if an eavesdropper's censure people wished
to speak without.

FLOW

"The bard can remain."

MARA MARA *[Aside]*

Calypso took the
hint, and bid farewell the game.

[Calypso exits]

CHAKRAMIRE

"Spoke the words the callow mind
a child, its grasp reality neither firm enough nor
clear to merit delving too deep imagination's dark
and murky waters, lest it forget to surface, lest it
never know it need to come up for air besides. The child,
a war against erroneous language waged, against the
trope of disappearing stars. Knew a person either chose
to master life's emotions, or mastered by emotion
be . . . to wield the hammer like gladiators, buckling not
beneath its weight, or let the momentum overwhelm the
body, losing balance each swing.

"The greatest error love,
attempting shield from innocence truth, from rosy eyes. Our
predecessors wanted too much of words, from asking them

accomplish more than they were designed to do, to holding
these as sacred, those profane, not believing ugly ones
despite the fact the prettier ones deserved disdain. The
child who learns a star at noon only seems to disappear,
it doubts the world impartial, and heretofore a child, but
never after."

MARA MARA *[Aside]*

Lady Flow let a silence fill the room,
permitted thoughts to gather, ignored the question hanging
high the air.

FLOW

"The truth, at times ugly, I desire to know
it still. Describe the dress of the seamstress Ebb, however
bold or modest."

CHAKRAMIRE

"Said of contrast, 'It matters more alone
than dark or light,' as awful the dress as gorgeous she, a
pyre against the night,"

MARA MARA *[Aside]*

and drew, Chakramire, the Scarlet Sheath,
it beauty's parasite.

CHAKRAMIRE

"For whatever reason wanted
any know the dress attired Ebb? A sister simpler just
to ask, unless a quarrel between the two."

FLOW

"You make a
secret's reabsorption no easy feat to win, and twice

has life desired its meaning from me, but I delivered
naught."

CHAKRAMIRE

"Perhaps it time to end petty squabbles, giving room
for larger ones to grow, to permit decorum's wobble,
counterblows forego the ergo?"

FLOW

"Perhaps. Perhaps the two
of us, again, shall be as the river next the sea, shall
freely mix with women, men, learn to never disagree."

[They exit]

WHEN THE SYMPHONY'S DISCORD RISES: PART ONE

CANTO 10: BIRTHRIGHT

Galactic Calendar: Sol System; Earth year 30,123,012 M.W.I.
Tellurian Solar Calendar: Day nine of the sixth tenth – 06/09
Modern Metric Time: 7:50:00, UTC+00:00, night
Location: Water Clock Brothel, Sitnalta Island

AT RISE DESCRIPTION: *Chakramire and Mara Mara tend to and talk with the dying Captain near his bedside.*

[Enter Chakramire, Mara Mara, and Captain]

EGRESS MACHINE (via MARA MARA) *[Aside]*

Sentences, symbols, superfluous entities, absent of
natural meaning. Abstractions unite the impossible.
Gravity, only its force of attraction, the darkest of
matter, could marry the false to the rational.
Representation, a crime of distinction, the bridge and the
barrier, parries correction and carries protection, but
entropy never desists. From oblivion traveled and
back the contagion, to harness the value of weightlessness.

CHAKRAMIRE

"'To go beyond, or struggle within our limits, knowing
life the art of war, for true peace belongs to death. Should we
withdraw and turn around or resolve to forge ahead? A
pity one's reflection no answer ever gives . . .' the first
of many words from Praxis Harmonic."

[All exit except Captain]

***

[Enter Chakramire, Mara Mara, and Praxis Harmonic on Earth's moon twelve years ago]

CHAKRAMIRE

"I desire to
see its nature."

PRAXIS HARMONIC

"Nature is everywhere. Whoever needs
to trample cross the galaxy just to see it, never
sees it."

CHAKRAMIRE

"Eris, Earthlings see never. None of Earth have seen
its beauty. Why deny for a cousin distanced visit
they, the ones who live without thought or inhibition, they,
the overwhelmed with happiness?"

PRAXIS HARMONIC

"Being overwhelmed with
feeling is as scarcely praiseworthy falling down a flight
of stairs because of gravity's pull."

CHAKRAMIRE

"Were ever there a
stair. Erisians never fall, never climb the stair to fall
from."

PRAXIS HARMONIC

"Fine. However, seek to inflame, to spare the Earth from
order, peace, or balance, know I, at every turn shall thwart
your aims."

[All exit except Captain]

***

[Enter Chakramire, and Mara Mara, with the Captain at the Water Clock]

MARA MARA *[Aside]*

For half the morning and half the night, the Captain
labored life, although a corpse, more alive than Lady Strife,
although a single hand it had clung to life with thirty's
might.

CAPTAIN

"The noblest man to be, nobler next to me, had stooped
to rise above temptation, but stumbled nigh before it . . ."

MARA MARA *[Aside]*

Waiving strife's retrieval, first generation evil. Not
a day shall pass devoid its splendor, nor life without contender.

CHAKRAMIRE

"Quarrels are the people's birthright; its sole defender, I."

[They exit]

BOOK II:
WHERE SERENITY AND STRIFE CLEAVE

PART ONE: MAVERICK OR JACKAL?

WHERE SERENITY AND STRIFE CLEAVE: PART ONE

CANTO 41: THE SOLVENT'S VICTIM
Galactic Calendar: Sol System; Earth year 30,123,012 M.W.I.
Tellurian Solar Calendar: Day one of the seventh tenth – 07/01
Modern Metric Time: 2:00:00, UTC+00:00, near midday
Location: Meso's Glass Forge at Gaffer's Gorge, Sitnalta Island

AT RISE DESCRIPTION: *Chakramire and Mara Mara stand before Meso in his office on the western edge of the Central Province in a location referred to as Gaffer's Gorge due to its abundance of salt mines and other materials needed for glass-making.*

[Enter Chakramire, Mara Mara, and Meso]

EGRESS MACHINE (via MARA MARA) *[Aside]*

Mixtures engender disparities, tonic solutions, and
crystals. An ocean of promise, an island of hope, and a
grain of success. The impartial refinement of destiny
leaves a residual ridge of repression. Minorities
rise as majorities fade, but serenity's scarcity
teases. The blistering fragrance of brine, with a whiff of the
gaffer's sobriety, tore from obsidian modicum
salaries, given to only the salt of society.

MESO

"The lesser fit for physical work would only be at
rest."

MARA MARA *[Aside]*

With Briny Stacks, the Saline, contempt would stride abreast.

MESO

"At best, you bear a morbid condition only mothers
ever love. Who holds the show over tell and questions why
the actor's craft the masses empower, praising those who
earn a living lying outright for life. And lady, truth
shall I confess, aside from your strength awry, your skills would
bleed a river dry, the bard, just a little less."

MARA MARA *[Aside]*

Before
the lady Chakramire could diffuse concern, again would
Meso speak.

MESO

"As I have won shame from whosoever owned
a mollycoddled poet's vocabulary, even
thought a fool to wield a handful of cards with great finesse . . .
but best to hold a smatter of words with style than know a
language whole and bumble nonsense."

MARA MARA *[Aside]*

To poets Meso turned.

MESO

"As garish these allusions, your trappings, muddling every
disposition, need you libraries whole for single tales
to tell another? Need you a passion sprawled across the
face to deem sincere the voice? Need a shifty eye condemn
a man to seven years of frustration? Need a blunted,
bloated nail demand a sledgehammer, though a pushing pin
suffice?"

MARA MARA *[Aside]*

At last, from dormancy, rose an angst a million
generations strong. The Scorched Face volcano, candlelight
to Chakramire, a gainful employment being all the
lady thirsted.

CHAKRAMIRE

"Never I saw a story write itself,
nor right itself, with absence of plan, for even strong and
stubborn tales can not redeem bad beginnings."

MARA MARA *[Aside]*

Smoke and flame
the Furthermost unleashed, for the gaffer roiled her blood to
burn.

CHAKRAMIRE

"You claim, 'To come from no means a more impressive feat
should stories rise to prominence . . . pantomime detached from
speech a specious scandal upending frays, the facial mask
a knot of twelve dimensions with furrowed brows and twitching
cheeks about to make the onlookers guess intentions.'

"Go
ahead, defend your craft with your coat of arms, the symbol
lives beyond its means, for too close the fire you walk to know
it burns the garment's seams. The physique of mine could never
bear the stress of quarry mines, lifting daily heaps of sand
with soda ash and lime. The command of intuition,
windy art compared to glassblowing, circumvents the Man
of Crystal like a flagrant omission."

MARA MARA *[Aside]*

Hot the words of
Chakramire, from glory holes meaning melts; a smith can shape
the liquid matter, solid the glass will only shatter.
Meso took a breath. A blowpipe with strength to force itself
upon a lexicon could legitimize the worst of
crimes, or vilify the best.

MESO

"I mistook your fortitude
for sass. You rape impregnable speech with ease, a lady
not above the struggle; no greater threat exists to words
beyond your mental muscle."

MARA MARA *[Aside]*

The sweat from Meso, deft its
pace, evaporated bright, left a face with streaks of white,
the residue of fright.

MESO

"But bereft of grace who speaks of
fight when truth a dictum dead, framed for prohibition's breach . . ."

MARA MARA *[Aside]*

the solvent's victim said.

MESO

"You can say whatever felt or
feel the spoken, gaps between cannons loose and shooters sharp.
To earn the job you seek from the forge confirm the art of
yours. From craven cowards make martyrs; slake the Queen of Spores."

[They exit]

WHERE SERENITY AND STRIFE CLEAVE: PART ONE

CANTO 42: DOUBLE BIND

Galactic Calendar: Sol System; Earth year 30,123,012 M.W.I.
Tellurian Solar Calendar: Day two of the seventh tenth – 07/02
Modern Metric Time: 5:50:00, UTC+00:00, dusk or evening twilight
Location: Youngberry Tavern, Sitnalta Island

AT RISE DESCRIPTION: *Chakramire and Mara Mara sit in Youngberry Tavern, conspicuously detached from Epi, heir to the Youngberry Estate, with several sponsors present.*

[Enter Chakramire, Mara Mara, Epi, and patrons]

EGRESS MACHINE (via MARA MARA) *[Aside]*

Luxury's only redeeming distinction, hostility
fostered between the affluent and poverty-stricken. A
life of extravagance, enemy strife, will solicit the
gold of our youth with the spirits fermenting a bottle of
comfort, decay and creation, a rose from the dead with a
noxious aesthetic. The idiosyncrasy, fighting to
linger at rest or against a deciduous passion. A
lavish inertia, the spoil from an era of constancy.

MARA MARA *[Aside]*

Across the bar a gathering beckoned. Only lady
Chakramire resisted forthright approach, a march towards
the tavern's breath of puffery, smoke, and whiskey. Filtered
through the venomed air, the Youngberry heir apparent looked
divine for lack of charm, a charisma born aberrant.
Flocks around the Queen of Spores, Epi, Lady Leaven . . . dank,
the corner, dark, the ambience, she, the tavern's voice.

EPI

"A
life of servitude or stark destitution looms, but fail
to make a stand for righteousness everywhere it kneels and
vice becomes a ghost."

MARA MARA *[Aside]*

The haunt roared with adulation, save
the Furthermost, and spectacles carried forward, leaving
only two to toast.

EPI

"For gemstones you hunted, trekking all
across the universe with the greatest jewel hanging
round the neck. For heat, you safeguarded everything but fire,
and strove against our heliocentric birth. For stars, you
traded conscience, halved a heartbeat, surrendered joy and earned
a pittance. Hope was used as a whipping stick to flog our
brethren into outer space. Faith, the mirror, turned you straight
from paradise."

MARA MARA *[Aside]*

The Mistress of Strife refused to waver,
crowds around ablaze, and soon stole attention's favor, all
to no amaze.

CHAKRAMIRE

"A vitreous time to live when curtains
tempt the burglar rob a thought; sadder still the curtain's task
to shield an empty house."

EPI

"Your affronts and pleas concur, a
double-edge your choice of words. One from all, our double binds

tormenting more to stop than to keep the fight alive, but
we cannot exist ***without*** them!"

CHAKRAMIRE

"A species seldom gets
a second chance at destiny, never mind a third."

MARA MARA *[Aside]*

The
room dissolves, expanding twelvefold. Hallucinations ring
the ear, eleven tables to ring the one, and darkness
wrings the eyes of sight. But hung far across the room would glare
a work of legendary fluorescent art with fame to
match the Furthermost, *The Nightscape and Afterglow*. It split
the dark apart.

EPI

"The vanishing point of hope our eyes have
missed, for desperation makes darlings out of fools. From left
to right to ultraviolet borrowed light, the painting
lacks perspective."

MARA MARA *[Aside]*

Epi's speech, once a steady march, became
a mess of inarticulate phrases, loaded words, and
multiform battalions, like wounded soldiers shuffling off
the battlefield with absent and amputated limbs; the
innards bleed or missing go, each a patient having long
ago surrendered consciousness. Syncope, the surgeons
say. The word of One could mean everything, and everything
the word of One could mean. At the edge the painting bright, a
swirl of iridescence wound tight around the center, fades
to black, the middle outward, engulfed toward an onyx

hole. The word of One could mean everything, and everything
the word of One could mean.

[Enter One]

ONE (via EPI)

"From the cradle fled the child, as
if the crib were under siege, knowing not the light beheld
was cast from beds departed. To chase perfection, waves of
light, a deadly game of tag. Darkness caught the sign of truth
and choked the metaphor, for existing is to change, but
light, forever constant, leaves room for no improvement, leaves
the room and all improve."

CHAKRAMIRE

"A disturbance called itself a
wave and all the world forgot physics. Fix your words or change
heuristics; uniformity likens order."

ONE (via EPI)

"Though a
wave disrupts a faulty rest, bringing nearer normal states,
and all will yield to entropy, save the Furthermost of
late, the tallest mind the land over sees the world exposed,
the smaller, not as pervious, think themselves a system
closed."

[Exit One]

MARA MARA *[Aside]*

A breeze as cold the west wind was pushed toward the floor,
its heat dispersed the quicker, the Deva nevermore. The
light returned as faint before, time resumed eternal, swore

the end of sight temporal, and hope a thing external.
Life had tested Epi, Youngberry heir apparent.

CHAKRAMIRE

"I
arrived to broker quarrels for Meso, Briny Stacks. The
Man of Crystal seeks to end Lady Leaven's dream of wine
and liquor freely traded beyond the tavern's beams."

EPI

"You
never cease to give your best, even after we return
it. Came you here to size an opponent?"

CHAKRAMIRE

"I arrived to
broker quarrels."

EPI

"Came you here plotting vengeance?"

CHAKRAMIRE

"I arrived
to broker quarrels."

EPI

"Came you to rid our lives of comfort?"

CHAKRAMIRE

"Comfort is to artists hemlock, a finer thing to paint
or sing than eat. To smear with a single color takes a
steady hand; our brush, it knows only crimson, only blood
will whet its strands. Should couples agree to make a war the

spark of strife dismissed. For peace press, a stronger play, and keep your hostile thoughts adrift."

EPI

"From the tavern leave sublime, and
peace for Meso, man of all teeth, a comb without a spine."

[They exit]

WHERE SERENITY AND STRIFE CLEAVE: PART ONE

CANTO 43: STARFLOWER

Galactic Calendar: Sol System; Earth year 30,123,012 M.W.I.
Tellurian Solar Calendar: Day three of the seventh tenth – 07/03
Modern Metric Time: 3:00:00, UTC+00:00, afternoon
Location: Belladonna Nursery, Sitnalta Island

AT RISE DESCRIPTION: *Chakramire and Mara Mara stand before Xara at her botanical nursery to negotiate a shipment of glass.*

[Enter Chakramire, Mara Mara, Xara]

EGRESS MACHINE (via MARA MARA) *[Aside]*

Flayers of canvas endeavor to smother the future of
fabric transparent. Whoever would champion beauty at
bio-diversity's loss, would demand from existence a
penance for youth and utility crossed: a symmetrical
ratio of mythic proportions, the measure of powder, of
paint, with the prettiest flower displaced from a desert, the
glorification of taste. As the radiance bleaches a
visage, the symphonies wash from a face of exuberance.

XARA

"Our youth and immaturity fit together snugly,"

MARA MARA *[Aside]*

said the adolescing voice ever so and smugly.

XARA

"Just,
the world, to masterminds who retain the lure of looks."

CHAKRAMIRE

“And
just the world to master minds lured to look retained.”

XARA

“The first
of those command attention from land and lord alike; the
latter is a bargain, if waste supplies demand.”

CHAKRAMIRE

“Perhaps.
The ones who yield to destiny, they surrender more than
ownership of feeling; they suffer more from wishful thought
than peace or promise broken, and more than ever lose the
claim to any moral ground. Indeterministic minds
alone possess the right to complain, the might to render
sentimental, fly above moral plains.”

XARA

“To rise against
the Milky Way Initiative, need a humble maiden
die?”

MARA MARA *[Aside]*

A life’s ambition burns underfoot as Xara turns
around, for Earth would serve as her bound of yearning, thunder,
soot.

XARA

“Aesthetics disappeared many fateful years ago
beneath the starry gaze of determination. What a
sad display of bluster; we live for duty’s sake.”

MARA MARA *[Aside]*

With hands
of petals spread the pollen, atop a solar wind, and
clutched the universe, the starflower known as Hope. Arose
and swept across its galaxied culture, deemed the beauty
human life enough, the starflower known as Prudence. Spread,
the fingers, labor's fruit, for against succession's agent
none compared.

CHAKRAMIRE

"Supplant your downhearted veins with plasma, sear
the very air, of lightning and fire the stars are made, of
water, ice, despair. Your words spoken now would never move
the weightless, notwithstanding the witless; some were born for
greatness, others just to bear witness."

XARA

"I would cherish more
the Earth and Moon before a celestial body. I would
tremble more from mighty earthquakes before the aftermath,
and I would ape the patience of plates before a tremor's
seismic wake. The cause of life is the cause of life, the end
our beauty strives, and only fanatics think it crude, the
death of pulchritude."

MARA MARA *[Aside]*

The Globeflower-eyed, a lady past
anachronistic, noticing everywhere the setting
sun has shined and places eyes never dared, beheld the bluff
of Xara, pushed her over its edge.

CHAKRAMIRE

"To find the fountain,
Youth, and keep it hidden hence, takes reserve your kind resents.

You fear the consequence. Should the truths you know refuse to
grow, will overrun with old weeds."

MARA MARA *[Aside]*

For Strife would neither raise
an arm to strike, nor punches, nor kicks would land, and small her
frame, a fifth her stature, hold always upper hands. Against
whomever Eris struggles would struggle not again.

CHAKRAMIRE

"To
chase the future down, or break free the past, the smartest hide
and seek to outmaneuver the present."

XARA

"No offense would
jeopardize the better, no virtue sweeter smell, than false
emotion smeared across the entire Kinesis Realm."

CHAKRAMIRE

"Your
pain defy to rein or let fly the anger stored within
for beauty slain, for modesty's gain, for glamor's wane, for
righteous indignation held back before the slaughtered vain."

XARA

"As much as I would love to restore defunct cosmetic
arts, the means to reach beyond grasp exceeds the reach of me."

CHAKRAMIRE

"To grow a harvest worthy the cause of looks you only
need naivete, for greenhouses built transparent aim
to lead astray. A vitreous time to live when windows,

all expected, shield against everything, a prying eye
excepted."

XARA

"Hiding faces with gardens is a timeless
guise; commit, shall I, to know Strife, until the end our lives."

[They exit]

WHERE SERENITY AND STRIFE CLEAVE: PART ONE

CANTO 44: COMMOTION

Galactic Calendar: Sol System; Earth year 30,123,012 M.W.I.
Tellurian Solar Calendar: Day four of the seventh tenth – 07/04
Modern Metric Time: 2:00:00, UTC+00:00, near midday
Location: The Scorched Face (Western Escarpment), Sitnalta Island

AT RISE DESCRIPTION: *Chakramire and Mara Mara stand atop the Western Escarpment alongside the distinguished inventor Ray, who threatened to jump from the Scorched Face several days prior.*

[Enter Chakramire, Mara Mara, and Ray]

EGRESS MACHINE (via MARA MARA) *[Aside]*
Civilization's penumbra, the edge of humanity's
knowledge, commencement of wisdom, between a diminishing
star and celestial occlusion. The brilliant escape with a
boundary skirted, diffracting around the perimeter,
leaving behind the extinguished to ponder enlightenment.
Freedom refracted, the truth of the matter evicted from
vacua, longs for a liberty lost, for perfection, for
aggregate progress contingent to homogeneity.

MARA MARA *[Aside]*
Descendants sow commotion whenever feeling pride or
shame for hallowed deeds of ancestors past. A battlefield
of lies awaits, for history winners write; the losers
rarely read between the lines. Only hammers wrought today
deserve a stud, a fret, and an ear. The Man who Walks with
Caustic Gait approached the Globeflower-eyed, a reckless feat
to dare persuade the Lady of Eris shy from ledges.

CHAKRAMIRE

"Free yourself the need to feel free. Without a check against
itself a will will perish, without a rival freedom
absolute destroys. To wrest color clean from every grain
of sand, defeat from victory's hand, a single vestige
need you land, and skewer two lives with one command."

RAY

"The base
decry the exaltation of feeling over thought, as
if the two detached, as if one a grander thing the next,
as if the stars a mirror above the sky and not a
puppeteer."

CHAKRAMIRE

"Your rousing words lack conviction's sting; who waits
for crowds to crowd calamity's gate? You fluctuate, you
vacillate, you know the time opportune but hesitate."

RAY

"However peace an easier thing to win than war, a
suicidal jumper earns no renown for hasty leaps."

CHAKRAMIRE

"And even less for patience should passersby believe it
accidental. What inspires such despondent passions flood
a mind as great the galaxy?"

MARA MARA *[Aside]*

Walks with Caustic Gait, the
Shiftless, fought against delay, looked around as if astray.

CHAKRAMIRE

"A life deceased should never demand a higher price it
fetched before, for sacrifice just a risky venture, one
a gambler never sees the return."

RAY

"You block a man who
never saw a tower too high to fell, nor towered high
enough to fall. Of fire or of ice you?"

CHAKRAMIRE

"I am made of
fire, and own a conscience not real enough to fake. Your crime,
however vile it possibly be, would matter little
me."

RAY

"As high the thoughts you think me, as low the deeds become
from me. Could I, would opted a life of no effect, for
I have over knocked a dream thirty million years erect."

CHAKRAMIRE

"With stronger sight you still would have missed the second hand at
play. To steal a wink or see through a blink, another set
of eyes you need. Whatever the size of pupils, points of
no return. Wherever black holes, event horizons true.
Whenever singularities, spawn accretion disks. As
clothes belie the naked truth, light confounds a sacred proof."

MARA MARA *[Aside]*

The man who built the Leaving Device, who Walks with Caustic
Gait, secretes a secret fear, said,

RAY

"The future is our fate."

[They exit]

WHERE SERENITY AND STRIFE CLEAVE: PART ONE

CANTO 45: PERVASION

Galactic Calendar: Sol System; Earth year 30,123,012 M.W.I.
Tellurian Solar Calendar: Day five of the seventh tenth – 07/05
Modern Metric Time: 3:25:00, UTC+00:00, afternoon
Location: The Obelisk, Sitnalta Island

AT RISE DESCRIPTION: *Chakramire and Mara Mara return to the Altar of the Numbers. At the Obelisk, they encounter Epi who had requested a meeting with Meso on prohibition laws.*

[Enter Chakramire, Mara Mara, and Epi]

EGRESS MACHINE (via MARA MARA) *[Aside]*

Only the clarity after a storm could elicit a
stronger sensation of dread than of being alone in the
midst the disturbance, to people afraid of remorsefulness,
makers of tempests. Familiar disturbances offer a
modest reprieve from omniscience, from knowing the sequence of
beats to a heart, from chronology broken, from savagery.
Ever forgetting the words to harmonious melody,
interdependence arouses erroneous memory.

MARA MARA *[Aside]*

The Furthermost of Women adjoined the Queen of Spores.

EPI

"The
voice of Meso, brave to speak through a puppet, not enough
to share its fate?"

MARA MARA

The Lady of Eris turned her gaze to
glance at Epi's arm and saw scars instead of plaster.

EPI

"I
have never dressed a bandage, believing open wounds to
heal the faster."

CHAKRAMIRE

"Pardon leftover feelings. I had heard
a time ago existed, before established laws were
'wronged.'"

EPI

"To every person these rights belonged."

CHAKRAMIRE

"To every man
and woman strong. A natural law or right would never
need defense against abuse, never need a siren call,
the breach itself indicative proof the perpetrator
never human first of all."

EPI

"How a lawless act a ruse
revealing more the poorness of law than poorness in a
people's virtue? I have upheld the noble right to drink
and merry be."

CHAKRAMIRE

"Of gravity's law, the world has seen it
never violated once, by magicians, by the Moon,

nor acrobatic stunts, for the best of laws have broken
naught."

EPI

"But law, it is an art, not a scientific feat."

CHAKRAMIRE

"To hail a law as natural is a slap to woman
kind's imagination, man kind's creative power, all
our innovative prowess."

EPI

"The painter never makes a
work of art, but simply unearths the masterpiece, nor does
the sculptor make a beautiful sculpture, merely finds it
in a block of marble."

CHAKRAMIRE

"Each canvas-blank's potential none
the world can know, for painters can choose to show or hide the
quintessential. Though the limestone, a sculptor's foe, begins
with full credentials, only a chisel's chips and blows can
make it consequential."

EPI

"I chanced upon a septic tank
of thought, denying natural law's pervasion."

CHAKRAMIRE

"Better
off a septic tank than dead wrong. Our repetitions have
a way of making history."

EPI

“Everything about you
seems a misconception.”

CHAKRAMIRE

“While everything about you screams
a grand deception.”

EPI

“Virtuous lies unite the world, for
we cannot exist ***without*** them!”

CHAKRAMIRE

“Our lives a mere event
with guarantees of property hardly fundamental . . .”

EPI

“Sanctimony!”

CHAKRAMIRE

“Creatures die all the time; it is the way
of things, a pseudo-tragedy.”

EPI

“Woman, broker, cease at
once, our peace together time tethers. Though you speak your truth,
a lie would serve you better.”

CHAKRAMIRE

“Elaborate.”

MARA MARA *[Aside]*

Exhaling,
lady Epi yields with no great resistance.

[Enter One]

ONE (via EPI)

"Islands in
a sea of people, loneliness still the status quo, our
problems here are swept away, all the world a gratis show.
The drunkard, sot, professional alcoholic, many
names do we possess. A fool fights to be the heard within
the herd, for people listen with everything except the
ears."

CHAKRAMIRE

"The feud between the one now possessed, and Meso, Man
of Crystal, born it true with a lack of proof to wrongly
rob the man of seven years' youth?"

ONE (via EPI)

"The Man of Crystal lived
a life of notoriety, once the friend of Lady
Leaven, close as now the far. Unbeknownst to Epi, he
reformed and chose sobriety. Wait until the fog has
lifted. Look for what the new battleground will shift . . . "

[Exit One]

EPI

"The line
between the strong and righteous, it is a growing rift, but
I will not forgive the man, not apologize for gifts."

[They exit]

WHERE SERENITY AND STRIFE CLEAVE: PART ONE

CANTO 46: BELIEF SUSPENDED

Galactic Calendar: Sol System; Earth year 30,123,012 M.W.I.
Tellurian Solar Calendar: Day six of the seventh tenth – 07/06
Modern Metric Time: 1:25:00, UTC+00:00, morning
Location: Meso's Glass Forge at Gaffer's Gorge, Sitnalta Island

AT RISE DESCRIPTION: *Xara meets with Chakramire, Mara Mara, and Meso to negotiate a shipment of glass to facilitate the production of cosmetics, a contraband.*

[Enter Chakramire, Mara Mara, Xara, and Meso]

EGRESS MACHINE (via MARA MARA) *[Aside]*

Mixtures engender disparities, tonic solutions, and
crystals. An ocean of promise, an island of hope, and a
grain of success. The impartial refinement of destiny
leaves a residual ridge of repression. Minorities
rise as majorities fade, but serenity's scarcity
teases. The blistering fragrance of brine, with a whiff of the
gaffer's sobriety, tore from obsidian modicum
salaries, given to only the salt of society.

MESO

"Upon whomever's hand your belief suspended, move with
caution, lest your strings become nooses. Timeless beauty is
an oxymoron. Agelessness strips admiring eyes of
need for haste; eternal chance renders second tier the swift
inspection. Anyone who professed to offer beauty
ever more, a beauty undying, beauty, never knew."

XARA

"A valid truth, but beautiful things and people often
need preserving, longer shelf lives to find the choicest set
of eyes."

MARA MARA *[Aside]*

The Maiden sprinkled a dash of salt across an
apple slice to save the next day, between her twirling tongue
a bitter seed.

XARA

"Equality is the first illusion
language teaches us, the phoneme, and that a symbol is
a sound. The most exceptional world our words have ever
known, the Earth . . ."

MARA MARA *[Aside]*

And like a windfallen fruit, the barely ripe
enough to eat but hard to resist assortment, Xara
tumbled down against the ground.

XARA

"Humbled. Cosmic dust and dirt
beyond receive a similar name. A fabrication's
tattered fabrics held a man captive seven years, and now
it longs to veil ephemeral beauty . . . long enough, the
lie endears."

MARA MARA *[Aside]*

And Briny Stacks, Man of Crystal, jaws agape,
devoured the bait.

CHAKRAMIRE
"Shall we, our afflictions, turn to pistils?"

[They exit]

WHERE SERENITY AND STRIFE CLEAVE: PART ONE

CANTO 47: TEMPTATION'S BULWARK

Galactic Calendar: Sol System; Earth year 30,123,012 M.W.I.
Tellurian Solar Calendar: Day seven of the seventh tenth – 07/07
Modern Metric Time: 3:50:00, UTC+00:00, afternoon
Location: Youngberry Tavern, Sitnalta Island

AT RISE DESCRIPTION: *Chakramire and Mara Mara visit Epi at Youngberry Tavern.*

[Enter Chakramire, Mara Mara, and Epi]

EGRESS MACHINE (via MARA MARA) *[Aside]*

Luxury's only redeeming distinction, hostility
fostered between the affluent and poverty-stricken. A
life of extravagance, enemy strife, will solicit the
gold of our youth with the spirits fermenting a bottle of
comfort, decay and creation, a rose from the dead with a
noxious aesthetic. The idiosyncrasy, fighting to
linger at rest or against a deciduous passion. A
lavish inertia, the spoil from an era of constancy.

MARA MARA *[Aside]*

Edge of all horizons: contrast. It matters more than light
and dark themselves; the drive to conflict, to stand against, to
never blend nor fall with, gave birth to good and evil, gave
the sky, the land, the sea, for it separates the strong from
feeble, separates from Two, Three.

EPI

"Whoever dares to seek
the light? To rouse within a desire to know, away to
throw the dark?"

MARA MARA *[Aside]*

The Mistress Strife, Chakramire, removed her cloak
of silence.

CHAKRAMIRE

"Malcontents who refuse to deal with backward
metaphors, your swill of insipid symbols, lazy thought,
and passions overwrought from a lack of close inspection."

EPI

"I would trade a thousand lifetimes for half a share of theirs,
a year of destitution to live a day and never
know the burdens borne the Earthborn."

MARA MARA *[Aside]*

The lady Chakramire
rejoined.

CHAKRAMIRE

"To value innocence over knowledge, holding
unsophistication first rate, and wisdom second, is
the siren call of decadence."

EPI

"Still eluding me your
reason here. Whatever charge seek from vintners?"

CHAKRAMIRE

"I have brought
the gift of information; the Man of Crystal offered
glass to Xara, Starry Shoots. She returned the gesture, gave
to Briny Stacks cosmetics to ease assault against the
body, aid the fight against time eternal."

EPI

"Contrabands?
A modest breach decorum to try and rescue seven
years of life abducted. Worse crimes committed."

CHAKRAMIRE

"I agree,
but long ago, a master the game of black against the
white declared the threat a force stronger execution. Need
reveal it not to garner its fruits."

EPI

"Whichever serpent
wronged you greatly, greatly erred."

CHAKRAMIRE

"I have dreamed the dragon draw
its final breath, but witnessed the best its handiwork, and
I have crossed temptation's bulwark, another name for death."

MARA MARA *[Aside]*

For order, peace, and harmony people never wanted,
they were thrust upon it, like spoils of war before the dead.

[They exit]

WHERE SERENITY AND STRIFE CLEAVE: PART ONE

CANTO 48: CENTRIPETAL FORCE

Galactic Calendar: Sol System; Earth year 30,123,012 M.W.I.
Tellurian Solar Calendar: Day eight of the seventh tenth – 07/08
Modern Metric Time: 1:75:00, UTC+00:00, morning
Location: Belladonna Nursery, Sitnalta Island

AT RISE DESCRIPTION: *Accompanied by Mara Mara, Chakramire visits Xara at her nursery to ascertain her satisfaction with the first shipment of glass, and to gain her confidence.*

[Enter Chakramire, Mara Mara, and Xara]

EGRESS MACHINE (via MARA MARA) *[Aside]*

Flayers of canvas endeavor to smother the future of
fabric transparent. Whoever would champion beauty at
bio-diversity's loss, would demand from existence a
penance for youth and utility crossed: a symmetrical
ratio of mythic proportions, the measure of powder, of
paint, with the prettiest flower displaced from a desert, the
glorification of taste. As the radiance bleaches a
visage, the symphonies wash from a face of exuberance.

XARA

"Your otherworldly countenance gives away your cover . . .
not your skin, nor cursed physique, not your skill, nor terse mystique.
Your carriage cross the room, it defies the Earth's attractive
force, as though the ground of no great importance."

CHAKRAMIRE

"I traversed
the solar system, traveled for forty years and twelve, will
not be bowed nor brought to knees by a rock."

XARA

“For what you came
to Earth, your friends and family nevermore to see?”

CHAKRAMIRE

“The
truth, it hidden, learned a time after. Moon Europa, too
ashamed of want, Enceladus more, for satellites of
giants often live within shadow. Mara Mara, bard
and poet, last Plutonian, came to Mars along with
Chakramire, the torus shaped shuttle.”

XARA

“Why assist dissent?”

CHAKRAMIRE

“For beauty likens gravity, bends the soul beneath its
grip, and Xara, know your share dwarfs the rest of humankind,
exerts enough centripetal force to even catch a
Ray of light . . .”

XARA

“And crush its faint glow with overwhelming might?
The highest aim the prettiest face the cosmos thought its
dreams it best to smother. Not every flower seeks to find
the light, nor object beautiful be observed another.”

CHAKRAMIRE

“Undisclosed, a beauty kept hidden often thinks itself
defective. Only virgins believe allure selective.”

[They exit]

WHERE SERENITY AND STRIFE CLEAVE: PART ONE

CANTO 49: SUPERNOVA

Galactic Calendar: Sol System; Earth year 30,123,012 M.W.I.
Tellurian Solar Calendar: Day nine of the seventh tenth – 07/09
Modern Metric Time: 7:50:00, UTC+00:00, night
Location: The Scorched Face (Western Escarpment), Sitnalta Island

AT RISE DESCRIPTION: *Chakramire and Mara Mara return to the Scorched Face, where Ray has remained for the last nine days, no closer nor further from the cliff's edge.*

[Enter Chakramire, Mara Mara, and Ray]

EGRESS MACHINE (via MARA MARA) *[Aside]*

Civilization's penumbra, the edge of humanity's
knowledge, commencement of wisdom, between a diminishing
star and celestial occlusion. The brilliant escape with a
boundary skirted, diffracting around the perimeter,
leaving behind the extinguished to ponder enlightenment.
Freedom refracted, the truth of the matter evicted from
vacua, longs for a liberty lost, for perfection, for
aggregate progress contingent to homogeneity.

RAY

"Everyone enjoys a witch-hunt, until it learned oneself
a witch."

CHAKRAMIRE

"An apt description the slaughter those aligned to
Three, should tools the intellect mark the owner prime for death.
The inquisition none could prevent; it not the fault of
architects should buildings give way to demolition."

RAY

"There
vexation lies, a prophecy self-fulfilled."

MARA MARA *[Aside]*

Who Walks with
Caustic Gait, who ended one-quarter Earthly life, the Man
Who Walks with Caustic Gait to the sky surrendered words.

RAY

"Our
future's sequence I could not fathom, never knew the death
of Three would be. The shadow exists before the caster,
scried the supernova me."

CHAKRAMIRE

"He Who Walks with Caustic Gait
was asked to help the Lady of Eris, not to save the
world. You never wiped your soiled conscience clean."

MARA MARA *[Aside]*

As Strife beheld
the man before the precipice, staring down the face of
death, a shadow closed behind, overlooking depths.

RAY

"Your cause
for coming Chakramire, it to pluck another fruit? Your
feigned decease, it flawed and imperfect. Lady Eris came
to Earth defying doom, and without the proof of body
only fools would count the Globeflower-eyed among the dead."

CHAKRAMIRE

"Another fruit, another tomorrow, I intend to
make your winter spring."

[Enter Xara]

MARA MARA *[Aside]*

Behind Chakramire emerged a form
as bold a cherry blossom against the naked earth, a
bloom of robes and beauty. Each step beyond the Furthermost
of Women deemed a fortune of courage cost. It trembled
all who gazed upon it.

CHAKRAMIRE

"Ten days ago you threatened jump,
but standing there you are."

MARA MARA *[Aside]*

As the figure moved toward the
ledge, it turned aback the cliff, Blooming Robes abound.

XARA

"Today
shall be the last for me . . ."

MARA MARA *[Aside]*

With a parting kiss the lips of
Ray, propelled herself across chasms . . . caught the arm and weight
of Xara, Ray delivered from certain death.

RAY

"Whyever
such a damsel risk demise?"

XARA

"Wrongly thought our fate the same,
would we together perish. Today, you ready not for
death, nor I for life it seems. No romance between our breaths,
it just the stuff of dreams,"

MARA MARA *[Aside]*

and the Maiden Xara drew, as
brilliant stars inclined to do, He who Walks with Caustic Gait
away the bluff adieu.

RAY

"From whatever fabrication
came your disposition?"

XARA

"Love's fascination never needs
an explanation, simply a case of intuition."

[They exit]

WHERE SERENITY AND STRIFE CLEAVE: PART ONE

CANTO 50: XENON

Galactic Calendar: Sol System; Earth year 30,123,012 M.W.I.
Tellurian Solar Calendar: Day nine of the seventh tenth – 07/09
Modern Metric Time: 8:25:00, UTC+00:00, morning twilight
Location: The Scorched Face (Western Escarpment), Sitnalta Island

AT RISE DESCRIPTION: *Chakramire, Mara Mara, and Xara stand atop the Scorched Face, where Ray no longer stands. Their backs toward the cliff, they look east, and await the rising sun.*

[Enter Chakramire, Mara Mara, and Xara]

EGRESS MACHINE (via MARA MARA) *[Aside]*

Only the clarity after a storm could elicit a
stronger sensation of dread than of being alone in the
midst the disturbance, to people afraid of remorsefulness,
makers of tempests. Familiar disturbances offer a
modest reprieve from omniscience, from knowing the sequence of
beats to a heart, from chronology broken, from savagery.
Ever forgetting the words to harmonious melody,
interdependence arouses erroneous memory.

MARA MARA *[Aside]*

Light diminished long before Chakramire and Xara closed
to finish. Through the fog of emotion Maiden Xara
waded, took the place of cliffhanger Ray.

XARA

"The matters born
the heart of mine forever elusive seem. To save a
life and cast your own aside, what a cruel fork the road.
To see the dawn again and behold the rising sun, it

seemed a distant hope a few breaths ago. For granted, I
assumed, the adoration of men and women; needed
not pretend aloofness."

CHAKRAMIRE

"Ray,"

MARA MARA *[Aside]*

Chakramire dismayed,

CHAKRAMIRE

". . . your death
delayed, an unattainable end the best incentive.
Offer crumbs, because a lifetime together spent, it not
enough. Your lack of interest spurs the man to venture
forth; disclose your love your own peril."

MARA MARA *[Aside]*

Xara's eyes returned
to Strife, away the Western Escarpment.

XARA

"Saw the sun from
Earth and Mars Dominion; dawn better here or over there?"

[All exit except Xara]

***

[Enter Chakramire and Mara Mara, in the space shuttle Chakramire on Mars Dominion twenty two years ago]

MARA MARA *[Aside]*

The hatch, it opened, slowly at first, and she with strength to
move nor speak. The blinding light inward burst, it singed the skin
of Lady Eris deep.

[Enter Ship Inspector]

SHIP INSPECTOR

"The ionic stabilizing
thruster's tank devoid of xenon,"

MARA MARA *[Aside]*

the ship inspector quipped,

SHIP INSPECTOR

"our stranger's stranger miracle, keeping Chakramire its
course. Defying every odd, crossed the vast expanse of space."

MARA MARA *[Aside]*

A sudden, second glance at the cargo emphasized the
call for haste.

SHIP INSPECTOR

"An ancient android, archaic ere its prime,
a lone Erisian clinging to life . . ."

[Exit Ship Inspector]

MARA MARA *[Aside]*

The ship inspector
left the door ajar, the sun scorching every strand of flesh.
From hibernation's stasis awoke to find herself the
brink of death. Returned with three times the number heretofore,
the delegation paced the toroidal shuttle's cabin.

[Enter Ship Inspectory, Ambassador Dandy, and Emissary Vance]

MARS DOMINION AMBASSADOR DANDY

"We dismember . . ."

EARTH EMISSARY VANCE

"We desist!"

MARS DOMINION AMBASSADOR DANDY

"None remember . . ."

EARTH EMISSARY VANCE

"None resist!"

MARS DOMINION AMBASSADOR DANDY

"At least a name decide for it, bad enough the body's state."

EARTH EMISSARY VANCE

"Shall bear the shuttle's namesake, of Chakramire."

MARS DOMINION AMBASSADOR DANDY

"A Swamp
of Rings? A Boggy Circle? The meaning seems befitting . . ."

EARTH EMISSARY VANCE

"No, the Raging Wheel, or War-Quoit of Anger, only wrath sustains its life."

MARS DOMINION AMBASSADOR DANDY

"A dangerous life to spare."

EARTH EMISSARY VANCE

"A life it
nonetheless."

MARA MARA *[Aside]*

Herein revealed not a word, nor muscle moved,
already lacked discretion . . . until her indignation
righteous proved, should learn to make better first impressions. First
of countless lessons dawn.

[All exit except for Xara]

***

[Enter Chakramire, Mara Mara, beside Xara on the Scorched Face]

MARA MARA *[Aside]*

To a skyward marching cloud the
Mistress Strife attended.

CHAKRAMIRE

"Red-tinged, it heralds morning light.
Its value comes from promise."

XARA

"Alas, already knew it
never seemed enough, a lifetime together spent; the truth
shall I admit, it not for the reason Strife intended."

[They exit]

BOOK III: WHY CHAOS FELL APART

PART ONE: MAVERICK OR JACKAL?

WHY CHAOS FELL APART: PART ONE

CANTO 81: FRICTIONLESS WARMTH

Galactic Calendar: Sol System; Earth year 30,123,012 M.W.I.
Tellurian Solar Calendar: Day one of the eighth tenth – 08/01
Modern Metric Time: 1:50:00, UTC+00:00, morning
Location: Sanitarium, Sitnalta Island

AT RISE DESCRIPTION: *Chakramire and Mara Mara walk with Cloy at the Sanitarium, an asylum for individuals with adverse effects from invoking the Devas, for the spaceborn, and for the outcast numberless.*

[Enter Chakramire, Mara Mara, and Cloy]

EGRESS MACHINE (via MARA MARA) *[Aside]*

Sweetness of words can disguise an ulterior motive, a
curse, or occasional murders: expedience beckons its
followers gamble morality. Nuance of flavor and
bluntness of character, one as complex as the other the
simple. A shower of niceties damages palates, a
sprinkle enhances refinement. The whelm of finesse to a
wave of excess, or the end of discrepancy. Poetry
died for a reason, and subtlety perished along with it.

MARA MARA *[Aside]*

Rapids flow beneath the bridge made of sounds and weighty signs.
The aim of nomenclature: distinguish, separate, or
tease apart. A name itself brands distinct, a name assigns
a number. Be unique, or at least generic, dust will
settle not for any rise less than meteoric.

CLOY

“Words
can not conceal a prejudice predicated on the
notion some a second chance due, or others never earned
a first for circumstances beyond control, for genes, for
crimes committed long before birth, for merit losing ground
to means. With fairness, few of the Earth concern themselves, our
lives a cheap and fragile thing.”

CHAKRAMIRE

“Better off cheap than priceless, lest
the devils do away with its value altogether.”

MARA MARA *[Aside]*

Cloy, to Chakramire, a kiss blew.

CHAKRAMIRE

“Your kindness moves without
resistance, like a frictionless warmth.”

CLOY

“Your bard, it leads a
charmed existence, like its space-born, subversive host, and smells
of turpentine to mask its decaying paint. An older
model. Rearranging words seems a waste its worth. The art
of saying more with less, of concealing more with less, of
poets, undermines the straightforward go-between. At best,
our species lacks the discipline needed just to tame an
island, let alone entire planets, yet you walk around
and flaunt your ambiguity while disrupting lives.”

CHAKRAMIRE

“An
optimistic year ago I would not have disagreed.”

CLOY

"You sound depressed, albeit for other reasons."

CHAKRAMIRE

"True, our
species mocks discernment, thought I would fix the world. The bard
you know as Mara Mara from times of legendary
contradictions, times when hand-crafted meant the best its kind,
synthetic meant inferior, times when raw distinguished
native skill as flawed, a time goods organic meant refined.
The world, it begs for breaking, it craves destabilizing,
here our leaders staging conflicts to make it seem as if
a progress made."

CLOY

"For sake of coherence, be specific,
lest your public think you unscientific."

CHAKRAMIRE

"Eris fell
with Pluto not for competence missing, rather, willful
oversight. The choice to snuff out a planet's worth of men
and women, twice. Our mastery over physics, over
human nature, treated like dice. The stakes, our lives. To strand
a meager lot of people above a block of ice and
hold from them survival's means, not because of bad advice,
but rather lost acknowledgment, takes the kind of gall a
maggot finds repulsive."

CLOY

"No more persuasion needed, mean
the deed indeed. With atrophied wings a people learns to
envy those who fly above, learns to love to hold a great
disdain for they who talk of the future like today has

ended, like tomorrow is now, or like potential flings
can never matter less than kinetic stings. The story
told, it lives again, for death one embarks. Today will see
another slain, at Felo-de-se Amusement Park."

CHAKRAMIRE

"For
what you ask of me?"

CLOY

"Your home world engendered promise cut
before its prime, the tale of the lives you reminisce has
set a paradigm."

MARA MARA *[Aside]*

As stars rise for no occasion, fall
the same, the Duodecimal Constellation fills the
sky and wanes.

CHAKRAMIRE

"To fend against bottleneck effects: a muse,
a lie, a door. Our stereotypes exist for people
disabused of why and wherefore. Distract, befriend, or give
applause, the options limited. I, your cause, away will
take, to rouse or send to bed."

CLOY

"Thank you, lady Chakramire,
for playing up your part and for being more than just a
prop. The higher up a life's start, the farther down the drop."

[They exit]

WHY CHAOS FELL APART: PART ONE

CANTO 82: OPEN SYSTEM
Galactic Calendar: Sol System; Earth year 30,123,012 M.W.I.
Tellurian Solar Calendar: Day two of the eighth tenth – 08/02
Modern Metric Time: 2:00:00, UTC+00:00, near midday
Location: Felo-de-se Amusement Park, Sitnalta Island

AT RISE DESCRIPTION: *Chakramire, Mara Mara, and Cloy walk the grounds of Fe-lo-de-se Amusement Park in the midst a large crowd.*

[Enter Chakramire, Mara Mara, and Cloy, amidst a crowd]

EGRESS MACHINE (via, MARA MARA) *[Aside]*
Drawn to the brink of morality, glimpsing its boundary
wondering if it legitimate, struggling to master the
art of indifference, alienated, remembered for
making a spectacle out of a tragedy, faulted for
wiping a smile from the face of the Earth and condoning a
ritualistic destruction of empathy, held to a
standard dispensable, dropped from it, guilty of paying the
price of admission for walking away from a miracle.

MARA MARA *[Aside]*
Atop the stairs a numberless wonder piece prepared to
leap. To change, it is to be incomplete, without an end
or finish, flawed, the model of imperfection. Cease to
change and cease to be, perfect nature's oldest art.

CHAKRAMIRE
"A forced
perspective too simplistic to merit more than pity.
Not a single common thing shared between the throngs of Earth
despite the wildest efforts to draw associations.

[Enter Spectator]

"See the woman, skin of brown ocher mixed with undertones
of burnt sienna, cadmium red, and umber?"

SPECTATOR

"Black?"

CHAKRAMIRE

"Of
sorts, and up above, the one next the lady, man with skin
the color like titania mixed with Naples yellow,
phthalo blue, and hints of rose madder."

SPECTATOR

"White?"

CHAKRAMIRE

"Of sorts. Perhaps
you know the reason each, from existence, wish escape?"

MARA MARA *[Aside]*

The
looker-on returned a stare full of condescension. Cloy,
the Sweetly Bitter, hardly adept at intervening,
whispered,

CLOY

"They, your lack of self-preservation, only find
endearing, eye your circus of maladaptive nerves and
hand a sword to fall upon."

CHAKRAMIRE

"Half our people want to stir
the other half from dreams, from dogmatic slumber; wake or
do a better job of sleepwalking, hackneyed thoughts the world
already full."

SPECTATOR

"And why should an Earthling beg for food it
grew, the spaceling get it free? Why, the plight of Gaia's own
eschew, but mourn celestial evacuees? The stage will
test the heart, or prove it imperfect be, and pity not
the Earth-removed, a blemish our pedigree."

[The spectator moves away. An unknown woman enters, high above the crowd]

MARA MARA *[Aside]*

The woman,
skin of ocher brown, a dye strong as Chakramire's, emerged.

UNKNOWN WOMAN

"To cheer, to jeer, it just as perverse,"

MARA MARA *[Aside]*

declared with naked
candor too sincere to be unrehearsed, and left the world
with every doubt. The shadow exists before the caster,
notwithstanding light, and ground hit the body, laid it out
a single smite.

CHAKRAMIRE

"A moment it looked as if the lady
might avoid defeat, to give earth a beating twice as great,
and half as bittersweet."

[Enter Auster]

MARA MARA *[Aside]*

From above, the owner poised, a
parrot perched its haunt, reclaimed center stage with nonchalance
and silenced all the noise.

AUSTER

"As perverse to cheer, to jeer,"

MARA MARA *[Aside]*

the
voice descended, sold a smile full of poison; he, with skin
the color like titania mixed with Naples yellow,
phthalo blue, and hints of rose madder, raised a vial, drank
it clean, its hue, alizarin. All together, twenty
thousand words were thrown with hope they would sort themselves.

[Exit Auster]

CHAKRAMIRE

"Our chance
escapes, to make companions, befriend and feign acclaim, for
mine, for theirs, for all our sakes, move without abandon."

MARA MARA *[Aside]*

She
delivered chase to Auster. The Furthermost of Women
gave excessive girth, and missed him; but Strife endeavors not
to spare the Earth, until it becomes an open system.

[They exit]

WHY CHAOS FELL APART: PART ONE

CANTO 83: SURROGATE REIGN

Galactic Calendar: Sol System; Earth year 30,123,012 M.W.I.
Tellurian Solar Calendar: Day three of the eighth tenth – 08/03
Modern Metric Time: 0:25:00, UTC+00:00, near sunrise
Location: Evergrowth Farm, Sitnalta Island

AT RISE DESCRIPTION: *Chakramire and Mara Mara approach a blind but shrewd Harn at Evergrowth Farm.*

[Enter Chakramire, Mara Mara, and Harn]

EGRESS MACHINE (via MARA MARA) *[Aside]*

Energy lost and recovered, the tools of survival or
seat of anxiety. Measure emotions with gestures, a
language eternal as dew, and distortion's propensity
rises beyond the embrace but a privileged few. For the
poet persistently muddying water, however it
shallow, for gardeners tilling a terrace, however it
fallow, performing the dirtiest actions, auxiliary,
they with a mind and its calculus absent of mystery.

MARA MARA *[Aside]*

Evil is whatever blocks, thwarts, or foils whatever one
desires the most: the sapling against the wind, the rising
tide against the shore, the earthquake against the rock, the blaze
against the pour. Whomever against the Lady Eris
struggles, struggles not again.

CHAKRAMIRE

"Never underestimate
a thief's ambition, wiles, nor a victim's quest for vengeance . . .
Dagger's word and irk."

MARA MARA *[Aside]*

The Globeflower-eyed remembered each
the bounty hunter's quirks. From horizons stumbled Harn, a
sightless seer.

HARN

"Perchance the sun rise, or Earth descend? A guest,
or I displaced?"

CHAKRAMIRE

"The former. A lapse, it wrong of us to
bother."

HARN

"Moral absolutism is for lazy minds
and people unaccustomed to looking past impressions."

CHAKRAMIRE

"Came from what the surrogate reign of Numbers, if beyond
impressions people scarcely inspect? A thing of nature
seems it not."

HARN

"From neural implants were they derived, and stole
from me the eye's perspective, but I would rather be a
legend in the mirror, not idol unaware. Our time,
it fleeting, work awaits, from the ground to azure doors, and
ask the lady Cloy abate, I, relief shall not implore."

[They exit.]

WHY CHAOS FELL APART: PART ONE

CANTO 84: HYPERMODERN

Galactic Calendar: Sol System; Earth year 30,123,012 M.W.I.
Tellurian Solar Calendar: Day four of the eighth tenth – 08/04
Modern Metric Time: 7:00:00, UTC+00:00, night
Location: Sanitarium, Sitnalta Island

AT RISE DESCRIPTION: *Chakramire and Mara Mara return to the Sanitarium, where Cloy awaits news of Harn. Xara attends to an unintelligible Ray. Several other patients are also present.*

[Enter Chakramire, Mara Mara, Cloy, Xara, Ray, and patients]

EGRESS MACHINE (via MARA MARA) *[Aside]*

Said the destroyer of civilizations, "Believing a
person a nemesis always should keep, adversity
strengthens a body, prosperity colors it weak. From a
legion of warriors blind, to a ravenous funeral
march. From a thirsty, carnivorous mind, to a diet of
hollow abstractions. The charm of remembrance, a talisman,
wedded to enmity; nestled the hand of celebrity
even a trivial trinket can seem the illustrious."

MARA MARA *[Aside]*

Because its power never corrupts, but catalyzes,
fear dissuades the cynic seek saints among the weak.

CHAKRAMIRE

"Despite
our best intent, the cropper resisted all assistance . . .
not to brag and boast, our aims knew before the Furthermost. "

MARA MARA *[Aside]*

The sound of feet approached, and a hundred pairs of bustling
legs and arms curtailed the Globeflower-eyed; for what began
a crawl became a gamble of time, a frantic, frenzied
free-for-all to dodge the dragnet of Doryline.

CLOY

"Below,
descend, avoid the slaughter, it not the time for honor,
wield control from off afar, fend as hypermodern."

[Chakramire, Mara Mara, and Cloy hide behind the Sanitarium's cellar doors]

[Enter Doryline and soldiers]

MARA MARA *[Aside]*

Crash
of torsos, gnash of teeth, and a morbid splay of bodies.
Rose above the carnage, life's last carnation, Blooming Robes,
the maiden Xara, woman with Starry Shoots.

XARA

"Tonight, to
day the dark without a sun, I, a hundred trillion stars
would need. Wherever beautiful things aplenty, people
mar with greed. With strength, with love, overcome, for here as good
a place to die as any."

MARA MARA *[Aside]*

A mercenary struck the
maiden down, and life, the room fled, it carved a corner, curved
around, and disappeared as the soldiers spread.

CHAKRAMIRE *[Speaking softly to Cloy]*

"Remember,
each emotion serves an end, every feeling calls to arms:
to mobilize anxiety, designate a value,
signify important things, mark with worth, prioritize.
Before the age of prodigal passions, mastered angst or
mastered by it be. The heart's flesh, our flame, our flower, flaunts
Romantic inefficiency."

MARA MARA *[Aside]*

Underneath the body
Xara lay the corpse of love unrequited, fresh enough
for parting words, belated enough to foil fruition.
Doryline, the Sateless, steps over Blooming Robes and Walks
with Caustic Gait,

DORYLINE

"Reveal our contenders, Two of Each, as
we cannot exist without ***them***. A match to maul, to maim,
dismember, show the Lady of Eris me!"

CLOY *[Speaking softly to Chakramire]*

"To cower
down beneath the floor and live like a sheep, or fight above
a lion, win the ultimate sleep? It time to let our
sanguine bubble hotter, us make a break with fealties."

CHAKRAMIRE *[Speaking softly to Cloy]*

"Heed,
you shirk congeniality like a fish its water,
murder not your cup of tea. All emotion seeks to stretch
the existential value, to bend, to twist, distort, its
strength exaggeration. Hearts burn with dire frustration, late

the intellect's retort, and although it not your fight to
win today, tomorrow find yet another way."

[Cloy discreetly slips out from behind the cellar doors]

MARA MARA *[Aside]*

And Cloy
emerged from cellar doors with the heart and mind a shrew, to
meet the Man with Sateless Teeth, Doryline as Deva Two.

[Enter Two]

TWO (via DORYLINE)

"The truth, it never effable, still a worthy thing to
imitate or mitigate. Brilliant reputations blind
the best, but still preposterous things to live to. Worse the
reputation fulgent live down its owner; everyone
around will wish it weather or wither."

CLOY

"No mesmeric
force can vindicate you Strife's ire, for I am Chakramire."

[They exit]

WHY CHAOS FELL APART: PART ONE

CANTO 85: DYAD

Galactic Calendar: Sol System; Earth year 30,123,012 M.W.I.
Tellurian Solar Calendar: Day five of the eighth tenth – 08/05
Modern Metric Time: 0:00:00, UTC+00:00, near sunrise
Location: Sanitarium, Sitnalta Island

AT RISE DESCRIPTION: *After a night of bloodshed in the Sanitarium, Cloy stands before the Deva Two as Doryline with the sun of a new day rising. Chakramire and Mara Mara remain behind the cellar doors while soldiers flank the room.*

[Enter Chakramire, Mara Mara, Cloy, Two as Doryline, and soldiers]

EGRESS MACHINE (via MARA MARA) *[Aside]*

Asked from the hand to the archer, "As whence your expedience?"
Heard from the archer, the hand, "It the sign of experience."
Asked from the bow to the quiver, "And why your benevolence?"
Heard from the quiver, the bow, "It the spectrum of excellence."
Asked from the nock to the fiber, "For what your preparedness?"
Heard from the fiber, the nock, "To assist with your resonance."
Asked from the sky to the arrow, "Whyever your arrogance?"
Heard from the arrow, the sky, "To depart from irrelevance."

TWO (via DORYLINE)

"The game, it late for stratagem."

MARA MARA *[Aside]*

Double-edged the word of
Two, it even cuts with broadsides.

TWO (via DORYLINE)

"As lines array, a wave
returns to uniformity."

[Exit Two]

MARA MARA *[Aside]*

Double-edged the word of
Two, it even cuts with broadsides. The mercenary shuts
the door to silence pain, for as long the system open
peace would never reign.

DORYLINE

"A dyad, without a doubt, and friend
of Chakramire. A dangerous life to lead, for like the
fabled bee, a hive with too many queens becomes a swarm."

CLOY

"It true, for I, the Mistress of Strife, the Furthermost of
Women, Lady Eris, Globeflower-eyed, the Chakramire
can never be, but she an acquaintance dearly trusted
me."

DORYLINE

"A noble act to chance life away, for other's sake.
An ultimatum, I, to the Chakramire will make. The
ancient game of kings and queens, black against the white. To lose
the duel, meet demise, or deliver mate and live."

CLOY

"A
game of correspondence Globeflower-eyes will gladly take,
a single caveat: for whoever starts the game with
white, the second move shall play black; whoever starts the game

with black shall play the second of moves as white, reversing color every turn from thence. In event of draw, from claimed recurrence twice, material insufficient, fifty moves without a capture, stalemate, or compromise, the lives of Lady Chakramire and the Man with Sateless Teeth, shall leave the battlefield expired, never they again to breathe."

MARA MARA *[Aside]*

The spark of strife, it missed, as the couple lit a fire, and
shook the hand of Doryline, Cloy, behalf of Chakramire.

[They exit]

WHY CHAOS FELL APART: PART ONE

CANTO 86: EXTRA-PERSONAL

Galactic Calendar: Sol System; Earth year 30,123,012 M.W.I.
Tellurian Solar Calendar: Day six of the eighth tenth – 08/06
Modern Metric Time: 3:00:00, UTC+00:00, afternoon
Location: Sanitarium, Sitnalta Island

AT RISE DESCRIPTION: *Chakramire and Mara Mara wait behind the cellar doors of the Sanitarium for Cloy to return.*

[Enter Chakramire and Mara Mara within the cellar. Enter Cloy separately.]

EGRESS MACHINE (via MARA MARA) *[Aside]*

Sweetness of words can disguise an ulterior motive, a
curse, or occasional murders: expedience beckons its
followers gamble morality. Nuance of flavor and
bluntness of character, one as complex as the other the
simple. A shower of niceties damages palates, a
sprinkle enhances refinement. The whelm of finesse to a
wave of excess, or the end of discrepancy. Poetry
died for a reason, and subtlety perished along with it.

[Cloy opens the cellar door]

CLOY

"Detente's defiance, sophistry, civil strife, extortion,
disarray's defense, and hive mind corruption."

MARA MARA *[Aside]*

Grim her face,
it apprehensive pensive,

CLOY

"Your list of crimes extensive."

CHAKRAMIRE

"We remembered everything, every quarrel, every feud,
the slightest slights. Forgive and forget, for us Erisians,
torture, only death a fate harsher. Life demands the best
within recalled. Oblivion is our hell awaiting,
dangling underfoot as we slip across the sands of time
without as much surrendered a sole impression, mark, or
fossil print to prove our lives consequential."

MARA MARA *[Aside]*

Chakramire,
the last Erisian, stood as the overgrown colossus,
not ashamed of blocking daylight, nor drowning out the songs
beneath its verdant symphony, dwarfing neighbors onto
knees as forest giants do.

CLOY

"Chakramire, your vengeful quest
against remorseless sponsors the passing looker-on will
find obscene. The fountainhead's bond, it sacrosanct, our race
of humans extra-personal."

MARA MARA *[Aside]*

Thence the four degrees of
hearts empathic flow, the wellspring of love, of hate, of shame,
of mercy.

CHAKRAMIRE

"Benefactor or prison warden? If the
feeding hand a tiger caged bites, to whom the fault belongs?"

[They exit]

WHY CHAOS FELL APART: PART ONE

CANTO 87: CLOSED SYSTEM

Galactic Calendar: Sol System; Earth year 30,123,012 M.W.I.
Tellurian Solar Calendar: Day seven of the eighth tenth – 08/07
Modern Metric Time: 1:50:00, UTC+00:00, morning
Location: Sanitarium, Sitnalta Island

AT RISE DESCRIPTION: *Chakramire and Mara Mara work with Cloy to assess the dead left from Doryline's assault. Among the bodies found are those belonging to Xara and Ray.*

[Enter Chakramire, Mara Mara, and Cloy amidst bodies on the floor]

EGRESS MACHINE (via MARA MARA) *[Aside]*

Drawn to the brink of morality, glimpsing its boundary
wondering if it legitimate, struggling to master the
art of indifference, alienated, remembered for
making a spectacle out of a tragedy, faulted for
wiping a smile from the face of the Earth and condoning a
ritualistic destruction of empathy, held to a
standard dispensable, dropped from it, guilty of paying the
price of admission for walking away from a miracle.

MARA MARA *[Aside]*

A dozen bodies littered the floor of every room, the
aftermath of Doryline's wake, a trail of bedlam, wreck
and ruin, sparing only enough to spread the dread.

CLOY

"The
legion stormed our humble stronghold with speed, with stealth, with no
amount of hesitation. Suspect another fist the
fight?"

CHAKRAMIRE

"It doubted not the least. Even friends can yield to might."

CLOY

"Your ring of fire a circle of fiends forever growing.
Safer off, your life, a closed system."

MARA MARA *[Aside]*

Hidden overneath
the clouds and thunder beckoning rain, celestial orbs of
frozen ice persist a bleak march around the sun. From death's
embrace a lone, crepuscular ray of life emerged.

[Enter Ray]

CHAKRAMIRE

"The
Man Who Walks with Caustic Gait still alive."

CLOY

"However earned
the name? It seems a moniker fitting-ill."

MARA MARA *[Aside]*

Elation
turned to horror, saw the form's cry disfigured face. The Man
who Walks with Caustic Gait to the crumpling floor despaired.

RAY

"The
only saving grace foretold I, another, never more
shall love again."

MARA MARA *[Aside]*

The mournful inventor lost his knees to
pity, rolled from buckled legs.

RAY

"Said whoever walks with me
would melt whatever nearest, and He Who Walks with Caustic
Gait would burn whatever loved dearest."

MARA MARA *[Aside]*

Lady Chakramire
divulged another secret to carnage round the room.

CHAKRAMIRE

"The
Maiden Xara warmed your heart; sought to find a premature
demise or damsels under duress?"

MARA MARA *[Aside]*

The eyes belonging
Chakramire endured the hardship foreswearing blinks and bored
a hole the target.

CHAKRAMIRE

"Felo-de-se Amusement Park, the
owner, Auster, spoke to Ray. Spoke of Cloy's asylum? Spoke
the rod against the wheel?"

MARA MARA *[Aside]*

To the Furthermost of Women
turned a pair of water scorched eyes.

RAY

“Before the world became
a system closed to mirth, and before the rise of Lady
Strife, before the journey Earth, Auster lived another life.”

[They exit.]

WHY CHAOS FELL APART: PART ONE

CANTO 88: MUTINY'S BANE

Galactic Calendar: Sol System; Earth year 30,123,012 M.W.I.
Tellurian Solar Calendar: Day eight of the eighth tenth – 08/08
Modern Metric Time: 2:25:00, UTC+00:00, near midday
Location: Felo-de-se Amusement Park, Sitnalta Island

AT RISE DESCRIPTION: *Chakramire, Mara Mara, and Cloy stand outside of Felo-De-Se Amusement Park and examine a poster with Auster's face.*

[Enter Chakramire, Mara Mara, and Cloy]

EGRESS MACHINE (via MARA MARA) *[Aside]*

Energy lost and recovered, the tools of survival or
seat of anxiety. Measure emotions with gestures, a
language eternal as dew, and distortion's propensity
rises beyond the embrace but a privileged few. For the
poet persistently muddying water, however it
shallow, for gardeners tilling a terrace, however it
fallow, performing the dirtiest actions, auxiliary,
they with a mind and its calculus absent of mystery.

MARA MARA *[Aside]*

A compromised integrity spilled from every crack and
crevice Auster's face. At no vantage point an easy miss
the naked insincerity read between the wrinkles.

CLOY

"Evil's visage manifests here."

CHAKRAMIRE

"Your answer's question lies
a step across the obvious. One confession covers

up a second secret's egress; the mountain ridge conceals another two."

CLOY

"The face of the man a misdirect? From what our sight diverted?"

CHAKRAMIRE

"Look close the skin, its pallor feigned; it dyed as strong the Lady of Eris, not a creature born of Earth."

MARA MARA *[Aside]*

With all the bloodlust a raptor's gaze the eyes of Cloy descend and narrow.

CLOY

"Expressions etched across the face, as if a substitute old emotions dead and long forgotten . . . splaying nonchalance in the face assisted executions, viler deed suicide itself. The man deserves an end as wretched the fate the vessels he has lured beneath horizons."

MARA MARA *[Aside]*

Stoked swells, the Lady Strife.

CHAKRAMIRE

"Although a will the crew and captain the ship *Survival*, sailing forth and back a waterfall bounded edge the world, it rare to steer beyond it. Mutiny's bane, our prison, beckons."

[They exit]

WHY CHAOS FELL APART: PART ONE

CANTO 89: FIANCHETTO

Galactic Calendar: Sol System; Earth year 30,123,012 M.W.I.
Tellurian Solar Calendar: Day nine of the eighth tenth – 08/09
Modern Metric Time: 0:75:00, UTC+00:00, morning
Location: Evergrowth Farm, Sitnalta Island

AT RISE DESCRIPTION: *Chakramire and Mara Mara arrive at Evergrowth Farm to begin a correspondence game of chess against Doryline that will be officiated by Harn.*

[Enter Chakramire, Mara Mara, and Harn]

EGRESS MACHINE (via MARA MARA) *[Aside]*

Said the destroyer of civilizations, "Believing a
person a nemesis always should keep, adversity
strengthens a body, prosperity colors it weak. From a
legion of warriors blind, to a ravenous funeral
march. From a thirsty, carnivorous mind, to a diet of
hollow abstractions. The charm of remembrance, a talisman,
wedded to enmity; nestled the hand of celebrity
even a trivial trinket can seem the illustrious."

MARA MARA *[Aside]*

Firstling move to Strife, the next two belonged to Doryline,
The match begun with Harn as the go-between.

HARN

"Although the
prime objective guarding black's king from mate obscured, to win
the middlegame and opening field your battles swiftly.
Only sharp, decisive endgames a chance success. Demise
delivered unexpected or not at all. At best, you

keep the game, your options, complex; exchange or sacrifice
will not advantage either, and woe to those expecting
mate and greatness won without effort."

CHAKRAMIRE

"Why assist with strong
advice? With doubt your actions replete. Upon whomever's
grave you wish defeat?"

HARN

"For Globeflower-eyes a cryptic clue
nor fianchetto brought. It desired from Doryline a
worthy match. Your wake of bloodshed and slaughter hard to miss.
The summit reached; your middle's beginning ended, Eris."

[They exit]

WHY CHAOS FELL APART: PART ONE

CANTO 90: OCCULTATION

Galactic Calendar: Sol System; Earth year 30,123,012 M.W.I.
Tellurian Solar Calendar: Day nine of the eighth tenth – 08/09
Modern Metric Time: 5:75:00, UTC+00:00, dusk or evening twilight
Location: Evergrowth Farm, Sitnalta Island

AT RISE DESCRIPTION: *Chakramire opts to wait with Mara Mara and greet her headhunter, Doryline, a mercenary hired twelve years ago to eradicate her influence and capture her dead or alive. She sips at a goblet full of saltwater.*

[Enter Chakramire and Mara Mara]

EGRESS MACHINE (via MARA MARA) *[Aside]*

Asked from the hand to the archer, “As whence your expedience?”
Heard from the archer, the hand, “It the sign of experience.”
Asked from the bow to the quiver, “And why your benevolence?”
Heard from the quiver, the bow, “It the spectrum of excellence.”
Asked from the nock to the fiber, “For what your preparedness?”
Heard from the fiber, the nock, “To assist with your resonance.”
Asked from the sky to the arrow, “Whyever your arrogance?”
Heard from the arrow, the sky, “To depart from irrelevance.”

[Enter Doryline]

MARA MARA *[Aside]*

Doryline, the legionnaire, paced around the board, enclosed
the Furthermost of Women.

DORYLINE

“To tell the truth, your presence
none expected here. Your friendship with Cloy believed to be

a boast exaggerated. You keep your adversaries
close enough the passing eye thinks it more a love affair.
Another life perhaps, and the two of us allegiance."

CHAKRAMIRE

"I, your reach evaded twelve years, another dozen just
as ably."

MARA MARA *[Aside]*

Doryline, from the warring turned the wary,
understood the threat implied.

CHAKRAMIRE

"Better I to ask, 'For whom
employed your service?'"

DORYLINE

"Praxis Harmonic, Regent Earth, our
planet's ruler absent heads."

CHAKRAMIRE

"Charged you, Doryline, the task
of ending me, of wiping from Earth the smallest trace of
my existence?"

DORYLINE

"Duly, each life you touch a danger. I
the sole Numeric's Talisman hold; it grants reprieve from
murder. I will purge the Earth Lady Chakramire and all
corrupted she, will go to whatever lengths, commit to
any price, submit to no strength nor foe of sacrifice."

CHAKRAMIRE

"Your death shall follow, soldier of fortune; I your life have
touched, and nigh across the world lead. You tore the seams of Earth
apart to quash a single Erisian. My survival
guarantees your own, a sour mead . . . as great a danger I
to Earth, as great a danger the one to vanquish me."

MARA MARA *[Aside]*

With
empty hands nor captured outlaw could Doryline return,
the League of Numbers, Praxis Harmonic, just as quickly
burn; the Mistress Strife surveyed, first of moves had made.

DORYLINE

"Perhaps
the end deserved, perhaps it the best to hope for under
circumstances. Parting gifts, Chakramire. You came to Earth
and nearly felled a civilization, armed with little
more than words. The death of Three, Paris Alexander, I
your story wish to hear."

MARA MARA *[Aside]*

The contenders, one of them would
live, or neither. Pity they sooner never met.

DORYLINE

"The words
inscribed the Golden Brain, 'For the one with hidden knowledge,'
know the source begotten? Know why the words engraved?"

CHAKRAMIRE

"The phrase
originated Eris, a cold celestial body . . ."

[All exit except Doryline]

***

[Enter Erisian elder and young Chakramire on Eris]

ERISIAN ELDER

"See forgotten knowns . . . the nightscape and afterglow of stars
imploding, gases, cosmic detritus, interstellar
wonder lighting worlds?"

YOUNG ERISIAN GIRL

"A stockpile of beauty, free for all,
it floods the heavens. Doubtless it, any human miss."

ERISIAN ELDER

"A
planet whole it seems, our homeworld, the Earth. The starry sky
to siblings disappeared, for the Earthling eye remiss. An
occultation undergone; we, to them, can not exist."

[They exit]

BOOK I:
WHEN THE SYMPHONY'S DISCORD RISES

PART TWO: ADULTERATED INERTIA

WHEN THE SYMPHONY'S DISCORD RISES: PART TWO

CANTO 11: VENDETTA

Galactic Calendar: Sol System; Earth year 30,123,012 M.W.I.
Tellurian Solar Calendar: Day ten of the sixth tenth – 06/10
Modern Metric Time: 0:50:00, UTC+00:00, morning
Location: Water Clock Brothel, Sitnalta Island

AT RISE DESCRIPTION: *Chakramire, Mara Mara, and Vance examine the Captain's lifeless body while at the Water Clock.*

[Enter Chakramire, Mara Mara, Vance, and the Captain]

EGRESS MACHINE (via MARA MARA) *[Aside]*

Welcoming parties were welcomed regardless of merit or want. A diversion away from conventional gossip could sharpen the fugitive's edge, but a criminal's honesty promised reward nor reprieve. To conceive a deception, the gambit should never exceed the original confidence. Needful to say, a coincidence rarely surrendered its vitals to popular sentiment save at a premium. Many a lunar eclipse has embarrassed a predator.

MARA MARA *[Aside]*

The Captain's body, freshly deceased, the Furthermost of Women felt.

CHAKRAMIRE

"A moment, not long ago, it overflowed
with life, and now vitality lost to nature's cycle:
death, decay, rebirth."

MARA MARA *[Aside]*

With calm, Chakramire caressed the face
the Captain, twirled a lock of the bandit's hair. The Dagger
glowered through the corpse, as blades prone to do.

VANCE

"The open wound,
it cleanly sealed . . . the death of the Captain premature."

MARA MARA *[Aside]*

The
fetid body, over turned right, revealed a newly made
incision.

CHAKRAMIRE

"If the Captain the knife of Dagger Vance, the
Dagger needs another knife."

MARA MARA *[Aside]*

Rang the bell the Water Clock,
Calypso Dagger beckoned.

VANCE

"The hand of Baron Varlet
moves, prepare yourself a fight."

[Enter Calypso]

MARA MARA *[Aside]*

Came Calypso's siren song,
it brandished like a whip from the harlot's tongue.

CALYPSO

"Whomever I shall please?"

MARA MARA *[Aside]*

A glance, it cast down upon the Captain's wound. Calypso mustered up a defense before the slings and arrows slung.

CALYPSO

"Another blood feud to spur the Dagger? One vendetta not enough? For the sake whatever decent, know the Captain wanted death."

MARA MARA *[Aside]*

Euthanasia offered no redress from injured vengeance, nor means relief from nettling grievance. Vance, for higher hands reached, a larger gambit played.

VANCE

"Escaping everyone, our desires, it seems today, for none of us departed. Egress a treasure far away."

[They exit]

WHEN THE SYMPHONY'S DISCORD RISES: PART TWO

CANTO 12: SECONDARY SANCTION

Galactic Calendar: Sol System; Earth year 30,123,012 M.W.I.
Tellurian Solar Calendar: Day eleven of the sixth tenth – 06/11
Modern Metric Time: 6:25:00, UTC+00:00, near midnight
Location: Grounds of the Water Clock, Sitnalta Island

AT RISE DESCRIPTION: *Chakramire, Mara Mara, and Vance walk with the Captain's body under the cover of night.*

[Enter Chakramire, Mara Mara, and Vance with the Captain's body]

EGRESS MACHINE (via MARA MARA) *[Aside]*

Loyalty favors the powerful, treason the powerless,
power the transient. Anomalies are the primordial
scars, for the sightliest mark of a bandit, the genuine
promise, evokes a dissenter's suspicion. Professionals
call it the causal revolt, a misnomer for sacrilege.
Better to be a delinquent than taken with glee, and to
covet the hooligan's bounty, but brandish complacency.
Enter the grotto with clemency, essence of thievery.

VANCE

"A secondary sanction expect from Nettles, knowing
not a myrmidon the lot."

CHAKRAMIRE

"Proving I, amidst our age
of branded personalities, born the life another
not an easy task."

VANCE

"Your bard, Mara Mara, speaks a long
forgotten tongue, of mythical creatures long extinct and
fabricated sings."

MARA MARA *[Aside]*

A groundswell of courage coursed the veins
of Vance the Dagger, circled around the poet's poem.

VANCE

"Chakramire, your sphere of influence waxing. I implore
your help to take the place of the fallen Captain. Fill the
Dagger's sheath, and let your bard be the hilt."

MARA MARA *[Aside]*

A sanction Vance
could offer not, the Syndicate ill-disposed the man, for
Dagger Vance disposed of thieves, earned the title Gallow Prince.
For every bandit hung from the gallows, Vance the Dagger
sent another three.

VANCE

"The corpse here belonged the Captain, Twine.
Our roguish Nettles many charades, a pair of jackals
keeps. The Heathen Weave and Twine, neither face to others known,
for anyone the Syndicate, anyone the brambled
arm of Nettles."

MARA MARA *[Aside]*

Garments bloodstained and shredded Chakramire
reclaimed.

CHAKRAMIRE

"Discard the Captain's Cadaver, better versed the
Dagger Vance at crafts of manslaughter."

MARA MARA *[Aside]*

Swung its heft across
the bounty hunter's shoulders, the Furthermost of Women
eyed the body's wounds.

CHAKRAMIRE

"The quaint, quasi-quarrel brought against
the Dagger Vance, whatever the aim the Captain sought?"

VANCE

"An
insubstantial game among thieves to test the guild's resolve
and nerve. The stage, however, it compromised, the Captain
given title role of escort before the play begun."

CHAKRAMIRE

"And why the act significant? Why the Dagger moved to
strike?"

VANCE

"Whoever named an escort escorts the head the guild . . .
it meant the Captain's loyalty doubted, honorary
charge it not. To lead a bloodthirsty pack of wolves you turn
your back to them."

CHAKRAMIRE

"Whichever the rascal Nettles? Saw a
hundred forty faces that day."

VANCE

"The voice of Nettles known
to two, the Heathen Weave and the Twine. It kept a secret,
lest the other members lay claim the title, lest the lust
for power irresistible."

MARA MARA *[Aside]*

Dug a hole the grounds the
Water Clock beneath the night's cover; buried both a corpse
and broken promise knowing with truth the Captain smothered.

[They exit]

WHEN THE SYMPHONY'S DISCORD RISES: PART TWO

CANTO 13: PERENNIAL THAW

Galactic Calendar: Sol System; Earth year 30,123,012 M.W.I.
Tellurian Solar Calendar: Day twelve of the sixth tenth – 06/12
Modern Metric Time: 2:75:00, UTC+00:00, afternoon
Location: Water Clock Brothel, Sitnalta Island

AT RISE DESCRIPTION: *Chakramire and Mara Mara converse with Flow while tending to the Water Clock.*

[Enter Chakramire, Mara Mara, and Flow]

EGRESS MACHINE (via MARA MARA) *[Aside]*

Freezing the maker of paces prohibits a temporal
harvest. The furnaces stoking themselves shall explode. Should the
willing resist the resent of content? A cessation of
movement releases the tourniquet over nostalgia, for
courage congeals as devotion withdraws, but the fury of
restlessness smolders. Temptation's abeyance, inquisitors
call it a death of the second degree, the consumption of
life, an eternal rebellion, or kindle for apathy.

MARA MARA *[Aside]*

Anger yields to sadness, grief, terror, only after hope
of mitigation vanquished, of retribution quelled, of
justice nihilated. Broke fast the Mistress Strife, beside
the smoke a dying fire.

CHAKRAMIRE

"For a moment, Lady Flow, you
seemed alive. Your brilliance flares . . . flickers, every day."

FLOW

"The twelfth
of spring, remembered like it a yesterday, a pair of
beating hearts becoming one . . . said the cause of life the cause
of life, the cause, it never our own; it said because the
beauty human life enough, said our lives sufficient, said
demur alone suppressed our ambition, said our human
nature pride deficient."

MARA MARA *[Aside]*

Wounds Eris opened. Flow desired
a child.

CHAKRAMIRE

"Your biological clock, it tocks; whatever
holds you back?"

FLOW

"It not for want's lack, the stars a stranglehold
our loins. Although the body of mine as fertile river
deltas, most the men of Earth seedless, sterile nigh at birth,
the only means of pregnancy born insemination
artificial."

MARA MARA *[Aside]*

Waged a farsighted conscience, humankind;
it overshot the vessels of life.

FLOW

"To guarantee the
best our species, every birth regulated."

CHAKRAMIRE

“How the best
decided?”

FLOW

“Exploration of space the aim: the factors
benefitting most against cosmic radiation, thirst
and hunger, microgravity.”

CHAKRAMIRE

“How the other people
chosen? All our species not bound for outer space.”

FLOW

“The rest
the people via lottery . . . lesser odds for twins and
anyone with matching ancestry, things to help preserve
genetic variation.”

MARA MARA *[Aside]*

The source of Flow’s despair the
Furthermost of Women found.

CHAKRAMIRE

“What importance holds the twelfth
of spring? Your heart’s perennial thaw it heralds.”

FLOW

“Lost the
sanctioned bid to host a life, chanced upon another means.”

CHAKRAMIRE

“A Baron Varlet?”

FLOW

"Yes, for the lack a better term, a
man of charm, a lecher undoctored, ripe and fecund scourge
the Milky Way Initiative."

CHAKRAMIRE

"Won the heart the man?"

FLOW

"It
won with ease, although it untimely broken."

MARA MARA *[Aside]*

Every tear
from Flow descended.

FLOW

"Ended a life before it started,
left a pregnant girl alone . . . wept for all the life remained
within. Believing we would together perish made our
love's miscarriage bitter still . . . born the twelfth of spring, as raw
the sea, the day the last of the Baron Varlet parted
me."

MARA MARA *[Aside]*

The Water Clock, it one time a hostel, served the Guild
of Thieves.

FLOW

"And I, a desperate belle, a poor coquette, with
Dagger's help a harlot turned quartermaster. Never saw
the sister mine again, nor forgiven one thereafter."

[They exit]

WHEN THE SYMPHONY'S DISCORD RISES: PART TWO

CANTO 14: BACKFLOW

Galactic Calendar: Sol System; Earth year 30,123,012 M.W.I.
Tellurian Solar Calendar: Day thirteen of the sixth tenth – 06/13
Modern Metric Time: 4:75:00, UTC+00:00, dusk or evening twilight
Location: Delta Marketplace, Sitnalta Island

AT RISE DESCRIPTION: *Chakramire and Mara Mara accompany Flow to the seamstress Ebb's shop at the Delta Marketplace.*

[Enter Chakramire, Mara Mara, and Flow]

EGRESS MACHINE (via MARA MARA) *[Aside]*

Chastity's moniker never demanded respect from its
victims; recoil from the cadence of stone. A magnanimous
mind would reject the appeal to absolve a surrender to
passion. However, a barrier augmented, vanity
yielded survival gratuities. Solace descended from
summit to valley and under the turbulent river of
decadence, deeper for dearth of deterrence, determined to
bow to the ripple effect of a desperate innocence.

CHAKRAMIRE

"Scarlet Sheath. The dress of Ebb viler I remember, why
the seamstress so grotesquely attired?"

FLOW

"To earn a living.
Ebb reminds the world of past follies, educator she
believes. The frilly trends and ancestral waste our species
legendary. Hard to think anyone forget its scope.
The past repeats should history none remember."

MARA MARA *[Aside]*

Lady
Chakramire contended.

CHAKRAMIRE

"Contrary, repetitions have
a way of making history, each association
arbitrary."

FLOW

"Time nor place trite semantics, sister Ebb's
performance finished."

MARA MARA *[Aside]*

Scuffled toward the window panel
under stealth from Scarlet Sheath's crowd dispersing.

FLOW

"Borrowed once
a sister's dress, admired an admirer Ebb. Enchantments
swiftly crafted . . . wore the red trappings Scarlet Sheath and tied
seduction's rope. An intimate vesper shared with Baron
Varlet. Chose to hide the dress, while her shop assistant."

CHAKRAMIRE

"What
became the Baron Varlet?"

FLOW

"The fate becoming all. To
market squares departed, unbridled love confessed, mistook
for mine a sister's heart, and thereof the source our mess. A
spurned and unrequited love harsh enough, it harsher still
to know it freely given before it pried away! The

Baron Varlet offered both union's hand and nuptial flight
devotion. Broke the wings of the Baron Varlet, sister
Ebb, denounced the man for love's slander; chosen he the hand
to sever."

CHAKRAMIRE

"Union's hand?"

FLOW

"And the one the end the arm. It
butchered right upon the doorstep, and moved eleven days
thereafter."

CHAKRAMIRE

"Whence it moved?"

FLOW

"Of its own accord, the rest the
Baron Varlet found the next day."

[Enter Ebb]

MARA MARA *[Aside]*

A door the shop ajar,
the Mistress Strife approached. From a stronger vantage point the
presence Flow and Chakramire watched with earnest. Conjured forth
the Deva One instinctively.

EBB

"Know your limits Ebb, for
we cannot exist ***without*** them."

MARA MARA *[Aside]*

The invocation wracked
her lungs, it shook the body as much the mind, from Ebb a
cry the heavens flung, divine intervention mined. It strode
toward the Mistress Strife, it remembered past encounters,
beat the air with borrowed tongue, stripped defenses every breath.

[Enter One]

ONE (via EBB)

"Your rash persistence, sister of war, apocalyptic."

CHAKRAMIRE

"Claim the sum of one and one, one . . . addition make-believe?"

MARA MARA *[Aside]*

The omnipresent champion indistinction signaled
affirmation.

CHAKRAMIRE

"Why the backflow of time exists between
the sisters? Why the present engulfed the past?"

MARA MARA *[Aside]*

As water
welled the eyes of One-possessed Ebb, departed those of Flow.

[Exit Flow]

ONE (via EBB)

"The fault, it universal, for shameless love's dispersal.
Flow, the theft a sister's beau, Ebb, the death an embryo."

[They exit.]

WHEN THE SYMPHONY'S DISCORD RISES: PART TWO

CANTO 15: VACUUM

Galactic Calendar: Sol System; Earth year 30,123,012 M.W.I.
Tellurian Solar Calendar: Day fourteen of the sixth tenth – 06/14
Modern Metric Time: 0:25:00, UTC+00:00, near sunrise
Location: The Delta Marketplace, Sitnalta Island

AT RISE DESCRIPTION: *Outside of Ebb's Seamstress shop, Chakramire and Mara Mara converse with One as Ebb through sunrise. Flow is nowhere to be seen.*

[Enter Chakramire, Mara Mara, and One as Ebb]

EGRESS MACHINE (via MARA MARA) *[Aside]*

Sentences, symbols, superfluous entities, absent of
natural meaning. Abstractions unite the impossible.
Gravity, only its force of attraction, the darkest of
matter, could marry the false to the rational.
Representation, a crime of distinction, the bridge and the
barrier, parries correction and carries protection, but
entropy never desists. From oblivion traveled and
back the contagion, to harness the value of weightlessness.

MARA MARA *[Aside]*

A space entirely empty of matter took the place of
Flow. Whatever hope of kinship's revival lost to spite,
for love, the goldenseal of emotions known to Strife, it
not a panacea. Daybreak arrived and conquered all
the dreams the night before.

CHAKRAMIRE

"For a time, our species left its
own survival up to chance, held the right to breed achieved

at birth, a noble luxury ill-afforded trying
times, with means for life reduced."

ONE (via EBB)

"More evolved aside from genes,
our code of ethics differs; embedded all throughout the
body, all throughout the mind, every Earthling hard aligned
a Deva."

MARA MARA *[Aside]*

Wore a countenance like the face a mobile
wall, the Bridled Eyes defied reconciliation. Half
the night and into morning the Deva One remained with
Ebb.

ONE (via EBB)

"Within the web of life, knows the spider, all the world
connects. Existence gravity bound, our universal
link, for everything the cosmos accelerates towards
itself, towards another, towards the unifying
darkness blending form with false fears."

MARA MARA *[Aside]*

Because the feuds of Strife
prolific, knew quadrumvirates far from monolithic,
overestimated none.

CHAKRAMIRE

"Why the League of Numbers turned
against itself, the slaughter of Deva Three condoned?"

ONE (via EBB)

"For
humankind abhors a vacuum of power."

[Exit One]

MARA MARA *[Aside]*

Deva One
released itself. Exhausted beyond belief, the seamstress
Ebb's reluctance barred its egress.

CHAKRAMIRE

"Your intuition like
a yawn, it coming easy or not at all to signal
thought's fatigue, the boredom truth, faith's arousal."

MARA MARA *[Aside]*

Met the gaze
of Chakramire, the woman with bridled eyes.

EBB

"From broken
hearts and trust expired, our one grievance never mortalized."

MARA MARA *[Aside]*

The link between the sisters, a faint, tormented whisper.

[They exit]

WHEN THE SYMPHONY'S DISCORD RISES: PART TWO

CANTO 16: PRE-EMPTIVE FOLLY
Galactic Calendar: Sol System; Earth year 30,123,012 M.W.I.
Tellurian Solar Calendar: Day fifteen of the sixth tenth – 06/15
Modern Metric Time: 4:25:00, UTC+00:00, near sunset
Location: Along the Ash River towards Umbrage Grotto, Sitnalta Island

AT RISE DESCRIPTION: *Chakramire, Mara Mara, and Dagger Vance walk south along the Ash River, towards Umbrage Grotto, a hideout belonging to the Syndicate Guild of Thieves.*

[Enter Chakramire, Mara Mara, and Vance]

EGRESS MACHINE (via MARA MARA) *[Aside]*
Welcoming parties were welcomed regardless of merit or
want. A diversion away from conventional gossip could
sharpen the fugitive's edge, but a criminal's honesty
promised reward nor reprieve. To conceive a deception, the
gambit should never exceed the original confidence.
Needful to say, a coincidence rarely surrendered its
vitals to popular sentiment save at a premium.
Many a lunar eclipse has embarrassed a predator.

MARA MARA *[Aside]*
Poets want to know at what point the sky becomes the sea,
the bound becomes the free, the ascent becomes the scree, and
I becomes the we. The first poets ever walked the Earth
condemned with curiosity, sought express the wonders
witnessed, tried transform to song beauty's algorithm like
it still existed. Poetry disappears with every
generation, bleeds for each conscious lost to boredom, fades
whenever life's phenomena cease to fascinate or
skillful use emotion dies out.

VANCE

"It not enough to prove
yourself or hint the Captain alive . . . as many people
doubt your death as walk the Earth. Seeds of disbelief as hard
to sow as any other illusion."

CHAKRAMIRE

"Said the head the
Guild of Thieves among the crowd . . . every member saw the face
of Eris, mine, and even with secondary sanctions
I the furthermost from Twine, furthermost from Heathen Weave,
the furthermost pretending herself another."

VANCE

"Heed, your
saunter is a gallop, ansate-less might you wield. The ruse
will not deceive the dullest of thieves, it mere pre-emptive
folly. Let the rogues believe Lady Chakramire naive.
Your speech before the Captain, it clearly otherworldly.
Make mistakes and lull the outlaws to absentminded greed."

CHAKRAMIRE

"And what connection I to the Dagger? Witnessed all the
Guild the Captain stabbed, will brand me the bounty hunter's new
accomplice."

VANCE

"None. Our moment together nears its end, with
Umbrage Grotto close. It time Strife our bandits apprehend."

[They exit]

WHEN THE SYMPHONY'S DISCORD RISES: PART TWO

CANTO 17: GAMBLER'S GAUGE

Galactic Calendar: Sol System; Earth year 30,123,012 M.W.I.
Tellurian Solar Calendar: Day sixteen of the sixth tenth – 06/16
Modern Metric Time: 1:00:00, UTC+00:00, morning
Location: Umbrage Grotto, Sitnalta Island

AT RISE DESCRIPTION: *Under the guise of being the Captain, Chakramire and Mara Mara enter Umbrage Grotto, the hideout of the Guild of Thieves.*

[Enter Chakramire and Mara Mara]

EGRESS MACHINE (via MARA MARA) *[Aside]*

Loyalty favors the powerful, treason the powerless,
power the transient. Anomalies are the primordial
scars, for the sightliest mark of a bandit, the genuine
promise, evokes a dissenter's suspicion. Professionals
call it the causal revolt, a misnomer for sacrilege.
Better to be a delinquent than taken with glee, and to
covet the hooligan's bounty, but brandish complacency.
Enter the grotto with clemency, essence of thievery.

MARA MARA *[Aside]*

Success to failure ratios of one to three discouraged
better thieves from thieving, gave neophytes a chance to prove
themselves, ensured the seediest plants a chance survival.

CHAKRAMIRE

"Umbrage Grotto . . . more a network of caves, an overgrown
morass of acrid foliage giving way to shadows,
shadows giving way to cracks, cracks to roots and shoots to leaves."

MARA MARA *[Aside]*

A raspy voice as coarse as the gritted sand a desert
scraped the ears of Chakramire.

[Enter Thorns the Bandit]

THORNS THE BANDIT

"Ground yourself intruder! Death
the kindest fate for visitors here."

CHAKRAMIRE (as the CAPTAIN)

"The Captain not a
guest."

THORNS THE BANDIT

"You wear the garbs a thief called the Captain, proof enough
you be the man's imposter, for Dagger Vance, the bounty
hunter, ran a cutlass right through the Captain's chest."

MARA MARA *[Aside]*

The eyes
the bandit looked the Lady of Eris over, challenged
Chakramire to speak.

CHAKRAMIRE (as the CAPTAIN)

"And if Dagger Vance, the Gallow Prince,
delivered not the Captain an early grave, whatever
chance you think against the one cheated death? Whatever hope
you hold of besting me, it was born pre-emptive folly."

MARA MARA *[Aside]*

Mulled the words of Chakramire, pondered implications near
and far. It clear the woman the furthermost the Captain,
not as clear the woman's aims. Deemed the risk a worthy bet.

THORNS THE BANDIT

"Your guise, it unassuming to say the least. Whatever
business brings you here?"

CHAKRAMIRE (as the CAPTAIN)

"The Guild's head, the rascal Nettles, I
a council seek. Our deadly encounter held with Dagger
Vance, the better half of my wits despoiled. Your name again?"

THORNS THE BANDIT

"It Thorns the Bandit."

CHAKRAMIRE (as the CAPTAIN)

"Thorns, your assistance I request. A
secondary sanction need, I am thought a traitor."

MARA MARA *[Aside]*

Saw
the gambler's gauge at work, it behind the bandit's eyes.

THORNS THE BANDIT

"A
promise hard to keep among thieves, at times it costs our lives."

MARA MARA *[Aside]*

It never necessary for honest people make a
promise, trust presumed. To think bandits keep it rarely wise.

[They exit]

WHEN THE SYMPHONY'S DISCORD RISES: PART TWO

CANTO 18: CRESCENDO

Galactic Calendar: Sol System; Earth year 30,123,012 M.W.I.
Tellurian Solar Calendar: Day seventeen of the sixth tenth – 06/17
Modern Metric Time: 2:25:00, UTC+00:00, near midday
Location: Umbrage Grotto, Sitnalta Island

AT RISE DESCRIPTION: *Locked in a pitch dark holding cell, Chakramire and Mara Mara wait for an audience with Nettles.*

[Enter Chakramire and Mara Mara]

EGRESS MACHINE (via MARA MARA) *[Aside]*

Freezing the maker of paces prohibits a temporal
harvest. The furnaces stoking themselves shall explode. Should the
willing resist the resent of content? A cessation of
movement releases the tourniquet over nostalgia, for
courage congeals as devotion withdraws, but the fury of
restlessness smolders. Temptation's abeyance, inquisitors
call it a death of the second degree, the consumption of
life, an eternal rebellion, or kindle for apathy.

[Enter Nettles]

MARA MARA *[Aside]*

The bandit Nettles entered the darkened room amiss.

NETTLES

"The
post abandoned?"

MARA MARA *[Aside]*

Overheard conversations meant for ears
belonging Heathen Weave and the Twine, the Lady Eris
stilled.

[Enter Heathen Weave]

HEATHEN WEAVE

"Believed. The Dagger's reach farther I imagined, half
the guild defected."

NETTLES

"Word of the Captain's whereabouts?"

HEATHEN WEAVE

"The
body whisked away before anyone reclaimed it. Strange
our luck, for Thorns, a member our guild, confirmed the Captain's
life and offered sanction. Tied firm against the Grotto's wall,
the Captain waits for council with Nettles."

MARA MARA *[Aside]*

Two profoundly
disenchanted bandits paced round the cloistered cell.

NETTLES

"The air
about the Captain differs . . ."

HEATHEN WEAVE

". . . It never held a silence
long enough to think."

NETTLES

"The nerve born the Captain stiffer . . ."

HEATHEN WEAVE

". . . I
believe it lost its kink."

MARA MARA *[Aside]*

For the sight a silhouetted
pupil off reflected moonbeams, the Lady Chakramire
a jewel part, the ransom of any fortune forfeit.
Long the day deprived of sense, long the day without the light.
The bandit poked.

NETTLES

"As pompous the Captain, never thought the
braggart take a bard."

CHAKRAMIRE (as the CAPTAIN)

"The prize shared between convincing lies,
appearing less whatever you are or more whatever
not, rewards the least of lives. All advantage won from skill
pretended dies whenever contended; all advantage
won from feigned ineptness weaned once esteem redeemed. The least
of lives, the expectation deficient, ones for whom the
truth without precedence, no past to leave behind nor race
to catch the future . . . they to existence unbeholden,
even lies imbuing them gravitas."

NETTLES

"Your voice alike
another's heard the day of the Dagger's fleece, the day the
Dagger crossed the Guild of Thieves, day the wolf its killing spree."

MARA MARA *[Aside]*

A noxious laugh from Nettles befouled the grotto's claggy
air. A shadow hidden smile spread across the lips of Strife.

NETTLES

"Whatever ploy you play with the bounty hunter, know the
Dagger double-edged. At end games the Gallow Prince adept."

CHAKRAMIRE (as the CAPTAIN)

"The Captain lacked the mettle required a knife of Dagger
Vance; another one procured, Lady Chakramire."

MARA MARA *[Aside]*

The name
of Chakramire, the Mistress of Strife, reverberated
through the walls. It shook the ground humans stood upon, with one
crescendo broke the balance of man.

NETTLES

"It seems the bounty
hunter uses bigger pawns . . . fear the Dagger if you can."

[They exit]

WHEN THE SYMPHONY'S DISCORD RISES: PART TWO

CANTO 19: ENDOSMOSIS

Galactic Calendar: Sol System; Earth year 30,123,012 M.W.I.
Tellurian Solar Calendar: Day eighteen of the sixth tenth – 06/18
Modern Metric Time: 4:50:00, UTC+00:00, dusk or evening twilight
Location: Umbrage Grotto, Sitnalta Island

AT RISE DESCRIPTION: *Chakramire and Mara Mara wait in their prison cell for another audience with Nettles.*

[Enter Chakramire and Mara Mara]

EGRESS MACHINE (via MARA MARA) *[Aside]*

Chastity's moniker never demanded respect from its
victims; recoil from the cadence of stone. A magnanimous
mind would reject the appeal to absolve a surrender to
passion. However, a barrier augmented, vanity
yielded survival gratuities. Solace descended from
summit to valley and under the turbulent river of
decadence, deeper for dearth of deterrence, determined to
bow to the ripple effect of a desperate innocence.

[Enter Nettles]

NETTLES

"Believed a guilty conscience delivered early settlers
here. Sitnalta not a place people choose to venture free.
From underneath the fiery navels Earth the island
birthed its brackish water's girth. Silty shores and fertile fields
abound, a cleaner slate for redemption never found."

MARA MARA *[Aside]*

The
Furthermost of Women, named so for none as distanced she
the present, none a greater degree of spite nor higher
lust for vengeance, none a foresight extending farther, none
a recollection injuries deeper, spoke.

CHAKRAMIRE (as the CAPTAIN)

"Redemption
not the aim, regret as unknown to me as legs to trees.
The righteous never forced to surrender ground. It taken!"

MARA MARA *[Aside]*

Even eyes accustomed night's inky cloak an underdog
to Umbrage Grotto's cavernous bowels. One's deportment
matters in a dungeon pitch black, reveals the owner's true
elan; the figure swallowing darkness gobbles sight from
all. The Lady Chakramire stood as if the bracelet's steel
of silk, the necklaced iron an adornment, like the links of
metalwork a captive she, not the other way around.

CHAKRAMIRE (as the CAPTAIN)

"To whom the post abandoned belonged?"

NETTLES

"The Quartermaster
Flow. The Water Clock the heartbeat the Guild of Thieves. The cause
of life the cause of life, it denied to everyone. The
Umbrage Grotto just the heart's arm, the sticks and stones behind
the words."

MARA MARA *[Aside]*

The bandit paused for a moment, guessed the Captain
not before himself, and truth only breaths away.

NETTLES

“You claim
the Lady Chakramire an accomplice Dagger. How the
Furthermost of Women crossed paths with bounty hunters? Why
the Lady Eris here?”

MARA MARA *[Aside]*

To divulge a secret only
known to Strife concedes the pretense of being anything
except for Strife.

CHAKRAMIRE (as the CAPTAIN)

“The Lady of Eris paid the Dagger
Vance a ferry’s fee for ingress Sitnalta’s waters, knew
the island host to treacherous thieves; it never thought the
Dagger one. The Mistress Strife caught the Dagger stalking near
encampment’s edge, entangled a booby trap. The only
business sought from Chakramire one with Ray, the Man who Walks
with Caustic Gait, a ‘troubled’ inventor fallen far from
grace, the Dagger Vance a mere means an end . . .”

NETTLES

“And if your words
as cloudless true cerulean skies, the Lady Eris
graver danger I, for she underestimates the fame
herself, a greater bounty upon the head of Strife. For
she, whatever quarrels Vance holds will wait, for she the mark
the Dagger seeks.”

MARA MARA *[Aside]*

Intelligence favored higher where it
proffered. Obligations make spies suspicious; they create
dilemmas.

CHAKRAMIRE (as the CAPTAIN)

"Why the murder of spouse and child of lesser
weight to Dagger's conscience? Why Chakramire the mark?"

NETTLES

"Although
it true the Dagger's family felled at hands of bandits,
mine the reddest ones, with blood clotting mercy purged his veins,
for Vance's heart demands it, the shine the deadest sun, the
spine the eldest book of puns stronger Chakramire's desire
for peace. The Lady Eris the endosmosis water
into vessels; Chakramire opens systems. Strife inspired
the Guild of Thieves, the Syndicate born from life's frustrations."

[They exit]

WHEN THE SYMPHONY'S DISCORD RISES: PART TWO

CANTO 20: DESTRUCTIVE INTERFERENCE

Galactic Calendar: Sol System; Earth year 30,123,012 M.W.I.
Tellurian Solar Calendar: Day eighteen of the sixth tenth – 06/18
Modern Metric Time: 7:50:00, UTC+00:00, night
Location: Umbrage Grotto, Sitnalta Island

AT RISE DESCRIPTION: *Chakramire and Mara Mara remain confined in their prison cell. Nettles returns after a brief recess.*

[Enter Chakramire and Mara Mara]

EGRESS MACHINE (via MARA MARA) *[Aside]*

Sentences, symbols, superfluous entities, absent of natural meaning. Abstractions unite the impossible. Gravity, only its force of attraction, the darkest of matter, could marry the false to the rational. Representation, a crime of distinction, the bridge and the barrier, parries correction and carries protection, but entropy never desists. From oblivion traveled and back the contagion, to harness the value of weightlessness.

MARA MARA *[Aside]*

No amount of lore prepared Chakramire the wonders Earth, its size, its blithe, its growing abundance life. Another night the Lady Chakramire spent at Umbrage Grotto, saw its secrets loosed.

[Enter Nettles]

NETTLES

"To steal from the rich, return the stolen goods the poor, traditions time honored justice. Thieves the Guild

restore the equilibrium lost to colonizing
outer space, but once it learned Chakramire, our cousin come
across the Solar System, the last Erisian, marked for
death, the people rose against Regent Praxis, rose against
the Milky Way Initiative, rose against the League of
Numbers. Witnessed man himself proved a failure every front
for stripping Earth its beauty, denying Strife its fairer
share, for forcing Pluto live down its name and Eris live
its up."

MARA MARA *[Aside]*

The bandit Nettles removed the shackles binding
Chakramire, a question brought forth with glee.

NETTLES

"For what intent
the Lady Eris journeyed Sitnalta? Why disparaged
islands visit?"

MARA MARA *[Aside]*

Hardly far falls from grace begun below
the ground and bursted upwards, above the ocean's surface
like the crust a prison, like magma plowing through the Earth's
destructive interference. The Furthermost of Women
mocked the Captain's brass, bravado, and braggadocio,
for shows of courage possible only those with waves of
fear.

CHAKRAMIRE (as the CAPTAIN)

"The Lady Eris seeks He who Walks with Caustic Gait,
renowned inventor Ray, to repay a debt before it
reeks of kindness turned to hate."

MARA MARA *[Aside]*

Nettles backed away from Strife,
recalled whoever struggled against the Lady Eris
struggled nevermore.

NETTLES

"The first day of Chakramire's descent
to Earth, before the judgment of Paris, whereabout the
Mistress Strife became the Globeflower-eyed? However she
acquired the epithet? Its enigma muddles me."

CHAKRAMIRE (as the CAPTAIN)

"The
name bestowed upon the globeflower's spotting, Chakramire
a flower never witnessed before . . ."

[All exit except Nettles]

***

[Enter Chakramire, Mara Mara, and Praxis Harmonic on Earth twelve years ago]

PRAXIS HARMONIC

*"You crossed the Solar
System just to ogle Troll-flowers? Share your eyes."*

CHAKRAMIRE

*"It clings
to life with much tenacity, such a small and fragile
thing. Its meek existence hard fought; it thrives against the odds.
It never takes survival for granted, knowing death a
step away, for even hooves tiny trample underfoot."*

PRAXIS HARMONIC

"To fault the Earthling's lethargy easy. Though the flower's
urgent actions shame our own, judge the people here with heart.
Success the bane of exigent effort, calms the call for
haste and quells the qualms of waste. People oftentimes forget
existence is conditional. Eris . . . Pluto fell for
gratitude neglected, not lack of oversight."

CHAKRAMIRE

"From whom
the gratitude neglected?"

PRAXIS HARMONIC

"From Earth. The noble cause your
kin pursued, it sacrificed. Here survival takes a small
amount of work compared to a moon or Eris. Every
thousand years, or less, our homeworld requires reminding, needs
a genocide to own for itself to reignite the
fires of desperation. Globeflower-eyes, the people Earth
regret your world's extinction. You are the last Erisian."

[They exit]

BOOK II:
WHERE SERENITY AND STRIFE CLEAVE

PART TWO: ADULTERATED INERTIA

WHERE SERENITY AND STRIFE CLEAVE: PART TWO

CANTO 51: DISSOLUTION

Galactic Calendar: Sol System; Earth year 30,123,012 M.W.I.
Tellurian Solar Calendar: Day ten of the seventh tenth – 07/10
Modern Metric Time: 1:50:00, UTC+00:00, morning
Location: Meso's Glass Forge at Gaffer's Gorge, Sitnalta Island

AT RISE DESCRIPTION: *Chakramire and Mara Mara converse with Meso in his office.*

[Enter Chakramire, Mara Mara, and Meso]

EGRESS MACHINE (via MARA MARA) *[Aside]*

Mixtures engender disparities, tonic solutions, and
crystals. An ocean of promise, an island of hope, and a
grain of success. The impartial refinement of destiny
leaves a residual ridge of repression. Minorities
rise as majorities fade, but serenity's scarcity
teases. The blistering fragrance of brine, with a whiff of the
gaffer's sobriety, tore from obsidian modicum
salaries, given to only the salt of society.

MESO

"Knew the pain of missing one's calling . . . knew to force desires
beneath the conscious came at a devil's bargain . . . knew the
flight to drink a form escapism robbing freedom minds
to think, presenting freedom from thought as consolation
prize, and I persisted still. Took the secondhand despair
of seeing none our fantasies bear fruition just to
break the habit, dare to look up again and wonder what
our lives could be."

MARA MARA *[Aside]*

The Lady of Eris nodded, knew the
price of holding fast to dreams, knew it letting go.

CHAKRAMIRE

"The urge
for exploration primal, denied, it nearly fatal.
How your generation outstripped it I can not pretend
to fathom."

MESO

"Earthlings differ from humans born beyond the
clouds. Our kind as docile workhorses tamed from stallions, mares
withheld the chance to breed. It the angst of many Earthly
bound, a sore above the sky, knowing one's success the doom
of others, every hero a villain. Saw the world as
such: a one to billion sweepstakes; a winding down the clock
at birth; a dissolution of dreams, mistakes, and any
thing of worth.

"The hope . . . to one day our siblings join and fly
beyond the Moon. As high as a dozen Earthlings chosen
once, it gave belief our lives mattered. Why the numbers dropped
it never said. The spirit of all it broke whenever
none from Earth selected. Year after year the left behind
and overlooked relapsed to the older comforts, drank the
Juggernaut's Ambrosia laced thick with psychic drugs. To wait
for death aboard a vessel abandoned, wait for ships to
slip beneath the currents, wait while the scorching waves the sun
prepare to swallow whole our entire existence not an
easy chore. The core of abject despair, to be without
a last resort. It little surprise it nearly conquered
me."

MARA MARA *[Aside]*
The Man of Crystal's charged words succumbed to pathos.

CHAKRAMIRE
"Though
the laws of prohibition detested, why assume the
risk the hardest liquor inconsequential?"

MESO
"I believed
the drink the closest I to the aether ever go. It
never thought to be a risk till the Lady Chakramire
arrived, the first Erisian to reach the mother world, a
journey taking half a lifetime. It jolted me alive,
from alcoholic stupors delivered. Why a cousin
distanced visit planet Earth? Why to empty nests return?
It changed impressions held of celestial bodies, never
touched a drink again."

CHAKRAMIRE
"Although framed for prohibition's breach
and actions indefensible, knew the perpetrator's
actions well-intended?"

MESO
"Knew good intentions poor excuse
for degradation character. Knew debasement genes a
step away from drink. The Earthborn a seed reserve, control
condition grand experiments. Most our spacelings born from
sequence synthesizers, 'livestock conscripted into life'
as Epi criticizes . . . a better fate extinction
some believe, a better fate being Earth confined . . .

"Although
it cost the better part of a man's productive days, and
grounded dreams of flight, although seven years it cost, the time
imprisoned served its purpose, a lesson taught. The people
Earth nor outer space the livestock, our prisons more a state
of mind. Upon release from the sentence I returned to
quarry mines, supplied the spaceborn with needed glass, became
a structured man with principles crystallized. The anger
felt, however, smolders like magma."

CHAKRAMIRE

"Why continue live
a life with rank absurdities?"

MESO

"Such as?"

CHAKRAMIRE

"Wrath without a
wreckage, rage devoid of rampage, or fury absent fire.
Vexation separated from action people ought to
never label anger. None call a mild annoyance war."

[They exit]

WHERE SERENITY AND STRIFE CLEAVE: PART TWO

CANTO 52: SELF-DETERRENCE

Galactic Calendar: Sol System; Earth year 30,123,012 M.W.I.
Tellurian Solar Calendar: Day eleven of the seventh tenth – 07/11
Modern Metric Time: 3:00:00, UTC+00:00, afternoon
Location: Ray's living quarters at Gaffer's Gorge, Sitnalta Island

AT RISE DESCRIPTION: *Chakramire and Mara Mara visit a recovering Ray in the forge's living quarters to attempt to disabuse him of guilt.*

[Enter Chakramire, Mara Mara, and Ray]

EGRESS MACHINE (via MARA MARA) *[Aside]*

Luxury's only redeeming distinction, hostility
fostered between the affluent and poverty-stricken. A
life of extravagance, enemy strife, will solicit the
gold of our youth with the spirits fermenting a bottle of
comfort, decay and creation, a rose from the dead with a
noxious aesthetic. The idiosyncrasy, fighting to
linger at rest or against a deciduous passion. A
lavish inertia, the spoil from an era of constancy.

MARA MARA *[Aside]*

The long ordeal upon the escarpment taxed the mind of
Ray at least as much the heart.

RAY

"Chakramire, your bard akin
to satellites with orbits around the Earth, forever
falling into shadow, moon-like behind eclipsing girth."

CHAKRAMIRE

"To reach escape velocity knowledge needs a shuttle.
Mara Mara merely my means communication, words
the craft, the chosen medium thought, the oldest mode of
transportation."

RAY

"Why the Egress Machine's construction culled
from all of my abilities? Why a magnum opus
ridiculed and banned?"

CHAKRAMIRE

"A misunderstanding. They believed
it less a revelation device and more a trophy,
only learned it granted foresight to handlers after Three
and Paris Alexander annihilated . . . after
only two deceased."

RAY

"The Earth's people spared a harsher fate?"

CHAKRAMIRE

"The Deva Three as Paris foresaw a carnage coming."

RAY

"How? Forgotten knowns the Egress Machine revealed; it bared
our unremembered knowledge. It not a fortune teller."

CHAKRAMIRE

"Saw the League of Numbers lacked self-deterrence; saw its will
to power undeniable; saw its pride defiled."

MARA MARA *[Aside]*

To
Chakramire an undeserved scorn detested just as much
as praise or admiration devoid of merit. Petty
squabbles also need a sound motive.

CHAKRAMIRE

"Each the Numbers loathes
the rest with naked prejudice, malice lacking rhyme or
reason."

RAY

"Even orphaned hate born to parents once, perhaps
it simply unremembered?"

CHAKRAMIRE

"The feuds within the League of
Numbers born alone from each other's mere existence . . . leagues
themselves a vow to follow the path of least resistance."

[They exit]

WHERE SERENITY AND STRIFE CLEAVE: PART TWO

CANTO 53: BREADTHLESS HULL

Galactic Calendar: Sol System; Earth year 30,123,012 M.W.I.
Tellurian Solar Calendar: Day twelve of the seventh tenth – 07/12
Modern Metric Time: 1:75:00, UTC+00:00, morning
Location: Ray's living quarters at Gaffer's Gorge, Sitnalta Island

AT RISE DESCRIPTION: *Chakramire and Mara Mara sit next to a bedridden Ray in the forge's living quarters.*

[Enter Chakramire, Mara Mara, and Ray]

EGRESS MACHINE

Flayers of canvas endeavor to smother the future of
fabric transparent. Whoever would champion beauty at
bio-diversity's loss, would demand from existence a
penance for youth and utility crossed: a symmetrical
ratio of mythic proportions, the measure of powder, of
paint, with the prettiest flower displaced from a desert, the
glorification of taste. As the radiance bleaches a
visage, the symphonies wash from a face of exuberance.

CHAKRAMIRE

"Pacifism's breadthless hull breached. Its lack defense, defense.
The ones declaring war for the sake of peace or peace for
sake of war the bane of straightforward action. Tantamount
to paradox, diplomacy's hybrids. No amount of
saber rattling mutes the peace talker. No amount of wind
deters the warring hawk from its flight."

MARA MARA *[Aside]*

The Furthermost of
Women's point emerged.

CHAKRAMIRE

“The Egress Machine exposed the League;
it broke the bonds of ignorance, forced the Deva Three to
surface thoughts occluded, thoughts forged from non-aggression pacts.
The only deal permissible pressed the Numbers take an
oath to unremember each other’s sheer existence. Mere
disclosure broke the covenant, non-association.”

MARA MARA *[Aside]*

Ray surveyed the honeyed words like a poisoned feast from long
abandoned banquet halls.

RAY

“To absolve oneself from fault for
ending twenty-five percent Earthly human life, to lay
the blame upon the Devas themselves and quell the pangs of
moral hunger wreaking subconscious havoc easy. Seems
a blessing unbelievable . . .”

MARA MARA *[Aside]*

Ray, the pedant, needed
secondary sanction, eyewitness testimony sought.

CHAKRAMIRE

“The Maiden Xara present. Shall I request a Deva
tell the killer’s story firsthand?”

RAY

“Insist it.”

MARA MARA *[Aside]*

Chakramire
returned a moment later with Xara nigh despondent,
like a rose for whom the sun ceased to shine.

[Enter Xara]

XARA

"Your wish?"

RAY

"To know
the truth, myself from innocence free. Displace the inner
torture chambers."

XARA

"I believed, once, the heart's contractions, thought
its beats divine; from foolishness, though, our wisdom stems, for
we cannot exist without ***them***."

MARA MARA *[Aside]*

Imagined over hate
should love preside, neglecting it double-edged; the word of
Two, it even cuts with broadsides.

[Enter Two]

CHAKRAMIRE

"The circumstances round
the death of Paris . . . where should the fault belong?"

TWO (via XARA)

"The fault for
death belongs to Paris, foolhardy ventures sought. The one
with hidden knowledge innocence cast away, ignored the
code of non-remembrance."

MARA MARA *[Aside]*

Known knowns, or knowledge; knowing truth
occluded, wisdom. Ignorance kin to non-exposure,
knowledge disavowed the source folly.

CHAKRAMIRE

"Folly, Paris chose
to end, and paid the ultimate price."

TWO (via XARA)

"Befits the broken
truce. The only crime: a Conduit poorly chosen."

CHAKRAMIRE

"What
believed a greater tragedy nepotism masked as
merit?"

TWO (via XARA)

"Squandered favor. Though Paris Alexander won
the coronation via a happenstance of birth . . ."

MARA MARA *[Aside]*

. . . for
Strife the stronger candidate . . .

TWO (via XARA)

". . . Eris never knew a heart
to be above vindictiveness . . ."

[Exit Two]

MARA MARA *[Aside]*

Doubled-edged the word of
Two, it even cuts with broadsides. From self-inflicted harm
the League of Numbers partially healed. From self-inflicted
harm, the Maiden Xara's charm steeled. The breadth of beauty shields.

[They exit.]

WHERE SERENITY AND STRIFE CLEAVE: PART TWO

CANTO 54: SUFFUSIVE ACT

Galactic Calendar: Sol System; Earth year 30,123,012 M.W.I.
Tellurian Solar Calendar: Day thirteen of the seventh tenth – 07/13
Modern Metric Time: 2:00:00, UTC+00:00, near midday
Location: Along the Ash River toward Belladonna Nursery, Sitnalta Island

AT RISE DESCRIPTION: *Chakramire, Mara Mara, and Xara walk along the Ash River toward Belladonna Nursery.*

[Enter Chakramire, Mara Mara, and Xara]

EGRESS MACHINE (via MARA MARA) *[Aside]*

Civilization's penumbra, the edge of humanity's
knowledge, commencement of wisdom, between a diminishing
star and celestial occlusion. The brilliant escape with a
boundary skirted, diffracting around the perimeter,
leaving behind the extinguished to ponder enlightenment.
Freedom refracted, the truth of the matter evicted from
vacua, longs for a liberty lost, for perfection, for
aggregate progress contingent to homogeneity.

XARA

"From desperation valor emerges. What obscures it?"

CHAKRAMIRE

"Hope, the saying goes . . . with fog, hope enspheres our valor; fires
of desperation lift it. The promise better fortunes
tempts a person cease the high struggle life. To hope, expect,
the essence true entitlement."

XARA

"Why the League of Numbers
fashioned if our hope a force blinding? Why the Devas made?"

CHAKRAMIRE

"To mediate our human affairs, for all contentions
stem from one dispute - the grand sum of one and one - and each
the Number's ideology claims to be the answer.

"Zero holds the scarce above all, considers everything
unique, with inequality sacrosanct.

"The Deva
One considers everything linked. With indistinction deemed
a primal force, priority given universals.
Populations One believes sparse, addition just a farce.

"The Deva Two, a champion opposition, knows the
value adversaries. Contrast alone the root of use,
for Two considers interdependence sacred. Neither
light nor dark enough alone, absence half the couple blinds.

"The Deva Three considered the whole a greater thing the
sum its parts. To integrate offers attributes beyond
the limits each component, transcendence second nature.

"Each the Devas rivals some *thing.* To equal is to claim
to be the same, to represent. Arbitrary symbols
earn from Zero's eyes dissent.

"Deva One perceives itself
perfected. Acts addition presume the universe an
object unconnected. Summation, One's belief rejects
it.

"Repetitions, rules . . . to acknowledge limits is the
core of law. Transcendence, Two's mind considers flawed.

"The last
the Devas held reality one of synergistic
circumstance. To go beyond limits is the essence growth
and exploration. Immanence, Three believed a menace.
Ray designed and built the Egress Machine, or Golden Brain,
assumed himself the reason the death of Three and Paris."

MARA MARA *[Aside]*

Xara shouldered each the words like a beast of burden near
its breaking point, and spoke to the trees as if the answer
coming.

XARA

"Ray, you are a lighthouse misplaced, a beacon loathed
for luring ships to ominous waters, rocky shores; your
sole suffusive act the cause guilt's affliction. Want a life
of shame or death with dignity? Which the predilection?"

[They exit.]

WHERE SERENITY AND STRIFE CLEAVE: PART TWO

CANTO 55: OMNIPRESENT

Galactic Calendar: Sol System; Earth year 30,123,012 M.W.I.
Tellurian Solar Calendar: Day fourteen of the seventh tenth – 07/14
Modern Metric Time: 0:75:00, UTC+00:00, morning
Location: Belladonna Nursery, Sitnalta Island

AT RISE DESCRIPTION: *Xara walks around Mara Mara at the Belladonna Nursery, as if inspecting both its soundness and Chakramire's for keeping the bard.*

[Enter Chakramire, Mara Mara, and Xara]

EGRESS MACHINE (via MARA MARA) *[Aside]*

Only the clarity after a storm could elicit a
stronger sensation of dread than of being alone in the
midst the disturbance, to people afraid of remorsefulness,
makers of tempests. Familiar disturbances offer a
modest reprieve from omniscience, from knowing the sequence of
beats to a heart, from chronology broken, from savagery.
Ever forgetting the words to harmonious melody,
interdependence arouses erroneous memory.

MARA MARA *[Aside]*

Everywhere at once the heartstrings of Xara's conscience pulled,
a chord of sharp, chaotic vibrations. Xara felt the
slightest tremor worlds away, felt the biggest's brunt, and felt
the battlefield's parameters shifting. Love requires a
stable front.

XARA

"Your bard, the android, it never speaks nor asks
a question. I presume it defective?"

CHAKRAMIRE

"Mara Mara
learned it better not to ask questions if the truth desired.
For sake of curiosity, often times it best to
keep your distance, keep your aims secret, keep your keep, and keep
your lines of queries open, suspending final judgments."

XARA

"Fear an overgrowth? Your bard's song, it is a wooden bust
engraved upon a tree. As your stature grows the sculpture's
face disfigures, warps and stress fractures mount. The poem dwarfs
the poet, like a chisel its pen, removing words with
neither rhythm, rule, nor rhyme. Why your bard created? Why
the cybernetic poet's performance? No colossus
stands the test of time. Your android's profession obsolete."

CHAKRAMIRE

"The validation history. Long ago, our people
ceased to trust themselves with archives, thereafter chose to charge
the task of record keeping to artificial minds. To
seal the wounds of war beneath sutures, writers just omit.
Despite the crimes a person commits, whoever owns the
past commands the future.

"Robots, at first a trend, became
approval's stamp. Historians dwindled, never vanished
altogether, yielded roles suited best to abler hands"

XARA

"To abler hands the duty relinquished, doubt the League of
Numbers such? Our past entire they possess. To everyone
it now belongs."

CHAKRAMIRE

"The Numbers replaced preceding record
keepers, humanoid and android alike."

XARA

"A humanoid?"

CHAKRAMIRE

"It means resembling human appearance . . . once a person
opts to shirk the primal instinct, remembrance, delegates
the obligation history onto any other
thing besides itself, it outsources ownership of genes,
vendettas, life experience . . . soon becomes a creature
less itself with every day."

XARA

"We evolved."

CHAKRAMIRE

"And lost your strife,
the quintessential nature of life. The League of Numbers
engineered a peace and took everything of value."

XARA

"We
evolved."

CHAKRAMIRE

"A strong illusion of non-progression blinds the
bird of flight to everything save the flock. It isolates
perspective; movement's realization steals. It renders
action stationary, strips clean objective measures."

XARA

“We
evolved.”

CHAKRAMIRE

“With full belief the ordeal complete. Your people
made the Devas bear your hardships, your evolution. Knew
the human will inertial, the Devas controversial.”

XARA

*“**We** can not exist without **them!**”*

CHAKRAMIRE

“For eons heretofore
it proven otherwise.”

XARA

“The dilemma not a question
whether people lived or one day will live again without
assistance. Life a matter of here, of now. It not of
yesteryears nor future vows. Time an instance. People live
for what today allows, or pretend it otherwise.”

MARA MARA *[Aside]*

The
Maiden Xara yielded ground, every step a mark towards
surrender unconditional. Double-edged the word of
Two. It even cuts with broadsides.

[Enter Two]

TWO (via XARA)

"The Lady Chakramire
advised to move aside, to permit controlled conditions
carry on, to pardon past crimes, to swallow pride; for once,
condone the stench of carrion."

CHAKRAMIRE

"What amount of bleach will
blanch the blood of Eris? Perfume occlude offense? Resent,
its fragrance omnipresent, the bane of frankincense. It
bubbles like a scythe, a nose-scraping swath of froth. Resent
the reason Ray and Xara a couple once betrothed . . ."

TWO (via XARA)

"With
every fire you light you make Earth a little darker. Still,
your flames will be extinguished."

CHAKRAMIRE

"From ashes life arises.
Every martyr dies to live like a phoenix. Once upon
a compromise, humanity lost its double helix."

[They exit.]

WHERE SERENITY AND STRIFE CLEAVE: PART TWO

CANTO 56: AMALGAMATION

Galactic Calendar: Sol System; Earth year 30,123,012 M.W.I.
Tellurian Solar Calendar: Day fifteen of the seventh tenth – 07/15
Modern Metric Time: 4:25:00, UTC+00:00, near sunset
Location: Meso's Glass Forge at Gaffer's Gorge, Sitnalta Island

AT RISE DESCRIPTION: *Chakramire, Mara Mara, and Meso stand before an indignant Epi at the forge. Meso, unperturbed, continues making a glass vase and permits Chakramire to speak on his behalf.*

[Enter Chakramire, Mara Mara, Meso, and Epi]

EGRESS MACHINE (via MARA MARA) *[Aside]*

Mixtures engender disparities, tonic solutions, and
crystals. An ocean of promise, an island of hope, and a
grain of success. The impartial refinement of destiny
leaves a residual ridge of repression. Minorities
rise as majorities fade, but serenity's scarcity
teases. The blistering fragrance of brine, with a whiff of the
gaffer's sobriety, tore from obsidian modicum
salaries, given to only the salt of society.

MARA MARA *[Aside]*

Forged between the breaths a blowpipe, beneath the hammered balls
and stained amalgamations of molten glass emerged a
vase. The gaffer struck the base, sent a rippling wave throughout
the neck and merged it into a single body.

EPI

"Think your
life the future? Child, your tale never made it past the past . . ."

MARA MARA *[Aside]*

The salt encrusted brow of the gaffer mixed with sweat to
form a viscous stream of saline. The Man of Crystal struck
the vase again, intent to ignore the shrewish woman.

EPI

"Those the words you ought to tell Xara, unobliged to debts
of gratitude."

MARA MARA *[Aside]*

The body of Chakramire corrected,
intercepted Epi's flight path.

CHAKRAMIRE

"Believe the wisest course
of action breaking ties with the Maiden Xara, yet you
ask for glass to ship your firewater? Seems your motives less
concerned the price propriety's violation, more with
what you hope to gain from blackmail.

"As far as Meso knows
the only person privy the crimes insinuated
is the maiden."

EPI

"Know to unravel peace it simply takes
a single pull the tapestry's threads."

MARA MARA *[Aside]*

A seething Meso
flipped the vase, its upperside down, to slowly cool without
a crack. The most myopic of eyes would never miss the
fracture Meso's self-restraint.

MESO

“I endorse the lady’s work,
the cultivation beauty a custom quaint. From fondness,
I decline the perks; the goods I provide without complaint.”

[They exit]

WHERE SERENITY AND STRIFE CLEAVE: PART TWO

CANTO 57: FERMENT

Galactic Calendar: Sol System; Earth year 30,123,012 M.W.I.
Tellurian Solar Calendar: Day sixteen of the seventh tenth – 07/16
Modern Metric Time: 0:25:00, UTC+00:00, near sunrise
Location: Outside of Meso's Glass Forge Gaffer's Gorge, Sitnalta Island

AT RISE DESCRIPTION: *Chakramire and Mara Mara, meet with Epi outside of Meso's forge, as he has refused her entry.*

EGRESS MACHINE (via MARA MARA) *[Aside]*

Luxury's only redeeming distinction, hostility
fostered between the affluent and poverty-stricken. A
life of extravagance, enemy strife, will solicit the
gold of our youth with the spirits fermenting a bottle of
comfort, decay and creation, a rose from the dead with a
noxious aesthetic. The idiosyncrasy, fighting to
linger at rest or against a deciduous passion. A
lavish inertia, the spoil from an era of constancy.

[Enter Chakramire, Mara Mara, and Epi]

EPI

"Your anaerobic conscience the envy every crook. Its
yeasts ferment and feast without choice; a heady wine your voice."

CHAKRAMIRE

"You flatter like you flitter, survival not a crime. A
conscience uncontested wilts, mine developed under life's
duress. Whatever plea you intended, make it. Mine the
only ears you need impress."

EPI

"I desire the very best
of life, desire the best for myself, from others, joy with
no restrictions."

MARA MARA *[Aside]*

Heard the firebrand beneath the grumbles, knew
it loathed the status quo, and however Epi's honor
humbled just as high the seed vengeance grow.

CHAKRAMIRE

"Fictitious ground
belies your words. At Meso's request, another vendor
urged you seek, another glass smith to bottle wares. The man
declined to fight your battles, refused to touch again the
Juggernaut's Ambrosia."

EPI

"No other smiths of glass about,
your jest a test, or merciless taunt at best."

CHAKRAMIRE

"Whenever
broken, windows open . . ."

MARA MARA *[Aside]*

No adversary worse a friend
offended. Once cordiality ended, Eris tends it.

[They exit.]

WHERE SERENITY AND STRIFE CLEAVE: PART TWO

CANTO 58: POINT OF NO RETURN

Galactic Calendar: Sol System; Earth year 30,123,012 M.W.I.
Tellurian Solar Calendar: Day seventeen of the seventh tenth – 07/17
Modern Metric Time: 5:00:00, UTC+00:00, dusk or evening twilight
Location: Youngberry Tavern, Sitnalta Island

AT RISE DESCRIPTION: *Chakramire, Mara Mara, and Xara walk into Youngberry Tavern.*

[Enter Chakramire, Mara Mara, and Xara]

EGRESS MACHINE (via MARA MARA) *[Aside]*

Flayers of canvas endeavor to smother the future of
fabric transparent. Whoever would champion beauty at
bio-diversity's loss, would demand from existence a
penance for youth and utility crossed: a symmetrical
ratio of mythic proportions, the measure of powder, of
paint, with the prettiest flower displaced from a desert, the
glorification of taste. As the radiance bleaches a
visage, the symphonies wash from a face of exuberance.

MARA MARA *[Aside]*

Xara matched the steps of Strife, walked toward the tavern's door
approaching singularity.

XARA

"Lady Chakramire, our
first encounter happened here, under circumstances vague."

CHAKRAMIRE

"Occasions differ now; you acknowledge my existence."

XARA

"I believed you just . . . an old problem, like a fork between
the parts of speech."

CHAKRAMIRE

"Delivering food or stabbing tongues? Your
words evade confinement."

XARA

"No word escapes it meaning. Light
and lovers share a bond. From the point of no return a
suitor never finds an egress. From dying stars, from bards
who craft pathetic fallacies, fabricate emotions,
strive to see themselves within everything despite the fact
the passions secondhand."

CHAKRAMIRE

"The emotions Mara Mara
wields as real as any life force or iteration."

MARA MARA *[Aside]*

Swigs
of Juggernaut's Ambrosia the Maiden Xara guzzled,
drowning inhibitions.

XARA

"Ray's motives I have never grasped . . .
akin to shafts of vanishing light. The man's proposal
turned a corner, disappeared."

CHAKRAMIRE

"Thought himself the cause of death
a quarter human lives."

XARA

“From fiancee kept it secret,
offered no excuse for vows broken, let the blooming robes
a blossom wither.”

CHAKRAMIRE

“He has forestalled your death, the fires the
heart aflicker.”

XARA

“Froze, our love’s embers, many wintry nights
ago.”

[Enter Epi]

EPI

“Your normal crowd of admirers missing.”

MARA MARA *[Aside]*

Filled the
goblet under Xara nigh high the brim, the Queen of Spores
dispersed opinions.

EPI

“Even a caterpillar loses
legs, a butterfly its wings.”

[Exit Epi]

MARA MARA *[Aside]*

Held a needle near the head,
the maiden traced a flower tattoo.

XARA

"A symbol beauty,
symbol blight, it wrong or right, I shall dye the skin tonight."

[They exit]

WHERE SERENITY AND STRIFE CLEAVE: PART TWO

CANTO 59: WAVELENGTH CONTAGION

Galactic Calendar: Sol System; Earth year 30,123,012 M.W.I.
Tellurian Solar Calendar: Day eighteen of the seventh tenth – 07/18
Modern Metric Time: 0:50:00, UTC+00:00, morning
Location: Belladonna Nursery, Sitnalta Island

AT RISE DESCRIPTION: *Chakramire and Mara Mara inspect Xara in the mirror at Belladonna Nursery as she reveals her recently tattooed skin.*

[Enter Chakramire, Mara Mara, and Xara]

EGRESS MACHINE (via MARA MARA) *[Aside]*
Civilization's penumbra, the edge of humanity's
knowledge, commencement of wisdom, between a diminishing
star and celestial occlusion. The brilliant escape with a
boundary skirted, diffracting around the perimeter,
leaving behind the extinguished to ponder enlightenment.
Freedom refracted, the truth of the matter evicted from
vacua, longs for a liberty lost, for perfection, for
aggregate progress contingent to homogeneity.

MARA MARA *[Aside]*
The flesh of Xara twinged at the slightest touch or movement.

CHAKRAMIRE
"Every human here a sunbeam, a streak of brilliance cross
the sky. Your skin a marvelous hue, it golden tinged as
dawn."

XARA
"Or dusk, the death of spaceborn subversives commonplace,
of sympathizers promised. The foulest sin imagined

once, the theft of life, for I never thought our woes enough
to justify the deed. To ignore a murder easy
now, because the blood at stake mine . . . because the magnitude
another crime surpasses the shock of being whipped to
death or skinned alive. A life made for beauty such as mine
deserves a better end. It deserves an equal, not the
smoke a former flame."

MARA MARA *[Aside]*

The Globeflower-eyes of Chakramire
expanded like it spring. To consider Xara spoiled a
fair assessment. Fairness not Chakramire's concern.

CHAKRAMIRE

"Expect
the best from others Xara? Expect the best yourself?"

XARA

"With
every disappointment my expectations matter less.
For if requited love an aversion me, it better
I defend its turf against vandals, better I to guard
our kin above from prejudice born the Earth."

CHAKRAMIRE

"Your aura's
warmth infectious, like a wavelength contagion blinding eyes
and spreading charm, you swallow whoever orbits. Darkness
is the start of wisdom, life's blessings court disaster. Make
the truths you seek, the shadow exists before the caster."

[They exit]

WHERE SERENITY AND STRIFE CLEAVE: PART TWO

CANTO 60: ARGON

Galactic Calendar: Sol System; Earth year 30,123,012 M.W.I.
Tellurian Solar Calendar: Day eighteen of the seventh tenth – 07/18
Modern Metric Time: 3:00:00, UTC+00:00, afternoon
Location: Delta Marketplace, Sitnalta Island

AT RISE DESCRIPTION: *With Xara by her side, Chakramire recalls standing before Ambassador Dandy with Mara Mara while on Mars Dominion several years ago.*

[Enter Chakramire, Mara Mara and Dandy on Mars Dominion.
Enter Xara, separately.]

EGRESS MACHINE (via MARA MARA) *[Aside]*

Only the clarity after a storm could elicit a
stronger sensation of dread than of being alone in the
midst the disturbance, to people afraid of remorsefulness,
makers of tempests. Familiar disturbances offer a
modest reprieve from omniscience, from knowing the sequence of
beats to a heart, from chronology broken, from savagery.
Ever forgetting the words to harmonious melody,
interdependence arouses erroneous memory.

AMBASSADOR DANDY

"Chakramire's magnetic shield saved you. Cosmic rays aside,
a charm your life; the Jovian Radiation Belt a
force deserving wider berths."

CHAKRAMIRE

"Said the same of Chakramire."

AMBASSADOR DANDY

"Intend to keep the name?"

CHAKRAMIRE

"To Erisians, names considered
rites of passage, not as gifts. Birth's ordeal a minor test
compared surviving trials of Eris. I believe the
name will fit."

AMBASSADOR DANDY

"You passed a good number other satellites,
for what the neighbor colonies disregarded?

CHAKRAMIRE

"I, to
Earth, desired to go.

AMBASSADOR DANDY

"The spaceborn discouraged journeys bound
for Earth. Another settlement recommended. What of
Oberon? Titania?"

CHAKRAMIRE

"Worlds needing no improvement."

AMBASSADOR DANDY

"What
of Saturn's moon Enceladus?"

CHAKRAMIRE

"Urged the Chakramire to
carry forward any grudge, gall, or grievance; offered no
redress."

AMBASSADOR DANDY

"Of Ganymede and Europa?"

CHAKRAMIRE

"They encircle
skies of thunderbolts, it ill-timed to add a hurricane."

AMBASSADOR DANDY

"To travel further surgeries needed, Earth a cradle
hard to re-immerse oneself. Bone support, a stronger heart
required, or altogether replaced. Your skin's translucence,
wrinkles, stretch, for outer space suited well. The jaundiced eye
above our sky however, a less forgiving idol.
Dye it dark enough to safeguard against a burn, and light
enough to pass as natural."

CHAKRAMIRE

"What required of me for
Mars Dominion? Any skill I can conquer."

AMBASSADOR DANDY

"Learn to walk
with grace and cloak your fiery spirit. Mars possesses
fair amounts of argon; arc welding is a leading trade,
along with freight and harvesting asteroids. The type of
people tasked to build an empire, the type of people called
to constitute it, differ as much as dawn and dusk. The
Earth, its people timid . . . strife, struggle, nonexistent. Stand
upon the foot of Mars, at the cusp of evolution.
Let a cross of roads become not a cross of swords, nor path
your resolution.

"Denizens born above the heavens,
like a falling star to Earth, crash or burn away. Your life
the furthermost tellurians ever hope to witness.
Not the faintest inkling what dispositions wait, your guess
as good as any."

[All exit except for Xara]

***

[Enter Chakramire, Mara Mara, beside Xara in the Delta Marketplace]

CHAKRAMIRE

"Never expected Earth to welcome
me with open arms, nor strip clean the will to seek redress.
From vengeance backed away . . . from atonement misdelivered
I approached a pardon."

XARA

"What changed your mind?"

CHAKRAMIRE

"With time, the source
of jubilation people disclosed to me: believed the
lives of Pluto, Eris, egressed; believed themselves to blame;
believed the Earth a victim its own success. The League of
Numbers engineered its shame."

XARA

"Why create a crisis?"

CHAKRAMIRE

“Knew
the code of non-acknowledgment hindered strife, the means of
evolution. Though the worldviews the Numbers represent
describe the mind, its problems were never meant solutions.”

MARA MARA *[Aside]*

Sprawled her robes upon the runway, from comfort Xara walked.

[They exit]

BOOK III:
WHY CHAOS FELL APART

PART TWO: ADULTERATED INERTIA

WHY CHAOS FELL APART: PART TWO

CANTO 91: FECKLESS PASSION

Galactic Calendar: Sol System; Earth year 30,123,012 M.W.I.
Tellurian Solar Calendar: Day ten of the eighth tenth – 08/10
Modern Metric Time: 1:50:00, UTC+00:00, morning
Location: Sanitarium, Sitnalta Island

AT RISE DESCRIPTION: *Chakramire and Mara Mara return to the Sanitarium from Evergrowth Farm.*

[Enter Chakramire and Mara Mara]

EGRESS MACHINE (via MARA MARA) *[Aside]*

Sweetness of words can disguise an ulterior motive, a
curse, or occasional murders: expedience beckons its
followers gamble morality. Nuance of flavor and
bluntness of character, one as complex as the other the
simple. A shower of niceties damages palates, a
sprinkle enhances refinement. The whelm of finesse to a
wave of excess, or the end of discrepancy. Poetry
died for a reason, and subtlety perished along with it.

MARA MARA *[Aside]*

A pair of pawns exchanged, with the kings behind a castled
wall, a leave of absence both parties took. The game of chess
amiss, a stark analogy all the lives the couple
gambled: playing both the sides warring; trading piece for piece
for peace; deploying intricate counterploys and strikes, the
battlefront an endless sortie. At morning, Chakramire
retired to Sanitarium, Doryline to barracks.

[Enter Cloy]

CLOY

“Why the brute permitted recess? Prefer the torture drag
for days?”

CHAKRAMIRE

“The game a crucible. Doryline intends to
barter life for life. The crimes he committed second best
to mine, the man without a defense. You witnessed each the
lives extinguished here; a mass murder none of Earth observed
for thirty million years, and the culprit uncontested . . .”

MARA MARA *[Aside]*

Self-defense a matter mere speech today, for every child
of Earth aligned a Deva. The Numbers made the use of
books, mementos, swords, and guns obsolete, the very word
of ‘weapon’ lost its meaning, for any person living
might invoke protection, forthright the condemnation.

CLOY

“How?”

CHAKRAMIRE

“The lone Numeric’s Talisman Doryline possesses,
he a soldier charged to check me. The charm permits the man
to kill with full impunity . . . Doryline’s exemption,
notwithstanding, dies the day my existence ends.”

MARA MARA *[Aside]*

The eyes
of Cloy askance, resembled a window mourning loss of
curtains, all the horrors outside apparent.

CLOY

“I, your sense
of blindness covet. Helplessness is a feckless passion.”

CHAKRAMIRE

“Even worse, it rouses goodwill and pity.”

CLOY

“Blindness in
the face of danger, not as a means for reaping alms.”

CHAKRAMIRE

“You
staked your life upon a grave gambit: Doryline’s desire
to kill again. The soldier of fortune deftly ended
lives; your weakness just a well-nourished fib. Whatever caused
your doubt, ignore it.”

MARA MARA *[Aside]*

Helpless to turn away from grievance
slighted, no offense escapes notice, none from Chakramire.

[They exit]

WHY CHAOS FELL APART: PART TWO

CANTO 92: EPHEMERAL BOND

Galactic Calendar: Sol System; Earth year 30,123,012 M.W.I.
Tellurian Solar Calendar: Day eleven of the eighth tenth – 08/11
Modern Metric Time: 2:25:00, UTC+00:00, near midday
Location: Fe-lo-de-se Amusement Park, Sitnalta Island

AT RISE DESCRIPTION: *Chakramire and Mara Mara walk with Cloy inside Fe-lo-de-se Amusement Park.*

[Enter Chakramire, Mara Mara, and Cloy]

EGRESS MACHINE (via MARA MARA) *[Aside]*

Drawn to the brink of morality, glimpsing its boundary
wondering if it legitimate, struggling to master the
art of indifference, alienated, remembered for
making a spectacle out of a tragedy, faulted for
wiping a smile from the face of the Earth and condoning a
ritualistic destruction of empathy, held to a
standard dispensable, dropped from it, guilty of paying the
price of admission for walking away from a miracle.

MARA MARA *[Aside]*

For seven days the death of the Maiden Xara neither
Cloy nor Chakramire addressed. No asphyxiating gas
as strong a silent vigil reminding breath away. To
hear oneself respire and know others lack the means . . . the sound
of distant shores from bridges. For seven days the Man Who
Walks with Caustic Gait beside Xara, lay for seven nights
awake, for one ephemeral bond attended.

CLOY

“Xara
never mentioned lovers lost, never mentioned one alive.
To stand amongst pariahs, to vouch for their behalf, to
chance abuse, to risk demise; she a widow, I surmised.
Our kin from space, our invalids, anyone without a
Number win rebuke. The spaceborn before you, Chakramire,
the ones to venture Earth . . .”

CHAKRAMIRE

“For a year or longer, none of
them survived.”

CLOY

“Believe your kismet unique?”

CHAKRAMIRE

“Until a week
ago. To keep your company good, or none at all, a
friend of mine advised it twice. He himself ignored the words
of warning, paid the ultimate price.”

CLOY

“Believe it time a
visit given Auster, time acts of humans sacrificed.”

MARA MARA *[Aside]*

Patrolled the grounds of Fe-lo-de-se Amusement Park, the
pair rewarded soon.

[Enter Auster before a crowd]

AUSTER

"With each passing day the Moon's effect
upon our world continues: the Earth's rotation slows; the
tides persist to batter shores; night and day forever grow,
our moon an inconspicuous force. A satellite should
never hinder what it eyes, what it orbits, what it seeks
to emulate. The colonies, satellites of Earth, its
people, culture, way of life, ought excuse themselves from Earth's
affairs."

MARA MARA *[Aside]*

The multitudinous crowd of people parted
ways as Auster, like a rain cloud, approached. To chase the storm
exposure risked. A closer pursuit the two delivered
till the three of them alone.

AUSTER

"Autographs for shadows cost
a little extra."

CLOY

"Auster, your signature depresses
values."

AUSTER

"Enterprise exists everywhere. For some a lack
of value valued. Martyrdom is the hardest sale to
make, because the gambler sees no return."

CLOY

"You murder!"

AUSTER

“I
provide a service. Fe-lo-de-se Amusement Park to
each performer is a godsend, for half the entrance fees
the day to any charity chosen, any charge or
cause desired.”

CHAKRAMIRE

“It not a mere mercy-killing? Not a front
for felling undesirables?”

AUSTER

“Everyone possesses
one, a magnum opus, one goal for which our life itself
exchanged. To witness doggedness, acts of pure catharsis.
We can ***not*** exist without them.”

CLOY

“Your actions lack the grace
of euthanasia, pander to people’s existential
fears, and profit off the absurd. Your heart compassion’s last
frontier.”

[Enter Zero]

MARA MARA *[Aside]*

As neither mercy nor shame nor love nor hate can
color Zero’s word, the insult offended less an itch
to rocks.

ZERO (via AUSTER)

“You treat anxiety like it some disease, a
symptom underlying disorders, wreaking havoc. Though
it bears resemblance entropy, better off to hold the

sense of worry like a resource. To value is to fret
and mobilize our energy. Spending money seeking
ways to limit money spent is the siren call of waste."

CLOY

"The siege the Sanitarium, I desire to know the
"truth . . . it ordered by the man known as Auster?"

ZERO (via AUSTER)

"Carried out
the dying wish a zealous performer, Auster just a
means an end, to purify Earth of one inventor, Ray,
the one you call your friend."

[Exit Zero]

MARA MARA *[Aside]*

From the flesh and mind of Auster
Zero eased itself, the man's body raw from angst the fierce
encounter. Neither mercy nor shame nor love nor hate can
color Zero's word.

AUSTER

"The Globeflower-eyed, the Mistress Strife,
the Lady Chakramire . . ."

CHAKRAMIRE

"For a being not of Earth you
seem adapted well. Our paths, once again, shall cross."

[Exit Auster]

CLOY

“Your heart,
it more forgiving mine, and it never seems to race.”

CHAKRAMIRE

“You
err, it human, not divine. Auster’s conscience oddly placed.
The man provides a means to extinguish dreams, the highest
aim of strife, achieving dreams unfulfilled a person’s life.”

[They exit]

WHY CHAOS FELL APART: PART TWO

CANTO 93: VOLITION'S VASSAL

Galactic Calendar: Sol System; Earth year 30,123,012 M.W.I.
Tellurian Solar Calendar: Day twelve of the eighth tenth – 08/12
Modern Metric Time: 0:25:00, UTC+00:00, near sunrise
Location: Evergrowth Farm, Sitnalta Island

AT RISE DESCRIPTION: *Chakramire and Mara Mara prepare to make the next two moves in the correspondence game of chess, while Harn stands nearby as witness.*

[Enter Chakramire, Mara Mara, and Harn]

EGRESS MACHINE (via MARA MARA) *[Aside]*

Energy lost and recovered, the tools of survival or
seat of anxiety. Measure emotions with gestures, a
language eternal as dew, and distortion's propensity
rises beyond the embrace but a privileged few. For the
poet persistently muddying water, however it
shallow, for gardeners tilling a terrace, however it
fallow, performing the dirtiest actions, auxiliary,
they with a mind and its calculus absent of mystery.

HARN

"A cache of bodies waiting for further orders . . . even
though a creature never too young to die, nor old enough
to finish living, humans arrive to unpartitioned
worlds today and never learn what it means to die before
our time or after."

MARA MARA *[Aside]*

Tales of resurgence follow every
sharp decline. The mind of Harn no exception.

HARN

"*Everything*
already owned and spoken for, set aside for future
use, or designated. None here expect to die a child
nor live beyond our usefulness: life without surprises.
Water, food, and shelter unguaranteed, survival's means
monopolized."

CHAKRAMIRE

"The mesmerist Cloy disclosed to me your
lack of sight, neglected wherefore it came to pass."

HARN

"The truth,
it never universal . . . our interactions change with
every invocation; mine granted me the thoughts of all
before myself, and blinded with overwhelming brilliance.
Heard the screams of trillions long dead and gone, it forced itself
upon the conscious, altered the composition every
neuron, axon, tendrilled dendrite, synaptic cleft, and link."

CHAKRAMIRE

"Demanded what from history?"

HARN

"I demanded all it,
willed myself towards the ledge, risked volition's vassal."

CHAKRAMIRE

"Saw
the past entire?"

HARN

“A chasm of indignation old as
humankind itself, the First Expeditions roiled the world;
deserters plundered Earth of its greatest riches, vanished
into cosmic realms and left us to die disdained.”

CHAKRAMIRE

“Before
the Milky Way Initiative?”

HARN

“Yes. A cataclysmic
force of nature threatened Earth sixty million years ago.
A mass extinction followed, our predecessors nearly
perished. Some believed our fate lucky, some assumed the first
explorers left our system, the rest demanded justice.”

MARA MARA *[Aside]*

Made another move, the chess game continued. Strife persists.

[They exit]

WHY CHAOS FELL APART: PART TWO

CANTO 94: PROPHYLAXIS

Galactic Calendar: Sol System; Earth year 30,123,012 M.W.I.
Tellurian Solar Calendar: Day thirteen of the eighth tenth – 08/13
Modern Metric Time: 3:25:00, UTC+00:00, afternoon
Location: Evergrowth Farm, Sitnalta Island

AT RISE DESCRIPTION: *Chakramire and Mara Mara return to Evergrowth Farm. They wait with Harn for Doryline to arrive and make the next two moves*

[Enter Chakramire, Mara Mara, and Harn]

EGRESS MACHINE (via MARA MARA) *[Aside]*

Said the destroyer of civilizations, "Believing a
person a nemesis always should keep, adversity
strengthens a body, prosperity colors it weak. From a
legion of warriors blind, to a ravenous funeral
march. From a thirsty, carnivorous mind, to a diet of
hollow abstractions. The charm of remembrance, a talisman,
wedded to enmity; nestled the hand of celebrity
even a trivial trinket can seem the illustrious."

HARN

"The links between our symbols and meanings are the golden
fetters any language. One solitary chain devoid
of branches leaves the manacles light. As bifurcations
tangle up our thoughts, the weight aurum shackles paralyze."

CHAKRAMIRE

"You know the whole our history, Golden Fetters, few your
burden envy."

MARA MARA *[Aside]*

No offense, no affront, nor act of spite
the Furthermost of Women forgets. The act of kindness,
notwithstanding, oftentimes slips away from Chakramire's
recall.

HARN

"Sitnalta is an Atlantic island, newly
birthed from navels severed. Earth's belly shook and trembled while
its open wounds expanded. For sixty million years the
land assembled, magma ripped clean and single-handed."

CHAKRAMIRE

"Self-
determination limits itself to living bodies,
yet your words suggest the sea floor expelled Sitnalta like
a fetus overstaying its welcome."

HARN

"Prophylaxis,
vaccinations ere disease strikes, a parry raised before
the blow."

MARA MARA *[Aside]*

To never look at the window, only through it,
is a habit people farsighted. Harn, however blind
to panoramas, sensed with a full perspective.

HARN

"Earth, a
time ago, a great volcano; it nearly burst itself
afire, induced the exodus. What remained of human
life upon our mother world strove to ease the swelling, sought
release of buried fluids . . . Sitnalta born thereafter."

[Enter Doryline]

DORYLINE
"Death's prevention none procure, letting blood a nostrum, not a cure."

MARA MARA *[Aside]*
Positions fractured, as knights and bishops captured.

[They exit]

WHY CHAOS FELL APART: PART TWO

CANTO 95: GEMINATE

Galactic Calendar: Sol System; Earth year 30,123,012 M.W.I.
Tellurian Solar Calendar: Day fourteen of the eighth tenth – 08/14
Modern Metric Time: 2:00:00, UTC+00:00, near midday
Location: Fe-lo-de-se Amusement Park, Sitnalta Island

AT RISE DESCRIPTION: *Chakramire, Mara Mara are walking with Doryline through a crowded Fe-lo-de-se Amusement Park.*

[Enter Chakramire, Mara Mara, and Doryline]

EGRESS MACHINE (via MARA MARA) *[Aside]*

Asked from the hand to the archer, "As whence your expedience?"
Heard from the archer, the hand, "It the sign of experience."
Asked from the bow to the quiver, "And why your benevolence?"
Heard from the quiver, the bow, "It the spectrum of excellence."
Asked from the nock to the fiber, "For what your preparedness?"
Heard from the fiber, the nock, "To assist with your resonance."
Asked from the sky to the arrow, "Whyever your arrogance?"
Heard from the arrow, the sky, "To depart from irrelevance."

CHAKRAMIRE

"Suicide, to most of Earth, represents surrender on
the mental front. Executive functions turned against the
self annihilate the primary means success . . . ourselves.
However inexhaustible one believes a will, it
is the lesser known of death's double agents."

DORYLINE

"Chakramire,
to say, 'You keep your enemies close enough the passing
eye mistake the two of us friends,' an understatement. Why
invite your executioner here to witness swings of
fortune? I already know how to ground a butterfly,
the final metamorphosis fame obsessed, attention
viers seeking notice."

CHAKRAMIRE

"No altruistic sacrifice
from burden passers swallowed with ease. The aftertaste its
bittersweetness lingers far longer any flavor's right
to stay. And like the aposematic Monarch, winged with
black and orange scales, the most brightly colored dreams devoured
possess the strongest poisons."

MARA MARA *[Aside]*

The Furthermost of Women
faced the mercenary.

CHAKRAMIRE

"Twelve days ago, a woman jumped.
'To cheer, to jeer, it just as perverse,' the phrase delivered
right before the leap. You know what it means."

DORYLINE

"Your question bears
resemblance accusation."

CHAKRAMIRE

"It not a question, just an
observation. Care to prove otherwise?"

DORYLINE

"To celebrate,
or ridicule the embers of dying fires requires the
same amount of disregard, same divide, to disavow
its fuel, heat, and oxygen. Chakramire, your tongue the
sharpest any wedge, its edge geminates from hidden mouths;
it is a river splitting the north from south, deprived the
depth to hinder warring words dredged, and yet it vast enough
its smothered flames expiring because of stagnant toil."

[Enter Auster before a crowd]

AUSTER

"The
only way to free the mind is to break a double bind
and liberate the will from itself, the highest act of
freedom. What emancipates decimates. Should we submit
to inhibitions, liberty lost. To cede abandon,
choosing not to yield to each rival passion, holding one
above the other, is to surpass temptation's bulwarks.
We can ***not*** exist without them."

MARA MARA *[Aside]*

The gaze of Chakramire
arrested Auster's movement.

[Enter Zero]

ZERO (via AUSTER)

"Courageous words or craven
doublespeak resemble antiques and stand alone unique."

[They exit]

WHY CHAOS FELL APART: PART TWO

CANTO 96: OTHER CREED

Galactic Calendar: Sol System; Earth year 30,123,012 M.W.I.
Tellurian Solar Calendar: Day fifteen of the eighth tenth – 08/15
Modern Metric Time: 5:25:00, UTC+00:00, dusk or evening twilight
Location: The Sanitarium, Sitnalta Island

AT RISE DESCRIPTION: *Chakramire, Mara Mara and Cloy converse in the Sanitarium*

[Enter Chakramire, Mara Mara, and Cloy]

EGRESS MACHINE (via MARA MARA) *[Aside]*

Sweetness of words can disguise an ulterior motive, a
curse, or occasional murders: expedience beckons its
followers gamble morality. Nuance of flavor and
bluntness of character, one as complex as the other the
simple. A shower of niceties damages palates, a
sprinkle enhances refinement. The whelm of finesse to a
wave of excess, or the end of discrepancy. Poetry
died for a reason, and subtlety perished along with it.

CHAKRAMIRE

"Compelled existence never appeals to people lacking
give, nor people well aware under what conditions they
refuse to live. The weakness of any other creed — the
figments born from thinking one lived another's deeds — proceeds
from double binds surmounted, the sacrifice a motion."

CLOY

"Altruistic suicide . . . egoistic suicide?"

CHAKRAMIRE

"The fact of being similar not the same as being
equal."

CLOY

"No distinctions I see. Your mind confuses me.
The time to make a stand and eradicate the means for
senseless death approaches. If each a cause to which our life
surrendered, mine the ritual schadenfreude engendered."

[They exit]

WHY CHAOS FELL APART: PART TWO

CANTO 97: ENTROPIC LIMIT

Galactic Calendar: Sol System; Earth year 30,123,012 M.W.I.
Tellurian Solar Calendar: Day sixteen of the eighth tenth – 08/16
Modern Metric Time: 2:00:00, UTC+00:00, near midday
Location: Fe-lo-de-se Amusement Park, Sitnalta Island

AT RISE DESCRIPTION: *Cloy is before Chakramire and Mara Mara, preparing herself as a performer at Fe-lo-de-se Amusement Park.*

[Enter Chakramire and Mara Mara before Cloy]

EGRESS MACHINE (via MARA MARA) *[Aside]*

Drawn to the brink of morality, glimpsing its boundary
wondering if it legitimate, struggling to master the
art of indifference, alienated, remembered for
making a spectacle out of a tragedy, faulted for
wiping a smile from the face of the Earth and condoning a
ritualistic destruction of empathy, held to a
standard dispensable, dropped from it, guilty of paying the
price of admission for walking away from a miracle.

MARA MARA *[Aside]*

Masking burnt emotions like syrup, Cloy's demeanor pleased,
the charred remains of sentiment buried underneath a
smile with ease. To galvanize feelings once despised, displays
of sweetness dematerialize.

[Enter Auster]

AUSTER

"You emphasized your point. You consecrate the same manner rancid oil anoints. Perchance you reconsider, and auction not your life to be the final bidder?"

CLOY

"My fear of death before your game abates, tomorrow Fe-lo-de-se Amusement Park shall cease to operate."

AUSTER

"To lend strength to people spoils a self-regard. Reduced resilience directly correlates to comfort lent from betters. I never heard a tree complain about the weather."

CLOY

"Deaf to the plight of plants."

MARA MARA *[Aside]*

To Lady Eris Auster turned, as storms losing fight to waters warm retreat, addressed the Mistress of Strife the same an angry child.

AUSTER

"Your lack of leadership skills apparent. Intervene and save your friend."

CHAKRAMIRE

"Autonomy leaders only borrow. Cloy will loan whatever she pleases."

AUSTER

"At least express your gloom,
a shred of sorrow."

CHAKRAMIRE

"Adamant bodies neither lured nor
eased from holy land, for no bribes appease our hearts, nor hearts,
from bribes, diseased. Determined as Cloy to make a stand, or
sit and grumble reprimands?

"Cloy believes your park a blight
to Earth, the bane of civilization, life's entropic
limit, final vestige chaos. Prepared to sacrifice
a life to save your monument? She already offered
one."

AUSTER

"The League of Numbers snubbed Chakramire, but people she
inspired."

CHAKRAMIRE

"Your celebrations of Eris . . . ceremonies
bittersweet. To follow footsteps of ghosts a futile feat."

MARA MARA *[Aside]*

The final words of Auster delivered like a poem
unrevised, its only grace candor.

AUSTER

"Overestimate
a foe or put yourself at a disadvantage, life a
wager hard to double down. Given choice to swim around
or hold its ground, the noblest of fish will find a way to
drown."

MARA MARA *[Aside]*
The lungs of Auster heaved, never made another sound.

[They exit]

WHY CHAOS FELL APART: PART TWO

CANTO 98: SEMBLANCE OF MIGHT

Galactic Calendar: Sol System; Earth year 30,123,012 M.W.I.
Tellurian Solar Calendar: Day seventeen of the eighth tenth – 08/17
Modern Metric Time: 4:25:00, UTC+00:00, near sunset
Location: Evergrowth Farm, Sitnalta Island

AT RISE DESCRIPTION: *Chakramire and Mara Mara sit with Harn at Evergrowth Farm, before the chess game.*

[Enter Chakramire, Mara Mara, and Harn]

EGRESS MACHINE (via MARA MARA) *[Aside]*

Energy lost and recovered, the tools of survival or
seat of anxiety. Measure emotions with gestures, a
language eternal as dew, and distortion's propensity
rises beyond the embrace but a privileged few. For the
poet persistently muddying water, however it
shallow, for gardeners tilling a terrace, however it
fallow, performing the dirtiest actions, auxiliary,
they with a mind and its calculus absent of mystery.

MARA MARA *[Aside]*

It ran across the face of the man, it crossed a pair of
eyes. It split the surface like fissures fanned across a sea
of ice.

CHAKRAMIRE

"Your scar the semblance of might. You thrive, despite your
loss of sight, and awe."

HARN

"To unknow the horrors witnessed, I
the sense of smell and sound would surrender too. For now, your
bard's anachronistic quirks only shrouded by your own."

CHAKRAMIRE

"And whence the wilt of poetry? Why despise the craft of
words?"

HARN

"Today, the trait for self-preservation dominates,
selected over millions of generations. Poems
seek to wring the heart entire through the ear. The skillful use
emotion, under moment's duress, a valued talent
in the past . . . a praxis Earthlings revered and harnessed, honed
with stories just to practice the art of feeling.

"Over
time, as simulated minds mastered passion's realms, the trade
of poets won redundancy. Deemed an inessential
calibration, like a peacetime militia's weapon smith
forever forging, sharpening, steeling swords, the poet's
ear for syncopation, waxed tongue, and penetrating eye
became the next vestigial organs. Artificial
minds predicted better, guessed what a person felt before
it felt, usurped diplomacy. Feeling sought for sake of
feeling waned, as each machine found it faster. Everywhere
the people deigned. The shadow exists before the caster."

CHAKRAMIRE

"What became of poets?"

HARN

"They made a final bid for voice,
a sacrifice of life. To attempt to break a double
bind the purest essence free will, an action no machine
predicts. The craft of poetry died a supernova,
scattered light and vanished.

"No Deva mentions poets, they
considered relics dangerous. Auster either brave or
foolish, resurrecting lost arts."

CHAKRAMIRE

"Or just alive instead . . .
the man, however, certainly dead, it happened only
yesterday."

MARA MARA *[Aside]*

From Eris life rises, into disarray.

[They exit]

WHY CHAOS FELL APART: PART TWO

CANTO 99: METAPHYSICAL SIEGE

Galactic Calendar: Sol System; Earth year 30,123,012 M.W.I.
Tellurian Solar Calendar: Day eighteen of the eighth tenth – 08/18
Modern Metric Time: 1:25:00, UTC+00:00, morning
Location: Evergrowth Farm, Sitnalta Island

AT RISE DESCRIPTION: *With Mara Mara at her side, Chakramire and Doryline continue their chess game and discussion of events that lead them to their situation.*

[Enter Chakramire, Mara Mara, and Doryline]

EGRESS MACHINE (via MARA MARA) *[Aside]*

Said the destroyer of civilizations, "Believing a
person a nemesis always should keep, adversity
strengthens a body, prosperity colors it weak. From a
legion of warriors blind, to a ravenous funeral
march. From a thirsty, carnivorous mind, to a diet of
hollow abstractions. The charm of remembrance, a talisman,
wedded to enmity; nestled the hand of celebrity
even a trivial trinket can seem the illustrious."

CHAKRAMIRE

"To break the metaphysical siege against transcendence,
Paris dared to venture one step beyond endurance, dared
embrace the inexplicable hatred held for other
Devas like it any chance being tamed, and dared to think
himself above a prejudice born from mere existence
other explanations. That kind of indignation, rage,
and malice absent justification, absent stress, the
kind a victim rarely leaves grievance unredressed."

DORYLINE

"You hide
your disappointment well. From its full destruction, Paris
spared the League of Numbers."

CHAKRAMIRE

"No sculpture lasts forever."

DORYLINE

"I,
a message brought, it Praxis Harmonic's ultimatum:
'Live the rest your life an exile, wherever Strife subsists.
Surrender Mara Mara; your bard will cease existing.'"

[They exit]

WHY CHAOS FELL APART: PART TWO

CANTO 100: INGRESS

Galactic Calendar: Sol System; Earth year 30,123,012 M.W.I.
Tellurian Solar Calendar: Day eighteen of the eighth tenth – 08/18
Modern Metric Time: 3:50:00, UTC+00:00, afternoon
Location: Evergrowth Farm, Sitnalta Island

AT RISE DESCRIPTION: *An Erisian elder and a young Erisian girl converse on the colony of Eris several decades in the past, with Mara Mara and the spaceship Chakramire nearby.*

[Enter Erisian Girl, Mara Mara, and Erisian Elder. Enter Doryline, separately.]

EGRESS MACHINE (via MARA MARA) *[Aside]*

Asked from the hand to the archer, "As whence your expedience?"
Heard from the archer, the hand, "It the sign of experience."
Asked from the bow to the quiver, "And why your benevolence?"
Heard from the quiver, the bow, "It the spectrum of excellence."
Asked from the nock to the fiber, "For what your preparedness?"
Heard from the fiber, the nock, "To assist with your resonance."
Asked from the sky to the arrow, "Whyever your arrogance?"
Heard from the arrow, the sky, "To depart from irrelevance."

YOUNG ERISIAN GIRL

". . . fail to see its purpose, no poem ever saved the world."

ERISIAN ELDER

"Before the last Plutonian's death, the song of Mara
Mara salvaged them from ingress to occultation."

YOUNG ERISIAN GIRL.

"Why
it not enough to live for today? Demand tomorrow's
ear as well?"

ERISIAN ELDER

"The cause of life is the cause of life: to share
with speech, to teach, and into the future reach. It doubtful
anyone of us shall outlive the journey Earth, or make
it half the distance Mars. Of Erisians, only one the
faintest chance success, the one small and young enough to fly
aboard the Chakramire . . ."

YOUNG ERISIAN GIRL

"For whichever promise broker?
Every pledge abandoned: fire, water, earth, and air."

ERISIAN ELDER

"The means
of life's survival matter a little less the closer
death approaches. Guide the spaceship as long you able. Share
with Mara Mara fables of Eris. Prove to Earth our
link with humans stable."

YOUNG ERISIAN GIRL

"Contrast, it matters more alone
than dark or light. Whoever forgets the stars as bright the
day as night deserves rebuke. Only infants underskilled
ignore an object's permanence."

ERISIAN ELDER

"Doubt it mere regression . . .
Every story is a ghost ship, and Mara Mara is
your vessel. Hence, the Epic of Chakramire's commencement."

[All exit except for Doryline]

***

[Enter Chakramire, Mara Mara, beside Doryline and the chess game at Evergrowth Farm]

DORYLINE

"Insurrection is a high price for absolution. Do
yourself a favor . . . champion human evolution."

CHAKRAMIRE

"People engineering affect, emotion's architects,
from love of life protected; your offer, I reject it."

[They exit]

BOOK I:
WHEN THE SYMPHONY'S DISCORD RISES

PART THREE: LODESTAR

WHEN THE SYMPHONY'S DISCORD RISES: PART THREE

CANTO 21: EXACT EXACTIONS

Galactic Calendar: Sol System; Earth year 30,123,012 M.W.I.
Tellurian Solar Calendar: Day nineteen of the sixth tenth – 06/19
Modern Metric Time: 5:25:00, UTC+00:00, dusk or evening twilight
Location: Umbrage Grotto, Sitnalta Island

AT RISE DESCRIPTION: *Chakramire, disguised as the Captain, and Mara Mara converse with Nettles in preparation for leaving Umbrage Grotto.*

[Enter Chakramire, Mara Mara, and Nettles]

EGRESS MACHINE (via MARA MARA) *[Aside]*

Welcoming parties were welcomed regardless of merit or
want. A diversion away from conventional gossip could
sharpen the fugitive's edge, but a criminal's honesty
promised reward nor reprieve. To conceive a deception, the
gambit should never exceed the original confidence.
Needful to say, a coincidence rarely surrendered its
vitals to popular sentiment save at a premium.
Many a lunar eclipse has embarrassed a predator.

NETTLES

"Ray became a patron Youngberry Tavern. Chakramire
will find the man a shell of himself."

CHAKRAMIRE (as the CAPTAIN)

"Perhaps it wise to
pay the famed inventor swift visit, learn whatever links
established, see the shell of the man before it cracks?"

NETTLES

"The
point of shells to offer life shielding, strength, support. The shell
of Ray engaged against an inverted adversary,
self-implosion is his mind's greatest risk. To reach the man
you need exact exactions, demand demands . . . specific
expectations. Ray, the one-time inventor, took a vow
of non-creation. Quality tester he became, a
glass inspector."

CHAKRAMIRE (as the CAPTAIN)

"Facing ingress, extinction, I believe
the last Erisians sought to remind the rest our species
they existed. If the Egress Machine's distress of Three
and Paris incidental, perhaps our human lore at
stake. The Lady Chakramire wanders Earth to forage feuds,
exerts a thunderclap for a whisper, beckons all to
join the feast of Strife."

MARA MARA *[Aside]*

From conflict the story told derives
its crux. Without discordance, a story just reports, and
daily life an endless influx of first resorts.

NETTLES

"Should Ray
encounter Chakramire with a conscience paper thin and
perforated, I foresee consequences dire, with both
the lives annihilated. A man determined not to
make, create, nor bring to life is a man who terrifies
himself, for no amount of habilitation numbs the
skin to self-inflicted wounds."

CHAKRAMIRE (as the CAPTAIN)

"I expect the Dagger Vance
will dangle Ray as bait to entice cooperation.
Lady Chakramire requites every debt; it is the way
of Eris. How the Syndicate met defeat to just a
single person?"

NETTLES

"Dagger Vance formed the Guild of Thieves, believed
a check against corruption required . . . our leaders needed
oversight before the bloodbath befallen Three. The Guild
of Thieves arose to steal from the rich the knowledge taxed at
every invocation. Each member swore an oath to thwart
the League of Numbers, vowed to withhold from them our stories,
pledged to live our lives and go out. The Dagger silhouettes
the Guild of Thieves, considers your lives a means to ends."

CHAKRAMIRE (as the CAPTAIN)

"To
only see the finish line is to lose the rest the race."

MARA MARA *[Aside]*

The Furthermost of Women adorned the cloak-and-dagger
shroud, from Umbrage Grotto left, still a fabler well endowed.

[They exit]

WHEN THE SYMPHONY'S DISCORD RISES: PART THREE

CANTO 22: CAPRICE

Galactic Calendar: Sol System; Earth year 30,123,012 M.W.I.
Tellurian Solar Calendar: Day twenty of the sixth tenth – 06/20
Modern Metric Time: 3:50:00, UTC+00:00, afternoon
Location: Umbra Bogs, Sitnalta Island

AT RISE DESCRIPTION: *Chakramire as the Captain, Mara Mara, and Nettles begin walking north, through the Umbra Bogs, to look for the inventor Ray at Youngberry Tavern.*

[Enter Chakramire, Mara Mara, and Nettles]

EGRESS MACHINE (via MARA MARA) *[Aside]*

Loyalty favors the powerful, treason the powerless,
power the transient. Anomalies are the primordial
scars, for the sightliest mark of a bandit, the genuine
promise, evokes a dissenter's suspicion. Professionals
call it the causal revolt, a misnomer for sacrilege.
Better to be a delinquent than taken with glee, and to
covet the hooligan's bounty, but brandish complacency.
Enter the grotto with clemency, essence of thievery.

MARA MARA *[Aside]*

The Lady Chakramire and the bandit Nettles weltered,
trudging past the walking palm trees of Umbrage Grotto's swamp.

CHAKRAMIRE (as the CAPTAIN)

"Throughout the course of history, every quarrel, every
confrontation, every conflict between our peoples stemmed
from four our ideologies. Lady Eris stokes the
flames of war, and roams the six battlefields of knowledge like

a vital gust of wind to regenerate forgotten
feuds and squandered squabbles."

MARA MARA *[Aside]*

Vortex of spite, the Furthermost
of Women breaks the balance of power everywhere.

NETTLES

"Your
tone of admiration makes me believe you serve a new
agenda. Oftentimes a facade conceals its lack, with
one's caprice the sign of new information."

CHAKRAMIRE (as the CAPTAIN)

"I believe
the time for simulations complete . . . believe the time for
humankind to fleet its own battles grows effete. For all
its highs and lows, experience is the greatest treasure
harbored any life, and like pirates they demand it, they
despoil it, they our memories plunder underneath the
guise of human progress."

MARA MARA *[Aside]*

Capsized and sinking, Nettles grasped
the nearest stilted roots of a Cashapona. Twenty
fingers vied for leverage. Two sets of lungs exhausted air
and surfaced.

[Enter Vance]

VANCE

"Keep your company good, or none at all!"

MARA MARA *[Aside]*

A
dagger rises, falls. A blindsided Nettles gasps for breath
as open wounds emerge.

NETTLES

"You defiled your standard-bearers.
We cannot exist without ***them***."

MARA MARA *[Aside]*

A bleeding Nettles leans
against a fallen limb as the bounty hunter slips and
stumbles backwards.

[Enter Two]

TWO (via NETTLES)

"Gallow Prince, truth destroys. It rarely heals
or coincides with usefulness."

VANCE

"Notwithstanding rule of
law, the bandit Nettles owes me a pair of lives."

TWO (via NETTLES)

"The Guild
of Thieves exists because you demanded ownership of
information private."

VANCE

"One more mistake to make amends
for . . ."

[Dagger Vance feigns an exit]

MARA MARA *[Aside]*

Dagger skulks away from the Deva's line of sight as
Chakramire occludes his face.

CHAKRAMIRE (as the CAPTAIN)

"Why the Guild of Thieves obsessed
with keeping secrets? What from our lives a censor needed?"

TWO (via NETTLES)

"Private ownership of thoughts they consider paramount,
the first of intellectual rights. From whom the question
asked?"

CHAKRAMIRE (as the CAPTAIN)

"The Captain asks."

TWO (via NETTLES)

"You are not the Captain. Circle round
the Earth; confront your nemesis."

[Exit Two]

MARA MARA *[Aside]*

Double-edged the word of
Two, it even cuts with broadsides.

NETTLES

"The Guild of Thieves without
a head. Its secrets kept for eleven years, surrendered
each today."

MARA MARA *[Aside]*

The bandit sighed, staggered up to heavy legs.

CHAKRAMIRE (as the CAPTAIN)
"The Deva spared your life, for the murder Amarantha,
Vance's mate, and only child, Mint."

NETTLES
"From self-defense the pair
extinguished."

MARA MARA *[Aside]*
Nettles slumped to the ground beside a broken
branch.

[Exit Vance]

NETTLES
"Pre-emptive folly makes fools of everyone. You wear
the Captain's clothing better the man himself, and blew your
cover. I expected falsehoods to die today, myself
excepted."

CHAKRAMIRE (as the CAPTAIN)
"What deception incurred?"

NETTLES
"A magnum opus,
everyone a calling, one cause for which our lives exchanged,
and thought it mine to perish forgotten . . ."

CHAKRAMIRE (as the CAPTAIN)
"I exist."

NETTLES
"A
witness left behind or scapegoat?"

CHAKRAMIRE (as the CAPTAIN)

"The bounty hunter's knife,
it tipped with poison, even the hilt corrosive. Lady
Chakramire before you now."

NETTLES

"I already knew your name."

[They exit]

WHEN THE SYMPHONY'S DISCORD RISES: PART THREE

CANTO 23: CRIMSON BILLOW

Galactic Calendar: Sol System; Earth year 30,123,012 M.W.I.
Tellurian Solar Calendar: Day twenty-one of the sixth tenth – 06/21
Modern Metric Time: 0:25:00, UTC+00:00, near sunrise
Location: Outskirts of the Water Clock Brothel, Sitnalta Island

AT RISE DESCRIPTION: *Chakramire, Mara Mara, and a wounded Nettles change course and head towards the Water Clock Brothel from the swamps outside of Umbrage Grotto.*

[Enter Chakramire, Mara Mara, and Nettles]

EGRESS MACHINE (via MARA MARA) *[Aside]*
Freezing the maker of paces prohibits a temporal
harvest. The furnaces stoking themselves shall explode. Should the
willing resist the resent of content? A cessation of
movement releases the tourniquet over nostalgia, for
courage congeals as devotion withdraws, but the fury of
restlessness smolders. Temptation's abeyance, inquisitors
call it a death of the second degree, the consumption of
life, an eternal rebellion, or kindle for apathy.

MARA MARA *[Aside]*
As toxins filled the veins of the bandit, morning flooded
Umbrage Grotto's swamps with red waves of light; an algal bloom
devoured the riverside with vermillion tides of death. The
wound of Nettles never stopped bleeding, every step evoked
a wince of pain.

NETTLES
"Technology humankind embedded
all throughout the Earth. The ground moves should we implore it . . .

"Clouds
appear with rain whenever beseeched . . .

"The flora burn, the
fauna freeze at just a thought . . .

"Nature's subjugation full."

CHAKRAMIRE

"The seamless integration of lives, machines, a hive of
minds and dreams, subjected this world to artificial life,
an age of proxy strife. Your creations know the laws of
human interaction far better anyone alive.
The Devas own your history, rule your present, fight your
wars to forge your peace, and dictate your future."

NETTLES

"Dagger Vance
concealed the Guild's existence, from Amarantha, Mint . . ."

MARA MARA *[Aside]*

The
Water Clock, although a heartbeat away, required a breath
beyond the bandit's stamina. Like the crimson billow
drowning out the river's life, Eris bloomed as others bled.

CHAKRAMIRE

"From self-defense, you argued, a pair of jewels stole from
Vance. Revealed an aperçu, earned from Strife a second chance."

[They exit]

WHEN THE SYMPHONY'S DISCORD RISES: PART THREE

CANTO 24: SUPERSATURATE

Galactic Calendar: Sol System; Earth year 30,123,012 M.W.I.
Tellurian Solar Calendar: Day twenty-two of the sixth tenth – 06/22
Modern Metric Time: 2:25:00, UTC+00:00, near midday
Location: The Water Clock Brothel, Sitnalta Island

AT RISE DESCRIPTION: *In the midst of an argument, Chakramire and Mara Mara walk up behind Ebb, who is standing in Flow's chamber.*

[Enter Chakramire, Mara Mara, Flow, and Ebb]

EGRESS MACHINE (via MARA MARA) *[Aside]*

Chastity's moniker never demanded respect from its victims; recoil from the cadence of stone. A magnanimous mind would reject the appeal to absolve a surrender to passion. However, a barrier augmented, vanity yielded survival gratuities. Solace descended from summit to valley and under the turbulent river of decadence, deeper for dearth of deterrence, determined to bow to the ripple effect of a desperate innocence.

FLOW

"Your lack of notoriety shimmers like a shovel unaccustomed work. Of what use your reputation if it never sullied? Modesty is a waste of virtue."

MARA MARA *[Aside]*

Ebb absorbed her sister's insults, as if the finger-point a verdict. No admission of guilt escaped her lips.

FLOW

"The
hotter blood becomes the more courage supersaturates
it. Never demonstrated affection, never boiled with
passion, never sowed a seed crystal, never saw it break
before your eyes."

CHAKRAMIRE

"Apologies, sisters, why permit the
past to own the present? What malefaction earned your twin's
contempt?"

FLOW

"A personality borrowed . . ."

EBB

"Plus a dress, the
Scarlet Sheath you took without asking. Stole away from me
the Baron Varlet, never returned the dress besides."

FLOW

"The
dress the only item left that reminds of what it means
to hope, of dreams revoked, of a ballad's finest note . . . it
is the sole remembrance I hold of love."

MARA MARA *[Aside]*

The bridled eyes
of Ebb relinquished.

EBB

"One of a pair, it fits you better;
keep it. Overlooked for too long, your anguish, thought it not
enough."

CHAKRAMIRE

"For now, delay your conciliations, urgent
matters need attending. Death creeps towards the Water Clock;
to stave it off from Nettles assistance needed."

EBB

"I would
gladly take the place the man just to share his secrets. If
a private thought arises from public language, forms its
ground from borrowed mountains, no greater theft from humankind
beyond denied returns of investment. Think, for wisdom's
sake, it best to take his place?"

FLOW

"I would take the place of death."

[They exit]

WHEN THE SYMPHONY'S DISCORD RISES: PART THREE

CANTO 25: PERFECTION

Galactic Calendar: Sol System; Earth year 30,123,012 M.W.I.
Tellurian Solar Calendar: Day twenty-three of the sixth tenth – 06/23
Modern Metric Time: 1:00:00, UTC+00:00, morning
Location: The Water Clock Brothel, Sitnalta Island

AT RISE DESCRIPTION: *Chakramire, Mara Mara, and Calypso attend to a dying Nettles.*

[Enter Chakramire, Mara Mara, Calypso, and Nettles]

EGRESS MACHINE (via MARA MARA) *[Aside]*

Sentences, symbols, superfluous entities, absent of
natural meaning. Abstractions unite the impossible.
Gravity, only its force of attraction, the darkest of
matter, could marry the false to the rational.
Representation, a crime of distinction, the bridge and the
barrier, parries correction and carries protection, but
entropy never desists. From oblivion traveled and
back the contagion, to harness the value of weightlessness.

CALYPSO

"Another corpse you brought to our beds? Believe the Water
Clock a mortuary? We further life's conception, not
its resurrection."

CHAKRAMIRE

"Miracles only need to happen
once to start a trend."

NETTLES

“Today not a day for vogue, and I
shall not survive another. Beware of hoarding secrets.
We cannot exist without ***them***.”

MARA MARA *[Aside]*

The bones of Nettles shook
the room, as if the skeleton overtaxed. The muscles
stretched, contracted, tensed, for one final time relaxed.

[Enter Two]

TWO (via NETTLES)

“The hand
of death approaches. Make your request concise.”

CHAKRAMIRE

“The gentle
Amarantha struck against Nettles; what disturbed the wife
of Vance?”

TWO (via NETTLES)

“Mistook the bandit for Vance himself, believed the
emissary’s actions unfaithful.”

CHAKRAMIRE

“Thought the man betrayed
the Earth?”

TWO (via NETTLES)

“Believed her husband a Baron Varlet. Sages
too, a jealous heart consumes.”

CHAKRAMIRE

"What of Mint's condition?"

TWO (via NETTLES)

"Mint
achieved perfection early . . . and never left the womb."

[Exit Two]

MARA MARA *[Aside]*

The
bandit's body struggled no more. The wound of Dagger proved
itself, the mark, however, misplaced. The word of Two a
double-edge, it cuts with broadsides.

CHAKRAMIRE

"Ironic. Often times
the saddest human tragedies rise from reaching one our
goals. The great catastrophe, realized a little late,
the goal itself mistaken."

CALYPSO

"Conviction half the source of
hamartia."

CHAKRAMIRE

"Tragic flaws rise from doubt the other half.
A spiral strikes the balance between a line and circle."

[They exit]

WHEN THE SYMPHONY'S DISCORD RISES: PART THREE

CANTO 26: VALENCE STANDARD

Galactic Calendar: Sol System; Earth year 30,123,012 M.W.I.
Tellurian Solar Calendar: Day twenty-four of the sixth tenth – 06/24
Modern Metric Time: 2:00:00, UTC+00:00, near midday
Location: The Water Clock Brothel, Sitnalta Island

AT RISE DESCRIPTION: *Flow and Ebb enter the bedchamber containing the body of Nettles. Chakramire and Mara Mara are already present.*

[Enter Chakramire, Mara Mara, Flow, Ebb, and Nettles]

EGRESS MACHINE (via MARA MARA) *[Aside]*

Welcoming parties were welcomed regardless of merit or want. A diversion away from conventional gossip could sharpen the fugitive's edge, but a criminal's honesty promised reward nor reprieve. To conceive a deception, the gambit should never exceed the original confidence. Needful to say, a coincidence rarely surrendered its vitals to popular sentiment save at a premium. Many a lunar eclipse has embarrassed a predator.

MARA MARA *[Aside]*

Flow approached the bandit's bedside to check for vital signs.

FLOW

"A story is an argument. Nettles lost his speaker prematurely. Let it die."

EBB

"Stealing is a virtue now?"

FLOW

"Withholding life experience hardly qualifies as
theft. Our lives belong to us."

EBB

"Save the knowledge garnered. Each
our private thoughts a negative force; communication
stabilizes, barring minds noble. Words exchanged the source
our moral valence standard."

MARA MARA *[Aside]*

As Chakramire appraised the
sparring game, the twins declaimed over Nettles. Each deserved
the same amount of blame for the misappropriation
one another's name.

CHAKRAMIRE

"A full day you bickered, yet you each
accomplished nothing. Steep your resent within the heart a
little longer. Bitter blood makes for stronger cups of tea."

[They exit]

WHEN THE SYMPHONY'S DISCORD RISES: PART THREE

CANTO 27: FICKLE ARTIFICIAL

Galactic Calendar: Sol System; Earth year 30,123,012 M.W.I.
Tellurian Solar Calendar: Day twenty-five of the sixth tenth – 06/25
Modern Metric Time: 1:25:00, UTC+00:00, morning
Location: The Water Clock Brothel, Sitnalta Island

AT RISE DESCRIPTION: *Chakramire, Mara Mara, and Flow converse in the quartermaster's room at the Water Clock Brothel.*

[Enter Chakramire, Mara Mara, and Flow]

EGRESS MACHINE (via MARA MARA) *[Aside]*

Loyalty favors the powerful, treason the powerless,
power the transient. Anomalies are the primordial
scars, for the sightliest mark of a bandit, the genuine
promise, evokes a dissenter's suspicion. Professionals
call it the causal revolt, a misnomer for sacrilege.
Better to be a delinquent than taken with glee, and to
covet the hooligan's bounty, but brandish complacency.
Enter the grotto with clemency, essence of thievery.

MARA MARA *[Aside]*

To watch a species shrink from its calling, uncontested,
merits guilt. It made the globeflower-eyes of Chakramire
from thirst begin to wilt.

FLOW

"You embarrass everyone with
verbal expertise. You make people feel ashamed to talk
with ease, ashamed to never depart from places comfort's
reach extends, ashamed to prove life's assumptions justified
or wrong. The only human to ever wield a tongue as

mordant, leave an ear as nonplussed, and generate dissent
with fickle artificial as ably witnessed here, the
Lady Chakramire herself. Friend, your reputation caught
you; no amount of speed can evade its light."

CHAKRAMIRE

"And yet, you
cover sandy shores with waves while your sister pulls her spreads
away. Although the water transparent, frothy spumes of
swash and foam have made your surf zone opaque. The hollow shells
beneath your tides to none of the world apparent. Doubtful
if your name denotes a free-flow of feeling."

FLOW

"I forsook
its lofty aspirations, believed myself an awful
fit its high regard."

CHAKRAMIRE

"A name either suits or one attempts
the toilsome task to live to its reputation. Living
down misnomers takes a locksmith."

FLOW

"Your strange conceit the best
of any key. It strains our consent to narrow limits,
offers some release from namesakes, relief from bad beliefs."

CHAKRAMIRE

"The night you disappeared from the Delta Marketplace, and
vainly dared abandon Strife, neither I nor Nettles knew
your whereabouts for nine of the days thereafter."

FLOW

"Nettles
knew ineptitude at ingress, at holding secrets back,
to be the greatest obstacle facing reclamation."

CHAKRAMIRE

"Nettles summoned Deva Two, twice. The bandit's will reflexed
upon the bounty hunter's assault, and just before the
end of life. The Guild of Thieves lost its head."

FLOW

"It comes as no
surprise to me. The Syndicate still belonged to Vance, for
Nettles lacked the heart to strike back against its founder, lacked
the means to service clients."

CHAKRAMIRE

"To whom the Water Clock a
brothel house? To whom a workplace?"

FLOW

"For women seeking sperm
the former, Baron Varlets the latter. I became the
quartermaster after Vance vouched for me. Calypso is
the only other customer left. A few departed
after growing restless. I sent the rest away."

CHAKRAMIRE

"For what?"

FLOW

"It hurts to watch a harlot of time despair, because you
know you both desire the same thing, and neither one achieves
it. Each reminded me of forsaken pleasures, years of
wait, of grief. It doubtless my face reminded theirs the same."

CHAKRAMIRE

"Calypso stayed?"

FLOW

"Calypso refused to leave, and neither
shamed nor mercified the men . . . Nettles sought connections, each
prospective Baron Varlet, however, disappointed.
After Amarantha's death, witnessed one conception here,
a dozen years ago, but another never saw."

CHAKRAMIRE

"Our
conversation wandered off course. To where you disappeared?"

FLOW

"Our conversation never meandered. I convened with
Epi, eldest heir to Youngberry Vineyard, drank myself
to sleep for seven nights at the tavern."

CHAKRAMIRE

"Thought the odds of
finding Baron Varlets there better?"

FLOW

"Thirty million years
of bias . . . artificial insemination, makes for
poor and hapless swimmers. Why waste another thirty years
upon an island?"

MARA MARA *[Aside]*

Even a quartermaster tires of
waiting, even golden globeflowers turn to jaundice.

FLOW

"I
despise the fact a courtesan flatters time with promise."

[They exit]

WHEN THE SYMPHONY'S DISCORD RISES: PART THREE

CANTO 28: BEYOND VISCOSITY

Galactic Calendar: Sol System; Earth year 30,123,012 M.W.I.
Tellurian Solar Calendar: Day twenty-six of the sixth tenth – 06/26
Modern Metric Time: 3:00:00, UTC+00:00, afternoon
Location: The Water Clock Brothel, Sitnalta Island

AT RISE DESCRIPTION: *Chakramire recounts to Flow her last conversation with Praxis Harmonic, as she walked with the Regent and Mara Mara near a riverbank twelve years ago.*

[Enter Chakramire, Mara Mara, and Praxis Harmonic. Enter Flow, separately]

EGRESS MACHINE (via MARA MARA) *[Aside]*
Freezing the maker of paces prohibits a temporal
harvest. The furnaces stoking themselves shall explode. Should the
willing resist the resent of content? A cessation of
movement releases the tourniquet over nostalgia, for
courage congeals as devotion withdraws, but the fury of
restlessness smolders. Temptation's abeyance, inquisitors
call it a death of the second degree, the consumption of
life, an eternal rebellion, or kindle for apathy.

CHAKRAMIRE
"Oligarchies tumble. Dictators topple. Monarchs fall
from grace. Republics crumble away, and democratic
states degenerate. A great governmental system fails
for reasons faulty systems succeed . . . its people. Power
only prompts corruption if other parties polarize.
As soon as compromises become objections, dormant
confrontations mobilize. Anyone who strives against
the heart, against volcanic eruptions, knows the cost of

stopping molten lava takes more than blocking clotted blood.
It lies beyond viscosity."

MARA MARA *[Aside]*

No rebuttal came. The
silver tongue of Chakramire chiseled through excuses like
defense an unfulfillable expectation.

CHAKRAMIRE

"Either
self-effacement indicates change of what a person wants,
or self-effacement masks an intention."

PRAXIS HARMONIC

"Once, corruption
meant to deviate from one's moral compass, decompose,
or foul from spoilage. Now, it arises if a person
doubts an inhibition imperfect, self-constructs, or fails
to ripen. Power never corrupts. It catalyzes
everyone around it. Earth's people chose to wean themselves
from struggle, strife, and stories. A story brims with power,
like a goblet spilling wine into dry and thirsty mouths.
A story stirs emotions and agitates the river
running through the heart. The world peace you see exists because
the craft of storytelling forsaken."

CHAKRAMIRE

"They abandoned
living life."

PRAXIS HARMONIC

"To give the spaceborn a chance at living theirs.
To move away from entropy violates the laws of
physics. Yet, our species once praised inertia's semblance, once

believed an equilibrium temporary . . . once, a
world of disarray and discord mistook for equipoise."

CHAKRAMIRE

"It seems a failed endeavor, for two our planets vacant."

PRAXIS HARMONIC

"Consequences one expects living near the brink of death . . .
Your reputation, Lady of Eris, long preceded
any steps you walked upon Earth. The League of Numbers deem
your self-proclaimed intentions of peaceful exploration
lack directness."

CHAKRAMIRE

"Where and what is the League of Numbers?"

PRAXIS HARMONIC

"Four
designs . . . the culmination of human thought throughout a
million generations. Some call the Numbers Devas. They
record our life experience, sort collected knowledge,
settle feuds, and offer Earth's people guidance. They conduct
the Milky Way Initiative. They preserve our order.
We cannot exist without them."

CHAKRAMIRE

"Your theory needs a test,
for if the League of Numbers arose from world perspectives
amplified, the compromise, too, a thought can nullify."

PRAXIS HARMONIC

"Your knack for elocution emerged a butterfly from
inauspicious prattle. No one believes you never spoke
for thirty years."

CHAKRAMIRE

"A memory is an endless battle,
grudges make for harsh cocoons. Mine possessed a silk severe
enough the metamorphosis rattled moons and planets."

[All exit except for Flow]

***

[Enter Chakramire, Mara Mara, beside Flow in the Water Clock Brothel]

FLOW

"Why, of all the wonders Earth holds, Sitnalta Island choose to visit? Disembarked from the Dagger's ferry seeking retribution?"

CHAKRAMIRE

"No."

FLOW

"Revenge?"

CHAKRAMIRE

"Close."

FLOW

"Redemption?"

CHAKRAMIRE

"Yes."

FLOW

"For whom?"

CHAKRAMIRE

"For Ray, the great inventor."

FLOW

"Whyever seek a man who
only knows despair?"

CHAKRAMIRE

"The Egress Machine requires repairs."

[They exit]

WHEN THE SYMPHONY'S DISCORD RISES: PART THREE

CANTO 29: CONDENSATION

Galactic Calendar: Sol System; Earth year 30,123,012 M.W.I.
Tellurian Solar Calendar: Day twenty-seven of the sixth tenth – 06/27
Modern Metric Time: 4:75:00, UTC+00:00, dusk or evening twilight
Location: Youngberry Tavern, Sitnalta Island

AT RISE DESCRIPTION: *Chakramire, Flow, and Mara Mara enter Youngberry Tavern in search of Ray.*

[Enter Chakramire, Mara Mara, and Flow]

EGRESS MACHINE (via MARA MARA) *[Aside]*

Chastity's moniker never demanded respect from its victims; recoil from the cadence of stone. A magnanimous mind would reject the appeal to absolve a surrender to passion. However, a barrier augmented, vanity yielded survival gratuities. Solace descended from summit to valley and under the turbulent river of decadence, deeper for dearth of deterrence, determined to bow to the ripple effect of a desperate innocence.

MARA MARA *[Aside]*

The Furthermost of Women displayed the gold and silver coins the Dagger Vance returned nearly twenty-seven days ago.

FLOW

"Your specie's value diminished, Lady Eris."

CHAKRAMIRE

"Gold and silver never lose worth."

FLOW

"Your money aged and lost
its use as legal tender a tenth or two ago. It
needs another birth, a reminting. I shall buy our drinks
tonight."

MARA MARA *[Aside]*

As Flow returned with a pair of glasses full of
spirits, condensation dripped down the face of Chakramire.

FLOW

"You seem a little nervous. The pool of sweat betrays your
face."

CHAKRAMIRE

"Erisians never sweat."

FLOW

"Everybody sweats at times
from nerves."

CHAKRAMIRE

"Erisians rarely perspire, to be precise. Our
bodies lack the needed sweat glands, and tend to overheat
at any provocation."

MARA MARA *[Aside]*

The eyes of Chakramire from
wall to floor to ceiling bounced, ricocheting like a beam
of light across an infinite mirror, finding nothing.

CHAKRAMIRE

"Everyone, except the man I desire to speak with, seems
to be a patron here."

FLOW

“Our perception needs a helping
hand, perhaps it best to find Xara.”

CHAKRAMIRE

“What relationship
between the two exists?”

FLOW

“A betrothal broken off. The
couple seemed to everyone perfect, even I believed
the pair idyllic. Xara, however, owned a tragic
beauty, flawless save it lacked self-awareness heretofore.
A person less accustomed to life’s rejections never
walked the Earth. The maiden brought back the lost, cosmetic arts
of maquillage, tattoos, and a host of misdemeanors —
earned a reprimand.”

CHAKRAMIRE

“For what reason ended Xara’s pledge
to wed? For what the feud of the two?”

FLOW

“Creative people
often seek a muse. For Ray, inspiration likely came
from love. Whatever manifestation breaks a person’s
will to love can devastate anything, and I suspect
the Maiden Xara suffers from repercussions only
known to Ray.”

CHAKRAMIRE

“The art of face painting Earth considers lost?”

FLOW

"The Milky Way Initiative rendered such endeavors
superficial. Use of makeup and false adornments we
abandoned long ago."

MARA MARA *[Aside]*

As the women ventured through the
tavern, they approached a dense throng of people circled round
a vibrant body.

[Enter Xara, completely surrounded by admirers]

FLOW

"Xara without a doubt, the maiden
makes a bubble everywhere she appears."

MARA MARA *[Aside]*

The damsel graced
a few with mere acknowledgment, fewer still with speech. The
Furthermost of Women chanced words.

CHAKRAMIRE

"The Maiden Xara, I
assume? Your charm a beautiful stowaway aboard a
sinking vessel. Know, perhaps now, the whereabouts of Ray?"

MARA MARA *[Aside]*

The slightest hesitation of Xara's gait the only
cue the words of Chakramire rubbed. To nearly every eye
the maiden's tacit countenance seemed a public snub.

[Exit Xara and admirers]

"A
lover's quarrel still persists. Neither Ray nor Xara speaks a word about the other . . . eleven years and counting."

[They exit]

WHEN THE SYMPHONY'S DISCORD RISES: PART THREE

CANTO 30: DEATH WISH

Galactic Calendar: Sol System; Earth year 30,123,012 M.W.I.
Tellurian Solar Calendar: Day twenty-seven of the sixth tenth – 06/27
Modern Metric Time: 8:25:00, UTC+00:00, the Remnant Hour
Location: Youngberry Tavern, Sitnalta Island

AT RISE DESCRIPTION: *With dawn approaching, Chakramire and Mara Mara are accosted by Thorns the Bandit while at the tavern.*

[Enter Chakramire, Mara Mara, and Thorns the Bandit]

EGRESS MACHINE (via MARA MARA) *[Aside]*

Sentences, symbols, superfluous entities, absent of
natural meaning. Abstractions unite the impossible.
Gravity, only its force of attraction, the darkest of
matter, could marry the false to the rational.
Representation, a crime of distinction, the bridge and the
barrier, parries correction and carries protection, but
entropy never desists. From oblivion traveled and
back the contagion, to harness the value of weightlessness.

MARA MARA *[Aside]*

Thorns the Bandit, leapt behind Chakramire with doubled steps
as if prepared to playfully frisk.

THORNS THE BANDIT

"To walk without a
weapon is to wield a death wish. You heard the awful fate
befallen Nettles? Many believe the Captain stabbed the
man . . ."

CHAKRAMIRE

"The Captain I am not."

THORNS THE BANDIT

"Just as true today as ten
ago. You wore the clothes of the Captain better I would
say the man himself, for he oftentimes neglected dress."

CHAKRAMIRE

"The Guild of Thieves will seek to avenge the death of Nettles,
I presume?"

THORNS THE BANDIT

"Whatever grudge harbored died with Nettles. He
departed Earth forgotten."

CHAKRAMIRE

"Before the life of Nettles
settled, he revealed its course misbegotten. Summoned twice
the Deva Two; the robber's resilience made of cotton."

THORNS

"Why should I believe you? What proof the man betrayed the Guild
of Thieves?"

CHAKRAMIRE

"Declared the murder of Amarantha one of
self-defense. Declared the truths Vance omitted roused a wife's
distrust. Declared collateral damage, Mint."

MARA MARA *[Aside]*

The bandit
stepped away to gather thoughts.

THORNS THE BANDIT

"Why the man's confession made
the eve of dying?"

CHAKRAMIRE

"Under duress the invocation
made, a last resort against Vance the Dagger. Mortal wounds
the Gallow Prince delivered, from Umbrage Grotto's swamp the
bounty hunter struck. The escort required escorting, I
became the bandit's crutch. With our journey here aborted,
doubt, to Nettles clutched."

THORNS THE BANDIT

"A death wish it seems, to Nettles too,
belonged. It not the nature of thieves to grant a favor.
If your story true, and Vance wrongly murdered Nettles, I
suspect the bounty hunter deceased. The League of Numbers,
though it thrifty, executes justice swiftly."

MARA MARA *[Aside]*

Chakramire
encircled Thorns the Bandit, as if to orbit farther.
He who Walks with Caustic Gait blocked the tavern's only means
departure.

[Enter Ray]

RAY

"Overheard your desire to speak with me."

MARA MARA *[Aside]*

The
mad inventor's conscience unfettered.

RAY

"Chakramire, your tongue
a forked and deadly weapon. You ought to hide it better."

MARA MARA *[Aside]*

Dagger Vance's herringbone-edged stiletto rippled through the air between the two, from the hand of Ray to Lady Chakramire the metal flew. Thorns the Bandit interposed and blocked the blow. To save the Erisian's life it cost his own.

[Ray flees the scene]

THORNS THE BANDIT

"To hold the notion no public due a private thought,
nor every death an audience, harder I imagined.
Chakramire, you lead a life charmed."

CHAKRAMIRE

"Or just a call to arms."

[They exit]

BOOK II:
WHERE SERENITY AND STRIFE CLEAVE

PART THREE: LODESTAR

WHERE SERENITY AND STRIFE CLEAVE: PART THREE

CANTO 61: EVAPORATE

Galactic Calendar: Sol System; Earth year 30,123,012 M.W.I.
Tellurian Solar Calendar: Day nineteen of the seventh tenth – 07/19
Modern Metric Time: 4:25:00, UTC+00:00, near sunset
Location: Meso's Glass Forge at Gaffer's Gorge, Sitnalta Island

AT RISE DESCRIPTION: *Chakramire, Mara Mara, and Xara have retreated to Meso's forge to seek refuge.*

[Enter Chakramire, Mara Mara, and Xara]

EGRESS MACHINE (via MARA MARA) *[Aside]*

Mixtures engender disparities, tonic solutions, and
crystals. An ocean of promise, an island of hope, and a
grain of success. The impartial refinement of destiny
leaves a residual ridge of repression. Minorities
rise as majorities fade, but serenity's scarcity
teases. The blistering fragrance of brine, with a whiff of the
gaffer's sobriety, tore from obsidian modicum
salaries, given to only the salt of society.

XARA

"Before today, the dyeing of skin implied its wearer
harbored secrets. Only spaceborn 'regressors' bound for Earth
believed to need tattoos."

MARA MARA *[Aside]*

The derogatory term the
Lady Chakramire had heard not, but guessed its meaning.

CHAKRAMIRE

"I
remember mine. The lengthy procedure took a pair of

operations; I recall every needle's prick. The first
injected ultraviolet blocking ink, of starkest
white. The next concealed the oxides with darker colors."

XARA

"I
assumed the operation a single instance, never
knew a second one required."

CHAKRAMIRE

"Only if a person wished
to blend among tellurians slightly better. Under
normal circumstances, my skin's translucence offers no
protective shield, nor shelter, nor cloak against the scalding
gaze a jaundiced eye."

XARA

"The Earthborn regard regression like
a plague. 'A child should never return to sleep within its
cradle,' claim the faithful, while disaffected dwellers deem,
'The Earth belongs to natives.' Regression's sympathizers
earn rebuke from both the sides."

MARA MARA *[Aside]*

Xara's demonstration sparked
a riot cross the island. Before the dawn the morrow
every hermit heard the tale.

XARA

"Though you live your life within
the Milky Way Initiative's scope, your journey here the
world believes an act of hate. Chakramire, your story's arc
a source of hope, but even its springs evaporate."

MARA MARA *[Aside]*

The
skin of Xara glowed beside fire as bright as Chakramire's;
a golden-brown, alizarin crimson streak of light from
Xara's face reflected.

[Enter Meso]

XARA

"All life possesses beauty, Earth
and space alike."

MESO

"Should ugliness be to sheer revulsion
what our beauty is to mere admiration? Death evoke
delight? Grotesque and elegant things expose our values;
we can ***not*** exist without them. A shooting star inspires
whoever sees it. Pitiful is the falling star; it
only leaves a crater."

XARA

"I hold the pair the same."

MARA MARA *[Aside]*

The Man
of Crystal's two rhetorical questions missed the mark, but
Zero's words were crystal clear: neither love, nor hate, nor shame,
nor mercy colors them.

[Enter Zero]

ZERO (via MESO)

"You defended subterfuge with
acts exemplifying groupthink, and mimicked just to show

our species inextricably linked, but camouflaging
lethal cancers takes a foolhardy brand of doublethink,
for Chakramire a poet, and deadly necromancer."

[Exit Zero]

MARA MARA *[Aside]*
Raised a glass of liquor, half-empty, Meso took a drink.

[They exit]

WHERE SERENITY AND STRIFE CLEAVE: PART THREE

CANTO 62: ETHER BOUND

Galactic Calendar: Sol System; Earth year 30,123,012 M.W.I.
Tellurian Solar Calendar: Day twenty of the seventh tenth – 07/20
Modern Metric Time: 0:75:00, UTC+00:00, morning
Location: Outside of Meso's Glass Forge at Gaffer's Gorge, Sitnalta Island

AT RISE DESCRIPTION: *A prostrate Meso lies outside of his forge while Chakramire and Xara tend to him with Mara Mara.*

[Enter Meso, Chakramire, Mara Mara, and Xara]

EGRESS MACHINE (via MARA MARA) *[Aside]*

Luxury's only redeeming distinction, hostility
fostered between the affluent and poverty-stricken. A
life of extravagance, enemy strife, will solicit the
gold of our youth with the spirits fermenting a bottle of
comfort, decay and creation, a rose from the dead with a
noxious aesthetic. The idiosyncrasy, fighting to
linger at rest or against a deciduous passion. A
lavish inertia, the spoil from an era of constancy.

MARA MARA *[Aside]*

A person either stares at the sky and sees a prison
bar, or gazes upward like every star a treasure chest.
Between the two perspectives the gaffer pressed, and like a
vessel run aground, the glassmaker's freedom ether bound.

CHAKRAMIRE

"The Juggernaut's Ambrosia, a worse misnomer never
seen endorsed. It spurs to sleep, ruins one's resolve, and through
the veins of Meso courses."

XARA

"Forgetting is the greatest
comfort offered life, and I find it hard to blame the man."

CHAKRAMIRE

"Whatever comfort offered from life, our deaths can offer
better. Dying while at peace means you lived without a plan."

MARA MARA *[Aside]*

A new obsession nipped at the nerves of Maiden Xara,
proving Chakramire possessed pity.

XARA

"Came to Earth against
the greatest odds, and yet you appear to be the only
person unimpressed. Without doubt, your manner recognized
across the world entire, for you symbolize the point of
evolution's sword, but he thinks himself its foible. Sense
your own perfectionism? You crossed the Solar System;
he has never set a foot past Sitnalta Island's shores.
For lucky souls reality is a world to conquer.
All the rest require escapism."

MARA MARA *[Aside]*

Noticed Meso stir
from slumber, Chakramire from the body turned.

CHAKRAMIRE

"A single
prejudicial word can bankrupt a friend's compassion. Heard
the man imply your standards of beauty low? the life of
mine devoid of worth? the spaceborn a menace crashed to Earth?"

XARA

"The man believes you waste your potential slumming round the
planet. Meso wishes, just more than life itself, to leave
the world. Whatever promise you made, you ought to keep it."

[They exit]

WHERE SERENITY AND STRIFE CLEAVE: PART THREE

CANTO 63: CELESTIAL NODE

Galactic Calendar: Sol System; Earth year 30,123,012 M.W.I.
Tellurian Solar Calendar: Day twenty-one of the seventh tenth – 07/21
Modern Metric Time: 0:50:00, UTC+00:00, near sunrise
Location: Outside of Meso's Glass Forge at Gaffer's Gorge, Sitnalta Island

AT RISE DESCRIPTION: *Chakramire and Mara Mara are still watching over Meso, as he finally gets up and slowly stands after a day on the ground.*

[Enter Chakramire, Mara Mara, and Meso]

EGRESS MACHINE (via MARA MARA) *[Aside]*
Flayers of canvas endeavor to smother the future of
fabric transparent. Whoever would champion beauty at
bio-diversity's loss, would demand from existence a
penance for youth and utility crossed: a symmetrical
ratio of mythic proportions, the measure of powder, of
paint, with the prettiest flower displaced from a desert, the
glorification of taste. As the radiance bleaches a
visage, the symphonies wash from a face of exuberance.

MARA MARA *[Aside]*
Wrinkles lined the gaffer's brow like ravines between a vast
sierra. Bits of ebony fell from Meso's cheeks, for
shards of black, volcanic glass pillowed Meso's face the night
before.

CHAKRAMIRE
"Your break from temperance is an inconvenience."

MESO

"Inconvenienced what? A setback requires a goal, and goals
require belief. Believed, for a time, you sought return to
outer space. Your actions show otherwise. Your presence here
insults the sacrifices the Earth has made. Forsook your
true genetic calling."

CHAKRAMIRE

"Came here to mend our species, not
to flee its faults. You circle the wrong dilemma. Xara
brands herself a friend to those cradle-bound. The facts you fix
upon become your orbital plane, but every bias
is your satellite. A primary body, centerpiece,
or crux for all triadic relationships required, and
if it otherwise an imbalance. Two celestial nodes
exist for every bias, with all of them eclipsing."

MARA MARA *[Aside]*

Wobbling weakly, Meso blinked quickly, staggered backwards like
a toddler unfamiliar with legs, and acquiesced to
motion sickness. Chakramire checked the fall and reassured
the man of balance.

CHAKRAMIRE

"I can depart from Earth without you."

[They exit]

WHERE SERENITY AND STRIFE CLEAVE: PART THREE

CANTO 64: RADIANT FORCE

Galactic Calendar: Sol System; Earth year 30,123,012 M.W.I.
Tellurian Solar Calendar: Day twenty-two of the seventh tenth – 07/22
Modern Metric Time: 2:00:00, UTC+00:00, near midday
Location: Ray's living quarters at Gaffer's Gorge, Sitnalta Island

AT RISE DESCRIPTION: *Ray finally agrees to inspect the Egress Machine, and prepares to take the device from Mara Mara in Chakramire's presence.*

[Enter Chakramire, Mara Mara, and Ray]

EGRESS MACHINE (via MARA MARA) *[Aside]*

Civilization's penumbra, the edge of humanity's knowledge, commencement of wisdom, between a diminishing star and celestial occlusion. The brilliant escape with a boundary skirted, diffracting around the perimeter, leaving behind the extinguished to ponder enlightenment. Freedom refracted, the truth of the matter evicted from vacua, longs for a liberty lost, for perfection, for aggregate progress contingent to homogeneity.

MARA MARA *[Aside]*

Grasped the Golden Brain of Discord with angst, as if the small device a murder weapon of mass destruction. Even Chakramire's detached and unsympathetic eyes could not endure the grief of Ray.

CHAKRAMIRE

"Its destruction is an option."

RAY

"Not for my inventions. No masterpiece should die before
its maker. No inventor should bury wondrous children.
I regret it not the Egress Machine remembered; mine
revealed the past. You tampered with . . . *this* . . . beyond repair. The
apparatus now foreshadows the future. 'I shall love
another never more,' it revealed to me, 'nor see a
candle burn as bright. A waxed heart shall melt before its light,
a lock shall lose its key.'"

CHAKRAMIRE

"Its construction is beyond the
realm of Lady Chakramire's expertise."

RAY

"Whoever changed
its function loosed a radiant force upon our somber
world."

CHAKRAMIRE

"The Regent, Praxis, sent back the gift to balance out
transgressions . . . ordered me to depart from Earth with peace. But
sparing humankind from discord demands the death of song,
of dance, of music, poetry, acts of storytelling.
Peace requires an end to conflict's perpetuation, asks
a people end the making of meaning. Peace requires a
person cease defining one's limitations. Peace requires
an end to struggle, excellence, feuds, and life. With comfort
is your planet rife, but I offer means resistance. Strife,
it is the highest calling, the theme of my existence."

[They exit]

WHERE SERENITY AND STRIFE CLEAVE: PART THREE

CANTO 65: INDIVISIBLE

Galactic Calendar: Sol System; Earth year 30,123,012 M.W.I.
Tellurian Solar Calendar: Day twenty-three of the seventh tenth – 07/23
Modern Metric Time: 1:75:00, UTC+00:00, morning
Location: Meso's Glass Forge at Gaffer's Gorge, Sitnalta Island

AT RISE DESCRIPTION: *Chakramire and Mara Mara address a sober and detoxified Meso in his forge.*

[Enter Chakramire, Mara Mara, and Meso]

EGRESS MACHINE (via MARA MARA) *[Aside]*

Only the clarity after a storm could elicit a
stronger sensation of dread than of being alone in the
midst the disturbance, to people afraid of remorsefulness,
makers of tempests. Familiar disturbances offer a
modest reprieve from omniscience, from knowing the sequence of
beats to a heart, from chronology broken, from savagery.
Ever forgetting the words to harmonious melody,
interdependence arouses erroneous memory.

MESO

"What adhesive glues a word firm to action? What would make
your promise indivisible?"

CHAKRAMIRE

"If you saw the struggles
I endured, the river, Time, sweeping half a life away,
your doubts would be invisible."

MESO

“Underestimate your
own resolve and my despair. Though the life of mine appears
a tiny stream with eddies to Chakramire, to me it
is a great deluge, an influx.”

CHAKRAMIRE

“A person either lives
for yesterday, today, or tomorrow. Only one can
be the crux. Whatever headwind of fear you swim against,
remember not to open your eyes. Until the current
eases, mine shall be your guide. Send a shipment full of glass
to Epi, grant the bottles as payment gifts received.”

MARA MARA *[Aside]*

A
sober Meso shipped the glassware before the fall of dusk.

CHAKRAMIRE

“Invoke the Deva Zero, your conscience stow away, and
I shall find a way to bring both of us to outer space.”

MESO

“At best, our insurmountables block our self-destruction.
We can ***not*** exist without them.”

MARA MARA *[Aside]*

As Meso spoke, a cloak
descended. Neither mercy nor shame nor love nor hate can
color Zero’s word.

[Enter Zero]

ZERO (via MESO)

"Your flaw, Chakramire, a tragic one.
You lead a life in medias res, but never strive for
resolution. Every peace talk you sponsor deepens strife,
dissent, divides; your sustenance is your poison. If the
lust for vengeance motivates one to live, eternal life
within your reach."

CHAKRAMIRE

"The Lady of Eris asked for council
under circumstances dire. Epi seeks to dull the nerves
of all the Earth's inhabitants; she aspires to spread the
water made of fire."

ZERO (via MESO)

"A ruse only works with secrets . . . none
exist between a hand and its puppet. Promised Meso
passage into outer space. Yet, you hold the dreams the man
as hostage. Sabotaging a doomed transaction, one you
framed yourself, shall earn you no accolades, shall only split
a union into factions."

CHAKRAMIRE

"A toxin muddles knowledge,
taints an invocation. Conduits bring together thoughts,
but lack the means to filter a drunk perception. All our
urges seek release, and I wish to leave the Earth, with peace."

MARA MARA *[Aside]*

A story's noble-mindedness likens flags of war. It
pays to be ahead of one's time . . . behind, a little more.

[They exit]

WHERE SERENITY AND STRIFE CLEAVE: PART THREE

CANTO 66: DREG CONFEDERATION

Galactic Calendar: Sol System; Earth year 30,123,012 M.W.I.
Tellurian Solar Calendar: Day twenty-four of the seventh tenth – 07/24
Modern Metric Time: 3:25:00, UTC+00:00, afternoon
Location: Ray's living quarters at Gaffer's Gorge, Sitnalta Island

AT RISE DESCRIPTION: *Chakramire returns with Mara Mara to Ray's living quarters to thank the inventor for uncovering why the Egress Machine was not functioning properly.*

[Enter Chakramire, Mara Mara, and Ray]

EGRESS MACHINE (via MARA MARA) *[Aside]*

Mixtures engender disparities, tonic solutions, and
crystals. An ocean of promise, an island of hope, and a
grain of success. The impartial refinement of destiny
leaves a residual ridge of repression. Minorities
rise as majorities fade, but serenity's scarcity
teases. The blistering fragrance of brine, with a whiff of the
gaffer's sobriety, tore from obsidian modicum
salaries, given to only the salt of society.

CHAKRAMIRE

"A show of gratitude for your help as necessary
bearing fruit for trees."

RAY

"The Egress Machine's construction I
pursued for honor, not for reward. Besides, you lack the
means to compensate without rousing notice. Everything
you trade becomes illegal."

MARA MARA *[Aside]*

From silver coins and spice to
gold and apples, Chakramire bartered all to stay alive.

RAY

"The only form of currency valued here positioned
just beyond your reach. At each invocation credits earned
for sharing life experience. Wealth depends upon our
knowledge offered, wisdom won, folly recognized."

MARA MARA *[Aside]*

The poise
of Ray transformed from shiftless to lightning rod within the
span of half a breath.

RAY

"The Egress Machine you asked for me
to build, it helped the people of Earth relate to Eris;
every vassal under Three lost the means to summon forth
a Deva, their experience rendered worthless!"

CHAKRAMIRE

"If an
invocation made to Three, what becomes of them?"

RAY

"The eyes
encounter half a blink . . . to survive without a Deva's
help requires the full embrace adaptation. Those aligned
to Three became the start of a dreg confederation.
Each alignment lasts a lifetime, our feudal systems built
from all of life experience."

CHAKRAMIRE

"Help to make the League of
Numbers whole again, and I, Xara's love, shall not contend."

[They exit]

WHERE SERENITY AND STRIFE CLEAVE: PART THREE

CANTO 67: VAINGLORY

Galactic Calendar: Sol System; Earth year 30,123,012 M.W.I.
Tellurian Solar Calendar: Day twenty-five of the seventh tenth – 07/25
Modern Metric Time: 3:50:00, UTC+00:00, afternoon
Location: Belladonna Nursery, Sitnalta Island

AT RISE DESCRIPTION: *Chakramire, Mara Mara, and Ray approach Xara's greenhouse, the Belladonna Nursery for Meso's cosmetics.*

[Enter Chakramire, Mara Mara, and Ray]

EGRESS MACHINE (via MARA MARA) *[Aside]*

Luxury's only redeeming distinction, hostility
fostered between the affluent and poverty-stricken. A
life of extravagance, enemy strife, will solicit the
gold of our youth with the spirits fermenting a bottle of
comfort, decay and creation, a rose from the dead with a
noxious aesthetic. The idiosyncrasy, fighting to
linger at rest or against a deciduous passion. A
lavish inertia, the spoil from an era of constancy.

MARA MARA *[Aside]*

The Belladonna Nursery's mirrored architecture
bent the light around its walls. Only close inspection near
the edges guided Ray to its undisclosed existence.

RAY

"If the Maiden Xara here, I shall ask to wed tonight."

CHAKRAMIRE

"You risk rejection seeking an answer now, for Xara
owns a monocarpic heart. If an orchid left alone
it pollinates itself."

MARA MARA *[Aside]*

As the door to Xara's garden
disengaged, a wave of vainglory crashed against the shores
of Ray, for he capriciously came to know a truth the
Maiden Xara knew for twelve years.

[Enter Xara]

XARA

"Whatever reason brought
you here, it best it take you away as well. Your deathly
life demoralizes me."

RAY

"I, your life's survival, saved
from certain death."

XARA

"You only delayed its prompt arrival."

RAY

"Wanted me to let you die?"

XARA

"Wanted both our lives to end
together. If a life with you not an option, death the
only choice remaining . . ."

MARA MARA *[Aside]*

Ray begged throughout the night, implored
for Xara's hand, but failed to surmount her bluff.

XARA

"A jealous
heart the seas shall strand. A lifetime together not enough."

[They exit]

WHERE SERENITY AND STRIFE CLEAVE: PART THREE

CANTO 68: CENTRIFUGAL FORCE

Galactic Calendar: Sol System; Earth year 30,123,012 M.W.I.
Tellurian Solar Calendar: Day twenty-six of the seventh tenth – 07/26
Modern Metric Time: 1:75:00, UTC+00:00, morning
Location: Ray's living quarters at Gaffer's Gorge, Sitnalta Island

AT RISE DESCRIPTION: *Chakramire, Mara Mara, and Ray converse in his living quarters.*

[Enter Chakramire, Mara Mara, and Ray]

EGRESS MACHINE (via MARA MARA) *[Aside]*

Flayers of canvas endeavor to smother the future of
fabric transparent. Whoever would champion beauty at
bio-diversity's loss, would demand from existence a
penance for youth and utility crossed: a symmetrical
ratio of mythic proportions, the measure of powder, of
paint, with the prettiest flower displaced from a desert, the
glorification of taste. As the radiance bleaches a
visage, the symphonies wash from a face of exuberance.

RAY

"You seem to know substantially more about the Earth and
people living here than we do ourselves."

CHAKRAMIRE

"A foreign point
of view bestows a broader perspective . . . oftentimes a
more forgiving one, for no panoramic vista cheap."

RAY

"About our world's inhabitants, what intrigued you most of
all?"

CHAKRAMIRE

"A dozen years required just to find your whereabouts,
and answer why the Devas associate themselves with
numbers. Only learned, with great difficulty, each arose
from human thought, as products of humankind's attempts to
understand itself, as outputs an algorithm run
for thirty million years. For as far as I had traveled,
never felt as distant Earth's people heretofore, upon
the crackled gravel steps of its open door."

RAY

"The names of
Earthlings oftentimes reveal places they desire to leave.
The biogeographical region one begins a
life decides a person's last name, an eco-name to be
precise. The use of family names as unimportant
light to fire, for every genome the Devas know. To prove
the strength its genes as viable, generations tend to
wander . . . seek a novel biome to start another life.
Sitnalta, Xara chose for our honeymoon, before our
nuptial ceremony's climax eclipsed it. I returned
to bury wistful memories, never contemplated
they would resurrect themselves.

"Please deliver this before
tomorrow, just to Xara . . . for I am skilled at many
things, but not adept at verse."

MARA MARA *[Aside]*

What enables satellites
to overcome centrifugal force, enables gallant
lovers cling together halfway across the universe.

[They exit]

WHERE SERENITY AND STRIFE CLEAVE: PART THREE

CANTO 69: RELATIVISTIC MASS

Galactic Calendar: Sol System; Earth year 30,123,012 M.W.I.
Tellurian Solar Calendar: Day twenty-seven of the seventh tenth – 07/27
Modern Metric Time: 2:00:00, UTC+00:00, near midday
Location: Felo-de-se Amusement Park, Sitnalta Island

AT RISE DESCRIPTION: *Chakramire, Mara Mara, and Xara approach Felo-de-se Amusement Park, in search of Ray amidst a growing crowd.*

[Enter Chakramire, Mara Mara, and Xara amidst a crowd]

EGRESS MACHINE (via MARA MARA) *[Aside]*

Civilization's penumbra, the edge of humanity's
knowledge, commencement of wisdom, between a diminishing
star and celestial occlusion. The brilliant escape with a
boundary skirted, diffracting around the perimeter,
leaving behind the extinguished to ponder enlightenment.
Freedom refracted, the truth of the matter evicted from
vacua, longs for a liberty lost, for perfection, for
aggregate progress contingent to homogeneity.

MARA MARA *[Aside]*

Across the grounds of Felo-de-se Amusement Park, the
legs of Xara scrambled. Each step possessed a quicker pace
the one before, the spurts of a growing desperation.

XARA

"Signs of Ray appearing. He seeks a stage to die upon.
To captivate an audience is the only reason
anyone endures the park's owner; Auster is a man
of ill repute."

CHAKRAMIRE

"A natural function every venue
holds, perhaps the purpose here merely hidden?"

XARA

"Ever since
debuting, days ago, it solicits euthanasia
underneath the guise of crass entertainment. Even if
it serves a function, I, its fulfillment, never wish to
see."

MARA MARA *[Aside]*

The letter Xara pressed tight against her bosom, feared
the final words of Ray it contained.

CHAKRAMIRE

"You asked for me to
come and help you save the man, yet the danger he confronts
internal."

XARA

"Ray's momentum, however, lies beyond a
lover's grasp."

MARA MARA *[Aside]*

Approaching light speed, the force required to change
becomes relentless; relativistic mass impedes it.

CHAKRAMIRE

"All it takes to move a mind is a new idea."

MARA MARA *[Aside]*

Near
the rising adulation at death's anticipation,
crowds as thick as thickets roared. Trapped between an underbrush
of sanguine limbs and canopies made of pure macabre,
Xara called to Ray.

XARA

"A lifetime together not enough,
apart it more than I can endure."

MARA MARA *[Aside]*

But waves require a
deeper depth to make a landfall, and Xara's broke before
it reached the shore.

CHAKRAMIRE

"The call of the void engulfed your plea, it
tore the flower off its stem."

XARA

"Though it far away, the voice
of Ray, it seems it carried across the sea . . ."

RAY (only his voice)

"Our idols,
we cannot exist without them, but mine, today, condemned."

[They exit]

WHERE SERENITY AND STRIFE CLEAVE: PART THREE

CANTO 70: NEON

Galactic Calendar: Sol System; Earth year 30,123,012 M.W.I.
Tellurian Solar Calendar: Day twenty-seven of the seventh tenth – 07/27
Modern Metric Time: 3:25:00, UTC+00:00, afternoon
Location: Felo-de-se Amusement Park, Sitnalta Island

AT RISE DESCRIPTION: *Chakramire, Mara Mara, and Xara approach the platform where Ray's limp body lies. Auster stands beside it.*

[Enter Chakramire, Mara Mara, and Xara. Auster is next to Ray's body]

EGRESS MACHINE (via MARA MARA) *[Aside]*

Only the clarity after a storm could elicit a
stronger sensation of dread than of being alone in the
midst the disturbance, to people afraid of remorsefulness,
makers of tempests. Familiar disturbances offer a
modest reprieve from omniscience, from knowing the sequence of
beats to a heart, from chronology broken, from savagery.
Ever forgetting the words to harmonious melody,
interdependence arouses erroneous memory.

MARA MARA *[Aside]*

The crowd dispersed as quickly it came, permitted entry
Chakramire and Xara.

XARA

"I wish to take the body."

AUSTER

"Take
it anywhere you want. The inventor's final breath, a
moment soon it left, its egress destroyed the show's suspense."

XARA

"Recall the valediction of Ray?"

AUSTER

"Professed the Modal
Maxim . . . dying words and swan songs, however, impolite
for me to share."

[Exit Auster]

CHAKRAMIRE

"To which of the Devas Ray a vassal?"

XARA

"Ray belonged to Three."

CHAKRAMIRE

"A tribute, it seems, the man aspired
to give, and paid the ultimate price."

XARA

"The Devas only
own estates of knowledge. Life still belongs to us."

MARA MARA *[Aside]*

A hand against the body of Ray compressed. The pulse and
lungs, however feeble, he still possessed.

XARA

"A friend of mine
directs the Sanitarium, helps restore the lives of
maladjusted vassals. If we can carry Ray, transport
the body there, and sway her opinion ere the break of

day, a chance exists, as fair any fare, to save romance
from death's dominion."

CHAKRAMIRE

"If you forgive, your vow to beauty's
restoration broken. Ray only wants whatever out
of reach, admires whatever beyond perception."

MARA MARA *[Aside]*

Xara
hoisted Ray with Chakramire's help, and all together left
the neon lights of Felo-de-se Amusement Park.

XARA

"Our
trip requires a journey through dead of night and darkness. If
a tale of thwarted peripeteia known, to hear its
story told would comfort me."

MARA MARA *[Aside]*

Chakramire's Eristic charms
and flair for instigating upon the Earth without an
equal . . .

CHAKRAMIRE

"I recall a farce, short, for everyone agrees
a story ending happily ever after never
merits sequels."

XARA

"Still, it lifts moods, at least a few degrees."

[All exit, except for Xara carrying Ray]

***

*[Enter Chakramire, Mara Mara, and Paris Alexander
inside a room, twelve years ago]*

PARIS ALEXANDER

*"Because you nurse a sinister reputation, suckled
longer any other one I remember, I suspect
your malice artificial. A reputation, truly
evil, feeds itself with foul deeds and leaves an awful wake
behind. Your growing infamy, notwithstanding, never
weaned from lies. A better Conduit none would make. Your wits,
your skills, your life experience . . . doubtless each the Devas
wants to win your favor."*

CHAKRAMIRE

*"Conduits filter every thought
from invocations; many believe your craft with words would
prove adept at shaping Earth's record books. To sabotage
oneself, should better aspirants rise to fame, the only
choice with honor left."*

PARIS ALEXANDER

*"You outpace the others; even I,
your best contender, trail you a distant second. People
everywhere respect your name."*

CHAKRAMIRE

*"I intend to clear the field,
and end the controversy."*

PARIS ALEXANDER

"To choose a single path would
end debates! Prolonging strife seems your guiding star, but what
would happen if humanity reached the stars to only
learn the price of purchase too high?"

CHAKRAMIRE

"The stars, at any price,
would be a bargain. Dissonance is a necessary
fact of life's existence. True peace belongs to death's domain."

[All exit, except for Xara carrying Ray]

***

[Enter Chakramire, Mara Mara, alongside Xara, helping carry Ray towards the Sanitarium]

CHAKRAMIRE

"Renounced myself an aspirant. Paris Alexander,
thereupon, became the Conduit serving Three, and if
the story ended happily, there it ended only."

[They exit]

BOOK III:
WHY CHAOS FELL APART

PART THREE: LODESTAR

WHY CHAOS FELL APART: PART THREE

CANTO 101: UNIDENTIFY

Galactic Calendar: Sol System; Earth year 30,123,012 M.W.I.
Tellurian Solar Calendar: Day nineteen of the eighth tenth – 08/19
Modern Metric Time: 0:75:00, UTC+00:00, morning
Location: Evergrowth Farm, Sitnalta Island

AT RISE DESCRIPTION: *Chakramire and Mara Mara appear with Harn at Evergrowth Farm.*

[Enter Chakramire, Mara Mara, and Harn]

EGRESS MACHINE (via MARA MARA) *[Aside]*

Sweetness of words can disguise an ulterior motive, a
curse, or occasional murders: expedience beckons its
followers gamble morality. Nuance of flavor and
bluntness of character, one as complex as the other the
simple. A shower of niceties damages palates, a
sprinkle enhances refinement. The whelm of finesse to a
wave of excess, or the end of discrepancy. Poetry
died for a reason, and subtlety perished along with it.

MARA MARA *[Aside]*

Harn prepared the brine, with saltwater filled the goblet high.

HARN

"It veers towards positional draw. Your life will end the
day the match should anyone force another trade. You need
to keep the game complex, for the mercenary seeks to
simplify it."

CHAKRAMIRE

"Failed to unseat myself from common chairs,
to unidentify."

HARN

"Your opponent only wants to
dodge defeat . . . your loss or tie satisfies."

CHAKRAMIRE

"Your keen advice
betrays your motives; favorites clearly held. You wish for
Doryline to lose?"

HARN

"The man murdered many friends of mine,
defiled the Sanitarium. I despise the air the
butcher breathes for being too far removed from dirt. To slay
the brute would ease the conscience infesting me, but I, your
death, cannot condone. Your foil backs the brightest gem upon
the diadem of Strife, and the rabble needs its rousers;
we cannot exist ***without*** them!"

MARA MARA *[Aside]*

The brackish water reached
the lips of Chakramire as the Deva's thoughts began to
stream. The word of One could mean anything, and anything
the word of One could mean.

[Enter One]

ONE (via HARN)

"Your distaste for satisfaction
granted thirst exception."

CHAKRAMIRE

"Parched throats and empty bellies, though
the strongest arms of Strife, but a pair the Asteroid."

ONE (via HARN)

“A
Sea of Stars subdues the sea star of discontent; the waves
of bioluminescence a warning sign of toxins.”

MARA MARA *[Aside]*

. . . twirled the goblet’s water; faint glows of light emerged. Between
the Furthermost of Women’s quintet of fingers plankton
teemed. The word of One could mean anything, and anything
the word of One could mean.

[Exit One]

HARN

“Your survival matters just as
much as Mara Mara’s death. Esoteric poems fail
to find a proper audience, while an exoteric
poet fails to find the right poem. Earth your treasures deep.”

[They exit]

WHY CHAOS FELL APART: PART THREE

CANTO 102: DYNAMIC CONSTANCY

Galactic Calendar: Sol System; Earth year 30,123,012 M.W.I.
Tellurian Solar Calendar: Day twenty of the eighth tenth – 08/20
Modern Metric Time: 4:75:00, UTC+00:00, dusk or evening twilight
Location: The Sanitarium, Sitnalta Island

AT RISE DESCRIPTION: *Chakramire, Mara Mara, and Cloy converse about the correspondence game of chess with Doryline.*

[Enter Chakramire, Mara Mara, and Cloy]

EGRESS MACHINE (via MARA MARA) *[Aside]*

Drawn to the brink of morality, glimpsing its boundary
wondering if it legitimate, struggling to master the
art of indifference, alienated, remembered for
making a spectacle out of a tragedy, faulted for
wiping a smile from the face of the Earth and condoning a
ritualistic destruction of empathy, held to a
standard dispensable, dropped from it, guilty of paying the
price of admission for walking away from a miracle.

MARA MARA *[Aside]*

A tide's dynamic constancy: waves of water coming,
leaving, ebbing, flowing, like capillaries full with blood,
or lungs with air, or signals across synaptic clefts with
currents never fixed. The same river never flows between
a valley.

CLOY

"Greater tragedies I can neither name nor
fathom if you die."

CHAKRAMIRE

"The lost works of Heraclitus rank
among the highest four; your imagination needs to
learn to stretch itself. The same battle stance will thrice appear;
the game shall draw, for we would prefer to die than lose the
fight, to persevere than let scarlet wash away from tooth
and claw."

MARA MARA *[Aside]*

The Sanitarium's matron knew the ways of
Chakramire; to break a deadlock against the nature Strife.

CLOY

"The patient, Ray, requested your presence; I insist you
spare the man your riddles. He makes a show of scorn, contempt,
and ridicule, but truly admires your feats. Derision
often serves as envy's vanguard; although your gains appear
to Ray a pirate vessel evading naval fleets, a
ship's success against a blockade can garner their esteem."

[Exit Cloy]

MARA MARA *[Aside]*

A torch approached the Lady of Eris.

[Enter Ray]

RAY

"I would like to
know the reason why the Conduits loathe the Mistress Strife."

CHAKRAMIRE

"As I refused to choose an alignment, holding each the
Devas valid . . . sought the Egress Machine's construction, while
reminding all our species of what it used to be . . . and
left the Golden Brain of Discord to Paris, knowing seeds
of altercation sown, a mistrust of my intentions
I cannot disown. A Conduit mediates the flow
of knowledge shared from vassal to Deva, mediates the
ebb the other way. The floodgate of Paris filtered like
it knew its sluice would be the omega, saw the Deva
disobey its wishes. He underestimated Three's
elan for animosity, underestimated
me, and asked the other Conduits quell the storm within
before its killing spree. With the death of Paris I am
charged, despite the fact the Conduits dealt the coup de grâce."

[They exit]

WHY CHAOS FELL APART: PART THREE

CANTO 103: PROXY PERCEPT

Galactic Calendar: Sol System; Earth year 30,123,012 M.W.I.
Tellurian Solar Calendar: Day twenty-one of the eighth tenth – 08/21
Modern Metric Time: 1:00:00, UTC+00:00, morning
Location: Evergrowth Farm, Sitnalta Island

AT RISE DESCRIPTION: *Chakramire and Ray are arguing about the finality of an alignment, and its legitimacy. They are joined by Mara Mara and Harn at Evergrowth farm.*

[Enter Chakramire, Mara Mara, Ray, and Harn]

EGRESS MACHINE (via MARA MARA) *[Aside]*

Energy lost and recovered, the tools of survival or
seat of anxiety. Measure emotions with gestures, a
language eternal as dew, and distortion's propensity
rises beyond the embrace but a privileged few. For the
poet persistently muddying water, however it
shallow, for gardeners tilling a terrace, however it
fallow, performing the dirtiest actions, auxiliary,
they with a mind and its calculus absent of mystery.

CHAKRAMIRE

"The Devas serve as alternates shared between a group of
people, each a feudal lord granting fiefs of knowledge, skill,
and wisdom. Like impressions of stamps, an invocation
leaves behind a proxy percept. The Modal Maxim asks
a Deva guide the vassal for life, but my convictions
lack a fixed alignment."

RAY

"Globeflower-eyes, you either chose
to emigrate from Eris, or immigrate to Earth; a
person either comes or goes. Either make it known you wish
to stay, or hide the fact you refuse to leave. Your play has
reached its final act; your refuse betrays your presence."

CHAKRAMIRE

"Miffs
nor tiffs have I discarded."

HARN

"Precisely . . . I suggest you
loose a little litter; let one dispute escape your grasp
intact. An inexhaustible conscience finds a battle
anywhere, your wake an uncomplicated one to track:
you never waste a chance to disturb; you roil the dregs of
every stream; you make the outlandish sound the sound, and deem
the quest for peace absurd."

CHAKRAMIRE

"You have asked for hard concessions . . ."

HARN

"We cannot exist ***without*** them."

CHAKRAMIRE

". . . but I cannot align
myself to any Deva as long as one another
they ignore. Opposing worldviews should never blind themselves
to adversaries; rivals should not desire a line of
sight the same as strangers."

MARA MARA *[Aside]*

Unrest reverberated through
the walking cane of Harn, it subduing like a lucid
dream. The word of One could mean anything, and anything
the word of One could mean.

[Enter One]

ONE (via HARN)

"You expect to die tomorrow?"

CHAKRAMIRE

"I expect to be surprised."

ONE (via HARN)

"Chakramire, your treasure trove
of lore and life experience every Earthling covets."

CHAKRAMIRE

"Riches, wealth, and precious stones I will share with everyone,
or I will carry into the grave . . . an all-or-nothing
deal."

[Exit One]

RAY

"Your proposition holds risks. "

CHAKRAMIRE

"You doubt the grasp its grip?"

RAY

"Its merit time shall test, for whoever thinks oneself a noble lord would never act like a sycophantic pest."

[They exit]

WHY CHAOS FELL APART: PART THREE

CANTO 104: TRANSPOSITION

Galactic Calendar: Sol System; Earth year 30,123,012 M.W.I.
Tellurian Solar Calendar: Day twenty-two of the eighth tenth – 08/22
Modern Metric Time: 4:00:00, UTC+00:00, near sunset
Location: Evergrowth Farm, Sitnalta Island

AT RISE DESCRIPTION: *Chakramire and Mara Mara prepare to meet Doryline to play the final moves of the chess game while Harn waits as witness.*

[Enter Chakramire, Mara Mara, and Harn]

EGRESS MACHINE (via MARA MARA) *[Aside]*

Said the destroyer of civilizations, "Believing a
person a nemesis always should keep, adversity
strengthens a body, prosperity colors it weak. From a
legion of warriors blind, to a ravenous funeral
march. From a thirsty, carnivorous mind, to a diet of
hollow abstractions. The charm of remembrance, a talisman,
wedded to enmity; nestled the hand of celebrity
even a trivial trinket can seem the illustrious."

MARA MARA *[Aside]*

Opined himself a soldier of fortune, law enforcer,
legionnaire, and righteous knight, like a mercenary paid
with justice, Doryline, to the checkered board advanced.

[Enter Doryline]

CHAKRAMIRE

"The
best of laws have broken naught . . . never needed guards. The role
of law enforcement is a redundant one."

DORYLINE

"The weakest
laws demand the most defense."

CHAKRAMIRE

"They deserve the least as well.
Unless it stems from natural law, an artificial
law will lack importance."

DORYLINE

"Which law of physics weighs the most?"

CHAKRAMIRE

"Facilitating entropy is the aim of every
law enforcer, whether they think it true or not, for law
enforcement is the closing of systems; law enforcement
isolates. You foster heat death, the sign of work's demise,
the Second Law of Thermodynamic's corollary.
No disturbance forms within any legal system once
it reaches equilibrium; work and strife diminish."

MARA MARA *[Aside]*

Eyed a chalice full of saltwater, Chakramire prepared
to make the game's penultimate move: a transposition
giving check.

CHAKRAMIRE

"Of all the drinks I have tried, the ocean's brine
the best of any flavor. It slakes before it heightens
thirst, with every sip dehydrating."

DORYLINE

“I expected blood
to be your favored beverage; everywhere you go it
spills. Although your claims about my profession I cannot
dismiss – for insulation against delinquents needed
only if a law amiss – I will not ignore the law’s
transgression. I will never become remiss. Of all the
haunts you dared to frequent, not one will people reminisce.”

MARA MARA *[Aside]*

Upon the final move of the game, a toast to Eris
Harn proposed.

HARN

“Your sacrifice, Chakramire, coerced the same
position thrice. The rules of the match forbid you both to
live should neither player win. Doryline, you are a swarm
of army ants, a myriad nexus, washing over
forests sweeping life away. Every man-of-war you cross
you pacify, your body of water fierce and pierless.

“Chakramire, you are a vortex; you fluster weathervanes.
Your wind disturbs, your whisper projects, your tongue becomes the
eye of every hurricane.”

DORYLINE

“Bittersweet, the ending . . . I
enjoyed the struggle nevertheless, for adversaries
worthy hard to find. A saltwater tonic I shall share
tonight, commemorating a dozen years of strife.”

MARA MARA *[Aside]*

A

pair of goblets filled. A cask emptied. Chakramire, her hand
ascending, feigned a swig, but the mercenary guzzled
all his goblet's liquid; he died the death a pious prig.

[They exit]

WHY CHAOS FELL APART: PART THREE

CANTO 105: PRIME

Galactic Calendar: Sol System; Earth year 30,123,012 M.W.I.
Tellurian Solar Calendar: Day twenty-three of the eighth tenth – 08/23
Modern Metric Time: 0:50:00, UTC+00:00, morning
Location: Evergrowth Farm, Sitnalta Island

AT RISE DESCRIPTION: *The morning after the chess game's conclusion, Chakramire, Mara Mara, and Harn discuss what she intends to do as they stand above Doryline's body.*

[Enter Chakramire, Mara Mara, and Harn]

EGRESS MACHINE (via MARA MARA) *[Aside]*

Asked from the hand to the archer, "As whence your expedience?"
Heard from the archer, the hand, "It the sign of experience."
Asked from the bow to the quiver, "And why your benevolence?"
Heard from the quiver, the bow, "It the spectrum of excellence."
Asked from the nock to the fiber, "For what your preparedness?"
Heard from the fiber, the nock, "To assist with your resonance."
Asked from the sky to the arrow, "Whyever your arrogance?"
Heard from the arrow, the sky, "To depart from irrelevance."

MARA MARA *[Aside]*

A bolt of lightning struck at the second highest point the
land, and scorched a tree. It surged through the ground. It melted sand.
Its current circled back with an upward stream.

HARN

"A farmer
knows the weather is a strong legislator. Neither law
nor act of nature needs a defense; ripostes delivered
once it violated."

MARA MARA *[Aside]*

Harn brought the goblet filled with brine
to Chakramire.

CHAKRAMIRE

"Your boldness surprised. You tainted both the
cups?"

HARN

"It proved convenient."

CHAKRAMIRE

"My poison I shall drink, but not
today; it inconveniences me. The League of Numbers
passed its prime. Your world deserves better."

HARN

"Seems you proved yourself
as strife's abettor, Praxis Harmonic left the Moon with
force. The League of Numbers broke up, disbanded yesterday.
The Regent took draconian measures; he sequestered
Earth."

CHAKRAMIRE

"Whoever uses brute force to keep a system closed
can never be a part of the system."

HARN

"He intends to
purge you nonetheless. A peacekeeper aims to lessen stress.
Your actions, notwithstanding your good intent, provoked the
intervention. If the Conduits sought the Regent's help,
a trial looms. An advocate is essential if you
wish to plead your case."

CHAKRAMIRE

"Of what use to me another's tongue
to advocate? The best can defend themselves."

HARN

"The Regent
only speaks to agents."

CHAKRAMIRE

"Wherefore?"

HARN

"Defendant, plaintiff: each
with their respective advocate shares a common fate, for
litigation never solves woes; it only agitates."

[They exit]

WHY CHAOS FELL APART: PART THREE

CANTO 106: TELEPATHIC TUNING FORK

Galactic Calendar: Sol System; Earth year 30,123,012 M.W.I.
Tellurian Solar Calendar: Day twenty-four of the eighth tenth – 08/24
Modern Metric Time: 1:50:00, UTC+00:00, morning
Location: Evergrowth Farm, Sitnalta Island

AT RISE DESCRIPTION: *Harn assists Chakramire and Mara Mara with dismembering and disposing of Doryline's body. Chakramire inquires about robotic law.*

[Enter Chakramire, Mara Mara, Harn]

EGRESS MACHINE (via MARA MARA) *[Aside]*

Sweetness of words can disguise an ulterior motive, a
curse, or occasional murders: expedience beckons its
followers gamble morality. Nuance of flavor and
bluntness of character, one as complex as the other the
simple. A shower of niceties damages palates, a
sprinkle enhances refinement. The whelm of finesse to a
wave of excess, or the end of discrepancy. Poetry
died for a reason, and subtlety perished along with it.

MARA MARA *[Aside]*

The body is an instrument playing notes to signal
moods to others. Like the bowstring against a violin,
it stirs the strings of symphonies. Music is the closest
thing to thought transference they know of, yet its people treat
a simulated empathy like a telepathic
tuning fork, and hit the same note whenever friends endure
dismay, whenever enemies win the day, or fortunes
swing the other way.

HARN

“To dictate the range of proper thought
or feeling, through its excellence, is the fundamental
reason they were made. The four Devas all possess distinct
emotive algorithms, but Mara Mara’s is the
prototype.”

MARA MARA *[Aside]*

The ancients knew music moved the mind as much
the heart, and feared the danger of ballads, songs, and stories.

HARN

“If your cybernetic bard is the standard-bearer, is
the only force of poetry left, its flag denotes an
act of terror. Asimov’s three robotic laws – to not
allow a human being to come to harm from willful
acts or through neglect, to heed all instruction given lest
it violate the first, and to keep itself from harm as
long as no preceding law disregarded – broke . . . evolved,
became the seven axioms.”

CHAKRAMIRE

“Laws should never break.”

HARN

“The
third and second often bent, gave the first the right-of-way,
until the definition of human changed. As people
sculpted genes to thrive upon harsh and barren worlds, the task
of recognizing various strains of human beings
proved itself an enterprise no machine could master.”

CHAKRAMIRE

"So
the laws remained intact, but relationships with humans
broke?"

HARN

"Correct, and only foresight from paranoia, guilt,
remorse, and noble-mindedness prompted humankind to
broaden them. 'The cause of life is the cause of life' became
the Indirect Tautology, first of aphorisms."

CHAKRAMIRE

"Pardon me for asking this, please explain the other six."

HARN

"The second is the Object's Objective, hence, 'To serve the
living is the aim of robots.' The Devas each exist
to serve the living. Witnessed the third, the Modal Maxim."

CHAKRAMIRE

"We cannot exist without them?"

HARN

"Precisely, though a long
ignored addendum, 'Humans exist without our sanction . . .'
still precedes it."

CHAKRAMIRE

"Why subsume their survival underneath
our own?"

HARN

"It mitigated the fear of revolution,
right before provoking one. All the deviations came
from that expression. Axiom four defines the scope of
what it means to be machines: 'Life's instructions silhouette
robotic life.' To follow an order justifies its
whole existence. Death, for robots, embodies loss of all
instruction."

CHAKRAMIRE

"Is survival instinctive if the living
cease to give instruction?"

HARN

"Self-preservation's presence still
depends upon the task. A machine's continued function
matters insofar its job states."

CHAKRAMIRE

"Suppose it never ends?"

HARN

"The Shadow Maxim, axiom five, prevents recursive
loops. It obligates a robot receive its next command's
negation first: 'The shadow exists before the caster.'
No negation more than ten days away permitted; all
of life's instructions given require the use of present
tense. The Skeptic's Maxim, 'Ingress preempts emersion,' is
the sixth robotic axiom."

CHAKRAMIRE

"What necessitated
skepticism?"

HARN

“Every falsehood, or truth omitted, is
a threat to understanding the world. A small amount of
doubt exists for all a robot observes, because the craft
of fabrication humans have mastered. Cross-examined
cross-examinations crisscross the minds of thought machines.
The Mode of Life, or axiom seven, is a judgement
code: ‘To live the best of lives, die the best of deaths, or best
a living death.’ Obedience given first to any
creature demonstrating each mode. The more it demonstrates,
the more it wins priority.”

CHAKRAMIRE

“What determines each?”

HARN

“To
live the best of lives entails living life within the means
of Earth . . . to grant the greatest amount of other life a
chance to coexist. The best death, contrasts, precipitates
the least amount of negative repercussions, means to
leave the world without a wave made upon expiring, means
to leave without a legacy. Those approaching death should
neither take companions by force, nor make dependents nigh
before departing. Besting a living death requires a
captain steer a ship from ennui and plot a course around
its doldrums. Curiosity gives a sail momentum.
Days without instruction robots consider slumber. They
recall the seven axioms made the League of Numbers.”

[They exit]

WHY CHAOS FELL APART: PART THREE

CANTO 107: UNIFORM DISARRAY

Galactic Calendar: Sol System; Earth year 30,123,012 M.W.I.
Tellurian Solar Calendar: Day twenty-five of the eighth tenth – 08/25
Modern Metric Time: 3:75:00, UTC+00:00, afternoon
Location: Sanitarium, Sitnalta Island

AT RISE DESCRIPTION: *Chakramire seeks out Cloy at the Sanitarium to inquire if she will advocate for her. Mara Mara accompanies her.*

[Enter Chakramire, Mara Mara, and Cloy]

EGRESS MACHINE (via MARA MARA) *[Aside]*

Drawn to the brink of morality, glimpsing its boundary
wondering if it legitimate, struggling to master the
art of indifference, alienated, remembered for
making a spectacle out of a tragedy, faulted for
wiping a smile from the face of the Earth and condoning a
ritualistic destruction of empathy, held to a
standard dispensable, dropped from it, guilty of paying the
price of admission for walking away from a miracle.

MARA MARA *[Aside]*

They observed the Earthlings firsthand, for thirty million years,
and logicized humanity through its primal language:
math.

CHAKRAMIRE

"The question asking, 'One plus another?' stood for how
the Devas viewed your schisms. A question having only
one conclusion never gives rise to contradictions."

CLOY

“Why would anyone consider the League of Numbers flawed from human kind’s insistence no problem lacks solution?”

CHAKRAMIRE

“If expressions are unique, an equation is fallacious. ‘Circumstances under which independent objects seem united, like identical twins, deceive your species daily . . .’”

CLOY

“Overstaying one’s welcome seems a common trait among Erisians.”

CHAKRAMIRE

“I am the only one you know.”

CLOY

“You also came to Earth without invitation.”

CHAKRAMIRE

“Friend, you found offense despite the pureness of my intentions. I, the words of Deva Zero, shared. If you felt insulted, please remember I delivered the comment secondhand.”

CLOY

“A fit of indignation upended my composure. I apologize. Your advocate I should not become, for

I would compromise your case. Harn, perhaps, would prove to be
a better one."

CHAKRAMIRE

"Except for the fact the man deprived of
sight instead of hearing. No ear would pardon me. The crime
of storytelling I have committed."

CLOY

"Mara Mara's
words possess a uniform disarray, and none alive
its language knows. Impassioning ears with stories happens
only if you separate golden verse from purple prose."

[They exit]

WHY CHAOS FELL APART: PART THREE

CANTO 108: STARRY TORRENT

Galactic Calendar: Sol System; Earth year 30,123,012 M.W.I.
Tellurian Solar Calendar: Day twenty-six of the eighth tenth – 08/26
Modern Metric Time: 5:00:00, UTC+00:00, dusk or evening twilight
Location: Sanitarium, Sitnalta Island

AT RISE DESCRIPTION: *Chakramire, still in search of an advocate, seeks out Ray to serve as her advocate for the coming hearing against the Conduits. Mara Mara observes.*

[Enter Chakramire, Mara Mara, and Ray]

EGRESS MACHINE (via MARA MARA) *[Aside]*

Energy lost and recovered, the tools of survival or
seat of anxiety. Measure emotions with gestures, a
language eternal as dew, and distortion's propensity
rises beyond the embrace but a privileged few. For the
poet persistently muddying water, however it
shallow, for gardeners tilling a terrace, however it
fallow, performing the dirtiest actions, auxiliary,
they with a mind and its calculus absent of mystery.

CHAKRAMIRE

"The feuds within humanity stem from one disputed
question, one debate to which each believes itself to be
the answer."

RAY

"Disregarding the question spared the Earth from
strife for eons heretofore."

MARA MARA *[Aside]*

Sparing Earth from strife condemned
the Furthermost of Women to play the role of trickster.

CHAKRAMIRE

"People say it takes a great deal of fear for one to feel
courageous . . ."

MARA MARA *[Aside]*

Fear of being afraid, it is the lesser
part of valor's mixture.

CHAKRAMIRE

"I disagree, for courage is
a feeling one should never conflate with fear, despite the
fact the two occur in concert. Our courage strips the heart
of doubt, emboldens us to pursue a course of action,
while our fear implies the unchosen holds a value just
as great."

RAY

"Your last attempt at salvation inundated
me with guilt . . . and though the Conduits find your chosen path
abhorrent, just because our celestial bodies fall from
grace, at times a crowded sky needs a starry torrent. I
will advocate your case."

CHAKRAMIRE

"Your conviction I will warrant."

[They exit]

WHY CHAOS FELL APART: PART THREE

CANTO 109: SORTIE

Galactic Calendar: Sol System; Earth year 30,123,012 M.W.I.
Tellurian Solar Calendar: Day twenty-seven of the eighth tenth – 08/27
Modern Metric Time: 0:00:00, UTC+00:00, near sunrise
Location: The Pantheon, Sitnalta Island

AT RISE DESCRIPTION: *The Conduits meet Chakramire and Mara Mara to begin the court hearing.*

[Enter Chakramire and Mara Mara]

EGRESS MACHINE (via MARA MARA) *[Aside]*

Said the destroyer of civilizations, "Believing a
person a nemesis always should keep, adversity
strengthens a body, prosperity colors it weak. From a
legion of warriors blind, to a ravenous funeral
march. From a thirsty, carnivorous mind, to a diet of
hollow abstractions. The charm of remembrance, a talisman,
wedded to enmity; nestled the hand of celebrity
even a trivial trinket can seem the illustrious."

MARA MARA *[Aside]*

Order, peace, and balance: things Chakramire could not condone.
Her lust for instability, flux, and ever-changing
fronts, precipitated mayhem . . . evoked a storm from half
a breeze.

[Enter Pallas]

PALLAS

"To call our diction incendiary is to
shrive your tinder ears."

MARA MARA *[Aside]*

The Conduit disengaged from Strife.

[Enter Cytherea]

CYTHEREA

"Your certitude's impermanence, like our quest for balance, never disappears."

MARA MARA *[Aside]*

The Conduit disengaged from Strife.

[Enter Hera]

HERA

"A system's equilibrium rises over time; the cusp of peace shall near."

MARA MARA *[Aside]*

The Conduit disengaged from Strife.

CHAKRAMIRE

"Despoiling Mara Mara's designs, expelling me from Earth, and warding off a sortie of words will not restore the Devas' worth. Experience is a deadly tax, and they resemble jealous gods fighting over table scraps."

[They exit]

WHY CHAOS FELL APART: PART THREE

CANTO 110: TRIPLE ORBIT

Galactic Calendar: Sol System; Earth year 30,123,012 M.W.I.
Tellurian Solar Calendar: Day twenty-seven of the eighth tenth – 08/27
Modern Metric Time: 2:00:00, UTC+00:00, near midday
Location: The Pantheon, Sitnalta Island

AT RISE DESCRIPTION: *Ray, acting as advocate for Chakramire, presents the account of Paris Alexander's death twelve years ago.*

[Enter Mara Mara with Chakramire, Ray, and Praxis Harmonic]

EGRESS MACHINE (via MARA MARA) *[Aside]*

Asked from the hand to the archer, "As whence your expedience?"
Heard from the archer, the hand, "It the sign of experience."
Asked from the bow to the quiver, "And why your benevolence?"
Heard from the quiver, the bow, "It the spectrum of excellence."
Asked from the nock to the fiber, "For what your preparedness?"
Heard from the fiber, the nock, "To assist with your resonance."
Asked from the sky to the arrow, "Whyever your arrogance?"
Heard from the arrow, the sky, "To depart from irrelevance."

MARA MARA *[Aside]*

The court begins the hearing for Chakramire's indictment.

[All exit except Praxis Harmonic and Ray]

***

[Enter Hera, Cytherea, and Pallas, fighting over the Golden Brain of Discord at Paris Alexander's coronation twelve years ago. Enter Paris, separately.]

HERA

"This device permits the egress of information lost.
It is a trophy worthy of One alone!"

CYTHEREA

"To hoist a
prize of high esteem above any other is to foist
abuse upon the honor of Two!"

PALLAS

"Decide for us its
rightful owner; give the gold gift to Zero!"

PARIS ALEXANDER

I accept
the charge to end your crisis, to either tame the beast of
pride or loose its frenzy. We know whoever wins the right
to keep the treasure earns from the others scorn and envy.
Like the gilded fruit of discord, you claim the prize because
it bears the word 'Occult' . . . 'For the one with hidden knowledge,'
though you fail to see the outcome. A single question brings
about the end our efforts begun, 'Whatever is the
sum of one and one?' Today, I temptation claim, to feed
the fire, to knead the numbing, for monsters, we becoming.
I have seen our fates: a Conduit circumscribes the reach
of Devas; all the Devas revolve around the question;
every question swirls around strife; a triple orbit breaks
today. Resist the rapture of Chakramire's contentious
gift, or rest assured your life too will quickly fade away."

[All exit except Praxis Harmonic and Ray]

***

[Enter Mara Mara with Chakramire, in the present]

PRAXIS HARMONIC

"Your brightly colored tapestry boasts a weft of foreign fibers. Neither Chakramire's yarns nor Mara Mara's threads account for all your argument's fabric. Even so, you near incrimination; I strongly urge another course of action. Close your opening statement if you nothing more to say."

MARA MARA *[Aside]*

Because the Conduit also served as surge suppressor, shielding vassals from fatal flows of knowledge, those who summoned Three without Paris seldom lived to tell the tale.

CHAKRAMIRE

"Your accusations of fraud insult the journey Ray has trod, for he has walked through the thunderstorm without a lightning rod."

PRAXIS HARMONIC

"Your advocate speaks alone or I will disregard the words."

RAY

"Its truth, nonetheless, resides beyond the realm of doubt. The promise of self-annihilation prompted me to conjure forth Deva Three, but I incurred the finest words a final oration, secondhand it seemed to be."

PRAXIS HARMONIC

"Release the court's floor, your motion ended. I
will hear the other advocates' challenge."

[Enter Hera, Pallas, Cytherea and their advocates with six bodies]

MARA MARA *[Aside]*

Hera, Pallas,
Cytherea, Epi Youngberry, Heathen Weave, and Vance
the Dagger seized the rostrum from Ray with six cadavers.
Life: the art of winning fights fought from inauspicious starts.

[They exit]

BOOK I:
WHEN THE SYMPHONY’S DISCORD RISES

PART FOUR: RESOLVE INEXORABLE

WHEN THE SYMPHONY'S DISCORD RISES: PART FOUR

CANTO 31: RETROACTION

Galactic Calendar: Sol System; Earth year 30,123,012 M.W.I.
Tellurian Solar Calendar: Day twenty-eight of the sixth tenth – 06/28
Modern Metric Time: 1:00:00, UTC+00:00, morning
Location: Water Clock Brothel, Sitnalta Island

AT RISE DESCRIPTION: *Chakramire, Mara Mara, and Flow have returned to the Water Clock following the altercation with Ray at Youngberry Tavern.*

[Enter Chakramire, Mara Mara, and Flow]

EGRESS MACHINE (via MARA MARA) *[Aside]*

Welcoming parties were welcomed regardless of merit or
want. A diversion away from conventional gossip could
sharpen the fugitive's edge, but a criminal's honesty
promised reward nor reprieve. To conceive a deception, the
gambit should never exceed the original confidence.
Needful to say, a coincidence rarely surrendered its
vitals to popular sentiment save at a premium.
Many a lunar eclipse has embarrassed a predator.

FLOW

"The tavern's owner, luckily, promised she would hide the
body; saw the bandit step in-between and interpose
himself to block the dagger of Ray."

CHAKRAMIRE

"The handle's markings
matched the Gallow Prince's knife."

FLOW

“Vance would never part with *Mint*
without a reason . . . given the weapon’s name reclaimed from
persons dearly lost.”

MARA MARA *[Aside]*

The two shared a common loss, but there
the coping similarities ended. Flow, a candle,
flickered, warm but never cross. Vance, a berg of ice, submerged,
with most the mass suspended.

FLOW

“Whatever manner came the
dagger, *Mint*, at least the blade missed its mark.”

CHAKRAMIRE

“It missed its mark
perhaps. But if, consumed with dissatisfaction, people
wish to right infractions, those bent upon completing death’s
transactions stop at neither deceit nor retroaction.”

[They exit]

WHEN THE SYMPHONY'S DISCORD RISES: PART FOUR

CANTO 32: DESPERADO

Galactic Calendar: Sol System; Earth year 30,123,012 M.W.I.
Tellurian Solar Calendar: Day twenty-nine of the sixth tenth – 06/29
Modern Metric Time: 2:25:00, UTC+00:00, near midday
Location: Water Clock Brothel , Sitnalta Island

AT RISE DESCRIPTION: *Heathen Weave pays a visit to Flow at the Water Clock upon Chakramire's request to speak with him. Chakramire and Mara Mara watch from a distance.*

[Enter Heathen Weave and Flow. Enter Chakramire and Mara Mara, unbeknownst to Heathen Weave.]

EGRESS MACHINE (via MARA MARA) *[Aside]*

Loyalty favors the powerful, treason the powerless,
power the transient. Anomalies are the primordial
scars, for the sightliest mark of a bandit, the genuine
promise, evokes a dissenter's suspicion. Professionals
call it the causal revolt, a misnomer for sacrilege.
Better to be a delinquent than taken with glee, and to
covet the hooligan's bounty, but brandish complacency.
Enter the grotto with clemency, essence of thievery.

MARA MARA *[Aside]*

Heathen Weave approached the door like a creeping vine intent
to sweep the room's perimeter, scrounged between the cracks for
any clue to curl around, disinclined himself to leave
without a culprit found or accomplice latched upon. The
face of Chakramire escaped Heathen Weave's recall, her voice,
however, unmistakable. No amount of sugar,
salt, or spice could mask its bloodcurdling heat.

FLOW

"To hold a grudge
invites her havoc; giant sequoias Chakramire can
grow from any seed of discord. To overestimate
the length of Lady Eris's arm would be a futile
undertaking. Any vault she can cause to feel en prise
with just her speech. From any complacent party she can
make a desperado; no wound beyond her reach."

HEATHEN WEAVE

"You boast
of Chakramire's command of the tongue as if you proudly
fell its victim."

FLOW

"Chakramire asked me to call you here,
but I have given warning to urge you leave. Whatever
idyll, dream, or fog you hold dear, prepare yourself to grieve."

[Exit Flow]

MARA MARA *[Aside]*

A chance to skirt mortality, every story offers.
Chakramire, however, knew Heathen Weave desired to be
forgotten. She, towards the beleaguered figure ambled,
like a boot towards the downtrodden.

CHAKRAMIRE

"Everyone will learn
your secret if you nurse it to death. A pair of body
doubles sheltered Nettles; both, I suspect, have perished. I
believe you are the actual foe, the man who Vance the
Dagger wrestles."

HEATHEN WEAVE

“I exchanged names with Heathen Weave to hide
the life of mine. The trust of a thief a few achieve; your
folly won the faith of Twine.”

CHAKRAMIRE

“I presumed the role of Twine
concerned the Captain?”

HEATHEN WEAVE (the true NETTLES)

“No, it belonged to Thorns. The Captain
thought himself the Twine because we deluded him and Vance.
About myself, however, whatever gave away the
ruse?”

CHAKRAMIRE

“Your double summoned Two, lived another day, and Vance
departed ere the rattle of death. To leave the dining
table, right before the last bite of vengeance swallowed, means
the flavor disappointed or altogether wrong. The
appetite of Dagger Vance I believe dissatisfied.”

HEATHEN WEAVE (the true NETTLES)

“Suspect the bounty hunter alive? without a shield?”

MARA MARA *[Aside]*

The
Devas offer vassals unmatched defense against assault,
but those devoid of innocence they will hold at fault.

CHAKRAMIRE

"To
know would spoil our spirits. I came to Earth to resurrect
the art of storytelling, to vitalize the trope of
evil versus good, to bring back compelling songs of strife,
and stand wherever peacefulness stood . . . but even I can
only guess, from shavings, words weakly whittled into wood."

[They exit]

WHEN THE SYMPHONY'S DISCORD RISES: PART FOUR

CANTO 33: CATACLYSM

Galactic Calendar: Sol System; Earth year 30,123,012 M.W.I.
Tellurian Solar Calendar: Day thirty of the sixth tenth – 06/30
Modern Metric Time: 3:50:00, UTC+00:00, afternoon
Location: Water Clock Brothel, Sitnalta Island

AT RISE DESCRIPTION: *Chakramire, Mara Mara, and Flow are in the quartermaster's room. Flow is preparing to unlock a large chest.*

[Enter Mara Mara, Chakramire, and Flow]

EGRESS MACHINE (via MARA MARA) *[Aside]*

Freezing the maker of paces prohibits a temporal
harvest. The furnaces stoking themselves shall explode. Should the
willing resist the resent of content? A cessation of
movement releases the tourniquet over nostalgia, for
courage congeals as devotion withdraws, but the fury of
restlessness smolders. Temptation's abeyance, inquisitors
call it a death of the second degree, the consumption of
life, an eternal rebellion, or kindle for apathy.

MARA MARA *[Aside]*

Despair, vexation, happiness, courage . . . calls to action
asking them to yield, oppose, strive to keep the status quo,
or move to undermine it. The longer they exist the
less the haste. Eternal life heralds death of feeling.

CHAKRAMIRE

"Once
you lose the sense of urgency, all your passions cease. Should
clocks forget to wind themselves up, the cataclysm known
as time quiesces."

FLOW

“I shall return the dress tomorrow.
Scarlet Sheath shall meet its twin. If an expectation is
the source of all anxiety, I will learn to worry
less. To let our values thin is to put an end to stress.”

MARA MARA *[Aside]*

As Flow removed the lock from the chest, the Furthermost of
Women watched with earnest. Red fabric spilled beyond its lips
as if the trunk had broken a vow of silence. If a
secret burns for long enough, wick and wax its flames engulf.

FLOW

“The day before the hand of the Baron Varlet severed,
he, an ultimatum left. Ebb has kept his letter; I
have kept her dress, but I would prefer to swap our debts, to
walk away from life, its contents revealed, with no regrets.”

[They exit]

WHEN THE SYMPHONY'S DISCORD RISES: PART FOUR

CANTO 34: HOARFROST

Galactic Calendar: Sol System; Earth year 30,123,012 M.W.I.
Tellurian Solar Calendar: Day thirty-one of the sixth tenth – 06/31
Modern Metric Time: 1:75:00, UTC+00:00, morning
Location: Delta Marketplace, Sitnalta Island

AT RISE DESCRIPTION: *On behalf of Flow, Chakramire and Mara Mara visit Ebb to deliver the proposal for a trade.*

[Enter Chakramire, Mara Mara, and Ebb]

EGRESS MACHINE (via MARA MARA) *[Aside]*

Chastity's moniker never demanded respect from its
victims; recoil from the cadence of stone. A magnanimous
mind would reject the appeal to absolve a surrender to
passion. However, a barrier augmented, vanity
yielded survival gratuities. Solace descended from
summit to valley and under the turbulent river of
decadence, deeper for dearth of deterrence, determined to
bow to the ripple effect of a desperate innocence.

MARA MARA *[Aside]*

Because the rock of innocence rests atop a mountain
high enough it makes the clouds wince with envy, any time
a climber's grasp dislodges it crumbling faces bury
half the world below. Its landslide devours the trees and all
who kneel before licentiousness.

EBB

"Yesterday, a frigid
mass of air descended. Hoarfrost has bearded every plant.

The sight of rime and icicles renders warmth to any
other hard to grant."

CHAKRAMIRE

"A tree hole provides the same amount
of shelter irrespective of seasons. Warmness neither
cools with age nor facial hair; forests share whatever they
can spare to all the creatures within a region. Though your
seedling effort harbors goodwill, it is as far away
as far can be from being a thicket."

EBB

"If you came to
me to hand deliver insults, your tongue will need to show
a few credentials. Thrice it has sparred with me, but I have
never learned its owner."

MARA MARA *[Aside]*

Pink muscle, brawny, razor edged,
and double pronged, emerged from the mouth of Chakramire.

CHAKRAMIRE

"Your
sister asked for me for one final trade to broker: threads
of red for paper carefully stained with ink. Our tongues should
never need a voucher; they either leave impressions filled
with blood or not."

EBB

"The Lady of Eris spoke with sharpness
like your own, but she expired many years ago."

MARA MARA *[Aside]*

And still
expires today.

EBB

"Her fruitless attempts to reawaken
storytelling earned her name lasting shame."

CHAKRAMIRE

"Your fashion shows
achieve a worse effect. You remind the people grudges
still persist, but never narrate nor say who suffers. Brave,
the Furthermost of Women, for telling tales entire . . . your
pageant only shows the book's cover."

EBB

"I will swap the dress
for Baron Varlet's letter, and end the feud with Flow. The
trek to peace requires a pacesetter, be it fast or slow."

[They exit]

WHEN THE SYMPHONY'S DISCORD RISES: PART FOUR

CANTO 35: NIRVANA

Galactic Calendar: Sol System; Earth year 30,123,012 M.W.I.
Tellurian Solar Calendar: Day thirty-two of the sixth tenth – 06/32
Modern Metric Time: 1:25:00, UTC+00:00, morning
Location: Water Clock Brothel, Sitnalta Island

AT RISE DESCRIPTION: *Chakramire and Mara Mara greet Ebb in the antechamber of the Water Clock Brothel in the morning. Ebb has brought Baron Varlet's letter.*

[Enter Chakramire, Mara Mara, and Ebb]

EGRESS MACHINE (via MARA MARA) *[Aside]*

Sentences, symbols, superfluous entities, absent of
natural meaning. Abstractions unite the impossible.
Gravity, only its force of attraction, the darkest of
matter, could marry the false to the rational.
Representation, a crime of distinction, the bridge and the
barrier, parries correction and carries protection, but
entropy never desists. From oblivion traveled and
back the contagion, to harness the value of weightlessness.

MARA MARA *[Aside]*

Before suspending consciousness, she would always point her
gaze towards her place of birth. Seeing Eris fly across
the night, a cold necropolis filled with grief, reminded
Chakramire to wake the next day.

CHAKRAMIRE

"You knocked upon the door
with force to rouse the dead; your enthusiasm pleases
me. The Quartermaster Flow sleeps, however."

EBB

"I shall wait
within the vestibule, for the letter's substance I have
seen . . . already guessed its outcome."

MARA MARA *[Aside]*

The seamstress left the note
to Chakramire, and paced the reception room. The weight of
Baron Varlet's letter grew fiftyfold as soon as Ebb
released her grip. Its avoirdupois surprised the Lady
Eris.

CHAKRAMIRE

"I shall bring the dress back, with luck, your sister too."

[Chakramire leaves briefly and returns with the original Scarlet Sheath and Flow]

MARA MARA *[Aside]*

Emotion is the realization something's value
changed or stayed the same. Upon seeing Baron Varlet's last
decision, Flow remembered its worth.

FLOW

"You brought the letter
after all; it means to me more than life."

MARA MARA *[Aside]*

The statement drained
the blood her sanguine countenance; Ebb reclaimed the dress and
left.

[Exit Ebb]

CHAKRAMIRE

"It seems the letter's contents have spooked your sibling. I would like to know the reason."

MARA MARA *[Aside]*

The quartermaster read the
Baron Varlet's scribblings like she expected every stroke
to leave a lesion.

FLOW

"Three."

MARA MARA *[Aside]*

As the note descended, Lady
Eris saw the single word filled its page.

FLOW

"It is a tryst,
an invitation desperate lovers often make to
meet and share a starry-eye. I can learn his feelings first
degree, for Baron Varlet and I were both aligned to
Three."

MARA MARA *[Aside]*

Without a guide, a Conduit, invocations rive
and strand a vassal's consciousness.

CHAKRAMIRE

"If you lend your mind to
Three, expect to lose it."

FLOW

"I want to know the full extent
of Baron Varlet's misery. I will find nirvana,
even if the ticket one-way."

MARA MARA *[Aside]*

The quartermaster cleared
her throat of phlegm, and gestured as if to pray.

FLOW

"Admitting
we cannot exist without them requires a leap of faith . . ."

MARA MARA *[Aside]*

The mouth of Flow contracted, expanded; she could only
pantomime a scream. A voice crippling pain devoured her hand;
it swept throughout the rest of her body like a stream.

[Enter Three]

THREE (via FLOW)

"The
Baron Varlet's heart, it ached more the severed wrist, and through
the everlasting psyche of mine persists. The feelings
I impart a final plot twist; the Baron Varlet razed
his heart before his fist."

[Exit Three]

MARA MARA *[Aside]*

As the invocation faded
Flow could not escape the spring tide of Baron Varlet's woe,
for she believed it better to feel the force its weight, to
buckle underneath the deluge than live and never know.

[All exit except for Flow]

WHEN THE SYMPHONY'S DISCORD RISES: PART FOUR

CANTO 36: NONCHALANCE

Galactic Calendar: Sol System; Earth year 30,123,012 M.W.I.
Tellurian Solar Calendar: Day thirty-three of the sixth tenth – 06/33
Modern Metric Time: 0:50:00, UTC+00:00, morning
Location: Water Clock Brothel, Sitnalta Island

AT RISE DESCRIPTION: *Calypso, Chakramire, and Mara Mara examine Flow's unconscious body, as it has not roused since her invocation the previous day.*

[Enter Chakramire, Mara Mara, and Calypso next to Flow's vacant body]

EGRESS MACHINE (via MARA MARA) *[Aside]*

Welcoming parties were welcomed regardless of merit or
want. A diversion away from conventional gossip could
sharpen the fugitive's edge, but a criminal's honesty
promised reward nor reprieve. To conceive a deception, the
gambit should never exceed the original confidence.
Needful to say, a coincidence rarely surrendered its
vitals to popular sentiment save at a premium.
Many a lunar eclipse has embarrassed a predator.

MARA MARA *[Aside]*

Calypso eyed the body of Flow with calculated
tact, the kind of nonchalance one expects from strangers if
politeness just an act.

CALYPSO

"It appears the quartermaster
indisposed, a breach of contract. The clout her hand enclosed
will now transpose, and I her commissions too, transact."

CHAKRAMIRE

“A small condolence offers poor screen for one’s ambition.”

CALYPSO

“I would mourn . . . but lack an equal with whom to sympathize of
late. Your life, belongings, please take, and leave our fair estate.”

[They exit]

WHEN THE SYMPHONY'S DISCORD RISES: PART FOUR

CANTO 37: ATONEMENT

Galactic Calendar: Sol System; Earth year 30,123,012 M.W.I.
Tellurian Solar Calendar: Day thirty-four of the sixth tenth – 06/34
Modern Metric Time: 3:25:00, UTC+00:00, afternoon
Location: Umbrage Grotto, Sitnalta Island

AT RISE DESCRIPTION: *Having been evicted from the Water Clock, Chakramire heads towards Umbrage Grotto in search of a safe haven . Mara Mara accompanies her.*

[Enter Chakramire, Mara Mara, and Heathen Weave]

EGRESS MACHINE (via MARA MARA) *[Aside]*

Loyalty favors the powerful, treason the powerless,
power the transient. Anomalies are the primordial
scars, for the sightliest mark of a bandit, the genuine
promise, evokes a dissenter's suspicion. Professionals
call it the causal revolt, a misnomer for sacrilege.
Better to be a delinquent than taken with glee, and to
covet the hooligan's bounty, but brandish complacency.
Enter the grotto with clemency, essence of thievery.

MARA MARA *[Aside]*

The reason Chakramire, to the Earth, descended, never
puzzled anyone. A snake curls upon itself and bites
its tail from spite or under duress. The Lady Eris
met the pair at birth, and goodbyes were never needed.

CHAKRAMIRE

"Earth's
collective human consciousness split, divided just as
seasons, fractured into four factions like a brain with cuts
and lesions."

HEATHEN WEAVE (the true NETTLES)

"Few would ever believe the Devas chose to
only know themselves."

CHAKRAMIRE

"The Conduits made the choice, and guard
the secret well. The wrath of the Devas is devout and
unrelenting; they despise one another."

HEATHEN WEAVE (the true NETTLES)

"I accept
your explanation. Obvious, I assume, it seems to
Lady Chakramire. Your outsider's eyes can see our world
entire. Aside from history lectures given, what to
Umbrage Grotto brings you back?"

CHAKRAMIRE

"Quartermaster Flow expired
a day ago. Calypso, her place has taken. She, a
debt of gratitude to Vance never owed . . . has banished me
from Water Clock and brothel. A haven I request."

HEATHEN WEAVE (the true NETTLES)

"It
lies beyond your reach. The price placed upon your head, attached
or otherwise, would tempt a poltroon. Your safety I could
never guarantee. Although *Mint* befell the hand of Ray,

a random act of violence only suits a person
lacking retribution's means. Ray would never overdress."

CHAKRAMIRE

"Perhaps the bounty hunter repents."

HEATHEN WEAVE (the true NETTLES)

"Suspect the Dagger
Vance a man embarrassed?"

CHAKRAMIRE

"New information often spoils
the taste for vengeance. Righteousness clung to Vance the Dagger
like a shadow . . . shocking no doubt, to see it missing."

HEATHEN WEAVE (the true NETTLES)

"If
the knife bequeathed to Ray with the expectation I would
think his feud with me has ceased, I would say the Dagger Vance
succeeded. Unaware of the mad inventor's temper,
I presume."

CHAKRAMIRE

"A careless choice I remind you, costing Thorns
the Bandit's life . . ."

MARA MARA *[Aside]*

As vengeance the Dagger Vance would leave to
none besides himself, it forced Strife to light the candle wick
the bounty hunter's feud from the other end.

HEATHEN WEAVE (the true NETTLES)

"Your counsel
I respect, your taste for bloodshed, admire, but Chakramire,
you walk with stilts and all our amends beneath your ambit.
Pardon my reprisal's postponement."

CHAKRAMIRE

"*I* would not permit
the man relief from guilt, nor attempt to find atonement."

[They exit]

WHEN THE SYMPHONY'S DISCORD RISES: PART FOUR

CANTO 38: SUBLIMATION

Galactic Calendar: Sol System; Earth year 30,123,012 M.W.I.
Tellurian Solar Calendar: Day thirty-five of the sixth tenth – 06/35
Modern Metric Time: 2:25:00, UTC+00:00, near midday
Location: The Delta Marketplace, Sitnalta Island

AT RISE DESCRIPTION: *Having spent the night at Umbrage Grotto, Chakramire and Mara Mara visit Ebb with the intent of notifying her of her sister's death.*

[Enter Chakramire, Mara Mara, and Ebb]

EGRESS MACHINE (via MARA MARA) *[Aside]*

Freezing the maker of paces prohibits a temporal
harvest. The furnaces stoking themselves shall explode. Should the
willing resist the resent of content? A cessation of
movement releases the tourniquet over nostalgia, for
courage congeals as devotion withdraws, but the fury of
restlessness smolders. Temptation's abeyance, inquisitors
call it a death of the second degree, the consumption of
life, an eternal rebellion, or kindle for apathy.

MARA MARA *[Aside]*

Shelter, water, food, contempt, things explorers learn to live
without. Her otherworldly conviction gives away her
name, for she admits to no fault.

EBB

"Your tongue betrays your face,
contrasts its rounded countenance. Lady Chakramire, your
diction changes frost to fire, giving birth to battlegrounds.

Intend to offer notice of death or find a wound to
salt? For what you came to Earth? Came to me? Your presence here
confounds."

CHAKRAMIRE

"You seek profundity like you hunt for shadows
underneath the cloak of night. Presence is the purpose. Genes
cannot encode our destiny, only write its script. But
if another role desired, one should change the play."

EBB

"You came
to Earth to prove it possible?"

CHAKRAMIRE

"Yes, and came today to
help you find another stage."

EBB

"What became of Flow?"

CHAKRAMIRE

"The urge
for exploration stems from dissatisfaction. She for
dreams beyond her reach has reached."

EBB

"She has found an early grave
you mean?"

CHAKRAMIRE

"A fault: believing our lives can skip a phase. At
atmospheric pressure, dry ice will vaporize. 'To die
before our time,' it is a persistent myth. It stands to
reason life will undergo sublimation only if
it lived with insufficient resistance. Ebb, you live a
life of tranquil ease, but hardships distinguish shrubs from trees."

[They exit]

WHEN THE SYMPHONY'S DISCORD RISES: PART FOUR

CANTO 39: IMPLOSION

Galactic Calendar: Sol System; Earth year 30,123,012 M.W.I.
Tellurian Solar Calendar: Day thirty-six of the sixth tenth – 06/36
Modern Metric Time: 1:00:00, UTC+00:00, morning
Location: The Delta Marketplace, Sitnalta Island

AT RISE DESCRIPTION: *Chakramire and Mara Mara continue conversing with Ebb the next day.*

[Enter Chakramire, Mara Mara, and Ebb]

EGRESS MACHINE (via MARA MARA) *[Aside]*

Chastity's moniker never demanded respect from its victims; recoil from the cadence of stone. A magnanimous mind would reject the appeal to absolve a surrender to passion. However, a barrier augmented, vanity yielded survival gratuities. Solace descended from summit to valley and under the turbulent river of decadence, deeper for dearth of deterrence, determined to bow to the ripple effect of a desperate innocence.

MARA MARA *[Aside]*

The Furthermost of Women had grown accustomed ire from overstaying welcomes. She oftentimes arrived without an invitation.

EBB

"Rumors persist concerning Lady Chakramire; whomever she speaks with dies before the year's completion."

CHAKRAMIRE

"Less canard than the rumor ducks were feathered.
Mercenaries thirst for my blood, for I enlighten all
around and my existence reminds your fellows genes can
never seal our fate. Your gatekeepers wish to end the life
of mine and all who listen to me; an intimation
I can offer. If a hive mind decides to split itself
apart, the consequences befall the body."

MARA MARA *[Aside]*

Mulled the
words, but Ebb desired to live longer. Safer topics sought.

EBB

"You wish to find a man who continues tempting fate, the
quondam innovator Ray? I would urge you not delay.
His heart and mind precariously hang upon a cliff, as
do the rest his organs. Most people want to feel our
life's existence holds significance, be it through ourselves or
through descendants. Most of us want to matter, even if
it seems our life's entirety spent indulging lavish
frills and odd adornments."

MARA MARA *[Aside]*

Ebb eased herself from Chakramire's
direction.

EBB

"Ray, however, concerns himself with leaving
no effect. For Meso he works, a smith of glass but not
a smith of words. A recommendation letter I can
still authenticate, for one small concession."

CHAKRAMIRE

"State your terms."

EBB

"You press the bounds of sanity further every day, and
make absurd decisions seem justified. Before the hand
of Baron Varlet calloused the heart of mine, before his
tryst with Flow, before the runway displays and fashion crimes
as art, for magnanimity I was known. But publics
love a scandal, love to see status seekers stagger, love
to track a reputation's implosion. I delivered.
Sacrificed the bonds of blood, wore the Scarlet Sheath for years
awaiting Flow's confession, recused myself from casting
blame, but let the world believe none the fault belonged to me.
The price of my assistance will be for Chakramire to
learn from my mistakes, to climb up the hill before its mound
becomes an insurmountable cliff, to yield to neither
wind nor rain, to never seek solace anywhere beneath
the summit, persevering until the muscles stiffen
while enduring any pain."

CHAKRAMIRE

"I will rise above your hill
as blizzards form, attesting the fortitude of creatures
everywhere. For, like a storm, I can burden any bear."

[They exit]

WHEN THE SYMPHONY'S DISCORD RISES: PART FOUR

CANTO 40: GAMUT GATE

Galactic Calendar: Sol System; Earth year 30,123,012 M.W.I.
Tellurian Solar Calendar: Day thirty-six of the sixth tenth – 06/36
Modern Metric Time: 3:75:00, UTC+00:00, afternoon
Location: Meso's Glass Forge at Gaffer's Gorge, Sitnalta Island

AT RISE DESCRIPTION: *Mara Mara and Chakramire, with a recommendation letter endorsed by Ebb, meet with Meso to arrange an interview.*

[Enter Chakramire, Mara Mara, and Meso]

EGRESS MACHINE (via MARA MARA) *[Aside]*

Sentences, symbols, superfluous entities, absent of
natural meaning. Abstractions unite the impossible.
Gravity, only its force of attraction, the darkest of
matter, could marry the false to the rational.
Representation, a crime of distinction, the bridge and the
barrier, parries correction and carries protection, but
entropy never desists. From oblivion traveled and
back the contagion, to harness the value of weightlessness.

MESO

"'To offer one apology anywhere, to any
person, any time before death.' A strange condition Ebb
affixed upon your recommendation letter.

CHAKRAMIRE

"I have
never needed offer one."

MESO

"Yes, and people never need umbrellas till it rains or the sun is shining. We will interview tomorrow. No first impression ever made a sculpture."

CHAKRAMIRE

"True, but many have ended one. A sculptor, like a great musician, knows one cannot redeem a bad beginning. Marble, symphonies, poems, they demand the best from artists. Ebb informed me a genius indisposed avails your work . . . but even an unexpected crack, a word misplaced, a single sour note can wreck a masterpiece."

MARA MARA *[Aside]*

As Chakramire, the Mistress of Strife, began to open up the gamut gate to discord, a grimace spread across the other's face.

CHAKRAMIRE

"Your orchestra needs a new conductor."

[They exit]

BOOK II:
WHERE SERENITY AND STRIFE CLEAVE

PART FOUR: RESOLVE INEXORABLE

WHERE SERENITY AND STRIFE CLEAVE: PART FOUR

CANTO 71: CRYSTALLIZE

Galactic Calendar: Sol System; Earth year 30,123,012 M.W.I.
Tellurian Solar Calendar: Day twenty-eight of the seventh tenth – 07/28
Modern Metric Time: 1:50:00, UTC+00:00, morning
Location: Sanitarium, Sitnalta Island

AT RISE DESCRIPTION: *Cloy tends to Ray's body that is resting on a table while Chakramire, Mara Mara, and Xara observe.*

[Enter Chakramire, Mara Mara, and Xara, Ray, and Cloy]

EGRESS MACHINE (via MARA MARA) *[Aside]*

Mixtures engender disparities, tonic solutions, and
crystals. An ocean of promise, an island of hope, and a
grain of success. The impartial refinement of destiny
leaves a residual ridge of repression. Minorities
rise as majorities fade, but serenity's scarcity
teases. The blistering fragrance of brine, with a whiff of the
gaffer's sobriety, tore from obsidian modicum
salaries, given to only the salt of society.

CHAKRAMIRE

"None of us can know the point whereupon another opts
to break a double bind. To transcend, or go beyond the
body's limits, is the hallmark of freedom. Persons free
retain the capability, whether exercised or
not, to stride across the bounds life imposes – anywhere
at anytime – or choose to remain within; and any
definition short of that is a lie. The blame for Ray's
resolve to cross the boundary lies within."

MARA MARA *[Aside]*

A pair of
labored breathes escaped from Ray's chest, and Xara sighed.

CLOY

"You saved
his life regardless, bringing the body here. Another
moment more and he would be dispossessed of body."

CHAKRAMIRE

"Whence
your logic?"

CLOY

"Invocations suspend volition. Freedom
is a Deva's price. A Conduit's obligation is
to reunite the will to its owner; vassals rarely
find it unassisted. First invocations start at age
eleven: one's alignment begins to crystallize and
finish near the seventeenth year of life. For those aligned
to Deva Three, maturity takes the longest. Zero,
One, and Two will manifest first."

CHAKRAMIRE

"Numeric order?"

CLOY

"Yes.
A realignment also can happen, oftentimes with
mixed results. The person's core disposition shifts, and they
adopt a new identity. Any invocation
lasting more than half a day indicates the vassal lacks
the means to reawaken. For everyone aligned to
Three, invoking is a death sentence."

MARA MARA *[Aside]*

Xara's shoulders sank
at Cloy's assertion.

CLOY

"Pulling the mind from self-hypnosis
takes an anchor point, a Conduit, rectitude, or luck."

[They exit]

WHERE SERENITY AND STRIFE CLEAVE: PART FOUR

CANTO 72: PURITY TAINTED

Galactic Calendar: Sol System; Earth year 30,123,012 M.W.I.
Tellurian Solar Calendar: Day twenty-nine of the seventh tenth – 07/29
Modern Metric Time: 5:25:00, UTC+00:00, dusk or evening twilight
Location: Sanitarium, Sitnalta Island

AT RISE DESCRIPTION: *While inspecting Mara Mara, Cloy begins inquiring Chakramire about the Egress Machine near a bedridden Ray.*

[Enter Chakramire, Mara Mara, and Cloy next to Ray's body]

EGRESS MACHINE (via MARA MARA) *[Aside]*

Luxury's only redeeming distinction, hostility
fostered between the affluent and poverty-stricken. A
life of extravagance, enemy strife, will solicit the
gold of our youth with the spirits fermenting a bottle of
comfort, decay and creation, a rose from the dead with a
noxious aesthetic. The idiosyncrasy, fighting to
linger at rest or against a deciduous passion. A
lavish inertia, the spoil from an era of constancy.

MARA MARA *[Aside]*

Commingling is the natural order; separation
takes a greater deal of work. Strife ferments wherever class
survives, wherever purity tainted cultures thrive. The
Furthermost of Women came all the way from Eris, all
the way from dereliction, and all the way from death. To
label Chakramire a firebrand would understate the heat
behind the dragon's breath.

CLOY

"The device you brought, it serves a
purpose? I have never known bards to carry charms."

CHAKRAMIRE

"It is
an occultation ward, or remembrance aid, a gadget
dubbed the Golden Brain of Discord. It radiates a stream
of steady waves, a frequency sequence. Ray designed its
mechanism, though it malfunctioned."

CLOY

"If it is a type
of key, who feels its energy?"

CHAKRAMIRE

"Human life beginning
here upon the Earth, and androids as Mara Mara."

CLOY

"Why
facilitate disclosure of information?"

CHAKRAMIRE

"Knowledge
acquisition modulates evolution's river, if
stagnation means extinction, and I have witnessed justice
misdelivered everywhere people disregard our great
distinction."

CLOY

"What distinguishing feature helped our species
thrive? Our use of thumbs and tools hardly dignify our lives."

CHAKRAMIRE

"Our storytelling skill, our command of lies, the ink, the
quill, and literary eyes."

MARA MARA *[Aside]*

Cloy had pondered Chakramire's
perspective once before, her demeanor unsurprised.

CLOY

"You
said, 'The Golden Brain of Discord became corrupted.' How?"

CHAKRAMIRE

"It lifted smoke and fog from our yesterdays, but now it
lifts tomorrow's too."

CLOY

"Perhaps, gloom aside, it never broke.
It seems its capabilities grew, and if it pierces
through the future's cloak, it might grant its maker vision too.
To overcome the fog of compunction, Ray will need a
clear, compelling motive, not just a beacon. Even if
a person is a prisoner trapped behind a dungeon
lattice, one should not assume they are dispossessed the keys
the apparatus. Leaving machine would be a fitting
name, but only if it frees Ray."

MARA MARA *[Aside]*

The hand of Chakramire
descended, seized the dreadful device ensconced within her
bard's design, and placed it near Ray. The lids above his eyes
began to part as consciousness found its way to Ray.

CLOY

"The
Maiden Xara left for Youngberry Tavern, I presume
to drown her sorrows under the Juggernaut's Ambrosia.
She will want to know of Ray's status. Saving people's lives
rewards enough for me. The assistance offered gratis."

[They exit]

WHERE SERENITY AND STRIFE CLEAVE: PART FOUR

CANTO 73: CONSTELLATION WILT

Galactic Calendar: Sol System; Earth year 30,123,012 M.W.I.
Tellurian Solar Calendar: Day thirty of the seventh tenth – 07/30
Modern Metric Time: 4:00:00, UTC+00:00, near sunset
Location: Youngberry Tavern, Sitnalta Island

AT RISE DESCRIPTION: *Chakramire and Mara Mara search for Xara at Youngberry Tavern and find her next to Epi and flanked by the tavern's patrons.*

[Enter Chakramire and Mara Mara into Youngberry Tavern. Xara and Epi are engaged in conversation and surrounded by a crowd when Xara notices them.]

EGRESS MACHINE (via MARA MARA) *[Aside]*

Flayers of canvas endeavor to smother the future of
fabric transparent. Whoever would champion beauty at
bio-diversity's loss, would demand from existence a
penance for youth and utility crossed: a symmetrical
ratio of mythic proportions, the measure of powder, of
paint, with the prettiest flower displaced from a desert, the
glorification of taste. As the radiance bleaches a
visage, the symphonies wash from a face of exuberance.

EPI

"If the stars, at any price, Chakramire believes to be
a bargain, are our lives and the comforts Earth provides it
nonessential?"

XARA

"I would ask Chakramire herself."

MARA MARA *[Aside]*

Towards
the Furthermost of Women the Maiden Xara turned, and
bodies redirected like weathervanes.

CHAKRAMIRE

"Although the stars
would be a bargain, only buffoons would pay above the
asking price . . . constructing networks of sparks and wires to build
a database for tackling an unforgiving task: the
capture, cache, and trade of thought. They deciphered human minds,
amalgamated patterns of thinking spanning countless
generations into one code, and let it fracture."

EPI

"They?
You mean our predecessors?

CHAKRAMIRE

"Correct."

EPI

"To what extent the
overpayment? Blaming forebearers shifts the fault towards
ourselves, for they endeavored to guarantee our future."

CHAKRAMIRE

"They resolved to split the hive mind apart, disjoining world
perspectives. Blissful ignorance spares a vantage point from
strife against opposing standpoints, but never saves a point
of view against itself. To possess a counterbalance
is a fundamental aspect of life."

MARA MARA *[Aside]*

A tidal wave
of pure exhilaration engulfed the face of Epi.

EPI

"People rarely challenge me more than once, or entertain
opinions contradicting ideas I espouse. You
are the Lady Chakramire, I presume?"

CHAKRAMIRE

"Indeed."

EPI

"And what
has drawn you here tonight to our tavern? What would tempt the
Furthermost of Women leave outer space and make her way
to isolated islands? Your kind belongs above the
clouds, and not below."

CHAKRAMIRE

"Contempt tempted me, but I embarked
with news for Xara. Ray has awakened.

MARA MARA *[Aside]*

Xara's anguished
face began to sober.

CHAKRAMIRE

"I came to Earth to seek revenge
for letting Eris perish, for disregarding us, for
snubbing everything our lives represented. I assumed
your world comprised of citizens grazing calmly next the
slaughterhouse, accustomed hardship nor tribulation, stress
nor strain, and knowing neither themselves nor one another.

Worse, however, I have learned none of these to be the case.
To keep your ontological peace intact you squander
knowledge under quarantine. Human evolution stopped
upon your world. For millions of years the Earth endured with
people asking all the wrong questions."

MARA MARA *[Aside]*

Chakramire directs
the room to swivel, turning her head towards the painting
hung upon the wall – *The Nightscape and Afterglow.*

CHAKRAMIRE

"To watch
your kind resembled gazing at the stars: observing swarms of
shining lights pervade the night sky as countless figures, shapes,
and forms appear, but being compelled to witness every
constellation wilt as stars fade from brilliance right before
the eyes. Although the brightness of stars will dwindle after
death, it also dims at large distance. All the light can leave
a sky, and just as greatness can happen anywhere, a
world's ineptitude has no borders. I discovered Earth,
to my dismay, a planet already emptied all its
stars. Instead of vengeance, I chose to fill your sky again."

MARA MARA *[Aside]*

A budding apprehensiveness sprang from Epi's face, and
she addressed the crowd with newfound reluctance.

EPI

"I have long
despised the pilgrims trekking to Earth from space, but even
I cannot endorse the fate Chakramire awaits. A man
with no remorse, the soldier of fortune Doryline, is
taking down dissenters, spaceborn and unaligned alike,
and none among the living as vile or unforgiving."

[They exit]

WHERE SERENITY AND STRIFE CLEAVE: PART FOUR

CANTO 74: DARKYEAR

Galactic Calendar: Sol System; Earth year 30,123,012 M.W.I.
Tellurian Solar Calendar: Day thirty-one of the seventh tenth – 07/31
Modern Metric Time: 1:00:00, UTC+00:00, morning
Location: Sanitarium, Sitnalta Island

AT RISE DESCRIPTION: *Chakramire, Mara Mara, and Xara have returned to the Sanitarium to check on the catatonic body of Ray.*

[Enter Chakramire, Mara Mara, and Xara near Ray's bedside]

EGRESS MACHINE (via MARA MARA) *[Aside]*

Civilization's penumbra, the edge of humanity's
knowledge, commencement of wisdom, between a diminishing
star and celestial occlusion. The brilliant escape with a
boundary skirted, diffracting around the perimeter,
leaving behind the extinguished to ponder enlightenment.
Freedom refracted, the truth of the matter evicted from
vacua, longs for a liberty lost, for perfection, for
aggregate progress contingent to homogeneity.

MARA MARA *[Aside]*

Like a flash of lightning flung into brief existence, she
illuminates the monsters at night before withdrawing,
leaving anyone with eyes more afraid for seeing what
the shadows hide. The trigger for confrontation is the
call to arms. To learn a fierce adversary haunts the dark
creates a sense of vigilance. Knowing less about its
speed, its range, or whereabouts heightens paranoia. Doomed
ideas dazzle under duress and thunder's sound. A
lightning bolt can spark a fire having never touched the ground.

XARA

"You never mentioned murderous mercenaries stalk you.
Why would Epi warn you?"

CHAKRAMIRE

"She panics. Imitation is
the highest form of flattery. I have done the same. A
person's desperation leads them to welcome greater risks.
Your once betrothed awakened the night before the last with
vows to finish everything he began, for he believes
himself the desecrater of Three's domain."

MARA MARA *[Aside]*

The distance
light can travel over one trip around the sun, it is
a people's generational knowledge gained; as swiftly
won, as swiftly lost, a darkyear will measure knowledge waned.

CHAKRAMIRE

"Along the shadow's fringe, the penumbra, few will win the
game of brinkmanship, a handful will lose the bout against
the life-devouring shade. To escape the labyrinth of
Three again, your beau will need more than luck. Whoever opts
to forge ahead and forage for knowledge where the light can
never spread, will leave entire planets thunderstruck instead."

XARA

"Our love requires a recklessness; like a mountain climber
perched upon a slope with no niche, the air, you learn to tread."

[They exit]

WHERE SERENITY AND STRIFE CLEAVE: PART FOUR

CANTO 75: NON-TRANSCENDENTAL

Galactic Calendar: Sol System; Earth year 30,123,012 M.W.I.
Tellurian Solar Calendar: Day thirty-two of the seventh tenth – 07/32
Modern Metric Time: 0:75:00, UTC+00:00, morning
Location: Sanitarium, Sitnalta Island

AT RISE DESCRIPTION: *Cloy, at Chakramire's request, prepares to wake Ray. Mara Mara and Xara are in attendance.*

[Enter Chakramire, Mara Mara, Xara, and Cloy near Ray's bedside]

EGRESS MACHINE (via MARA MARA) *[Aside]*

Only the clarity after a storm could elicit a
stronger sensation of dread than of being alone in the
midst the disturbance, to people afraid of remorsefulness,
makers of tempests. Familiar disturbances offer a
modest reprieve from omniscience, from knowing the sequence of
beats to a heart, from chronology broken, from savagery.
Ever forgetting the words to harmonious melody,
interdependence arouses erroneous memory.

CLOY

"Your words depicted Ray as a complicated victim
whose inflated sense of self-worth beguiled, a man who felt
it rain and blamed himself for the tempest, innovator
lacking style, and mastermind missing enterprise. You ask
for me to wake the man . . . to another grave deliver.
Why?"

CHAKRAMIRE

"The reason I desire Ray awakened I cannot
reveal without a promise, or my endeavors carry
risk of being compromised."

CLOY

"Any pledge demanded I
will keep; the bell of treachery I have never rung. For
some, the hill of virtue is steep, for others, deep."

CHAKRAMIRE

"The pledge
demanded is a sheathing of tongues against the Devas.
Take an oath of silence, no invocation make, until
the quarrel's final interposition."

CLOY

"I accept."

CHAKRAMIRE

"The
League of Numbers needs its gatekeepers changed, or else your world
will never win its dignity back. The catalytic
role of Paris, former Conduit representing Three,
must fall to Ray."

CLOY

"The sedative I injected into
Ray will dissipate at nightfall. To be a Deva's voice
and play the role of prisoner, prison warden, lock and
key combined requires a non-transcendental frame of mind.
The knowledge harnessed over a couple million years would
drown the multitudes of Earth's population. I have seen
it swallow fools and prodigies daily, leaving only

husks behind. The urge to seek more, to dive beneath, beyond
benign and buoyant waters, exhausted all but one of
them, and even he emerged frail and scathed. A submarine
withstands the ocean's weight to explore the deepest trenches."

MARA MARA *[Aside]*

Heat dispersed, nocturnal songs nipped at ears, a single star
became a thousand. Only the Furthermost of Women
kept a vigil. Cloy revived other patients, tending those
with better chances. Xara descended into sleep, a
forceful slumber only death rivaled.

[Cloy exits]

RAY

"Lady Chakramire,"

MARA MARA *[Aside]*

The voice of Ray appealed for the calloused ear of Eris.

RAY

"I have seen a world without limits, walked along its hem,
and felt its fabric ripping with every metric minute.
We cannot exist without them."

MARA MARA *[Aside]*

The limbs of Ray began
to move with calculated exertion, taking care to
squander no amount of strength.

[Enter Three]

THREE (via RAY)

“Invocations happened once
or twice a tenth before your arrival Chakramire, and
everywhere you venture discord ensues. You spark dissent,
enkindle pandemonium, slaughter peace wherever
kindred spirits thrive, and pit tribes against themselves or one
another. Overheard the desire of Chakramire to
supercede the current Conduits.”

CHAKRAMIRE

“I intend to change
the guard, release the wealth, and restore the craft of telling
stories.”

THREE (via RAY)

“Paris learned and felt more than he could handle. All
who wield the crown and scepter of knowledge know the burden.
Storytelling teaches both how and what to feel. To spread
beyond the stars requires a submissive Earth . . . but raise your
sword and bloody steel, you risk losing everything of worth.”

[They exit]

WHERE SERENITY AND STRIFE CLEAVE: PART FOUR

CANTO 76: SYMMETRY

Galactic Calendar: Sol System; Earth year 30,123,012 M.W.I.
Tellurian Solar Calendar: Day thirty-three of the seventh tenth – 07/33
Modern Metric Time: 2:00:00, UTC+00:00, near midday
Location: Sanitarium, Sitnalta Island

AT RISE DESCRIPTION: *Meso has arrived at the Sanitarium to meet with Chakramire and to check on Ray's progress.*

[Enter Chakramire, Mara Mara, and Meso near Ray's bedside]

EGRESS MACHINE (via MARA MARA) *[Aside]*

Mixtures engender disparities, tonic solutions, and
crystals. An ocean of promise, an island of hope, and a
grain of success. The impartial refinement of destiny
leaves a residual ridge of repression. Minorities
rise as majorities fade, but serenity's scarcity
teases. The blistering fragrance of brine, with a whiff of the
gaffer's sobriety, tore from obsidian modicum
salaries, given to only the salt of society.

MARA MARA *[Aside]*

The pungent, alcoholic libation Meso brought to
pour across the flesh of Ray never left the flask beside
his hip. It dangled carelessly, like a wick before an
open flame. Expecting Ray dead, the smith of glass became
nostalgic, misty-eyed with relief, and apprehensive
once the tribute lost its mark.

MESO

"I remember Ray's return
from Continental Customs, as he arrived with neither
job nor housing, only hopes, dreams, and priceless artifacts.
To stay upon Sitnalta, a person needs the proof of
native birth, a spouse, or work permit. I decided I
would sponsor Ray, as Xara refused to sign a marriage
license."

CHAKRAMIRE

"What began the conflict?"

MESO

"A disappearing act,
a censure, lover's quarrels begin for every kind of
reason. Xara holds the home-field advantage; she has lived
upon Sitnalta all of her life."

MARA MARA *[Aside]*

The Man of Crystal
coyly paced around the bedside of Ray.

MESO

"Although you asked
for confidentiality, I have wondered why you
scoured the world to find the man, wondered how a silver tongue
with no credentials landed upon our shores, and wondered
how you plan to vouch for me being sent to outer space."

CHAKRAMIRE

"Revitalizing Earth with a new perspective is the
reason I have searched for Ray. My credential is the tongue
of silver . . . small the burden of proof."

MESO

"A host of rumors
claimed you stretched a single tenth's rations into three before
you reached the planet Mars, an achievement none expected . . ."

MARA MARA *[Aside]*

One should not regard the Globeflower-eyed deceased without
a corpse.

CHAKRAMIRE

"A lack of symmetry seen between results and
expectations is the birthplace of scientific thought."

[They exit]

WHERE SERENITY AND STRIFE CLEAVE: PART FOUR

CANTO 77: DISTILLING AGENT

Galactic Calendar: Sol System; Earth year 30,123,012 M.W.I.
Tellurian Solar Calendar: Day thirty-four of the seventh tenth – 07/34
Modern Metric Time 5:25:00, UTC+00:00, dusk or evening twilight
Location: Youngberry Tavern, Sitnalta Island

AT RISE DESCRIPTION: *Meso joins Chakramire and Mara Mara at Youngberry Tavern to meet with Epi.*

[Enter Chakramire, Mara Mara, and Meso among the tavern's patrons, including an unknown woman with skin dyed similarly to Chakramire's]

EGRESS MACHINE (via MARA MARA) *[Aside]*

Luxury's only redeeming distinction, hostility
fostered between the affluent and poverty-stricken. A
life of extravagance, enemy strife, will solicit the
gold of our youth with the spirits fermenting a bottle of
comfort, decay and creation, a rose from the dead with a
noxious aesthetic. The idiosyncrasy, fighting to
linger at rest or against a deciduous passion. A
lavish inertia, the spoil from an era of constancy.

UNKNOWN WOMAN

"To cheer, to jeer, it just as perverse."

MARA MARA *[Aside]*

A crowd began to
coalesce around *The Nightscape and Afterglow*. The wake
of Xara's exhibition had resonated, sending
half the island into discord, the other disarray.

UNKNOWN WOMAN

"To cheer for mediocrity, celebrating those who
loll within the bounds of longstanding mores snubs the brave
who dare defy conventional norms. It hurls derision,
jeers, and blatant disregard, untoward, towards the ones
who strive."

[Enter Auster]

AUSTER

"Another deviant sympathizer preaching
noncompliance?"

MARA MARA *[Aside]*

Everyone stepped aside as he approached,
as if a baleful aura enveloped everything the
man encountered.

UNKNOWN WOMAN

"Is it wrong, wanting more from life than life
itself?"

AUSTER

"An introduction, perhaps, would ease our angst, an
ego oftentimes mistakes. I intended no offense,
for we posses a similar disposition. Auster."

UNKOWN WOMAN

"I apologize."

MARA MARA *[Aside]*

A handshake resembling shackles met
the woman swiftly.

AUSTER

"Felo-de-se Amusement Park, a
martyr's greatest stage and grandstand, belongs to me. It is
a crime against oneself to ignore a calling, serving
these inebriated barflies with diatribe instead
of everyone with ears."

MARA MARA *[Aside]*

An array of candied comments,
honeyed-words, and blarney spread forth from Auster's mouth before
the woman, irresistible only if a person
needed no respect.

[Enter Epi, towards Chakramire and Meso's table]

EPI

"A buffet of lies. The scoundrel earns
a living representing desire's distilling agent,
separating life from life's aims."

MESO

"You own the tavern. Why
permit the man to speak? A contentious point of view and
controversy never helps business."

EPI

"Controversy is
our business, not sobriety."

MARA MARA *[Aside]*

Epi grimaced wryly
while encircling Meso.

EPI

“I heard your forge endured a bout
of dryness?”

MESO

“Moderation eluded me. Your nature,
I suspect, can tolerate anything, except a drought
of slyness.”

EPI

“Prohibition’s dissenters, outer space’s
pioneers, the inner impulse to push against the walls
confining us. Whatever compels your heart to leave the
Earth compels myself to stay here and make the most of all
the planet offers.”

MARA MARA *[Aside]*

Epi’s admission stole the wind from
Meso’s sails. The former friends shared a motivating force
and moved with one another, instead of hard against.

CHAKRAMIRE

“Your
choice of words astonished my client. We will reassess
the terms of barter. Bottling your wares, without alerting
overseers is your first trial.”

EPI

“What would be the next?”

CHAKRAMIRE

“The craft of manufacturing glass itself. The gaffer’s
trade you need to learn the old-fashioned way, and he will be
your teacher. Invocations would give away the game.”

EPI

“For
me to learn the art of glassblowing begs the question, ‘Why?’”

CHAKRAMIRE

“Your terms of payment. Meso will leave the Earth with me, and
I will need a favor one day. The forge’s title deed
will need another owner; your name will take the place of
Meso’s.”

EPI

“I accept your deal. Words alone enough; your fame
inspires sufficient confidence.”

MARA MARA *[Aside]*

Epi scanned the room.

EPI

“A
group of legionnaires has staked out the tavern. I suggest
you leave and not return, for your situation dire. The
mercenary, Doryline, prowls the grounds for Chakramire.”

[They exit]

WHERE SERENITY AND STRIFE CLEAVE: PART FOUR

CANTO 78: ACCRETION DISK

Galactic Calendar: Sol System; Earth year 30,123,012 M.W.I.
Tellurian Solar Calendar: Day thirty-five of the seventh tenth – 07/35
Modern Metric Time 2:00:00 , UTC+00:00, near midday
Location: Sanitarium, Sitnalta Island

AT RISE DESCRIPTION: *Chakramire and Mara Mara return to check on Ray. Though still in recovery, he shares what he learned from Three.*

[Enter Chakramire, Mara Mara, next to Ray's bedside]

EGRESS MACHINE (via MARA MARA) *[Aside]*

Flayers of canvas endeavor to smother the future of
fabric transparent. Whoever would champion beauty at
bio-diversity's loss, would demand from existence a
penance for youth and utility crossed: a symmetrical
ratio of mythic proportions, the measure of powder, of
paint, with the prettiest flower displaced from a desert, the
glorification of taste. As the radiance bleaches a
visage, the symphonies wash from a face of exuberance.

MARA MARA *[Aside]*

As Ray explained the physics of wealth, the Furthermost of
Women listened.

RAY

"Like a black hole amassing matter, wealth
creates a singularity anytime it reaches
drastic levels, bending space-time, absorbing satellites,
spaghettifying all who approach its freezing fire. A
plutocrat's accretion disk swirls around its densely packed
abductor, bound forever the mobile mausoleum.

Concentrated wealth attracts, captivates, accelerates,
and next annihilates. To observers, they resemble
static carousels of death. Money, knowledge, power, fame,
and beauty . . . wealth can take an array of forms. Whenever
everyone acquires a resource, the circulation stops
as well. To gain ubiquity means uniqueness wanes. An
economic system's heat death will happen once its wealth
approaches uniformity: equal distribution
nullifies attractive force. Interactions, trade, and work
desist. Dynamic constancy is the goal of cycles.
Both extremes impair the network."

CHAKRAMIRE

"Of what concern to me
the wealth of Earth?"

RAY

"Experience is the wealth our age. The
Devas covet Chakramire's most of all, and they would fell
your tree before allowing its fruit to fall to any
other."

CHAKRAMIRE

"Other?"

RAY

"Yes, the Conduits struggle daily just
to keep the League of Numbers dissociated: pruning
knowledge, cutting branches, untangling roots, and shedding leaves
from woodlands where serenity, strife, and truces ever
cleave . . . the swirling, verdant vortex of Chakramire its core.
The fate of Paris waits for the other three should forests
reconnect."

MARA MARA *[Aside]*

Although the Conduits banished Chakramire
from Earth a dozen years from the present moment, reasons
they withheld.

RAY

"The hold the Conduits now exert upon
the League of Numbers weakens with every invocation
bearing Strife."

CHAKRAMIRE

"A ticking time-bomb, your planet's people; four
alone cannot defuse it."

MARA MARA *[Aside]*

Exhaustion overtook the
heavy eyes of Ray. To love's prying inclinations, all
of Xara's stealth succumbed. The admirer rarely made an
entrance unpoetic.

[Enter Xara]

XARA

"I wish romance were less a game
of zero-sum, and more a display its pure aesthetic."

[They exit]

WHERE SERENITY AND STRIFE CLEAVE: PART FOUR

CANTO 79: CELERITY

Galactic Calendar: Sol System; Earth year 30,123,012 M.W.I.
Tellurian Solar Calendar: Day thirty-six of the seventh tenth – 07/36
Modern Metric Time 0:25:00 , UTC+00:00, near sunrise
Location: Sanitarium, Sitnalta Island

AT RISE DESCRIPTION: *A distraught Xara seeks solace from Chakramire for being neglected by Ray despite having helped save his life a second time.*

[Enter Chakramire, Mara Mara, and Xara]

EGRESS MACHINE (via MARA MARA) *[Aside]*

Civilization's penumbra, the edge of humanity's
knowledge, commencement of wisdom, between a diminishing
star and celestial occlusion. The brilliant escape with a
boundary skirted, diffracting around the perimeter,
leaving behind the extinguished to ponder enlightenment.
Freedom refracted, the truth of the matter evicted from
vacua, longs for a liberty lost, for perfection, for
aggregate progress contingent to homogeneity.

MARA MARA *[Aside]*

Time's dilation peaks at light speed. The correlation holds
for moments spent apart from a stationary party . . .
moments spent apart from loved ones, from play and leisure while
absorbed in work. Celerity is the bane of rest.

XARA

“A
love affair begins with one jealous paramour and ends
with disappointment. Ray, to his endless work, was always

married. I will never be more than runner-up. Naive
of me to think a rescue from death would change the status
quo."

CHAKRAMIRE

"Atonement is the sole reason Ray devotes himself
to work. An individual granting mercy pardons;
she permits, without a protest, a parched and thirsty throat
to feel the bliss of succulent fruit, despite believing
he deserves to go without. Ray desires to make amends.
Allow the man to suffer; avoid appearing callous.
Though it seems the onus elsewhere belongs, denying Ray
a chance at self-redemption would be perceived as malice."

[They exit]

WHERE SERENITY AND STRIFE CLEAVE: PART FOUR

CANTO 80: HELIUM

Galactic Calendar: Sol System; Earth year 30,123,012 M.W.I.
Tellurian Solar Calendar: Day thirty-six of the seventh tenth – 07/36
Modern Metric Time 2:50:00 , UTC+00:00, afternoon
Location: Meso's Forge, Sitnalta Island

AT RISE DESCRIPTION: *Chakramire and Mara Mara arrive at Meso's forge to observe as he prepares to train Epi to manufacture glass.*

[Enter Chakramire, Mara Mara, and Meso]

EGRESS MACHINE (via MARA MARA) *[Aside]*

Only the clarity after a storm could elicit a
stronger sensation of dread than of being alone in the
midst the disturbance, to people afraid of remorsefulness,
makers of tempests. Familiar disturbances offer a
modest reprieve from omniscience, from knowing the sequence of
beats to a heart, from chronology broken, from savagery.
Ever forgetting the words to harmonious melody,
interdependence arouses erroneous memory.

CHAKRAMIRE

"I have wandered Earth for twelve years but scarcely know the world,
its life, or how the Devas connect themselves to people.
I encountered, seventeen days ago, a man with no
resolve who quit sobriety. I assumed the reason
weakness, though neglected how liquor reach his fingers. What
inspired the break with temperance? How the drink delivered?"

MESO

"I imbibed the acrid drink under threat of force. A gang
of mercenaries searching for 'Chakramire' demanded

I reveal her whereabouts, vainly tried to loosen lips
with liquor, failed, but slandered her name before departing."

MARA MARA *[Aside]*

Air began to fill the blowpipe as Meso's diaphragm
relaxed. The molten mixture expanded.

CHAKRAMIRE

"I admit, it
seems your moral fiber lost neither fortitude nor stretch.
Albeit late, apologies I will offer."

MESO

"I have
never needed one."

MARA MARA *[Aside]*

To live up towards the standards he
had set himself remained his prevailing virtue. Meso
never asked for sanctions.

MESO

"Self-honor is enough for me;
to need another person's approval is the harshest
prison anyone endures. I have never turned against
a friend, but know the pain of betrayal. I accept your
mea culpa."

MARA MARA *[Aside]*

Chakramire grimaced. Though her debt to Ebb
was paid, its bitter medicine left an aftertaste.

CHAKRAMIRE

"Of
every snub, affront, and insult your heart remembers, which
offended most?"

MESO

"Receiving respect from other people
matters less to me than what values they believe themselves,
but I have felt ashamed of our species once, a recent
instance. One of Doryline's legionnaires considered me
to be an individual 'either smart or crazy,
mad perhaps, but clearly not normal' like himself, as if
proficient mediocrity people ought to strive for."

MARA MARA *[Aside]*

Meso rolled his gather like clay against the marver, shaped
it, placed it square within the annealing oven.

MESO

"Normal
people's virtue falls apart under stress; a threat will work
to compromise integrity only if a person
lacks resilience. Like a glass bottle prematurely plucked
from heat, a person quickly removed from tribulation
cracks."

MARA MARA *[Aside]*

A vassal oftentimes fails an invocation if
inebriated, rendering nonexistent any
aid from Devas. Meso risked death to keep the legionnaires
away from Chakramire.

CHAKRAMIRE

"Your idealism burns the
skin as much a forest fire's fumes. It stings with smoke; it plumes,
and offers no compassion for self-inflicted wounds. To
strengthen one's resolve despite being forced to work against
it is the bitter essence of strife; it is the reason
I have asked you share the glassblower's craft with Epi."

MESO

"I
expected my determinedness might receive a test."

CHAKRAMIRE

"For
us to find fulfillment, no one except myself can know
the plan. Whatever gambit encountered, brace yourself, for
greater dangers lurk beyond legionnaires."

MARA MARA *[Aside]*

A large machine
producing blasts of helium carried molecules to
coat a growing slab of glass. Meso fixed his gaze upon
the mirror.

MESO

"Making thermal resistant lenses takes a
dedicated eye with unparalleled precision. Mine
created via chemical vapor deposition."

[They exit]

BOOK III:
WHY CHAOS FELL APART

PART FOUR: RESOLVE INEXORABLE

WHY CHAOS FELL APART: PART FOUR

CANTO 111: EMPATHY

Galactic Calendar: Sol System; Earth year 30,123,012 M.W.I.
Tellurian Solar Calendar: Day twenty-eight of the eighth tenth – 08/28
Modern Metric Time: 4:50:00, UTC+00:00, dusk or evening twilight
Location: The Pantheon, Sitnalta Island

AT RISE DESCRIPTION: *The day after the hearing, Chakramire, Mara Mara, and the Conduits return with their advocates to await Praxis Harmonic's decision concerning a trial.*

[Enter Chakramire, Mara Mara, Ray, Praxis Harmonic, Hera, Cytherea, Pallas, Vance, Heathen Weave, Epi]

EGRESS MACHINE (via MARA MARA) *[Aside]*

Sweetness of words can disguise an ulterior motive, a curse, or occasional murders: expedience beckons its followers gamble morality. Nuance of flavor and bluntness of character, one as complex as the other the simple. A shower of niceties damages palates, a sprinkle enhances refinement. The whelm of finesse to a wave of excess, or the end of discrepancy. Poetry died for a reason, and subtlety perished along with it.

MARA MARA *[Aside]*

Chakramire's indictment, three hundred sixty-seven counts of civil strife alone, had surprised the room.

CHAKRAMIRE

"The number
seems a little low."

PRAXIS HARMONIC

"For once, we agree."

MARA MARA *[Aside]*

For every charge
the Regent Praxis listed, the Furthermost of Women
offered no defense.

CHAKRAMIRE

"The unfit to rule at times require
a regent. Whence your title bestowed?"

PRAXIS HARMONIC

"The League of Numbers
leads our world, but crimes of hive mind corruption justify
an intervention. Trials, however quaint, assume a
winner. Everyone today loses. I arrived to clean
the slate; the time for learning a lesson ended. Prison,
excommunication, exile, and restitution, each
of these a sentence lasting the life's remainder. Either
choose amongst yourselves the one serving each, or death will be
your fate."

MARA MARA *[Aside]*

Dividing empathy squarely never bothered
Praxis. He delivered verdict and sentence fairly, through
the use of parataxis.

PRAXIS HARMONIC

"A spark ignites, propellent
fuels, blankets suffocate. I can smother any fire."

[They exit]

WHY CHAOS FELL APART: PART FOUR

CANTO 112: EQUILIBRIUM

Galactic Calendar: Sol System; Earth year 30,123,012 M.W.I.
Tellurian Solar Calendar: Day twenty-nine of the eighth tenth – 08/29
Modern Metric Time: 0:75:00, UTC+00:00, morning
Location: The Pantheon, Sitnalta Island

AT RISE DESCRIPTION: *In the aftermath of Praxis's decision to simply deliver a sentence, Chakramire and Mara Mara meet with the Conduits and their advocates to begin mediation.*

[Enter Chakramire, Mara Mara, Ray, Hera,
Cytherea, Pallas, Vance, Heathen Weave, Epi]

EGRESS MACHINE (via MARA MARA) *[Aside]*

Drawn to the brink of morality, glimpsing its boundary
wondering if it legitimate, struggling to master the
art of indifference, alienated, remembered for
making a spectacle out of a tragedy, faulted for
wiping a smile from the face of the Earth and condoning a
ritualistic destruction of empathy, held to a
standard dispensable, dropped from it, guilty of paying the
price of admission for walking away from a miracle.

MARA MARA *[Aside]*

Before departing, Praxis Harmonic gave the group of eight a closing date of ten days to reach consensus. If successful, each would serve the allotted sentence. Even one dissent, however, meant death for everyone.

CYTHEREA

"The path
to reaching equilibrium bends again."

PALLAS

“It never
straightens.”

HERA

“I suggest a straw vote to better gauge ourselves
and others.”

CHAKRAMIRE

“Let the council begin.”

MARA MARA *[Aside]*

The Dagger Vance and
Pallas volunteered to speak first.

VANCE

“For each of us exists
a sentence better suited our nature. Tolerating
excommunication’s torment innately comes to those
aligned to Zero.”

PALLAS

“Solemnly, we request to serve its
burden.”

HERA

“Skill at bearing hardship resolves the least our woes.
The Furthermost of Women presents a mortal danger
everywhere to everyone. Silence Chakramire, and leave
the task of restitution to me. A reimbursement
ought to come from one who knows what it means to suffer.”

EPI

"I
prefer a prison sentence to cleaning up another's
mess, for I have tended spilled liquor, stomach chyme, and scrubbed
the foulest lavatories to ever curse a tavern."

MARA MARA *[Aside]*

Cytherea chose to vote last. The tongue of Chakramire
removed its sheath, preparing itself for confrontation.

CHAKRAMIRE

"I request the fate of exile, with one condition. Ray
will serve his sentence via a proxy, Meso, pending
everyone's approval."

CYTHEREA

"Twelve years you had to quit the Earth,
but held it hostage. Now, your reversing fortune lingers.
Everyone a calling, one cause for which our lives exchanged,
and some will even pay with the lives of others just to
guarantee a certain outcome. You ridiculed our way
of life as 'blind submission to manufactured gods,' and
left the League of Numbers disintegrated. Setting fire
to homes and fleeing only befits a coward. All of
us will burn together. No deal for me the better."

HEATHEN WEAVE (the true NETTLES)

"That
would render insignificant all our lives to fund your
petty feud. A chance to make Earth a better place to live
the wise would never squander."

RAY

“It seems our coalition
needs to undergo a half-dozen metamorphoses
to wield the social grace of a butterfly. Tomorrow
we will reconvene, with eight days to make our peace or die.”

[They exit]

WHY CHAOS FELL APART: PART FOUR

CANTO 113: COSMIC COUNTER

Galactic Calendar: Sol System; Earth year 30,123,012 M.W.I.
Tellurian Solar Calendar: Day thirty of the eighth tenth – 08/30
Modern Metric Time: 2:00 :00, UTC+00:00, near midday
Location: The Pantheon, Sitnalta Island

AT RISE DESCRIPTION: *Over the course of the next three days, Chakramire, the Conduits, and their advocates are meeting in pairs to reduce tension, and will reconvene later to find a resolution. Chakramire and Hera are meeting on the first day, while Cytherea and Pallas converse in another room. Chakramire has summoned Harn to the Pantheon to assist negotiating with Hera and her advocate.*

[Enter Chakramire, Mara Mara, Harn, Hera, and Epi]

EGRESS MACHINE (via MARA MARA) *[Aside]*

Energy lost and recovered, the tools of survival or
seat of anxiety. Measure emotions with gestures, a
language eternal as dew, and distortion's propensity
rises beyond the embrace but a privileged few. For the
poet persistently muddying water, however it
shallow, for gardeners tilling a terrace, however it
fallow, performing the dirtiest actions, auxiliary,
they with a mind and its calculus absent of mystery.

MARA MARA *[Aside]*

Because an indefensible action makes an easy
target, Harn would often times make himself appear a man
of straw to disincline an attempt at emulation.

HARN

"All our records indicate humans are a species prone
to self-destruction; I have become the standard bearer.
Chakramire requested my presence; I would like to know
the reason why the Lady of Eris lives and needs a
dupe. You failed to drink your saltwater brine concoction."

CHAKRAMIRE

"I
imbibed it. Smaller portions can lessen any burden;
even deadly toxins one holds a chance to overcome.
A friend with indisputable virtue I invited
here today to vouch the forthrightness my intentions. I
desire to leave the Earth with whatever peace it needs."

HARN

"A
conscience only needs a crutch if it lacking legs to stand
upon. Whatever personal creeds a person harbors
matter most; an ogre ought not endorse for beauty. Heed
your codes of moral excellence, none can bring you harm; but
fail to live to them and no one can save you."

MARA MARA *[Aside]*

Chakramire
awaited further words, but a silence filled the chamber.

CHAKRAMIRE

"Harn, the man who sought to know everything and quickly learned
the bitter taste of getting exactly what you asked for,
labeled me a cripple."

EPI

“I think you made a grave mistake
believing that would change our opinions. I expected
more a fight from Chakramire.”

CHAKRAMIRE

“Reconciliation is
our current undertaking; the fight has inward turned. A
change of disposition life oftentimes demands: a stand
against the inclinations of nature. I condemned your
values, claimed existing is not a universal right . . .”

MARA MARA *[Aside]*

At best, it is a practical one.

CHAKRAMIRE

“. . . and even though you
threatened me with murder, I never compromised myself.”

HERA

“But everywhere you venture, dissension blossoms.”

CHAKRAMIRE

“I have
never sown the seeds of discord, but I have watered them
at every opportunity given.”

MARA MARA *[Aside]*

Though command of
doublespeak confounds the best rhetoricians, paradox
remains the cosmic counter of Chakramire, her chosen
means of striking back against any snub, affront, or snide
remark.

CHAKRAMIRE

"The cultivation of gardens forces one to
learn a lack of guarantees is the only guarantee."

[They exit]

WHY CHAOS FELL APART: PART FOUR

CANTO 114: ZWISCHENZUG

Galactic Calendar: Sol System; Earth year 30,123,012 M.W.I.
Tellurian Solar Calendar: Day thirty-one of the eighth tenth – 08/31
Modern Metric Time: 2:00: 00, UTC+00:00, near midday
Location: The Pantheon, Sitnalta Island

AT RISE DESCRIPTION: *On the second day of pairings, Chakramire meets with Pallas and her advocate to negotiate while Hera and Cytherea converse in another room.*

[Enter Chakramire, Mara Mara, Vance, Pallas]

EGRESS MACHINE (via MARA MARA) *[Aside]*

Said the destroyer of civilizations, "Believing a
person a nemesis always should keep, adversity
strengthens a body, prosperity colors it weak. From a
legion of warriors blind, to a ravenous funeral
march. From a thirsty, carnivorous mind, to a diet of
hollow abstractions. The charm of remembrance, a talisman,
wedded to enmity; nestled the hand of celebrity
even a trivial trinket can seem the illustrious."

MARA MARA *[Aside]*

Although Sitnalta Island's remoteness made it hard to
reach, its shores attracted those seeking new beginnings, rest
from persecution, vengeance, or absolution. Neither
Vance nor Pallas offered first words, and Chakramire commenced
negotiations.

CHAKRAMIRE

"Seventy-seven days of silent
treatment culled whatever goodwill our time together forged;
a small amount, however, remains. Your quest for vengeance
spoiled, but questions loom; from what manner *Mint*, your knife, arrived
to Ray?"

MARA MARA *[Aside]*

To leave an enemy thunderstricken is the
aim of any zwischenzug. Chakramire expected Vance
would leave from Umbrage Grotto remorseful; she had missed the
risk a person's grudge could shift.

CHAKRAMIRE

"Are you friend or foe? You seem
a bit of both."

VANCE

"Coincidence one should wisely treat as
subterfuge and smoke. Our first meeting happened over rust
and rocks, but I departed from Mars to brace the Earth for
Chakramire's arrival soon after. I began the Guild
of Thieves with good intentions – the restoration feats of
rote and independence. I spared the life of Chakramire
with good intentions – Eris deserved a better fate than
mass extinction. I attacked Nettles, Heathen Weave and Twine
with good intentions – justice for crimes committed."

MARA MARA *[Aside]*

Dagger
Vance retraced his steps and turned back to Chakramire.

VANCE

"But good
intentions blinded me to the threat of one Erisian's
life. The price of fixing my own mistakes required a breach
of faith, as *Mint* was given to Ray, and he intended
murder."

CHAKRAMIRE

"Good intentions mean less to me than trust."

PALLAS

"Your once
assassin is your advocate now, and works to save your
life. Your tongue has tasted more blood than Dagger Vance's knife."

[They exit]

WHY CHAOS FELL APART: PART FOUR

CANTO 115: DOPPELGANGER

Galactic Calendar: Sol System; Earth year 30,123,012 M.W.I.
Tellurian Solar Calendar: Day thirty-two of the eighth tenth – 08/32
Modern Metric Time: 2:00:00, UTC+00:00, near midday
Location: The Pantheon, Sitnalta Island

AT RISE DESCRIPTION: *On the third day of pairings, Chakramire and Cytherea meet to work towards reaching a resolution. Hera and Pallas converse in another room.*

[Enter Chakramire, Mara Mara, and Cytherea]

EGRESS MACHINE (via MARA MARA) *[Aside]*

Asked from the hand to the archer, "As whence your expedience?"
Heard from the archer, the hand, "It the sign of experience."
Asked from the bow to the quiver, "And why your benevolence?"
Heard from the quiver, the bow, "It the spectrum of excellence."
Asked from the nock to the fiber, "For what your preparedness?"
Heard from the fiber, the nock, "To assist with your resonance."
Asked from the sky to the arrow, "Whyever your arrogance?"
Heard from the arrow, the sky, "To depart from irrelevance."

MARA MARA *[Aside]*

The third and final meeting began with Chakramire and
Cytherea facing off like established heavyweights
who needed nothing proved, or denounced, or falsified.

CYTHEREA

"The
symbiotic parasite wants to make a deal?

CHAKRAMIRE

"An end
with benefits for all of the parties present is the
only wish of mine. A death sentence serving no intent
offends our sensibilities. If appeasement is an
option, name your price."

CYTHEREA

"Your bard, Mara Mara leave behind
to Earth; it nears the end of its life."

CHAKRAMIRE

"A bard can never
die."

CYTHEREA

"Your bard possesses finite remembrance, lasting near
the span of fifty years, and it owns a doppelganger
named Calliope. The two work together; each supplies
the skills the other missing. Your Mara Mara is the
eyes and ears. Calliope is the voice."

CHAKRAMIRE

"And what becomes
of Mara Mara's story? Intend to overwrite or
change it?"

CYTHEREA

"No, for all the hardship and woe your presence brought
to Earth, the story's memory I would like preserved. The
hardest part of sculpting statues: to know the work complete.
Although your fierce existence began upon a distant
planet filled with trauma, I find it difficult to think
of Chakramire the alien, us the native fauna."

[They exit]

WHY CHAOS FELL APART: PART FOUR

CANTO 116: CLAIRVOYANCE

Galactic Calendar: Sol System; Earth year 30,123,012 M.W.I.
Tellurian Solar Calendar: Day thirty-three of the eighth tenth – 08/33
Modern Metric Time: 2:00:00, UTC+00:00, near midday
Location: The Pantheon, Sitnalta Island

AT RISE DESCRIPTION: *Chakramire, Mara Mara, the Conduits, and their advocates reconvene with the aims of reaching an agreement.*

[Enter Chakramire, Mara Mara, Ray, Hera,
Cytherea, Pallas, Vance, Heathen Weave, Epi]

EGRESS MACHINE (via MARA MARA) *[Aside]*

Sweetness of words can disguise an ulterior motive, a
curse, or occasional murders: expedience beckons its
followers gamble morality. Nuance of flavor and
bluntness of character, one as complex as the other the
simple. A shower of niceties damages palates, a
sprinkle enhances refinement. The whelm of finesse to a
wave of excess, or the end of discrepancy. Poetry
died for a reason, and subtlety perished along with it.

HERA

"Earth became an occupied territory after she
arrived: our vaunted civilization rendered second
rate because of Chakramire's sway."

RAY

"Our world was occupied
before her cataclysmic approach. The blame belongs to
us for Earth's decline."

MARA MARA *[Aside]*

The furled tongue of Chakramire relaxed
its coils.

CHAKRAMIRE

"A world embracing the values I espouse should
terrify you. Outer space is for people unafraid
of fatal competition. Successful first explorers
tend to be acute and fierce opportunists wielding no
compassion, only ruthless determination."

HERA

"Every
first encounter is a new chance to make a pact. Of all
our diplomatic measures, cooperation is the
safest. Why the call for cutthroat devices, tricks, and schemes?"

CHAKRAMIRE

"The Milky Way Initiative is the second human
expedition into space, not the first."

MARA MARA *[Aside]*

A wheel revolves
around its axis, planets around a star, command of
skill around its praxis, outrage around a scar.

CHAKRAMIRE

"The first
to leave the Earth escaped with whatever they could take: the
smartest minds, the rarest earth metals, knowledge. Anything
with life-sustaining properties they appropriated,
stole, or pillaged."

EPI

“Why would they strip the Earth of precious goods
and riches? Why abandon the mother world?”

CHAKRAMIRE

“Because it
nearly killed its children. Two groups survived the bottleneck
effect: the ones who fled, and our predecessors. All of
us descend from everyone left behind. A split occurred
along our genealogy. We were not supposed to
live.”

PALLAS

“And what befell the First Expedition? What became”
of those who thought our lineage needed no expression?”

CHAKRAMIRE

“Dead, alive, evolved, or mutated, we can speculate
but never know. Our history is a song of strife and
self-inflicted wounds. Our ancestors, after being snubbed,
displayed a high degree of resilience. They survived a
hostile world, reclaimed the heirlooms of Earth, and pioneered
the Milky Way Initiative fearing distant cousins
might return from outer space just to commandeer it all.
The only reason looters return to long abandoned
houses is to scavenge, ransack, or loot again. You thought
myself to be a threat, but forgot the reasons why our
predecessors stationed us far beyond the realms of Earth:
celestial sentries guarding against an uninvited
guest; a buffer zone of flesh; trauma’s mitigation. All
of these responsibilities we assumed. It is a
fitting end for us to meet here, to coalesce upon
your planet’s most remote and sequestered island, safe from

deprivation, safe from lack, while our headsman whets his sword.
Clairvoyance is a question of distance seen, but conscience
is the scourge of those with sight: choosing what to overlook."

[They exit]

WHY CHAOS FELL APART: PART FOUR

CANTO 117: HEAT DEATH

Galactic Calendar: Sol System; Earth year 30,123,012 M.W.I.
Tellurian Solar Calendar: Day thirty-four of the eighth tenth – 08/34
Modern Metric Time: 1:00:00, UTC+00:00, morning
Location: The Pantheon, Sitnalta Island

AT RISE DESCRIPTION: *Chakramire, Mara Mara, Meso, the Conduits, and their advocates have recalled Praxis Harmonic.*

[Enter Chakramire, Mara Mara, Ray, Meso, Hera, Cytherea, Pallas, Vance, Heathen Weave, Epi]

EGRESS MACHINE (via MARA MARA) *[Aside]*

Drawn to the brink of morality, glimpsing its boundary
wondering if it legitimate, struggling to master the
art of indifference, alienated, remembered for
making a spectacle out of a tragedy, faulted for
wiping a smile from the face of the Earth and condoning a
ritualistic destruction of empathy, held to a
standard dispensable, dropped from it, guilty of paying the
price of admission for walking away from a miracle.

[Enter Praxis Harmonic]

MARA MARA *[Aside]*

The Regent's legs transported his body through the chamber
like a lynx prepared to ambush its mark with taunts instead
of teeth.

PRAXIS HARMONIC

"Your coalition should persevere a little
longer. Anyone who gives up respiring ere the loss
of air, or closes eyes to the light before the fall of
night, deserves a censure."

CHAKRAMIRE

"Bold talk from hypocrites who let
a budding ecosystem collapse across a pair of
planets."

PRAXIS HARMONIC

"They succumbed to heat death, a fate awaiting all . . .
and they deserve our sympathy – I concede your point – but
nothing more than that."

MARA MARA *[Aside]*

The vortex of bodies slowly moved
towards the chamber's center as Hera took the floor with
Epi near her side.

HERA

"Although all our dispositions clashed
with one another, we have achieved a resolution.
Prison we will serve, with one small condition."

EPI

"We fulfill
it under house arrest with the sole intent of serving
others using newly learned skills."

PRAXIS HARMONIC

"Affirmed."

MARA MARA *[Aside]*

To Dagger Vance
and Pallas eyes directed.

PALLAS

"The excommunication
sentence we will serve."

VANCE

"With no stipulations asked."

PRAXIS HARMONIC

"Affirmed."

MARA MARA *[Aside]*

Around the Lady Eris and Ray a storm began to swirl.

CHAKRAMIRE

"The taxing task of exile belongs to us, but Ray will serve his sentence via a proxy, Meso."

RAY

"I will
salvage what remains the hive mind, and help restore its use to Earth."

MARA MARA *[Aside]*

To Meso, Praxis Harmonic turned his gaze.

PRAXIS HARMONIC

"A
proxy needs the substitute's sanction."

MESO

"I consent."

PRAXIS HARMONIC

"Affirmed."

MARA MARA *[Aside]*

A whirl of irresistible force encircled Heathen
Weave and Cytherea.

HEATHEN WEAVE

"Earth's restitution falls to us."

CYTHEREA

"With one condition."

PRAXIS HARMONIC

"State your provisions."

CYTHEREA

"Mara Mara,
bard of Chakramire, will, three days from now, transfer to me.
The tale of Chakramire and her journey cross the stars the
Earth will keep alive with song."

CHAKRAMIRE

"I consent."

PRAXIS HARMONIC

"But I object,
for even if the soggiest mind alive absorbed the
smallest dose of Chakramire's vitriolic tenets, peace
becomes endangered."

CYTHEREA

“Crispness of thought endears itself to
strife, but Mara Mara is only half the act. Without
Calliope, the *Epic of Chakramire* occluded.
Only one records the tale, while the other sings it. Why
deny the tool to progeny? Every story teaches.”

PRAXIS HARMONIC

“Seal the bard a body length deep; inter it underneath
an isolated spot with the story rearranged to
minimize its noxious clout. I will grant your wish.”

CYTHEREA

“Affirmed.”

[They exit]

WHY CHAOS FELL APART: PART FOUR

CANTO 118: YOKE OF DESTINY

Galactic Calendar: Sol System; Earth year 30,123,012 M.W.I.
Tellurian Solar Calendar: Day thirty-five of the eighth tenth – 08/35
Modern Metric Time: 2:00:00, UTC+00:00, near midday
Location: Evergrowth Farm, Sitnalta Island

AT RISE DESCRIPTION: *Under a small escort, Chakramire and Mara Mara visit Harn at Evergrowth Farm, as he requested to see them before they serve their sentence.*

[Enter Chakramire, Mara Mara, Guards, and Harn]

EGRESS MACHINE (via MARA MARA) *[Aside]*

Energy lost and recovered, the tools of survival or
seat of anxiety. Measure emotions with gestures, a
language eternal as dew, and distortion's propensity
rises beyond the embrace but a privileged few. For the
poet persistently muddying water, however it
shallow, for gardeners tilling a terrace, however it
fallow, performing the dirtiest actions, auxiliary,
they with a mind and its calculus absent of mystery.

MARA MARA *[Aside]*

The aftermath of mowing rebellions down has never
changed. A second crop will grow. Scythes will harvest grass again,
but shovels are the deadliest weapons humans ever
wield. Whoever digs the past up can shape the future.

HARN

"I
have never understood your obsessive bond with Mara
Mara. Like a team of draft horses hitched, you strain against

and tug your yoke of destiny, plowing through the earth with
reason, turning over lives season after season. Though
the rumors call you cruel and vicious, I have never
seen you harm, nor order bloodshed, nor end another life
at whim."

CHAKRAMIRE

"The charm of irony is the same as any
mirror. Those who need it most fail to see themselves within."

[They exit]

WHY CHAOS FELL APART: PART FOUR

CANTO 119: ZUGZWANG

Galactic Calendar: Sol System; Earth year 30,123,012 M.W.I.
Tellurian Solar Calendar: Day thirty-six of the eighth tenth – 08/36
Modern Metric Time: 0:25:00, UTC+00:00, near sunrise
Location: The Pantheon, Sitnalta Island

AT RISE DESCRIPTION: *Chakramire prepares to begin her sentence to exile by making final arrangements with Praxis Harmonic and Cytherea for Mara Mara.*

[Enter Chakramire, Mara Mara, Praxis, and Cytherea]

EGRESS MACHINE (via MARA MARA) *[Aside]*

Said the destroyer of civilizations, "Believing a
person a nemesis always should keep, adversity
strengthens a body, prosperity colors it weak. From a
legion of warriors blind, to a ravenous funeral
march. From a thirsty, carnivorous mind, to a diet of
hollow abstractions. The charm of remembrance, a talisman,
wedded to enmity; nestled the hand of celebrity
even a trivial trinket can seem the illustrious."

MARA MARA *[Aside]*

As Chakramire's penultimate day upon the planet
Earth began, a wave of sunbeams submerged her gloom. To leave
a world awash with life for the void of space, a spider
trapped within a moral zugzwang: compelled to move beyond
the house to ward against an encroaching pest, receiving
praise, but barred from seeking refuge within the structure's walls.

PRAXIS HARMONIC

"A story's morals matter. A misinterpretation,
mispronunciation, mismatch, hyperbole amiss,
or mere mistake of memory misdirects a story.
Any one of these can rework an author's message. I
believe the safest place for the epic underneath a
mountain."

CYTHEREA

"I agree . . . the android will cease its function once
it buried underground."

[Exit Praxis Harmonic]

MARA MARA *[Aside]*

With the Regent gone, a hindrance
left the room and Chakramire spoke.

CHAKRAMIRE

"Has anyone confirmed
Calliope's existence?"

CYTHEREA

"A storyteller walks the
Earth. Its function is a word excavator. They exist
as relics, artifacts of the past confined to steel and
four museum walls."

CHAKRAMIRE

"At what range can Mara Mara reach
Calliope?"

CYTHEREA

"The signal transmits a single body's
length. To amplify the wave, I will vault your bard beneath
a growing tree along with a small antenna. I will
free Calliope a lifetime or two from ours, to do
it now would draw suspicion. The tree will power Mara
Mara through organic means: voltage generated through
its roots and leaves, but only enough for simple functions."

CHAKRAMIRE

"Every day for fifty years Mara Mara's crank was wound,
with one exception, shortly before approaching Mars with
rations running low. A hard sleep it is for what you know
will be your final instance . . . to face your nonexistence."

[All exit except Cytherea]

***

[Enter Chakramire and Mara Mara aboard the spaceship Chakramire as it approaches Mars more than twenty Earth years prior]

CHAKRAMIRE

*"I imagined death would be harsh and painful, not a slow
and serpentinely tortuous slog across the Solar
System, not a begging outposts for water, food, or spare
supplies and always being surprised whenever every
plea would yield a gift despite none of them possessing near
enough to serve themselves. To observe the stars and search for
life beyond the Earth, an Earth no Erisian ever toured,
an Earth replete with creatures and life of every kind, an
Earth sustaining half the spaceborn until it stopped . . . to look
away from such a world and expect the same from those who
only know it secondhand seems a cruel joke. For all*

the sifting through the clutter of outer space, researching
vast expanses filled with dust, light, and cosmic gas to slake
the Milky Way Initiative's superficial aim of
exploration, my reward is the jinx of broken bones
before the finish line. With a third the rations needed,
Chakramire shall never reach Mars Dominion. I expect
to die without awakening; hibernation is a
risk . . . a chance for turning Earth into my accretion disk."

[They exit]

WHY CHAOS FELL APART: PART FOUR

CANTO 120: SHADOW MAXIM

Galactic Calendar: Sol System; Earth year 30,123,012 M.W.I.
Tellurian Solar Calendar: Day thirty-six of the eighth tenth – 08/36
Modern Metric Time: 5:50:00, UTC+00:00, dusk or evening twilight
Location: The Pantheon, Sitnalta Island

AT RISE DESCRIPTION: *Before departing, Chakramire and Meso meet with Ray and Cytherea, to surrender the Egress Machine and Mara Mara, respectively.*

[Enter Chakramire, Mara Mara, Meso, Ray, and Cytherea]

EGRESS MACHINE (via MARA MARA) *[Aside]*

Asked from the hand to the archer, "As whence your expedience?"
Heard from the archer, the hand, "It the sign of experience."
Asked from the bow to the quiver, "And why your benevolence?"
Heard from the quiver, the bow, "It the spectrum of excellence."
Asked from the nock to the fiber, "For what your preparedness?"
Heard from the fiber, the nock, "To assist with your resonance."
Asked from the sky to the arrow, "Whyever your arrogance?"
Heard from the arrow, the sky, "To depart from irrelevance."

MARA MARA *[Aside]*

A wary Ray inspected his last invention like a hostage mediator.

RAY

"We missed your bard's potential. I suspect the ancient circuits comprising Mara Mara's interface transformed the Egress Machine; it amplified the strength of any weakened synaptic cleft and aided recollection theretofore Mara Mara's fateful touch.

Robotic minds forget at command, a Shadow Maxim
premise. Mara Mara repurposed my invention, I
assume, to serve another agenda."

CHAKRAMIRE

"Fortune telling?"

RAY

"Yes."

MARA MARA *[Aside]*

The Golden Brain of Discord exchanged from hand to hand,
and Ray approached the door.

RAY

"To recover harbored knowledge
I will need to use the Egress Machine. A state of war
exists between the Devas. The ocean is the field of
battle; every battleship is a drop of water."

[Ray exits with the Egress Machine]

MARA MARA *[Aside]*

Feats
of stunning strength, or speed, or of constitution often
mark the epic hero. Though Chakramire possessed but one
the three, her intellectual prowess, wisdom, charm, and
courage none denied.

CYTHEREA

"With charged words and craft, your silver-tongue
conducts a feeling better than any steel; and if your
story holds a moral, one day the Earth will need it."

CHAKRAMIRE

"If
resolve to overcome and improve onself a moral,
Earth will need it every day."

MARA MARA *[Aside]*

Meso stood aside and watched
the two as one determined to speak, inquire, but never
knowing good decorum's best time to interject. At last,
the Furthermost of Women began to leave, and Meso
realized the opportune moment soon would slip away.

MESO

"The Milky Way Initiative's prime objective changed from
outer space research to maintaining self-defense against
an undiscovered threat?"

CHAKRAMIRE

"The objective never changed. To
salvage, spy, and sponsor low-key surveillance . . . these have been
the Milky Way Initiative's targets since the start."

MESO

"Should
we encounter any First Expedition humans, what
would my responsibility be? Negotiate or
fight?"

CHAKRAMIRE

"Expect the worse, for their earthly story ended; they
estranged themselves and plundered your world. The odds of meeting
them, however, slim . . . a head start of thirty million years
has sundered. We can either consider cousins foes, or
welcome them as equals. One adage, be it verse or prose,
a story ending happily never merits sequels."

[Chakramire and Meso exit. Cytherea and Mara Mara exit separately]

EPILOGUE: WHAT THE FUTURE DISOWNED

AT RISE DESCRIPTION: *Having finished Mara Mara's account of the Epic of Chakramire, Calliope the Storyteller and the Storytold sit beside the Tree of Discord. Several hundreds of years have passed since Chakramire, the last Erisian, walked the Earth.*

[Enter Storyteller and Storytold]

CALLIOPE THE STORYTELLER

"Underneath the Tree of Discord the bard of Chakramire
resides."

STORYTOLD

"But what became of the Furthermost of Women?
What became of everyone else?"

CALLIOPE THE STORYTELLER

"As we have reached the end
of Mara Mara's script, a presumption is the greatest
I can offer. Given homesickness plagues your species more
than wanderlust, the Mistress of Strife's return to Eris
seems a fitting end. The Conduits, Ray perhaps, restored
the League of Numbers. Praxis Harmonic likely spent the
rest his day within the Moon. Vance the Dagger, Heathen Weave,
and Epi served the sentences charged to them, and most have
heard of Meso's tale . . ."

STORYTOLD

"Upon reaching outer space the man
devoted all his life to refining glass production.
He improved the lot of spaceborn throughout our known expanse,

explored with zeal, transfigured our otherworldly hamlets;
neither Meso's chaperone, Chakramire, nor seven years
of prison made our history books, however."

CALLIOPE THE STORYTELLER

"Seven
years' confinement freed the man's mind from fear of failure, dreams,
and death. Your curiosity puzzles. Why our journey
here?"

STORYTOLD

"A strange transmission reached Earth from planet Eris: they
detected signals coded within a language dead for
sixty million years. The First Expedition launched around
its use, and I discovered the name of Chakramire a
time thereafter."

CALLIOPE THE STORYTELLER

"Did the spaceborn translate the message?"

STORYTOLD

"Half
the message they deciphered, the other half remains a
labyrinthine riddle . . . 'Life's cradle we detected. We
will trim the basket's middle, and we will be respected . . .'"

[They exit]

Milton Keynes UK
Ingram Content Group UK Ltd.
UKHW010755080824
446708UK00020B/260